PRAISE FOR
MILLY TAIDEN AND HER NOVELS

"Taiden introduces readers to the Alpha League Federal
Agency (A.L.F.A.), a secret group of shapeshifters who
work for the government. The chemistry between Parish
and Melinda is off-the-charts hot, but there is also a great
story that goes along with it. Readers will enjoy the intro-
duction to a new type of paranormal romance with characters who have fascinating backstories. A job well done
by Taiden!"   —*RT Book Reviews*

"Would I recommend this author? Yes! Milly Taiden does
not disappoint with this funny, sexy storytelling! This
author should be on all must-read lists!"
                          —Twin Sisters Rockin' Book Review

"I can always rely on Milly Taiden to write a fun, quick,
sweet and sexy romance."   —Angel's Guilty Pleasures

A.L.F.A. MATES

MILLY TAIDEN

BERKLEY SENSATION
New York

BERKLEY SENSATION
Published by Berkley
An imprint of Penguin Random House LLC
375 Hudson Street, New York, New York 10014

Copyright © 2017 by Milly Taiden
Excerpt from *Dangerous Mating* © 2017 by Milly Taiden
Penguin Random House supports copyright. Copyright fuels creativity, encourages diverse
voices, promotes free speech, and creates a vibrant culture. Thank you for buying
an authorized edition of this book and for complying with copyright laws by not
reproducing, scanning, or distributing any part of it in any form without permission.
You are supporting writers and allowing Penguin Random House to continue to
publish books for every reader.

BERKLEY and BERKLEY SENSATION are registered trademarks and the B colophon
is a trademark of Penguin Random House LLC.

ISBN: 9780399585838

Berkley Sensation mass-market edition / October 2017
InterMix ebook editions / July & October 2017

Printed in the United States of America
1 3 5 7 9 10 8 6 4 2

Cover design by Annette Defex
Book design by Laura K. Corless

For my husband, Mr. T.

Thank you for always having my back,
for picking up my slack so I can do more writing,
and for being the best friend and the most wonderful
husband a woman could have. I love you!

ELEMENTAL MATING

CHAPTER 1

Melinda gaped at the hunk of man standing in the doorway and her gulp of tea almost came out her nose.

Holy shit. Could a guy be any hotter? Even though he had a plastic protector in his lab coat's pocket, geeky glasses, and a bow tie, she'd take him here on the conference table with everyone watching. Well, not everyone watching, or this table. But she'd definitely take him.

The stranger took a deep breath and his eyes zeroed in on her. She startled and blushed as the group around the meeting room table glanced at her. "What? I don't know him."

Mr. Kintu, the senior principal research officer, who everyone called the senior PRO, smiled. "Of course, you don't, Miss Caster." He turned toward the man standing in the doorway. "Dr. Hamel, please come in."

More like Dr. Hump-him. Oh, yeah. She'd hump him if she got the chance. She kept her face tilted down, letting her hair fall forward to hide her hot cheeks. The man moved effortlessly despite his tall stature. She noted how the lab coat stretched across his shoulders. *Hot damn!* This guy might seem like a nerdy research scientist on the outside, but she bet when the clothes came off, things looked quite different. Suddenly the image of him doing the *Magic Mike hand glid-*

ing down his chest into his pants move sent her brain cells into nuclear meltdown.

Dr. Hamel took another deep breath and his fingers slightly balled into a fist before relaxing. That was interesting. Mr. Kintu greeted him with a handshake then turned to the table. "Everyone, this is Dr. Parish Hamel from the government's Oversight Committee."

All smiles in the room drooped. Anyone with "Oversight" in their title usually wasn't welcome. Especially to Melinda. The reason she ended up there in the African country of Uganda at the Uganda Virus Research Laboratory was because of another male with "Oversight" in his title. More asshole than male.

Good thing he wasn't there to watch over her. Currently, her focus was on a newly discovered virus that seemed to be related to the Zika virus. With no outbreaks and no "cure" needed, she wasn't doing much that seemed important to the government.

Mr. Kintu laughed at the attendees' reaction to the visiting doctor's title. "No worries, everyone. Dr. Hamel is only here for Miss Caster."

"What?" Melinda sat straight up in her chair. "What did I do? I'm not working on anything important."

Mr. Kintu raised a brow. "Didn't you say you were close to a breakthrough?"

Well, shit. She did. That was the last time she opened her mouth in front of the senior PRO. She nodded. "Yeah, sorta."

Her boss smiled. "Now Dr. Hamel is here to assist you in the documentation."

Oh, yay. She plastered on a smile. "Wonderful. I'm always happy to have overstep, I mean, Oversight helping."

Mr. Kintu cast her a veiled glance before turning to the table. "The meeting is dismissed. Everyone have a good rest of the week."

Melinda quickly gathered her notes to get the hell out before—

"Miss Caster, would you please remain."

She set her notes down and sighed. Her best friend and colleague leaned into her. "Girl, at least he's cute under all that garb. Maybe you can finally get you some."

Mel gasped and playfully smacked Dembe on the arm. "You did not just say that."

"Oh, yes, I did." Dembe gave her a huge smile and snuck out of the room, closing the door behind her.

Strange thing was this man was the first to spark her interest in a couple years. And not just her interest, but her libido. Oh, god, did she just think that out loud? Her face heated.

Sex and everything concerning it was almost taboo for her. Growing up in a highly religious home where sex was strictly for having children, and women were not to enjoy it, she had never really explored that part of herself. Not that she hadn't tried.

Her senior year in high school began her rebellion against the vast chains that strangled her. A little late, but considering it happened at all was a minor miracle.

During a school-sanctioned event, she'd slipped out with the boyfriend she wasn't allowed to have. The normal teen hormones flowed within them. In the backseat, she lay with her head crammed against the door armrest, the stupid seat belt gouging into her kidney.

When he finally lay on top of her, she tried to relax, but couldn't, too worried her parents would somehow find out. Shit would hit the fan and she'd be grounded for years. Then she'd have to pull a *Carrie at the prom* to escape the house. And wouldn't that be fun—

Her boyfriend flattened on top of her, smashing her neck farther into the door. He let out a sigh then sat up. *Was that it?* she thought. She'd felt him do something down there, but she was expecting overpowering pain, and blood from a stuck pig and brimstone and hell. What was the big deal? And why did people keep doing it?

Soon after, she accepted a full scholarship to an out-of-state college, which her parents forbade her to take. With a backpack loaded with all her wanted possessions, she took the bus away from her home and never ventured back. In the last twelve years, she'd called a couple times, to let them know she was alive.

The last time, she actually listened to the damnation speech a few minutes before she hung up. It was nice to know nothing had changed.

Her choice of career was also decided by her loving parents. In second grade, the class learned dinosaurs had lived millions of years ago. When she told the teacher her mom and dad said the earth was only several thousand years old, the teacher looked dismayed. "I'm sorry, Melinda. I forgot about you. You are supposed to believe what your mother and father tell you."

Even now, she recalled the sarcasm and disdain in her instructor's words. From that moment on, Melinda decided she'd believe only what the books in school told her. In her later years, she learned even her educational materials were not the "real" story. She had to do her own research and make her own decision.

Hard, steady, non-negotiable facts. That was where she found her peace, her way. With facts, no one could tell her she was wrong. Two plus two equaled four and there was no getting around that.

So when she was offered a research position with the Centers for Disease Control, she jumped at the opportunity to work with a prestigious organization whose mission was to better the world through finding the truth with science. Then she learned about the world of politics and how it affected almost everything.

Office politics made as much sense as her zealot parents. If she wanted to have the perks and money, she had to play the game. Which she hated. She was into discovery and advancing science to benefit mankind. All the other things someone else could deal with.

Two years ago when a position opened at the world-famous Uganda Virus Research Lab, she couldn't pass up the chance to get away from a place ruled by money. Certainly the UVRL had its issues, as all places did, but Melinda doubted they were any worse than she'd already experienced. At least in Uganda the temperature seldom rose higher than the seventies, nor fell lower than the sixties. And there weren't any roads to cause road rage. After being there for over a year, she'd learned the climate and customs pretty quickly.

"Miss Caster." She looked at her senior PRO. Oh, right. The hunky, geeky Oversight guy.

With an over-the-top grin, she tilted her head like a star-struck teen. "Yes, Mr. Kintu."

Her boss rolled his eyes. "Dr. Hamel, as I warned you earlier, Miss Caster has a strong . . ." He paused. Mel raised a brow. What had he told this guy about her already? "A strong sense of doing what she thinks right—"

You'd better believe it. "Aww, thanks, Mr. Kintu. I didn't know you cared."

He wasn't finished. "Whether or not she comes off as a—what do you call it?—smart-ass." Their visitor burst out a laugh. Mel, not so much. Mr. Kintu winked at her. If she had one person she wanted in her life in a father role, he would be that man. "Dr. Hamel, please have a seat."

Parish sat across the table from her. His glasses didn't look right. Maybe more like he wasn't used to wearing Coke bottles. Her sight was horrible as a kid. One of the first things she did when she'd saved up enough money was have laser surgery done on her eyes. It was indescribable how much that changed her self-image. It was the first time she could remember waking and seeing the clock without having to feel around for her glasses.

Dr. Hamel slipped off his own glasses and slid them into his pocket. Interesting. Maybe he only needed them for driving. Mr. Kintu turned to Melinda. "Miss Caster, in no way have you done anything wrong. I hope I didn't imply that earlier. Dr. Hamel is here to learn from you—"

"Learn from *me*?" What the hell? She was a researcher; all she did was learn, not teach.

Mr. Kintu turned to the visitor. "She also has a tendency to interrupt."

"I do not." Her cheeks flooded red.

"As I was saying," he continued, "a tendency to interrupt, which is a sign of a strong, quick mind."

Dr. Hamel nodded. "I am warned. Thank you, Mr. Kintu."

Her senior PRO turned to her. "Now, Miss Caster, Dr. Hamel is here to assist you. To take notes as you dictate your experiment's progress. Everything you do concerning this undiscovered virus is vital to log. We will not be blamed again for 'failing to act' against a new potential health threat.

"We discovered the Zika virus in 1947, and seventy years later, they act as if a nuclear bomb has exploded under our noses. We are well aware of every disease on this planet. And written records will continue to prove that."

"I fully agree, Mr. Kintu," Mel said. "Who's accusing us of not knowing?"

He mumbled under his breath and looked down at papers in front of him. He might've been blushing, though it was hard to tell with his dark-colored skin. "Anyway, Miss Caster, please show Dr. Hamel around the facility and introduce him to those you work with." He stood, signaling the meeting was over.

He turned to the newcomer and offered a hand. "Thank you for coming, Doctor. Your attendance is appreciated." He swiveled toward her. "Miss Caster, please don't beat him up too much. We need to return him in one piece."

CHAPTER 2

—✂—

Melinda set her laptop and notes on a table in her lab. The room was fairly large for only one person to work in, thus when a piece of equipment or box needed to be stored someplace, it usually ended up in her lab.

Dr. Hump-him—Hamel—followed her in. He took another deep breath. What was up with that? Did he smell something strange? She took a shower this morning. Her little home even had electricity.

Actually, most buildings did in Entebbe. The Ugandan town was one of the larger ones in the small country. It sat on the shore of Lake Victoria in Africa, much like Chicago butted up to Lake Michigan.

"You keep a clean lab, Miss Caster."

"Yeah, you can't have microbes from lunch floating onto a petri dish."

"Penicillin was discovered in such a way."

"Of course; how do you expect a man to discover anything?" She eyed him for his reaction. If he could handle her man-bashing, they'd get along just fine. No woman-bashing, though. Yes, it was a double standard, but it was her lab. If he didn't like it, he really was more than welcome to leave.

"Agreed, Miss Caster. Men are usually not associated with cleanliness."

Did he just agree with her? Holy shit. Maybe she'd found a keeper. Wait, he's Oversight. Never mind.

"Miss Caster—"

"Melinda"—yes, she interrupted, dammit—"please call me Melinda." The big guy smiled.

"As long as you call me Parish, I will."

She inwardly cringed. "Parish" reminded her too much of her parents. "No offense, Dr. Hamel, but may I call you by your last name?" She waited for his indignant reply.

"I prefer that, actually," he said.

Holy double shit! He agreed with her again. This hadn't happened since the guys on the vaccination floor agreed to move their beer to another fridge. She would've hated for one of them to accidently drink a virus. Though, how one could confuse a test tube for a beer, she didn't know. But she had no doubt, the men would've found a way.

"Hamel it is, then," she said. Her eyes glanced around the room while her brain scrambled for something to say. She was never good at the whole human-communication thing. That was another nice thing about being a researcher; they were known to work constantly, thus excused from social interaction.

Hamel saved her from herself and spoke first. "How about we start from the beginning and you tell me how you came across this new virus." That she could do.

She opened her laptop, logged into the network, then turned to him. Damn, he was standing close. She hadn't noticed in the awkward moment spent trying to find something to say. He smelled different, a good different. Woodsy, fresh, like he just came in from a run in the forest. Her favorite smells.

That was another thing she loved about where she lived. Before when she thought of Africa, two things came to mind: dense jungle with monster snakes that squeezed you to death, and desert sands that went on forever, unmercifully killing anyone stupid enough to get lost.

But surrounding Africa's largest lake, trees and cleared land dominated the populated areas. Waves gently lapped against the shore on Entebbe's public beaches. As soon as the narrow swaths of sand ended, forests sprang, giving shelter from the sun. Town sidewalks and parks roamed the lake area, letting tourists and natives alike easily dip their toes into the warm water.

Her balcony at home faced the water, always catching the cool winds. At night, she usually sat outside, listening to the waves come in. Sometimes a radio played pop hits in the distance, and happy screams of children chasing the retreating water, only to be caught by the incoming deluge, floated in the air.

Shit. She realized why he was so close to her. Not because she was alluring or exotic. No, he was close so he could watch her type in her network password. Damn. She'd have to change it again. It was time, anyway. She was sure administration wouldn't be happy if they found out *"fuckingpassword1"* belonged to their lab technician. It fit the criteria: more than eight letters, number included, and she wouldn't forget it. Worked for her.

"Melinda." The nerdy man stepped closer, bringing her back to reality. Damn, he smelled ever better. Tingles ran up her arms. Fortunately, her lab coat covered them. A low, intoxicating grumble reached her ears. It penetrated her senses. Her heart raced. Sweat beaded on her upper lip.

Her eyes popped open, looking for the source. Dazzling golden irises met her gaze, just inches away. Ohmigod. She sucked in a breath and tried to step back, but she was against the table. She wanted to put her hand on his chest to move him away, but she was afraid of what touching him would do to her.

He cleared his throat and stepped to the side. "Sorry about that. Didn't mean to invade your personal space." He walked to the other side of the table, hand brushing his buzzed hair. Shit, she thought, he could invade her anytime he wanted. A mental slap reprimanded her. *Stop that thinking. He's Oversight.*

Once again, she stood speechless, remembering they had started talking about something. What was it?

CHAPTER 3

———✦———

Hamel took in quick shallow breaths so as not to breathe her in. Fuck. Why now? Why did he have to find his mate in the middle of his tour of duty? He was ecstatic to have found her finally, but during duty he wasn't allowed to touch her. Not to mention she was his ward for the next several weeks. At least until intelligence reports came back saying the threat had been neutralized.

How would it look on his record if he was caught sleeping with his assignment? Well, there wouldn't be much sleeping going on. It took everything he had not to set her on the table right now and slide in balls deep. Fuck. He had to keep his identity covered for her safety. And that wasn't going to be as easy as originally thought.

She was fucking smarter than shit. He wouldn't be able to get away with laziness on this job. In a way, that made him proud. His mate was a tough adversary; no pansy for his family.

Right away in the meeting room, she suspected something. He'd smelled it. He should've never worn the damn glasses. She could tell he wasn't comfortable in them. Her file said she'd worn thick lenses her entire life. Only someone like that would pick up on the facial nuances that gave away his secret.

And now, standing so close to her to peek at her password—which he thought was hilarious; he wouldn't forget it, that's for sure—she smelled so freaking good. He was about to say screw the job. He'd whisk her off this continent and to a secluded island where he would be sure to put babies in her stomach.

Well, fuck. His balls ached thinking about it. He turned his back to her and walked away. Anywhere, just not so close. He rounded the end of the table and spoke across the gap between them. "You were telling me how you found the virus."

"Yes, the virus. Of course."

He hadn't missed her reaction to him. Heart suddenly racing, chills on her skin. She probably had no idea what hit her. His jaguar wanted its little mate, and it would have her, no matter what. He only needed to remind his animal they were on duty to protect her first. No sex. All they got was slapping the monkey, and that would have to wait.

Melinda continued with her story. "The wildlife reserve not too far away called us about three baby monkeys that died for no apparent reason. The workers had noticed strange things happening, also."

"Strange how?" he asked.

"Like things being moved from where they placed it. Food disappearing. They thought they had a prankster spirit. I saw a witch doctor last time I was at the animal medical facility. I'd heard about him, but never saw him until then.

"So, anyway. The three babies were ready for testing. I took blood, saliva, all the normal stuff. Then I noticed a stream of dried blood in one of the babies' ears. We brought that animal back to do cranial scans to see if it had any head trauma. What we discovered was this."

Melinda turned her computer around to show him images of what looked like the top view of a brain. The only time he'd seen anything like that was on TV crime shows. He scowled. What the hell was he supposed to say? He was a soldier, not a doctor. Though, he played one undercover. He scoured his head for something that didn't sound idiotic. "Really? Did you rescan to make sure there were not imaging errors?"

"That's the first thing we did. You're looking at the third rendition. All are identical."

He crossed his arms, pretending to be pondering. His job was to protect her from the perceived threat his agency knew existed, not challenge her mental abilities or work theories. He should've kept to the original plan of helping with "paperwork" and such. But when he discovered she was his mate, he wanted to be closer to her. Know more about her and what she was doing. Now he had her thinking he was a doctor. Well, fuck. *Now what? Think, think, think.* Had to be real. "Uh, this is good, but let's get to the bottom line. What are your conclusions?"

She raised a brow, but continued. "My conclusions are these three babies had highly developed nervous systems." She paused, looking at him. Like he had a clue what the fuck she just said. The babies were nervous all the time. So?

Melinda pointed to the center of the image. "As you see here, there are many more synaptic connections than normal."

He tried to sound unimpressed. "Of course. Go on." She paused a second before continuing.

"Therefore, I believe the babies overly developed in the womb and were born with extrasensory . . . abilities."

He scowled at her again. "Extra what?"

She hurried away from the laptop. "I know that sounds ludicrous. But what else can occur when you have a trillion more synaptic connections firing all the time?"

Beat the hell out of him. What?

"It's like having another brain smashed in with yours to make it twice of everything. The brain is extra strong. And with the additional fiber links, the brain can process tremendous amounts of information, taking it to the next level, per se."

"Next level? As in . . ." Overly ADHD?

On the other side of the lab, she opened a cage on a countertop and pulled out a little white mouse. She grabbed a handful of treats and put them into her coat pocket.

"I'm going into the next room and calling you." She pointed to a phone attached to the wall. "You answer and we'll go from there." She left, closing the door behind her.

What the hell was going on? What did all this have to do

with a virus? And the biggest question: Who the hell would kill to get their hands on an unknown biological weapon?

The phone rang. He picked it up. "Yeah."

"Okay. After I hang up, count to five and watch what the mice do. Ready? I'm hanging up." He ticked off a handful of seconds, then the mice went berserk in their cage. The phone rang. "Did you see that?"

"The mice made a lot of noise and stuff, but that's it."

"Okay, after I hang up count to ten and watch." He placed the receiver in the cradle and did as instructed. Same thing with the mice. They went nutso for a few seconds. He waited for the phone, but Melinda came through the door instead.

"Wasn't that exciting?" she asked.

"Overly. What's your point?"

Her expression turned harsh. Maybe he needed to back off on the asshole-doctor shtick. "I apologize if I sound a bit skeptical."

She softened. "I understand. Here's the point." She turned her back to the far side of the room, where the small animals were. She held a treat in front of the mouse she held so it could smell it. The others immediately erupted into a scuttle. She repeated the process after waiting a few seconds.

Holy living fuck. "Are you saying those mice in the cage know when this one here is given a treat and they get fussy wanting one, too?"

Her smile blew him away. So warm and inviting. Her eyes twinkled with happiness at sharing this with him. "That's exactly what I'm saying. The additional brainpower gives the animal clairvoyant abilities."

He put his hands up in supplication. "Whoa, here. Let's back this train up." He held his hand out. "May I hold the mouse?"

She started to hand it over, but when she got close to his hand, the mice exploded into screams and began bashing the sides of their cages on the other side of the room. The one in her hand wriggled, trying to get away. He snapped his hand back and they settled down. "Huh, guess they don't like me." More like they didn't like his big bad kitty smell. He forgot about that. "Okay, I don't need to hold it. I see the correlation.

I'm not seeing how this relates to dead monkeys or viruses, though."

Melinda turned toward the other side of the room. "Hold on a second. There are several working parts to this." She put the mouse into a cage and gave them all treats. Returning to the table and her laptop, she brought up another image, which looked identical to the other one, but the center of the brain was dark, where before it was light. She pointed to the mid-section again.

"This is the same image of the brain, but in its original state. We had to lighten it so we could see all the synapses that are hidden by the shadow in this one. We don't know what we're looking at. Why they are all black."

Good, he didn't feel so stupid that he didn't know, either. This doctor gig was not going to work much longer if she expected him to sound intelligent. He was so screwed.

CHAPTER 4

Melinda loved this part of her work. Showing the data she'd collected and the logical hypothesis based on that information. And when the other person really understood it, that made it so much more fun.

On her laptop, she brought up the slide of the blood samples. She turned the screen so she and Hamel could both see it. In her excitement, she'd forgotten her body's reaction to his. She'd have to ignore it because if she moved away, he'd know she was somewhat attracted to him. Which she totally wasn't. Just her stupid body.

"Look at this first blood sample on the left." She tapped the screen with a pen. "You see the erythrocytes, leukocytes, right?"

"Absolutely, all right there, plain as day."

She clicked the mouse pad and another image came up on the right side of the screen. She watched his reaction. His brows drew down. He asked, "What are all those squiggly things floating around?"

"Those squiggly things, Dr. Hamel, are the virus. This is the infected blood sample compared to a similar, normal blood sample." She turned toward the screen. "Interesting thing with this virus, like several Zika cases, is that the carrier doesn't appear to have any physical symptoms. No sickness or tiredness or anything else we would associate with a virus.

"Seems the effect is only to the offspring, advanced brain development giving sensory abilities beyond normal scope. I've dubbed it Espee."

Hamel shifted around. "That's appropriate. ESP as in extrasensory perception."

"No. As in Emily, Steven, and Paul," she said. She sighed at his baffled look. "Those are the three baby monkeys who died with this virus. I could've called it SEP, but that's too close to 'septic.' The only other option is PES and we couldn't have kids walking around saying 'pes,' too similar to 'piss.' But doesn't matter what I call it. The powers that be will name it when we release the data to the WHO."

"To who?" he asked.

"Yes," she said, pulling a small flash drive from her laptop's side and sliding it into a pocket. "We do the grunt work and they take the credit. Which is fine by me. I don't need my name in lights. Just pay me a fair wage. I love what I do, so it's not really work."

They had both relaxed a little, being together for a while now. With nothing to say, she looked at him a bit shyly, realizing she was getting into the personal side of things.

Hamel cleared his throat and shoved his hands into his pockets. "So, the mother carried the strain with no obvious signs of sickness, and the children had special connections. Could the children be the answer to the weird things the medical facility mentioned?"

She shrugged. "Could be, but it sounds more like they have someone playing tricks on them. Halloween is this weekend. They're getting an early start on their scaring."

"They have Halloween in Uganda?" Hamel asked, his brows snapping up.

"It's just another reason to stay up late and drink beer for most of the population. Lots of clubs have costume contests and fun stuff. Nothing big."

"Do you like Halloween?"

She frowned and thought about it for a second. "I love paranormal movies and over-the-top scares. I do have a hard time believing any of it, but it's all for the fun of it, you know?"

He grinned. "So you don't believe in ghosts, vampires, werewolves, or anything paranormal?"

She raised a brow. "Come on, Dr. Hamel. I've spent my life studying facts. I believe what I see, not what anyone else tells me. I learned long ago that people have wild imaginations. So, no, I don't believe in ghosts, vampires, werewolves, or anything that goes bump in the night. I'm sure there is an explanation for everything."

"I guess that means you won't be watching *The Exorcist* on Halloween, huh?"

His smile made her blink and realize he was kidding with her.

"Maybe. I do like that movie. The creepy factor is out of this world. It was one of the first movies I watched when my parents let me go to a sleepover. Let me just say, there was little sleeping and lots of lights on for the rest of the night."

He chuckled and nodded. "Back to the virus strain. What did you do after you discovered the wiggly lines in the blood?"

Wiggly lines? "I isolated the virus to create a serum for testing with the mice. We stumbled upon the clairvoyance accidentally when we were separating and running the maze."

"Running the maze?" he asked. "Is that for the mice to find the end?"

She hiked a hand onto her hip. "Dr. Hamel, I'm so glad they're teaching you something over there. It surely isn't hematology."

His eyes narrowed. She might have pissed him off. Darn. Maybe he'd leave. "My job isn't to know—" He cut off abruptly and she waited for him to finish, but he didn't. She decided to help.

"Your job isn't what?" She held his eyes, refusing to back down. She would not be intimidated by this or any man. She'd grown up cowering to those stronger than her, those who yelled at her. In college, her BS degree wasn't only a Bachelor of Science, it was also Balls of Steel. In a male-dominated laboratory, she'd learned to hold her own or get run over.

Hamel sighed and leaned against a cabinet. "Look, Melinda.

I'm not here as a threat to you or anyone. I just need to get the lay of the land and an idea of what we're dealing with. I won't get in your way. In fact, I'll even bring you coffee in the morning. How about that?"

Her own personal secretary with a body she bet would make any pair of undies shrivel into nothing, at her beck and call? Sounded too good, but she'd take if for now. "Okay, but I don't drink coffee. I'll show you how I make tea." *Then take all your clothes off,* she wanted to add.

She pulled a beaker from the sink and partially filled it with water from the filtered tap. From her coat pocket, she pulled out a six-inch packet, ripped the top off, then poured the powder contents into the beaker. She shook it, making a brown liquid. "Voila. Tea. Now we just need sugar." She dug through her lab coat pockets, pulling items out then shoving them back in.

"Melinda," Hamel started, "why is there a label with 'ESP' on the beaker you have your tea in?"

Oh, she'd forgotten about that. "Long story."

"I've got time," he said, the corner of his mouth quirking up.

"It's not a big deal. I'm the only one with access in here."

"What's not a big deal?" Amusement shone brightly in his eyes.

Fine. He was going to make her admit to being an idiot. "I set up everything for the serum last week, including putting a label on the beaker with the virus name I gave it. Well, when it came time to need it, I couldn't find it. Somehow it walked away. I don't know. But the beaker was too big anyway, so I pulled a test tube and used it.

"Then when I went to make tea for the day, I found the beaker next to the sink, so I used it instead. I tried to peel the label off, but as you can see, it kept tearing in slivers, so I said forget it." True enough, it looked like the label had been unsuccessfully picked at from both ends. She pulled a precarious handful of sugar packets from her side pocket and lifted them for Hamel to see.

"I like to use real sugar—" A couple packets came loose and fell through her fingers. She heard a plop and her tea showed a round wave moving outward from the center. When she looked down to see what she dropped, her heart stopped.

"SHIT." She dumped the beaker upside down on the countertop. Liquid spilled in all directions. She scooped her thumb-sized flash drive from the mess and shook it vigorously while looking in all directions for something to save it. She wiped it on her coat then ran for the ladies' room. Inside, her hand slammed on the button to the blow dryer. "Please, please, please."

Everything pertaining to the virus was on that drive. A lot was on her laptop, but the final solution for the serum was on the flash. Fortunately, this wasn't a disaster to end all disasters or her career. Her eidetic memory could re-create the serum, if needed. But some of the paperwork Mr. Kintu spoke about needing to prove discovery was gone.

She heard a knock on the bathroom door. "Melinda," a deep voice said, "everything okay?"

"Yeah, Hamel, sorry. I dropped my flash drive into my tea." She greeted him at the door and he held it open for her to exit. "It's not too big of a deal. I'll plug it in to see if it will work." Not likely.

At her laptop, the machine recognized the drive, but nothing showed in the directory for files. She pulled the piece out and shoved it into her pocket. Maybe one of the computer gurus could get something out of it.

She glanced at her watch. Thank god it was time for lunch. "Do you have plans for lunch? I bring mine and sit in the lunchroom with the others. You're welcome to join us."

His expression turned thoughtful. "Thank you, but I have plans with Mr. Kintu. I may not see you again until tomorrow."

She was surprised how disappointed she was at the possibility of not seeing him later. Damn, she was pathetic. No, not pathetic, just highly interested in a new man who made her girl parts take notice. Okay, yeah, pathetic. She knew better than that. Hamel was here for work. Not like he was going to up and offer to make all her sexual daydreams come true. She spent the rest of day with the techy guys trying to get data off her flash.

Late in the afternoon, she had a headache and was ready to toss her flash and laptop from the roof of the building. Giving it a good heave might make her feel better, but wouldn't improve the situation any.

She put the remainder of her second beaker of tea in her lab's fridge in front of several beakers, then locked it. She gathered her laptop and useless thumb drive and locked them in a cabinet along with anything else that could walk off. Theft wasn't a problem, but she hated to dangle an irresistible opportunity.

As soon as she stepped out of the building, she felt eyes on her. She looked around, but everything seemed as it always did. She hurried to her car and headed home.

CHAPTER 5

⌒

Stripped of her work clothes and shoes, Melinda relaxed into the hammock chair strung up on her balcony overlooking Lake Victoria. The lake was nearly as big as one of the Great Lakes in the U.S., so with no land to see on the other side, it seemed like she was on the ocean. A wooded area that had grown a bit too wild separated her home from the narrow strip of sand and mud—more mud than sand—that was her personal beach.

Glass of Moscato in hand, she let out a sigh. Good wine was not easy to come by in Uganda. And when she could find it, paying out the nose was normal. But if she ever needed wine to wind down, it was tonight after her crazy day. The oddest part being Hamel showing up out of the blue.

She found it hard to push the man from her mind. It had been a while since she'd seen someone from the States. After working, talking, and living with the native people for two years, it was weird.

But she'd forgive him that if she could just get a peek at the body under the clothes. She knew he had to be ripped. Her hormones decided to go along with her thinking. The way he filled out his shirt and the lab coat. The way he moved;

it was like he glided across the floor. Like a cat, steady and sure after its prey.

Tingles of pleasure gave her a full-body shudder. A growl came from somewhere in the woods. It was faint, which was good. She did not like the idea of being dinner for a huge creature. She'd been told stories by those she worked with about monster everything in Africa: monster snakes, bugs, cats, reptiles, fish. It was like Texas; everything was bigger.

The sunset was bloodred tonight. Crimson smeared from one side to the other. The lake mirrored the heavens, turning the rolling waves into a sea of blood. Which brought Hamel back into her mind, of course. Because, why the fuck not? The man was hot and she hadn't gotten laid in more time than she cared to remember.

He needed a refresher in his biological studies, though. She felt like he had no clue what she was talking about in the lab today. Typical for the American government. Those not qualified, but who have plenty of money, lead those who work their tails off to make a living. It's all the politics she ran from. Sorta.

A little piece of hurt pinged her heart. She didn't want to think about him tonight, or any night, for that matter. After two years, her heart and pride were still bruised. Still tender to the touch.

Like Hamel, Kenneth had shown up from out of the blue and attached himself to her. She was just beginning her career with the CDC, and her life was in a huge upheaval with finding a place to live, getting her belongings there, selling her old house, and starting a new job with high expectations. So when he stepped in to help her get settled, she didn't ask questions.

Kenneth was a recent grad, like her, and working in her area of study. Again, when he suggested they work together, she never asked questions. Kenneth made her feel pretty, feel worthy of love, which was something she didn't get on the home front. He made her laugh, he watched chick flicks with her, and he was cute. Too cute for someone like her. But she never questioned, until it was too late.

She and Kenneth had been working on a vaccine to develop a meningococcal conjugate vaccine as a tool for eliminating epidemic meningitis as a public health problem in sub-Saharan Africa. Early on, Melinda made a discovery that led directly to a cure. When they were ready to show their bosses what they found, Kenneth set her up for having little part of the find. He took all the credit.

She pleaded her case, explaining the truth. But in the end, it came down to he said, she said. And the *she said* side wasn't picked to win. She'd learned a lot with that experience, mainly that people didn't do anything without motive. That motive usually involved them winning something and her losing. Nobody had your best interest in mind. Well, maybe parents, but the point was she couldn't trust anybody for anything. Only herself.

Shitty backstabbing wasn't as much of a problem in Uganda. People here were honest and usually willing to help. She knew her neighbors, and they were all nice.

Slowly swaying in the hammock chair, wineglass in hand. Just the light crash of waves on the shore, the tweet of a passing songbird. Her eyes growing heavier and heavier.

Then exactly twenty minutes after she snuggled in, her phone went berserk with "WARNING. WARNING." The deep voice repeated to evacuate immediately. A scratchy horn blasted its shriek along with the high-pitched sirens associated with fire engines.

It scared the living shit out of her.

She scrambled forward in her hammock chair. In her haste and pumping adrenaline, she leaned too far to the side, causing the rope-constructed seat to dump her on the spot. Still holding the wineglass in one hand, she only had one way to catch herself.

Her free hand slammed on the edge of the side table, more specifically, on a tray overhanging the edge, loaded with crackers, sliced fruit, the bottle of Moscato, and of course, her phone. She watched as the food and drink launched into the air and sailed over the balcony's rail.

She lay on her back staring at the first stars appearing for the night. Goddammit, motherfucking son of a bitch with a corncob up her ass. Why did this kind of shit happen to her all the time? First she dropped her flash drive in her tea. Now, an expensive bottle—with its cap on, thank god—lay somewhere in the woods. Her phone had stopped roaring, at least. Just in time so she wouldn't be able to find it in the dark. Somebody above must hate her.

With a groan, she pulled herself up from the floor. Then she realized she still held her glass, wine still in it! Ha. Maybe that somebody above really did like her. She tipped her head back to chug the remaining alcohol and headed toward the kitchen.

With her first step, her pinky toe smashed into the out-of-position table leg, sending a sharp stab of pain through her foot. Without thinking, she lifted her knee, grabbing at the injury, fingers frantically rubbing the toe to stop the sting. Shifting her weight, she hopped around on the other leg, trying to remain upright. Dammit! Why did the little things hurt so damn much?

But she still had her pristine wineglass. She felt like a winner. Nobody could crush her spirit. *Go me!*

She limped to the kitchen to take out the food from the oven for dinner—the whole reason this fiasco happened. She forgot to set an alarm last time and fell asleep to wake up to a home filled with burnt-smelling smoke and an inedible chicken. Dinner could cool while she hunted for her phone and wine. At the back door, she slipped on her flip-flops and stomped down the back stairs to the woods. She looked up at her balcony and eyeballed where her stuff should've landed.

On hands and knees, she brushed at dead leaves and vines. This sucked. If she had to, she'd borrow a phone from someone and dial her number. Problem was none of her neighbors had phones. Yes, the gods that be hated her. Noises came from the dark ahead.

It was amazing how different the woods sounded from the safety of her balcony. Off to the side, something scuffled, stepping on brittle leaves. She stopped. Oh, no, no, no! Shit. It had to be a big animal or human to crunch leaves. Climbing to her feet, she spotted the wine bottle and hurried to scoop it up.

Movement close to the ground caught her eye. It looked like a pile of material. When she got close enough, she toed the dark bundle. The white tag on a black T-shirt fluttered in the breeze. That's what got her attention. She lifted the shirt and realized this was an entire outfit, shoes included, in black. What the hell?

Well, shit. Looked like they had another naked person running around. Same thing happened last year at this time. Some older kids thought it'd be fun to skinny-dip in the lake. Seemed they were so drunk, they couldn't remember where they stripped and wandered around the woods until someone called the authorities. But this was rather far from the beach.

Another crinkling of leaves came farther to the side. She wrapped her hand around the neck of the bottle. "Hey, whoever you are, you need to put your clothes on and get out of here. This is private property." Sorta. She got no reply back. "Hey. Did you hear me?"

Maybe she could scare him away. Eh, that was a dumb idea. It wasn't like she was the Bionic Woman and could kick his ass if he didn't run. She turned and retraced her steps.

The sound of sirens and trumpet blasts led her to her phone. It was buried under leaves she pushed to the side. She turned off the repeat alarm option so it would stop going off now that she didn't need it. After she climbed the stairs, she paused and looked over her shoulder.

On top of the neighbor's concrete wall stood a monstrous black cat. Shit, it could've been a lion as far as she knew. The thick fur swallowed the moonlight, not letting her see many details, only a silhouette. The sight took her breath away. So majestic, so confident, so strong.

She felt like it was looking directly at her, drilling into her, searching for her soul to see if she was worthy. She wasn't. No question about it. The cat turned and jumped down on the other side of the wall. She really hoped the naked guy wasn't the cat's dinner. Eww. Gross thought.

Hurrying inside, she shut and locked the door.

CHAPTER 6

Fuck. That was close. Hamel in his jaguar form slinked through the growing darkness toward the wooded area outside Melinda's bungalow.

He needed to pay more attention instead of staring at her and daydreaming of their first night together. But *fuck*. She was his mate. It took extreme willpower to keep from going into her home and claiming her there and then. His cat liked that idea. *Let's go up the stairs.*

Not happening, fur ball. Respect. A hole torn in a long piece of aluminum siding offered the perfect opportunity to get to the tree side of the fence. His cat stepped through, careful not to get cut on sharp edges.

He didn't smell her nearby, so he knew it was safe to shift and redress. He wondered if he should move to a different location. No, the position he had was strategically the best place to watch her house. For his mate, only the best of everything would be acceptable.

Ah, fuck. His mate. His mom always said he'd never know the time or place he'd meet his other half. He didn't have to worry about that now. The thought of mating and having a family sent an electric thrill through him. That was every shifter's dream. So many were never that lucky and ended up alone or marrying a non-mate.

He wondered if the boss knew his mate was here and that was why he was sent. How could he? Two of the ALFA team were on assignment undercover, and the third was recovering from a battle with a wolf pack. The whole pack had turned against him. Damn, that guy was a man's man and a shifter's shifter. He was the Alpha League Federal Agency's best.

So Hamel was the only soldier available. It had to be fate. Did he really believe that? During his life, he'd had problems accepting things he couldn't touch, couldn't verify with his own eyes. Fates, ghosts, gods, demons, magic. They were all the same. No solid evidence of their existence. He'd probably doubt the existence of shifters if he wasn't one.

Reaching the tree he had parked himself under, he looked into the high branches. Yup, his backpack was still there, hanging on a limb. He'd had no choice but to heave it somewhere Melinda wouldn't see it. Earlier, he saw the wine bottle fly over the balcony railing and wondered what she was doing. He about shit when she walked out her back door.

His best option was to strip and shift. If she saw any of the human side, she'd be wary and maybe overly suspicious.

Going on what he'd learned today, he was a bit confused about this whole virus thing. He understood what could happen if something like the bubonic plague was released. But this virus Melinda was working with didn't make people sick. It evolved their brains to another level, and only the children, at that. Who would find it beneficial to have a world of clairvoyant kids?

Well, they'd have tremendous military use for locating hidden bunkers, buried ammo stashes, and current hideouts for the bad guys. If that's how it worked. He wasn't sure. Again, he couldn't feel it or see it . . .

How was he going to explain shifters to her? He was sure her brain was even more logical than his. He might have time to build a relationship if he could get her a step up from just tolerating him. He didn't like the idea of simply taking her with him when it was time to go. She might have something to say about that.

He'd learned from others' mistakes, and it was putting it mildly to call it a mistake when his uncle thought he could pull a caveman when he met his own mate. Holy shit, he'd never witnessed anything so deadly and funny at the same time.

They'd met in the grocery store, of all places. She was buying snapper at the meat counter, and Hamel and his uncle were sent to pick up fresh steaks for dinner. After his uncle scented her, you couldn't pull him away with a crowbar. Hamel followed at a distance waiting for the shit to hit the fan. He knew it would. His uncle was one of those people who attracted bad luck like a magnet. If something could go wrong, it would.

So on that day at the grocer's market, he learned to never assume his mate would welcome him with open arms. Never think his little lady couldn't kick his ass and toss him onto the pie and cake display, thanks to her black belt in martial arts. And never, *ever*, get up in her face and tell her what she must do. That was the quickest means of getting your balls shoved *up* your throat.

But in the end, it had all worked out. They were as perfect for each other as destiny had planned. After a few times of him landing flat on his back for trying to boss her around, he came to the conclusion that offering options and letting her decide would keep his body in one piece much longer.

Now Hamel needed to come up with solutions to negate all the things she'd throw at him to keep from loving him—while watching out for bad guys, keeping his cover solid by not sounding like an idiot in the lab, and forcing his animal to wait until she said yes. That required multitasking. Men weren't known to be good at that kind of stuff. Just give them a spear and they'd come back with supper.

There was no way this would end well.

CHAPTER 7

＿＞＜＿

Melinda knew right away she had to be dreaming. She'd experienced this before: being cognizant in the dream, but unable to do anything about it. What clue did she have for that decision? First, she was in the swimsuit on this year's *Sports Illustrated* swimwear cover. That would never happen. She was happily built for a tankini with a skirt covering her cute ass.

Second, she stood in sugar-soft white sand outside her place on the lake. Last she'd looked at the beach, though, moss had covered the rocks and a couple dead fish floated in the waves, belly up.

Third, there was a four-poster bed with long sheer draping hanging off it on the beach. The material floated around the posts. There were a multitude of pillows. A soft breeze caressed her skin. The scent of nature made her almost believe she was really there. Except she'd never gone outside and seen any beds just lying around. Ever.

And fourth, the man walking toward her was the most gorgeous specimen she had ever encountered. His chest rippled when his powerful, broad shoulders swayed with his stride. His abs must have been Photoshopped; they didn't get that yummy-looking in real life.

She sucked in a sharp breath, seeing he wore a black Speedo that did nothing to cover what god gave him. Raised as she was with anything related to sex being a sin, this made her uncomfortable, and she looked away. When she glanced back, he wore loose-fitting swim trunks, which made her feel much better about this whole encounter. Not that it was real or anything.

His defined thighs rolled with each step he took, a well-oiled machine looking better the closer he— What the . . . ?

"Hamel, why the hell are you in my dream looking so freaking good? I don't remember inviting you to this party."

He smiled with perfect, bright white teeth. His eyes sparkled, full of happiness. From seeing her? He stopped inches from her, cupped her face in his hands, and kissed her until she almost came on the spot. He pulled back, his hand still curled around her face and his body flush against hers. "You're mine, baby girl."

She blinked. Damn. Even in her dreams, he was able to make her knees buckle. "Hamel, you're cute and all, but this is my dream."

He took her lips again, a low growl emanating from him. That sound was so . . . animalistic it made her instantly wet. Her legs hit the back of the bed and she fell back on the giant, plush mattress with him on top of her. His strong, powerful body was warm to touch. Their kiss went on while her hands roamed over his exposed torso. Lord have mercy!

She moaned into his mouth, her breathing ragged and her libido in overdrive. His delectable arm muscles shifted under her touch. He sucked on her tongue, and a soft rumble sounded in his chest and made her body shudder.

Her bikini top disappeared off her body. Yep, definitely a dream. She sucked in a gulp of air and watched his fire-rimmed irises brighten with need.

"You're mine."

She licked her lips, loving the taste of him still on her lips. "Right now, I can be anything you want."

It was a dream. She might as well live it up. His hands cupped her breasts, thumbs flicking over her tight nipples.

"You like that?"

Like it? She couldn't move; her bones had melted into the mattress. "Oh, yes."

"That's good, baby. I want you to tell me everything you like. Tell me how you want it."

She bit the inside of her mouth. She'd never been the dirty-talking sexual person. But Hamel was giving her such a domineering, hungry look, she wanted to say something to keep him going. To make him lose control. "Hard."

She did want it hard. The feel of his erection pressing at her bikini-covered crotch was driving her insane. He lowered his head, took her breast in his mouth, licking and biting her nipple before sucking it deeply between his lips.

"Oh. My. God!" she moaned, her belly quivering and her bottoms soaked from how turned on she was.

He massaged her other breast, thumbing her nipple and tugging lightly. The pricks of pain were enough to send fire shooting straight to her clit. She'd never realized how sensitive her nipples were. Holy crap, his touch was making her so wet. She was ready to come from every lick, every bite. Then there were his growls. She'd never been with a man so animalistic. It should worry her how hot she found his wildness, but all it did was turn her on more.

He pulled back. The glow in his eyes held her captive. "You have such a beautiful body. I can't wait to be deep inside you, making you mine."

She blinked and swallowed against the dryness in her throat. Her brain told her to say something, but she'd forgotten how to speak. Besides, what would she say? Thank you?

He slid a hand down to her bikini bottom and pushed the material at her pussy aside, dipping his finger into her slick sheath. "Ah, sweetheart. You're wet. So fucking wet," he rumbled, leaving a damp trail from her nipple to her belly. She leaned back on the bed, grabbing two pillows and shoving them under her head. What a view.

She moaned with each slide of his digits into her channel. Good god, that felt amazing. He undid the ties at the sides of her bikini bottom and pushed the flimsy material away from her sex completely. She inhaled an unsteady breath. "Hamel . . ."

"Shh." His lip curled into a wicked grin. "You will be

screaming out my name in a minute, beautiful." His voice held a rough quality she hadn't heard before. "You might not realize this yet," he told her, "but you're mine." He spread her folds and rubbed his thumb on her clit. "Fuck. You make me desperate to shove my face between your legs. Your tight little hole's searching for my cock."

She whimpered, her muscles tensing as he flicked his thumb over her clit again. "Oh, dear god!"

Lust raged in her blood. She'd never been with a man who made her feel so . . . so much. So much need. So much desperation. Lack of control. She wanted everything at that moment and she didn't give a shit that it was only a dream.

"You want me to eat your pussy, don't you?" His voice was even rougher than before, almost impossible to understand. "I know you do. I saw it the moment our eyes met. You want me to fill you with cock. My cock. Right?"

She nodded, her chest rising and falling with short bursts of air. He rolled two fingers into her and coated them with the moisture gathered there. To make things even dirtier, he brought them to his lips. She watched, wide-eyed, as he inserted both into his mouth and *mmmm*'d as he sucked.

Goddamn that was all kinds of dirty and sexy. And why was this the first time she'd seen a guy do that? Hamel might be a porn star acting as a scientist, because no man she'd been with in forever had looked at her like that as he sucked her off his fingers. "Damn, Hamel. I had no idea you were this kind of freaky."

He flared his nostrils and glanced between her legs, his fingers pressing at her clit once more. She wiggled into his touch, her body tensing with the need to come. "This isn't near freaky enough, baby girl. I don't just want your taste on my fingers. I want my tongue in your pussy, lapping at the source."

Her eyes widened. Oh, hell no. Guys didn't do . . . that. Not to her. She was too shy to try it. But watching Hamel's head lower between her legs, his gaze stuck on hers, she could do nothing more than gape.

He circled her entrance, licking and swirling his tongue up to her clit.

"H-Hamel," she moaned.

"Yes. That's it. Moan for me," he grunted. "I'm going to make you come hard, my love."

Oh, boy. He'd called her "*my love*." That right there would normally scare the shit out of her, but since this was a dream she loved it. She could let herself believe during this dream that everything was fucking awesome.

"Your pussy's so pretty." He licked her clit, pressing his tongue on the little pleasure center. "So pink and swollen." A quick swipe over her folds and she was arching off the mattress, the wind caressing her nipples and puckering them even tighter. "So fucking wet." He gave a long, slow lick up from ass to clit. "You're mine. I want your scent all over my face. All over my cock." He rubbed his mouth and chin on her pussy, his tongue curling and dancing over her hard button.

Holy mother of men with motorized tongues. He really knew how to work his mouth. While his tongue danced over her clit in furious strokes, he rubbed a finger over her asshole. Oh, good gracious. Things were getting really freaky now. She'd only read about this kind of stuff in romance novels. A girl needed something to unwind and those romances with men who did the wild thing and knew how to treat a girl were the stuff of her dreams.

Hamel's slick finger went in and out of her ass at the same time his tongue went in and out of her pussy. She gave a loud groan. With every thrust of his tongue into her, he slid the finger farther into her ass.

"Oh my god," she cried, her pussy grasping at nothing.

"That's it, baby. Come on my mouth. Let me taste you on my tongue."

Her muscles tightened with tension and her legs shook. Her pussy clenched, and a loud cry sounded from her as her release rode through her in an angry, forceful wave. Holy fuck, that was amazing. Like she'd never experienced before. Moisture dripped from her onto the bed. His tongue lapped at her, low growls sounding from between her legs.

Shudder after shudder rocked her body. She breathed hard. Her pussy felt empty. She wanted him, and he'd heightened her desire tenfold. She sat up, not trusting her legs for a second. He met her gaze, his mouth dewy from her climax.

Her blood felt aflame. She could barely form a coherent

thought. He slid a finger ever so slowly between her labia, pushing into her. A loud groan left him when her pelvic muscles sucked him in.

"After making you come and watching you struggle to catch your breath, you want me to fuck you, don't you?" He licked his lips and glanced at her sweat-laden torso. "You want my cum inside you, coating your pussy and filling you with my seed. Don't deny it. I know what you want."

This was unlike her. She didn't do the dirty talking or have men promise her hard sex. They definitely didn't suggest coming inside and promise to make her a baby. But instead of being embarrassed or ashamed, like she'd been raised to believe, she was turned on. He was right. She wanted every word he said, and this was her dream, dammit! She could get as freaky as she wanted.

She watched him pounce on the bed. The movement caught her off guard and her jaw dropped open. "How did you—?"

He gave a low growl. She wondered why Hamel was so animalistic in her dream. And why did that turn her on so much? He pushed her legs open with a wiggle of his hips. His cock went straight to her entrance and slipped inside her just a fraction. Enough to make her tense and want to lift her hips, looking for deeper penetration. God! This guy was going to kill her with his teasing.

"You need to—"

"No. Don't even think it. I'm not moving." He rumbled the words out. He sucked her lip between his teeth and nibbled on her mouth. Fuck, that was so good. "I'm staying right where I am, teasing you. Feeling your pussy suck at the head of my cock until you admit you're mine." He jerked his hips enough to give her a taste of what was to come and pulled back.

"Oh, my," she whimpered.

"It only gets better. When you tell me you're mine," he grunted, his lips pressing hard over hers before he met her gaze again, "that this hot, tight pussy is mine. I'm going to take you, fuck you, own you, and stamp myself so far inside, you will never forget who you belong to," he rumbled, caging her head with his hands.

What in the hell had she been secretly wishing for to get this kind of dream? Oh, who cared? She damn well loved it.

His features had gone from handsome man to feral and wildly sensual. "Say it," he encouraged. "Say the words, baby girl. Then, and only then, will I fuck you raw and fill you with cum. Fill you with my seed and my babies."

She couldn't think at all. Just the image of him coming inside her had broken her thinking process. All she wanted at that point was to experience him fully inside her, making her his. This was a dream, and so he could get his way and she could get hers. "Yes," she moaned softly. "I'm yours. All yours."

He pressed his lips roughly over hers, demanding entrance, and thrust into her mouth with his tongue at the same time he plunged with his cock. She didn't expect her body to unravel so quickly. Tension unfurled like a flower opening at the first sign of spring. How could he do that? Make her come with a single thrust?

He swallowed her scream through their kiss, fucking her hard and rough, not stopping for a second. Not through her mind-ripping orgasm or the follow-up shudders that left her legs shaking. He thrust fast, deep, and pulled back just as quickly, taking her pussy with wild, quick strokes. Her body was his and he took and gave equally. He sank his cock into her with swift moves. Each faster than the last. Building her up again, closer and closer. She'd come again soon.

She couldn't speak, could barely breathe. Her perspiration-slicked body allowed him to slide farther into her. It didn't matter that they were outdoors and there was a breeze; her body was on fire from the inside. She pulled back from their air-stealing kiss to gasp a breath. Feral grunts and moans came from both. Sex was never like this. This was more. He was marking her as his and she loved it. She dug her nails into his back, urging him deeper into her body. God, yes! More. More. More. His cock branded her like scorching iron. Her pussy quivered with her need for him.

He grabbed one of her thighs and pulled it to his waist, giving a tilt to her hips. Holy shit, this was it. She was so close, she could taste it. The move allowed him to rub against her hard clit with his pelvis. The first rub and she choked on an inhale. The second rub and she went flying.

Her back curved off the mattress. A hoarse scream flew from her lips as contractions made her pussy flutter. She was tasting colors. Her blood sang and her muscles went lax. He tensed, riding the wave of her orgasm. Her pussy sucked hard at his dick. Her nerve endings felt one hundred times magnified, until he slowed, taking shallow plunges. He tensed, readying for his own release. His cock pulsed, thickening with another orgasm coursing through her body.

Then he roared. A loud, wild sound of ownership with the word "mine" ushered from his lips. He brought his mouth down and scraped his fangs on her shoulder at the same time he bit his claws into her leg, leaving a fiery scratch on her thigh. She came hard at the feel of his bite. So hard she saw white spots dance behind her lids. It didn't end there.

Hot spurts of semen filled her channel as he gave in. She loved it. This dream had gone from sexy to *holy shit it needed to repeat itself every night for the rest of her life*. She didn't give a damn if this was a dream, she wanted him to make her his, make her pregnant, and make her come as many times as possible.

She didn't get much of a chance to enjoy Hamel and his expert-level lovemaking, though. As she glanced into his golden eyes and wondered what made them that way, he brushed his lips over hers and whispered, "I have to go."

"Wait . . ." She cleared her throat and sat up, watching him get off the bed. What the hell? This was her dream. She should be able to control this. "Where are you going? This is my dream. I haven't been with a man in real life in forever. I want to enjoy my time with you here."

The sun started to set. All she could think was that they'd been having sex for hours. If only. He stepped away. She stood, ready to go after him and figure out why her dream wasn't going as planned. "Hamel, wait."

He was about ten yards away now, moving farther away. "Hamel?"

He turned to face her, and the look of ownership wasn't disguised. "You're mine, Melinda. Mine."

She opened her mouth but nothing came out. Did she really want to argue with her dream? She thought better and decided to ask him back on the bed, when something unreal happened. Hamel changed. He fucking changed from a big, buff and hot guy with an amazing tongue and a cock she wanted to worship, into a giant black cat. Holy fuck!

She stumbled back, unsure what to say or do. The cat's eyes glowed, the same color Hamel's eyes had been throughout her dream. Then the cat was off. It darted so fast into the trees, she felt immediately lost without it. Hamel had turned into a kitty. This just proved one thing: She'd lost her fucking mind.

CHAPTER 8

Melinda woke with the sheets wrapped around her and sweating. Holy fucking on sugar sand, her dream was . . . was . . . fucking great! First sex she'd had in years. Not the usual way it was done, but damn, her body didn't know any different. To her brain, she had real sex without any soreness or wet spot the next morning. Hell, she should bottle that. Then she realized a male teen's wet dream was the same thing. That kinda ruined the romantic vibe she had going.

Her phone played "Sweet Home Alabama," telling her it was time to get up. She rolled and stretched, working out any stiffness—and she'd definitely worked out his stiffness—remaining from sleep. She laughed at herself. How pathetic could she be? Finding satisfaction from a wet dream. Granted, it was a freaking hot as hell with multi-orgasms wet dream, but still.

After a shower, breakfast, and driving to work, she'd returned to her normal boring self. "Hey. Melinda, wait up." Her face instantly flushed to sweating. The man in her dreams, the man who'd eaten her pussy like it was his last meal, was standing beside her. Thank freaking god he couldn't read her mind. He took a deep breath.

"Something bothering you this morning?" he asked.

She kept her eyes firmly on the glass door entrance to her building. "Nope, woke up feeling pretty good. How about you?"

"I woke up stiff. The hotel's beds aren't the best."

She bet he woke up more than stiff. She'd be willing to work it out again, after locking her lab room's door. She was going to hell. That's the only place this could lead to. She laughed and let out a sigh. "Wish I could help you there, Hamel. But outside the brain's REM state, I'm pretty useless."

He looked at her like she was crazy, which made her laugh more. "Inside joke, sorry," she added. "Besides waking up stiff, how did you sleep?"

Hamel rubbed the back of his neck. "I feel like I was rode hard and put away wet." She almost fell to the floor, she was laughing so hard.

Gasping for breaths, she laid a hand over her chest. "I apologize again, Hamel. It's just the way you said it was so funny." She pulled her key from her purse and unlocked the lab.

After stepping over the threshold, she froze. One gasp was all she could take in. No words came to mind. Hamel stopped close behind her. "Holy fuck."

Most of the lab had been destroyed. Machines and hardware lay busted, scattered on the floor. Cabinet doors hung open with contents scooped out, joining everything else on the floor. Every file with papers or binders was ripped open and tossed, as if someone systematically rifled through them.

The first thing that came to her mind was the defenseless little white mice. Were they here or even alive? She dashed in, pulling away from Hamel's grip on her arm. His voice registered in her head, but not his words. Whatever he thought could wait a few minutes.

Immediately she saw the cages on the far cabinets were there and didn't look disturbed. Her heart began to beat again. Focusing on the beloved critters and not where she was walking, her foot caught on something and the sheets of loose paper she stood on slipped on the smooth floor. Well, shit. She was going down.

She braced for a hard impact that didn't come. One of her squeezed-closed eyes popped open to see why. Large but gentle hands had her around the waist, a very strong arm gliding around to lift and pull her against a hard body.

Her heart beat so hard from the adrenaline, fear for the mice, and the dash to get to them, all she could do was lean against the hot body and listen to the soothing words in her ear. The words told her to calm down. The mice were fine and everything else could be replaced. She was safe as long as she didn't run off and do something stupid. So much for soothing words.

That brought her out of her fear-induced haze. And made her angry. She'd never *run off and do something stupid*. Who the hell said that? She fought the arms that held her tightly, but they didn't let her go. Fine. She twisted around to push away and found herself chest to chest with Hamel.

Her heart jumped. She wasn't thinking he would be the masculine strength wrapped around her. The Hamel of her dream, sure. But the Oversight guy in a lab coat and pocket protector, no.

His expression was intense on her. Fear and worry shined in his eyes. She felt the same. Who would do this to her lab? Then his hand cupped the back of her head and his thumb brushed her cheek. A rush of electric hot sensation burned through her. This was the first time his skin touched hers.

The top button of his shirt was opened and his rustic smell filled her senses. A fire she'd never felt before lit in her stomach. She swallowed hard. Her knees gave. He scooped her up and set her on the counter. With her head spinning, she couldn't think straight. What should they do now, besides find a sugar-soft beach and get naked?

A light vibration tickled her arms. A low grumble hummed in her ears. What was that? Hamel's hands holding her shoulders jerked, jarring her out of her sensual doze. She snapped her eyes to his.

Gold surrounded his hazel irises, making them exotic, fascinating. She wanted to stare into them to discover all the secrets she knew were there. Who was Parish Hamel? And how was she able to dream of his eyes in that same color?

CHAPTER 9

Hamel hung on by a thread. As if last night hadn't been hard enough for him. Now that his jaguar recognized her as his mate, it allowed for their mate bond to click. He'd been expecting to sense her deeper emotions, but he'd forgotten the ability to participate in her dream world.

Being with her, even if it was just a dream, had woken him up with a severe hard-on and the need to touch himself while reliving the things they'd done. Damn. It took everything in him to control his need to take her the moment she'd looked at his face. Her blushing and the scent of her need made his animal insane. He knew what she was doing the moment they saw each other. She'd thought back to her dream. Hell, he'd done the same thing.

Still, he'd controlled himself. Right now, though, he was losing his control. His mate sat on the counter, him between her knees. She breathed hard, her blood pumping through her veins, adrenaline coursing through her. Prey. All signs of prey being hunted. And occasionally, her smell tossed out scents screaming "sex" and "fucking." *Fuck*, he was going to break.

He didn't realize he was even growling until her huge eyes met his. His jaguar would be in full force, rimming his eyes with gold. But she showed no fear. The opposite, in fact. She scented like she wanted more of him. Like in the dream. No, not yet.

He stepped back abruptly, startling her. "Sorry, Melinda. I didn't mean to scare you. I was in your private space again. I seem to have a habit of that." He gave her a sheepish grin. She continued to stare at him, saying nothing. All right, then. This wasn't awkward.

He ran a hand over his bristly head. "We should talk with Kintu. Get security on this."

Melinda scooted off the counter. "Yes, of course. Let me put my purse away." Her eyes locked onto something on the far side of the lab. He followed her line of sight to see a wall cabinet with its doors blown off. He followed her dash across the room.

"What do you keep in here?" he asked.

"My laptop and other expensive stuff not bolted down." She seemed to take stock. "Only my laptop is missing. Oh, damn. This is so not good." She reached in, but he grabbed her arm.

"Don't touch anything. We need to get a forensics team in to dust for prints and search for possible DNA residue. I'll get the mice cleared first so you can take them elsewhere for the day. We'll pull security footage to see what happened." For the first time all week, he felt in control of the situation. What a great feeling. He hated feeling like an idiot. "Anything else missing? Look carefully."

Her eyes methodically swept the room, occasionally moving to different spots to look on the floor. When she reached the refrigerator, her face paled. The lock on it had been pried open. "I need to open it," she said.

He took a pen from his pocket and wedged it along the lower side of the door and levered it open. After a second, she said, "That's strange. Only my tea is gone."

"Your tea?"

"Yeah, there was still a lot in the beaker, so I put it in here for today. They didn't touch any of the experiments or serums."

Then it dawned on him. "Your tea was in the beaker with the ESP label partially scratched off."

"So? Other stuff in here has labels. In fact, the only thing without a label is the ESP serum." Then he saw it click in her head. "They were after the virus?"

"That's my conclusion, for the time being. We need to talk to Kintu." He took her hand and led her through the obstacle course to the back hall entrance. They came across the senior PRO leaving another lab. "Kintu." The man turned. "We have a security breach in Miss Caster's lab."

The senior's face looked puzzled. Melinda said, "Someone has broken into my lab and stolen my laptop and what they think is the unknown virus serum." Kintu's expression changed to one of alarm, then determination.

"Let's go to my office." Hamel and Melinda followed Kintu down a series of halls to a corner office. He noticed that Melinda hadn't tried to take her hand from his. Maybe this relationship thing wouldn't be so hard after all. He stopped himself from going further with that train of thought with the image of his uncle lying in a grocery store's dessert display, cake and pie on his face.

They took the seats in front of the senior PRO's desk and watched patiently as he made phone call after phone call. After a few minutes, he put the phone on speaker and turned his twenty-four-inch monitor toward them.

A male voice spoke through the phone speaker. "Here's footage from camera four on the south side of the lab's building." They watched the video fast-forward from daylight to nighttime. Cars zipped in and out of the front parking lot.

Then after what seemed like nothing for a long time, Hamel said, "Stop. Back up." The screen showed rewinding, then playing in real time. A shadow slithered down the side of the building from the roof, opposite side from the guard shack.

"Let me see if we can zoom in some." The man on the phone issued instructions to someone and the image stopped and reconfigured. When in focus, the screen clearly showed a person on a rope extending down the side of the building.

The way the person moved with confident, sure movements told him whoever this was had done this kind of thing before. He watched as the person attached suction cups with handles to the window and cut a large section of glass from the middle. He then pushed forward, easily entering the lab.

A few minutes later, the camera showed him leaving with a backpack.

"My laptop and tea are probably in there. Jerk."

Kintu turned to her. "Your tea?"

She sighed. "Long story. But my tea was labeled as the virus."

"What time was this last night?" Hamel asked.

The man on the phone pointed out the numbers running across the bottom of the footage. The time was the first numbers: 22:30. About five hours after most employees left yesterday.

How did this happen in such a facility? Guards were stationed at the gate up front. Security cameras were posted around the perimeter. He'd memorized every route the security patrol took every hour. There were guards in each building after hours.

He scrubbed hands through his hair, frustration setting in. What could've happened if his mate had been in the lab during that time? Would she have been killed? A pain like he had never experienced cut him—worse than being shot, worse than the six-inch bowie knife, worse than when he smashed his pinky toe against a chair leg. And fuck, that hurt.

No. Losing his mate was not an option. He'd carry her to the airport if it came down to it. He leaned toward the phone. "What about the camera in lab two? Can you bring up its recording?"

"We've been working on it," the phone voice said, "but it seems the cameras to this building were offline at that time. No data recorded."

Fuckity fuck fuck. That meant they were dealing with some damn serious enemies.

"Mr. Kintu, sir"—a different, more commanding voice was on the phone—"do you want this reported to the local authorities?"

"Good god, no, Captain. We'd have a circus on our hands. Order your men to keep this under wraps. If the outside world gets a whiff of this, the media will descend like a pack of sharks."

"Yes, sir," the captain said.

Hamel asked, "I don't suppose you have an in-house CSI team?"

Kintu laughed. "We have all the equipment you could possibly want, but no street team."

"Ironic, isn't it?" Hamel smiled. He glimpsed at Melinda's dazed face. Poor thing was probably overloaded with what the hell was going on. If he wasn't careful, he'd blow his cover with her. Fortunately, Kintu knew who he was, but it stopped there. "Mr. Kintu, I don't think Melinda here is too interested in what happens next. I think she just wants to get back to work in a different lab." He gave Kintu a look that said *Go along with this*.

The senior PRO swiveled his chair around like he'd forgotten she was there. "I'm so sorry, Melinda. Of course, you should get back to work. Don't let us stop your experiments."

Hamel stood, taking Mel's hand again. "If you'll give me a few minutes, we'll get her set up and then we can talk about the boring stuff." He flashed a wide smile at her, trying to play off any suspicions she may have. When she smiled back, he hoped he'd gotten away with it.

CHAPTER 10

He walked them to the back door of her lab. He needed to keep her from touching anything until he could get a forensics team in here. Once he made a couple calls, it wouldn't take long. Until then, he had this under control.

He asked, "Are you just playing with the mice today?"

She jerked her hand away. So much for having this under control. "What do you mean *playing* with the mice?" She crossed her arms over her chest. Oh, shit. His aunt did that after his uncle said something stupid. He put his hands up in supplication. Too late.

"I'll have you know, my *playing* has saved millions of lives. Maybe even the life of someone you care about, if that's possible."

He raised a brow and looked at her. "What does that mean? Do you think I'm incapable of caring?"

She huffed. "I don't know. Are you, Dr. Oversight? Everyone I've met like you is like you." She paused at what she just said. "You know what I mean."

He realized his mate was even hotter when riled. This could be fun. But not now. He needed to stay focused. She was in potential danger and he had to take care of her.

"Okay, I apologize for insinuating your work isn't important. I know it is. Let's just get the cages and whatever else you need to a different lab."

"Fine with me." She walked past as he took in a deep breath. There had to be clues to who the culprit group was. The local infidels were probably not highly skilled in rappelling down the sides of buildings, nor at turning off security camera systems.

He found the window that had been cut. He took in another deep breath. Interesting that the burglar chose to tape the pane in place upon leaving. There must've been a purpose. That in itself kept the crime hidden until someone walked into the room in the daylight. But why risk the few extra minutes? How much time did he need to get away?

Wanting to check out the cabinet that had held Mel's laptop, he made his way in that direction, sucking in a deep breath here and there. He worried about why he wasn't smelling anyone but his mate in this room. At the cabinet, he ran his nose along the frame. The sharp bite of chemicals used in explosives made him draw back. It wasn't a large explosion, but enough to do the trick. The intruder knew exactly what he was doing.

But there was no fucking scent of anything alive. This made no sense. His hands fisted into balls. He hated when others purposely hid their smell— Oh, fuck. They purposely hid their smell. Someone knew he was a shifter and was there. Only a handful of people knew. Shit. He needed to talk with HQ.

Without turning to Melinda on the other side of the room, he asked, "Is there any place in particular you'd like to go?" When she didn't answer immediately, he looked over his shoulder. She leaned against a counter and stared at him with a bemused look.

After a second, she replied, "There's a small room down the hall that has mazes the mice and I can *play* in." She narrowed her eyes at him, and he laughed. She was so damn cute.

He grabbed the two cages while Melinda loaded her lab coat pocket with treats. She led them to an unlocked room and held the door for him.

"Just put the cages on the counter. I'll take it from there." He did so and turned to leave. "Parish— I mean, Hamel." He stopped. Her cheeks were flushed, eyes focused on the floor.

"Thank you for your help this morning. I've never dealt with that kind of thing and I was shocked and lost. You knew what to do, and I appreciate that." Her eyes lifted to meet his. Their beautiful, glassy shine took his breath away. Yup, his mate had him wrapped around her finger already.

He took a bow. "You're welcome, milady. Dr. Oversight at your beck and call." He winked at her then closed the door behind him. He took a calming breath and pulled his phone from his pocket. After pushing the speed-dial button, he headed for Kintu's office.

Before he could get the phone to his ear, a voice was already yelling. "It's about fucking time, Jag. I was beginning to wonder if you'd gone AWOL." Right, like that'd ever happen.

"Don't be a douchebag, man. You won't believe all the shit that's happened in the past thirty hours."

"Ha, try me." Okay, maybe his boss would believe him. That man had probably seen some weird shit in his day.

"Fine, I take that back. But you'll never guess who I met."

"Christ, Jag. What is this, Twenty Questions?"

"You know, you've been the biggest pain in the ass since that fight with the wolf pack. Did they kick your sense of humor along with your ass?"

"In your dreams, dickhead."

Hamel smiled. "There's the prick we all love."

"What do you got, Jag?"

Good-relations social hour was over. That was one of the things he loved about his boss: He really cared. Most of the time. "Not looking good. There may be backing to the threats issued. Last night they pulled off a smooth gig after killing security cameras in a building as tight as Fort Knox."

"I'm not sure you want to use that analogy," his boss said.

What the hell was the guy talking about? It's Fort Knox. "Why not?"

"You know, there's no money there anymore. Hasn't been for forty years."

"No shit," Hamel said. "How do you know that?"

"I was one of the army's grunts lucky enough to load the shit and haul it away."

"Where'd y'all take it?"

"If I told you that, I'd have to kill you." Hamel kept his

mouth shut. His boss could be serious or blowing smoke up his ass. Either way, Hamel didn't want to know. "All right, back to the job at hand, Jag. What else do you know?"

"The target you sent me to protect happens to be my mate. Did you know that going in?" The silence on the line made him wonder if the call dropped. "You still there?"

"Yeah, I'm here." The tone of his voice had changed. It was filled with . . . uncertainty. He didn't like that.

"What's going through your head, boss man?"

A resigned sigh reached him. "You're not going to like this, but it may be in your best interest if you're reassigned."

Hamel froze in his tracks. "Bullshit!" Several people within hearing distance looked at him. He turned down another hall. "Don't even think about reassigning me. I won't leave. I can't leave. She's my mate and I will do whatever I have to to protect her."

"That's what I'm afraid of, Jag. A protecting mate's mind turns to violence and killing as the first defense, not logic and communication. I can't have you shooting first and asking questions later. Do you understand that?"

Hamel wanted to put his fist through a wall. "Yes, I understand it, goddammit. And I don't fucking care. You can send in someone else, but I'm staying with her no matter what."

"You know damn well I don't have anyone to send."

Hamel grinned. "I know." His boss laughed.

"You stay for the time being, Jag. Keep her safe and find out what you can to help us here with who wants her serum and why."

"Yeah, got it."

"And, Jag, don't be a stranger. Believe it or not, I do like to hear your voice. Most of the time." Hamel's phone beeped signaling the call had ended. He smiled and opened the door to Kintu's office. Time to get back to work.

CHAPTER 11

Melinda scooted old equipment and boxes from the side of the room and set up a table to place the older portable maze they once used. Seemed the establishment had a bit of a hoard mentality, which in this case worked for her. She needed to keep her mind occupied while Hamel took care of her lab.

Which in itself seemed a bit weird. He was a PhD-level person who appeared more in the know with CSI than CDC. But what did she know about a real Oversight job description besides the required asshole part? Pretty much zilch.

And what the hell was with all that sniffing and deep breathing? If he needed a tissue, all he had to do was ask. For a moment, she was going to offer him a box, but he was so intense in what he was doing, she didn't want to disturb him. Snot or not.

Whatever. Everyone had their little idiosyncrasies. Her habit of having a place for everything and being predictable—her ex complained about that once—could bug the crap out of others. But those two attributes were good for a research scientist to have. Especially when having virus-covered stuff sitting around.

She placed a treat in the far corner of the maze then

walked around the table to put the baby mouse in the far gated slot. She looked at the clock above the door to mark the time, then realized she didn't have her laptop to record her notes.

She sighed and searched the room for paper. Twenty drawers, six cabinets, and three shelves later, she found an old set of large sticky notes. That would work. She doubted much would happen on this first trip through. She just needed to know if the smells of unknown mice on the path would affect the baby's willingness to complete the journey.

Walking back to the beginning of the maze, she noticed the treat she thought she put there was gone. She had put one down, hadn't she? After placing another at the end, she rounded the side, glancing at the clock. Then she realized she didn't have a pen to write with. She slapped a hand on her forehead to keep from screaming her frustration. She couldn't get her laptop back soon enough.

Knowing there wasn't a writing utensil in the room, she raided a nearby unused office to find a pink pen with yellow and green fuzzies on the top. No wonder it was there; no one wanted to use it.

Already tired and not caring, she snatched it up and headed back to her temporary lab. Again, passing the end of the maze, she noted the treat was gone. What the fuck? She glanced at the mouse still behind the wire gate on the other side.

Her eyes searched the room, making sure no one else was hiding or playing a prank on her. Now was not the time. Her nerves where shot from the invasion of her lab this morning. Seeing nothing out of the ordinary, she laid another treat in the maze then leaned against the cabinet.

Maybe she should go home and sit on her balcony, relax to the waves for a while, and come back later. About a glassful of wine was left in the bottle. Even though Moscato had the lowest alcohol rate, it would still help—

The baby mouse squeaked and shuffled around in its spot, drawing her attention. The treat on her side of the table began to roll. Melinda didn't move. Didn't even breathe. She watched the treat clear each turn of the maze, never needing to backtrack, ending up in front of the mouse, who reached under the gate to pull the treat in and nibble it.

Holy teleporting freaky moving shit. Her heart pounded.

She felt better knowing she had put treats down earlier and wasn't losing her mind. But wow! Reaching for the desk phone, she dialed Dembe. "Hey," she almost hollered into the receiver when her friend picked up, "can you do a Mickey hat right now?" Getting a reply of yes, Melinda snagged the mouse on the run out the door, down the hall, and into Dembe's lab.

"Oh my god!" Melinda yelled as she slid through the door. "You're not going to freaking believe this."

Dembe stood next to the scanning machine, tiny metal hat with protruding wires in her hand. "Jesus, Melinda, you're scaring me. What happened this morning?"

This morning? "Oh, yeah. That's something totally different. Someone broke into the lab."

"That was the rumor. Are you all right? Last I knew you were in Mr. Kintu's office."

She waved a hand through the air, brushing off any concern. "Yeah, everything's fine. Hamel is taking care of it. I've got something more amazing."

She reached toward her pocket to see her baby mouse's front paws and head sticking up, looking at the world. It was soooo cute. "Come on, little guy. We're gonna put Mickey ears on you and see what your brain's doing."

Dembe pointed to a medium-sized wire cage. "Put him in that and bring it over here. What did you discover?"

Melinda set the critter in the container, then wrapped her arms around it. "Just you wait—" When lifting the cage, she didn't raise it enough to clear the soda can on the counter. "Oops." Dembe always had at least one Diet Coke sitting around. "Sorry, Dee. I'll buy you another one."

Her friend shrugged. "Don't worry about it. After you called to say you were coming, I put another one in the fridge to cool." Melinda laughed. Dembe knew her well. Melinda carried over her load while Dembe called housekeeping for cleanup on aisle five.

"Okay," the cocoa-skinned woman said, "let's get this cute little thing wired." For the next five minutes, the ladies wrestled a miniature brainwave detector onto an even smaller, constantly wiggling head. "You know," Dembe started, "if you could tell these pests to sit still, this process would be a lot easier."

Melinda smiled. Dembe liked to tease her about her affection toward the four-legged animals her friend considered nuisances. "Sure, Dee. I'll sign up for Mouse Speak 101 next semester."

A knock on the door broke their concentration. A man Melinda hadn't seen before stuck his head in from the hall. In native Ugandan, he said he was sent with a mop. Dembe pointed him toward the soda spilled on the floor. He pushed the door open and rolled in a yellow bucket with a squeegee attachment.

With the Mickey ears firmly in place, she set the mouse in the cage. Dembe fired up the equipment. "Okay, Mel. Show me what you got."

CHAPTER 12

Melinda was about to prove beyond a shadow of a doubt that something that once belonged in the realm of charlatans and witchcraft existed, with hard evidence to back it up. Stories and movies about ESP abilities flashed through her head.

She wondered if this was the first step to a better or worse world. Either way, there was no stopping science or the truth. Things happened for a reason and she was along for the ride.

Melinda took a treat from her pocket and held it next to the metal enclosure to get the mouse's attention. Once the critter had sniffed a couple times, she laid the treat on the table, a few feet away.

The passive brain image on the screen exploded to life. Vibrant orange lit the screen from deep inside the brain. Yellow streaks of light flashed and zipped from one neuron path to another like comets shooting through the sky.

"There." Dembe pointed to the screen. "Those pops and flashes are the extra neurons firing. Look how many signals are going at once. This is incredible." She leaned closer to the screen. "I've never seen anything like it."

Greens and red bloomed in various regions, lighting up like cloud lightning on a hot summer's night. "The red represents the most active parts, and then yellow, down to green and blue. See how quickly they come and go? It's like a symphony conducted by an invisible maestro."

The whole display was a fireworks show on steroids. Melinda had a new respect for the brain and the inherent abilities.

"Holy shit," Melinda said. Dembe said the same in her language.

As quickly as it started, it ended. Both ladies looked down to see the mouse nibbling on the treat that was once well out of reach. They remained speechless. Behind them, a male voice sounded in awe. He said the TV showed beautiful color pictures. It looked like the sky sometimes at night when the gods were active and noisy.

When Dembe explained the pictures were from the animal's head, the janitor looked at the mouse, then the screen, then back to the mouse. He smiled, a few teeth missing, and said something to the effect of, "You're joking, right?"

Dembe shook her head. The man gave the mouse the evil eye, crossed himself, and rolled his mop bucket out the door. This worried Melinda. He wouldn't do anything to hurt the mouse, would he?

"Dembe, I don't remember seeing that guy around much."

She shrugged. "Walog's been here for a few months. He lives in a shack with his wife and kids. Like many on the outskirts of town, they have nothing and barely make a living. When Mr. Kintu asked if we trusted anyone to fill in a couple janitor spots, I thought of him immediately."

"So you know him well?" Melinda asked.

"Well enough, I guess. I know his wife from the Saturday markets. They sell vegetables and everything they can. They're a good, god-fearing family. He'd do anything to give his children a better life."

Melinda thought back the last couple of months. "I don't remember seeing him here before."

"When I spoke to his wife last, she mentioned he'd been given a raise and shift change from nights to days. He's here from noon to ten, I think. He's always here after I leave. His wife thanked me profusely and gave me enough *nakati* and *borr* to last me three years."

She laughed. "I'd wondered why you were eating so much of those veggies lately."

Dembe grunted. "I can't get to anything else in my kitchen. I have to eat my way in." Both laughed. Dembe typed on her keyboard and hit enter. "Okay, the test is saved to the network. You can download it anytime."

Melinda groaned. "My laptop was stolen this morning in the break-in. It'll have to wait."

Dembe's eyes grew wide. "But your research? Is all of it on there?"

"All but the serum info. I saved that to the flash so I could take it home at night to study the day's results."

Dembe raised a brow at her. "You know the rules about taking data outside the building."

"I know." Melinda rolled her eyes. "That's why it was on a flash. No one would know. But it's a moot point. I dropped it in my tea and ruined it."

Her friend busted out a laugh. "Only you, Mel. Only you."

Melinda looked sideways at her best friend. "We've both been acting like we're not coming out of our skins with excitement over our telekinetic mouse."

Dembe looked like she was trying to hold back a smile, and failing. "I'm trying to be professional. Big brother is watching." Melinda then remembered cameras were in each lab room. "Otherwise, I'd be peeing my pants." The last words were almost a screech with excitement. "But you know we have to run another test for confirmation."

"Yeah." Mel smiled. "But you know what this means, right? This damn virus we found gives real psychic abilities."

"No wonder your research was stolen," Dembe said.

"Yeah, but the drawback is the three monkeys died extremely young. Remember their burned-out brains?" Melinda looked down at the mouse finishing the treat. "I wonder how long these babies have."

"Has the third mouse shown anything unusual?" Dembe asked.

"I haven't worked with it yet. We had the clairvoyant one yesterday, and this one today. I'm so glad the thief didn't think about taking the mice. But they think they have the serum, though."

"If I were you"—Dembe turned to her keyboard—"I'd switch out your mice with others to keep them safe. Mr. Kintu won't let you take them out of the building. Unless you want to hide them down your clothes on the way out."

Melinda gave a full-body wiggle. "I love the little things, but not *that* much." She gave another shudder. "The only hands down my clothes will belong to a hunky man prior to getting into my bed."

"That was quite bold from you, little Miss Hasn't Had It in Years."

Melinda hip-bumped Dembe. "I can't believe you said that."

"True, isn't it?"

"Maybe." She grinned. They had this conversation all the time. Teasing each other about who had the most pathetic love life. That was the only way to survive: Laugh about it.

A sly grin spread across her friend's face. "Any particular man in mind? Perhaps a doctor, say?"

She gasped. "I don't think so."

Dembe laughed at her overly dramatic reply. "Thou doth protest too much."

"Whatever." Melinda grumped. "Since when doth thou read Shakespeare? Push the freaking button and let's watch the light show again. I have to get the paper typed before we talk to Mr. Kintu tomorrow morning."

Even though she was trying to hide it, she didn't deny the feelings the dream and her time in the lab with Hamel ignited. God, she'd been so gullible before, allowing herself to be set up. That would not happen again.

After running another successful brain scan, she and her mouse headed back to their temporary lab home. Yellow crime-scene tape draped both doors to her usual lab. She needed to get her purse from inside before she could go home. Hopefully the guard at the door would let her in. Hamel could even do it for her. But she hadn't seen him since this morning.

She wondered what he'd been doing. For supposedly helping her, he wasn't around much. Granted, he helped her move the mice and sort of get set up in the smaller lab, but after that, nada. And heavens, no, she wasn't complaining one bit.

Something seemed wrong about him.

In the small lab, she put the mouse with the others and called up her friend at the CDC in the States. Atlanta was seven hours behind, so they were still in the morning hours there. Melinda got the voice mailbox of the Human Resources department and left a message to contact her about the credentials for Dr. Parish Hamel.

She leaned against a counter and rubbed her dry eyes. A day this productive hadn't occurred in a while. It was nice to know breakthroughs could still happen.

The security guard outside her lab door was kind enough to allow her to get her purse, as long as he followed her and she didn't touch anything more than she needed to. The room hadn't been fully swept for clues nor had photos been taken. She grabbed her purse, and a cloth she used to wipe down counters.

Her feet carried her to the refrigerator with confident, purposeful steps. With the open fridge door hiding her actions, she grabbed the ESP virus, wrapped it in the cloth and stuck it in her purse. She moved test tubes and beakers around to make it look like she was doing something important, then closed the fridge.

She said to the guard. "Guess I don't need to worry about locking up my laptop anymore, huh?" She stood in front of the destroyed cabinet and sighed. Time to go home. It was a bit early, but the day had still been long.

Plus, she wondered if the black cat she saw last night was still around.

CHAPTER 13

Hamel lay in his jaguar form in the woods behind Melinda's home. The events of the day really wore on him. Normally, he didn't worry about things he couldn't control, but with his mate so close to the action, he couldn't help but stress over "what if."

He'd spent the day scouring the facility for smells, clues, and any information that would shed light on their culprit. Early on he'd figured out the trespasser used hunter's block to keep his personal smell and identity hidden. Which could mean a couple things: Hamel knew this person, thus the need to block the scent, or Hamel would come across this person during the day.

Perhaps he should dig deeper into the background of the guards at the facility. The captain of security he spoke with on the phone in Kintu's office was a very capable ex-military Ugandan. Nice guy at face value. He held his men in tight formation and ran a clean ship. This made it hard to believe that someone outside the compound could get in and out without detection. Never overlook the possibility of an inside job.

But the big question for Hamel was why. Why did this person want a virus no one knew anything about? He wondered how long ago Melinda discovered the additional brain connections in the monkeys. The intel about someone taking the virus to "end the world" that his office received on the emerging threat was a week ago.

Did that mean someone understood the full implications of the added brain mass? That they already knew the virus would create the ability the mouse showed?

After the results come back from the forensics team, they would hopefully have more answers. The crew should've been in and out already. Even though the Ugandan virus lab could process the evidence, he'd ordered lab results from another location just to keep everything clean and at arm's length. He didn't want any cross-contamination affecting anything.

His tail flipped up, swatting at the flies buzzing around his fur-covered head. He'd decided to come in his animal so he wouldn't be caught with his pants down, or needing to be down, like last night. That could've been bad for this operation. He'd never blown an assignment, and didn't plan to start now.

His lovely mate had been home for about an hour. She'd opened her balcony doors, which seemed to be the norm for her, but had yet to sit in her hammock chair. Last night she was safe since the bad guy had been busy raiding her lab. Tonight, he wasn't sure if she would be safe since they had all her research, or if there was more they wanted. Either way, he would watch her until it was time to go back to the hotel.

Since he started working with the American government according to their "agreement," he and his cat had become a tightly knit team. At first, he had wanted no part in the contract between shifters and humans. But in the fifty years since his species was discovered, they'd had no choice but to go along with what the government cooked up. In exchange for volunteered assistance from alpha-level shifters, the U.S. military and president would do everything in their power to keep the shifter community unknown to humans.

In reality, the powers that be didn't want the shifters to be exposed because of the potential chaos and violence that could erupt. Humans weren't known for sharing or tolerance, even though they liked to pretend they were.

His grandfather had been one of the original members of the Alpha League Federal Agency. Their mission statement said they would uphold the laws of the United States of America and protect her people no matter where in the world they may be. That was still the case today, but the ALFAs were usually called upon when a job required agility and resilience humans didn't possess.

Melinda's back door opened, catching him by surprise. He didn't see anything fly over the rail, like another bottle of wine, so he wasn't sure what she had in mind. He moved into a low crouch and slinked behind a tree to watch her.

She slowly came down each step, staring into the woods intently. What was she looking for? After passing the first few trees, Melinda stopped and looked around. "Here, kitty, kitty."

She couldn't be serious. Kitty, kitty? He could take her down in a single leap and eat her whole. His tongue licked his feline lips. Eating her little kitty would be divine. Oh, fuck.

When his back foot came down, it slid on leaves, making enough noise to grab her attention. *So much for stealth, cat. Good thing we're not prey.* His animal growled at him.

Melinda moved directly toward him. Shit. He should stay away from her. But how could he watch over her then? Why did women always make things more difficult than they had to be? He headed for the concrete wall. It worked for a good escape route the first time.

His mate must've had the same idea. She stopped coming toward him and hurried through the trees parallel to him. Dammit, woman.

He really should be happy with his mate for wanting to see him. Ultimately, that's what he desired, for her to want to be with him. But not like this. Not in his other form. He put on a burst of speed to get to and over the wall before she could get too much of a glimpse of him.

Behind him in the woods came a short cry, as if Mel had fallen and skinned her knee. Then her scream filled with terror froze him in his tracks. He smelled a touch of her blood and a flood of adrenaline in her system. He turned and sprinted along his path. Then the seriousness of her plight hit him.

Snakes. He smelled a momma cobra, pissed off because her nest was invaded by a human. *Fuck.* Hamel had seconds to reach Melinda before the cobra attacked. Dodging tree after tree, he was finally close enough to see the cobra floating side to side with the sides of its head flared. And Melinda, not seeing in the dark or knowing where she was crawling, headed straight for the nest. Not on momma's watch.

The cobra reared back to strike. He would be too late. She'd die before he could get her to the hospital. He let out a sharp hiss, hoping to distract the agitated mother. Didn't work. His legs pushed him from the ground, through the air between the snake and his mate.

Melinda screamed as a sharp sting bit into his shoulder. His forward momentum dragged the attached snake with him, tearing the skin, letting more venom pump into his veins. He'd never been bitten by a cobra, or any snake, for that matter.

Far enough from his mate, his cat rolled, smashing the serpent's head, but forcing its fangs into the bone. He swatted the putrid thing off and headed back to his mate to make sure she was okay.

How strange. She had doubled; two of her sat where one had a minute ago. Then the earth tilted up. Or was it him falling to the ground. The ache that punched his nose suggested he just did a face-plant. In front of his mate. Shit. But seeing that he couldn't move any of his body, he'd worry about his pride later.

First, he needed—

CHAPTER 14

‾‾‾‾‾

Coming down the back stairs from her bungalow, Melinda had hoped the gorgeous cat would still be in the woods. She wondered what kind of feline it was. Uganda has several big cats and she couldn't tell from her long-distant view last night what it might have been.

She'd never seen anything so graceful or with such raw power. She was drawn to it in ways she couldn't explain. The wildness, freedom, sang to her, telling her to come home. She belonged here.

She saw a shadow move ahead in the trees. When he raced away, she knew it had to be him, as dark as the night itself. He ran the same direction as last night; must be going for the concrete wall again. This time she was ready. Making sure she was at a safe distance, she verified her phone was on the camera app, ready to snap pictures as soon as she cleared the trees.

Quickly, Melinda realized flip-flops were not the best choice for dashing through the woods. She should've thought this through better. Picking up her feet as best she could, she rushed toward the wall, hoping to catch a glimpse of her visitor.

Not able to see well in the waning light, her foot landed crooked and she fell and slid headfirst. When she came to a stop, a black-and-gold cobra raised its head a couple feet in front of her face. Instinctively, she screamed and scuttled away. The snake followed as if chasing her. Snakes didn't do that. They normally ran, unless cornered, or their nest was threatened.

Melinda froze, eyes wide, lungs pumping for air. Was she moving closer to the cobra's nest? She put weight on her ankle and a stab of pain streaked up the side of her leg. Okay, she would stay on the ground, trying not to move. Maybe it would go away if she didn't look like a threat.

The slender head started to fan out, like the cobras' did before they struck. So not good. She had to move, but which way? The last thing she wanted was to step or crawl into a slithering batch of babies, or eggs, or whatever the hell might be there.

As if hearing her words, the mother snake reared back, ready to attack. Mel screamed and her body moved without her thinking where. Then a black blur moved in front of the snake, and both were gone from in front of her.

A crash to the side snapped her head around. It was too dark to make out details, but something big rolled through the leaves. She stared until she saw her beautiful cat, her guardian cat, stumble toward her.

What was wrong with him? Was he bitten? When he collapsed, she shot to her feet then skidded to a stop on her knees before her savior. The cat panted, sides heaving up and down. Melinda laid a hand on his shoulder and felt tremendous heat and blood where fur was torn away. Oh, god. He was more than bitten; he'd had the entire venom sack drained into him.

Shit, shit, shit. What should she do? She felt panic creeping in. She rubbed her hands over her face and told herself to get a grip. If she didn't, the beautiful creature would die from saving her.

Melinda took off her long sweater, laid it on the ground, and rolled the animal onto it. Damn, it didn't look as heavy as it was. Her flip-flops had to go. Her ankle pain had pretty much gone away with the adrenaline rushing through her system. Didn't matter what she stepped on. Sore feet were a small price to pay to return a favor of life.

Dragging the sweater and animal through the yard, she saw the neighbor boys playing basketball under a floodlight. She yelled to them to help her. When they reached her, they were agog with the sight of the giant cat lying helplessly. She heard the word for "jaguar" muttered several times. Was that what the cat was? A jaguar?

In broken Ugandan, she told the boys to put the animal in the back of her car. She ran into her house, grabbed her purse and keys, and was back out before the front door closed from her coming in.

One of the boys asked where she was taking him. She said the Reptile Wildlife Center. She was sure they had antivenom for all the snakes in the area. Mel helped the boys wrestle the cat into the backseat. The same boy said the center would be closed by now. She cranked the engine in her car, praying the kid was wrong.

Flying down the pothole-infested road, Melinda avoided the bigger ones and couldn't care less for the others. She was on a mission. Car maintenance be damned. The tires squealed making the turn from the road into the center's concrete medical parking lot.

At the sliding emergency doors, two men argued. The younger one was dressed in scrubs and standing outside the open doors. The older—much older—guy stood with his arms crossed, face stoic as if making a point. She wasn't sure what the older man wore, but it wasn't medical gear.

As she came around the emergency entry like a bat out of hell, both men stared at her. She skidded to a stop in front of the door. "I have a jaguar bitten by a cobra. He needs anti-serum now."

The young man looked at the older one, who had a satisfied look, then whipped his head back to her. "Ma'am, maybe you have a large house cat. Jaguars are very rare around here. There hasn't been a sighting for many years."

She slammed her car door shut and ran around to the other side. "That's fascinating, but this jag needs medicine now or he will die." She whipped open the backseat door, revealing a sickly black jag.

The man's eyes popped open and words she didn't know left his mouth. She turned to the old man, but he was gone, nowhere in sight. The technician rolled a gurney up to the car and together they loaded the feline onto the bed and wheeled him inside.

Melinda followed the man into a triage-like area, where he whipped aside a curtain and stopped the gurney. Quickly and efficiently, he set up an IV line and needle. He raced toward tall cabinets, opened one, and pulled out two handfuls of vials. He hurried back and laid them on the bed. Over the next several minutes, he slowly fed six vials through the IV.

He watched the animal's face intently. She asked, "What are you looking for?"

"Watching for allergic reactions. Need to make sure we don't need an Epinephrine shot, too."

"Oh" was all she could think to say. This was so different than her use of vials and needles and IVs. The work she did usually didn't determine if the patient lived or died in the next few moments. Her legs began to give. She plopped in a chair by the curtain.

The man continued moving around the gurney, listening to the animal's heart and lungs. "So what's the story? How did a jaguar end up in the backseat of your car?"

Melinda laughed. "When you say it that way, it sounds rather crazy, doesn't it?"

"Miss, any way you say it, it sounds crazy." He smiled.

Her insides started to calm down. He had a soothing way about him that made the emergency situation seem like the everyday. "My name is Melinda. I work at the virus lab."

"I'm Nsubuga. Friends call me Buga."

"Nice to meet you, Buga. About our story: not much to tell. I saw the gorgeous cat last night in the woods between my home and the lake. I was hoping to get a picture of him with my phone. So I went out to see if I could find him and ran into a cobra and her nest. Just before the snake attacked me, the jaguar jumped in front of me and took the bite before killing it. It was amazing. I had no idea a jaguar would do that."

Buga grunted. "They don't."

That was an odd reply. He almost sounded mad. "After that, some boys helped me load him into my car to bring him up here. I'm glad you were still open."

"You can thank my grandfather for that. He wouldn't leave yet. Said it wasn't time, despite what the clock said."

"Was that the older gentleman I saw you talking to?"

Buga laughed. "He's no gentleman. He's a witch doctor."

Her eyes widened slightly, but she kept her mouth shut. Witch doctors were in the same league as ghosts and magic. But she would've said that about telekinesis a few days ago. "Why was he here?"

"Technically, he owns all the land the Wildlife Refuge is on, but I think he's mainly here to irritate me."

"Ha." The other man she saw at the main entrance entered the large room. "Don't think yourself so high because I spend time with you, grandson. My time very precious. Not much left, but lots to do."

"Don't say that. You'll be here as long as I am so you can torment me." Buga winked at Melinda. Being closer and in a lit area, she saw this older man more clearly. His skin was very dark and roughly weathered. Deep lines were etched into his forehead and around his mouth. He wore a white button-down shirt buttoned all the way to the top and a long dark coat over khaki pants. Melinda wouldn't have guessed he was a witch doctor, but he did look very wise in the old ways of things.

"Ha, grandson. You have sad sense of humor." The old man laid a hand on the unconscious cat, then turned to Melinda. "Your mate be fine. Transformers hard to kill. Go home. Sleep. You need rest for what is to come."

CHAPTER 15

"Sweet Home Alabama" played in Melinda's dream until she woke. Her dream slipped away like sand through fingers. She wasn't one to remember her dreams, but these past few days had been stressful. Maybe that was the reason for the sudden change in her not only remembering her dream, but it being so real.

Realizing it was only Thursday, she groaned and rolled in her warm covers. This was the longest week from hell. Would it ever end? Maybe she should buy out the local market's stock of chocolate and eat it all herself for Halloween. It was on a Saturday, so she had all day to gorge.

Even though Uganda had an official six-day workweek, her contract with the lab allowed her both weekend days off. She rarely took them, though. It's not like she had lots to do around the house. Besides that, she loved what she did, so it didn't feel like work. Most of the time. This week was an anomaly.

She wondered how the jaguar was. Later in the day, she'd call. The old man had assured her that it would be fine. What did he mean when he said "mate" and "transformer"? Obviously he didn't have strong command of the English language, but she was thankful he was considerate enough to speak it so she could understand what they were saying.

By "mate" he must've meant someone who stands beside you, like a bodyguard. She could see the big, beautiful cat being her protector, her guardian. Maybe he just liked the smell of mouse she probably had soaked into her clothes and hands. That was a funny thought. A badass jaguar hanging out with her because she held mice all day.

"Transformer" was not as easy to figure out. The only transformer she knew was the kind that sat on a telephone pole and carried electricity between houses. When she was a kid, she'd seen lightning strike the top of a pole and sparks flew everywhere as a big metal thing virtually exploded. Then the family sat in the dark for hours waiting for the electric people to bring the lights back on.

So whatever the old guy meant by transformers being hard to "kill," she had no clue. She let it go. It was too early to ponder such deep issues. She needed a shower and tea to get going.

At the research facility, her door no longer had the yellow tape, nor the guard from yesterday. She sighed with relief. She could get back to normal now. She had a lot of paperwork and testing to re-create for the file. Fortunately, it was more of a time thing than actual running of tests. She had the images of each page in her head, so it was just the arduous task of making them real.

She needed to bring her mice back into the lab also so she could get some work done. She'd figure out later where the best place to keep them safe would be. Hopefully their night in the strange room didn't affect them any. She considered it a sleepover party at someone else's house.

That thought made her angry. Because of her parents, she didn't experience half the life most kids did. She'd missed out on so much. If she were to ever have a family, she'd make sure her children got to see and explore everything the world had to offer. She would never hold them back and tell them they couldn't do something because of their gender or that they weren't smart enough.

She'd never really thought about a family before. Shit, she was thirty years old. How long was she going to wait? She didn't feel like she was waiting as much as the time simply hadn't come yet. Inside, she felt confident it would happen; there was no anxiety over it. Okay, there was some anxiety, but mostly because her dream man had mentioned babies, and boy, had that made her hormones remember what nature had intended. As of that night, her biological clock had decided to start making itself known.

Maybe she just wanted a friend with benefits. Unfortunately, that friend was more of the make-believe kind. She'd still need help from her toy. The thought of him and her toy brought a flush to her face. Good god, she was so pathetic.

After unlocking the lab door and flipping on the lights, she was relieved to see everything back to where it had been. Tables were upright, machines off the floor, papers in stacks. She'd have to do an inventory to see which items were broken beyond repair.

From her purse, she pulled out the tissue-wrapped virus serum she'd snuck out of the building last night, ready to put it in the fridge again. Then she noted the complete destruction of the refrigeration unit on the other side of the room.

Seemed the thief realized her tea didn't make a good virus serum. Every piece of glassware in the fridge was either gone or smashed on the floor. And the door had been completely shattered.

A bad vibe rolled through her. How did someone do this twice in a row? There were guards at each door. For a while, anyway. She wondered when they'd left. She never would've guessed a second attack would have happened the next night. That's why she wasn't a thief; she didn't think outside the box enough to get away with that kind of thing. Predictable, she was.

She put the vial in her lab coat pocket and headed to Mr. Kintu's office.

CHAPTER 16

⤙

Melinda held the dustpan in front of the destroyed fridge in her lab room while Walog brushed the broken glass into it.

Mr. Kintu about threw his chair out the window when Melinda had told him of the damage to her lab and what she thought they were after this time. He'd profusely apologized for the facility's inability to keep her lab safe and asked her if she felt threatened. She had to admit she felt safer when Hamel was close, but she wouldn't say that out loud. Not like he was her bodyguard or anything.

She hadn't seen him this morning and asked if he was coming in. Kintu gave her his cell phone and asked her to call Hamel while he visited the security department. Didn't look like a friendly drop by to say hello.

She stopped by another lab and asked to store her vial with theirs until her fridge was fixed. The guys promised not to drink it—as long as it didn't taste like beer. She smiled for the first time that morning. "No," she said, "it's mouse urine mixed with male bug bits."

One of the guys smiled. "Sounds better than the beer."

When she'd gotten back to her lab, one of the janitors had

already wheeled his big gray trashcan in and was cleaning up the debris.

"Miss Caster," he began, "why keep breaking your lab? Someone angry?"

"Please call me Melinda. I guess somebody wants what I'm working on badly."

"*Panya* okay? No see," he asked.

Oh, her mice. She had to bring them in. "I think so. I moved them last night and haven't checked on them yet."

He set the broom against a table. "Me help. Cage heavy for woman." He started toward the door. That ruffled her feministic feathers, but she knew he was only trying to help. He followed her and carried back the cage. After he set it on the table in her lab, he stuck a finger through the wire meshing. "Hmmm. Not good." He poked one of the small babies lying unnaturally still.

She came around the side and saw a second baby unmoving. She let out a sad sigh. Both the clairvoyant and telekinetic mice were dead. The baby monkeys had lived several months. She'd hoped to have more time with the mice. Did they have more than one ability? Could they have developed more? How powerful could the ability grow to? Would offspring be stronger or weaker?

So many questions left unanswered. Her eyes floated to the one baby remaining, running around, not knowing it was now an only child. Well, sort of. Technically, it had more than a dozen brothers and sisters elsewhere in the building.

"Miss Melinda, I take babies for you. Bad. Make sick."

"Thank you, but not yet. I have to see why they died. I think their brains burned out."

He looked at her, questioning expression on his face, as if he didn't understand what she said. Or he did and thought she was nuts.

"Okay, you call me when."

"Thank you."

He gathered his broom and equipment and rolled his trashcan through the back hall door.

Melinda leaned against the table and blew out a breath. She called Dembe to see when she had time to run scans. One of the other techs was finishing up and she would be ready shortly. She could prep more analysis or trials, but she'd have to stop in the middle when Dembe was available.

Now what? It was too early for lunch. Since Hamel still hadn't shown up, she dialed his number. After several rings, he picked up.

"Go away."

Melinda snorted. "Nice, Doctor. Sporting a hangover from too much drinking last night?"

"Yeah, you could say that. They may as well have given me an IV so I could've taken it straight."

"What's the occasion? Or does Oversight require that type of work?"

"My job description mentions fieldwork, but doesn't mention anything about the local flora or fauna."

"You gotta stay out of those clubs, Doc. They'll kill you."

"No shit."

"So, you coming in?"

"Of course. I gotta keep an eye on you." Did she detect a bit of playfulness in his voice? And what was she doing joking around with him? That wasn't like her. She didn't like talking on the phone if she didn't have something specific to say.

"Well, too late for that."

He asked why, and she went into how the morning had been so far. To her, he didn't sound happy at all. And the more she talked, the madder he got. She heard a door close through the phone line.

"I'm on my way. Don't go anywhere. In fact, stay in your lab. Don't let anyone in."

Was he serious? Did he think she was a child, unable to take care of herself? She blamed it on his being a male. She didn't appreciate his demanding patronizing tone. "Listen here, buddy. No one has told me what to do since I left my parents' house. And it won't start here. I have mice brains to scan, and you can't stop me." Dear god, she sounded like a four-year-old having a tantrum. "I'll see you when you get here." She disconnected the line and crossed her arms. Men.

One more call, then she'd continue with her day. From her

purse, she fished out the business card for the medical center she'd brought the jaguar to last night. She asked for Buga. When he picked up the phone, he said he was glad she called.

He told her that his grandfather came in sometime in the morning mumbling that the animal was fine and had left the medical center. Buga laughed. "The cat may be fine, but he'll have one hell of a hangover. I pumped enough antiserum in him to counteract a gallon of venom. I was hoping to take some pictures of the beautiful animal. But as my grandfather said, he let the cat loose." He laughed again.

"Did he say something else, too? What are you laughing at?"

"Grandfather actually said he let the cat loose, reprimanding it for getting bitten and telling it not to do it again."

Melinda smiled. "Like the cat could really understand him? That's cute. He really cares for the animals, doesn't he?"

"He does," Buga said. "Almost too much. It kills him when poachers get in, take what they want, then leave the rest to rot. Things like that bring out the voodoo in him."

"Voodoo? Is that part of him being a witch doctor?" Thinking back on the old man, she hadn't expected him to be a witch doctor. For one thing, she didn't think they believed in modern medical science. Obviously, that wasn't true with this one.

Buga laughed again. "If you believe in that kind of thing. Grandfather gets out his herbs, rattles, and dead chicken blood and puts a 'hex' on the bad men so their exotic goods never make it into market to make them money."

"That doesn't seem too wise," Melinda said. "Then they'll just come back for another one."

Buga cleared his throat and seemed to hesitate. "Well, there's more to the hex, but I'm not going there. It seems to work, because I never see the same poachers twice."

Melinda didn't know what to think, except that this was getting weird. "So the cat is safe and back to where it wants to be, then?"

"Yes, everything should be fine. If you see it again, let me know how it's doing. It is so rare to see a jaguar in this part of the world anymore. Too bad they aren't native. They are beautiful."

"I agree. I'll look for him and see how he's doing. He may not come back since he was released at your place, though. He'll probably find somewhere around there to roam." Melinda was surprised how sad this made her. "At least he's safer on the refuge than wandering the woods."

"Not from snakes."

Melinda smiled. "True. Keep in touch." She slid her phone into a pocket, grabbed the mouse cage, and left for Dembe's lab.

CHAPTER 17

"Look here," Dembe said, pointing to the monitor with the end of a pen. "Just like the monkeys. All the center sections with the additional synapses are black."

Melinda sat back in the rolling chair and stared at the images on the screen. "What if these connections were burned out from overuse, like having no fuse pop when overloading to save the wire from damage? Too much for the tiny DNA available."

"That makes sense," her friend replied. "We need to study these fibers to see if they are identical to the original ones. They could be weaker in structure, or could be the same and the psychic use is too much, like you just said."

"Either way, though, not including other factors, this brain burnout is likely to be the cause of death for the mice and monkey babies."

"I'd agree with that. Did you get anything written last night to present to Kintu?"

She rubbed her face with exhaustion. "No. I had something else come up. Besides, without the mice, the show is much less impressive. But I will get the whole experiment together soon. I need to get a new laptop, too."

"You're looking really tired. Are you not sleeping?"

"Not restfully. I've been dreaming these past few days. Some I remember and some I don't. Plus, the stress with the robberies, and Dr. Oversight being all weird—"

"Weird? What's he doing?"

Melinda groaned. "I don't know. I'm just worn out. And it's only Thursday."

"Take vacation time. Heaven knows you have enough to take a month off."

Melinda sighed. "Just sleep and spend all day in bed. That would be nice." And dream about Mr. Beach Man. Her phone rang in her pocket. She took it out and looked at the caller ID. "I need to take this. I'll see you after lunch." She grabbed the cage while pushing the answer button and headed for the door.

"Hello." Melinda jammed the phone between her ear and shoulder as she opened the door and stepped into the hall.

"Melinda, hi. This is Sheri from HR in Atlanta. How are you way over there in Africa?"

"I'm good. It's beautiful here. The lab is awesome. I couldn't ask for anything more." Well, Beach Man came to mind, but eh . . .

"I looked up a Dr. Hamel. We don't have anyone by the name Parish. We have a Nevel, but no Parish. Could that be a middle name?"

"Could be. I didn't ask. But I'd pick Parish over Nevel if I had to choose." She opened the door to her lab and carried the mouse cage to the cabinet under the windows, then leaned against the countertop.

"Yeah, me, too. Sorry I couldn't have been more help."

"No, you are definitely a help, Sheri. Thanks for getting on it so quickly."

"Anything for you, girl. Whenever you come back to the States, let us know. We can all go to the Mexican grill. Bet they don't have much of that around there." The baby mouse started running around its cage, banging against the sides like it was trying to get out.

Melinda laughed at the food reference from Sheri. "You so got that right. I'd like to talk longer, but my mouse is having a panic attack or something. Tell everyone I said hi." The mouse squeaked and she swore it screamed. "Okay, calm down." She slipped her phone into her pocket, then picked up the cage and headed for the table. Halfway there, the window-pane that had been cut and taped back up the other night came loose and smashed on the counter exactly where she had been standing.

She stumbled toward the table, barely able to get the cage on it before she fell. Her knee smacked on the hard floor, but the pain didn't register. Her mind was occupied with the splintered glass on the cabinet and ground.

She would've been cut badly, with no one around to help her. My god, she could've bled to death. If the mouse hadn't thrown a hissy fit— Oh shit. No way. Did the mouse know it was going to happen? A cold chill rolled down her back, goose bumps prickling her legs.

Leaning away from the table leg, she eyeballed the now quiet mouse. It jumped into its running wheel and took off like nothing happened.

She climbed to her feet and the mouse jumped off its track and ran to the farthest corner from the opening. Melinda reached in and pulled it out. "Sorry, buddy. If you know the future, then I gotta know. We'll only do a couple things so you don't burn out. How's that sound?"

Placing the critter in the middle of a wide, open pen, she pulled out a treat to put in the upper right corner. The mouse scampered to that area. She gave it the reward then paused to think this through.

The mouse could've seen the window come loose, ready to fall. But it wouldn't understand the consequence of that. She watched the little guy sniff along the side of the pen as he walked along. He could've read her mind and seen where she was going to put the treat. But that didn't work for the window event since she didn't know about it. What were the other options?

One more experiment, then she'd stop so she wouldn't burn out his connections. It wasn't possible the mouse could know the future. It hadn't happened, so how could it know? She hated time-continuum paradoxes and books and movies that tried to get around it. It simply wasn't possible—she thought, anyway.

Ripping a piece of paper from the pad she carried, she tore it into quarters then wrote numbers one through four so each torn section had one numeral on it. She wadded these into small balls, gathered them into her hands, and shook them as she walked to the pen.

"All right, baby mousey, which corner am I going to pick?" She laid the paper wads on the pen's floor. The mouse still moved around with what looked like no purpose. When she put a finger on a ball, the mouse scuttled to the lower left corner. "Okay, let's see if number three is under my finger. If it is, I'll give you two treats."

Her heart thumped as she picked up the ball. Fingers shook as she peeled the paper apart. Slowly, the numeral three came into view. Her breath caught. She put two treats in the corner, then repeated one last time with the same results. She even put down the first selected ball and chose a second one. She leaned against the wall. The magnitude of what this meant to the world scared her. She slid down the wall to sit on the floor.

The world would go to war to get their hands on this virus. They would kill anyone in the way to acquire this miracle bug. No wonder her lab had been broken into twice. She froze when realizing the next logical step. Someone knew what the virus was all about. How far would they go to keep her from learning the full potential?

CHAPTER 18

Hamel had spent hours poring over security footage, retracing the footsteps of the thief, figuring out how the camera system kept being turned off with no one knowing, and how no guards heard anything. He even rappelled down the wall to re-enact the first incident.

Now, on his way to find his mate, frustration set in. Nobody was this good at getting away. They would make a mistake and he'd be there to find it. No one threatened his mate and lived. He finally began to understand all the strange behavior he'd seen from mated men while he grew up.

He had always thought the males were overprotective to a fault when it came to their mates. He never understood why, but he'd never been in love, either. His feet stopped short. Was he in love? Could love happen in three days?

She saved his life, or at least made it less painful. The snake venom probably would've been neutralized in his system, but it would've taken much longer than with the antiserum. He loved how she loved animals, big and small. He loved how she laughed, how she smiled at him, how her eyes sparkled when she was happy. He even loved how klutzy she tended to be.

He loved her mind and her body. He loved how she moved around the room, sure and confident in herself. Loved how she called him out when he tried to boss her around about staying in her lab today. His mate couldn't be a wimp. She'd have to stand up for herself.

With that many loves, he figured he was in deep. Damn, this would really rock his world after the mission was over.

When he opened the door to her lab, he smelled her fear. "Melinda!" he called out as he flung the door open. Immediately, he noticed the window section was missing, some of the tape flapping in the breeze. He jumped a table to get to the far side of the room. Then he saw her sitting on the floor against the opposite wall.

He pulled her up by her shoulders and held her to him. His arms slipped around her. She felt so good pressed to him. Her hair smelled like strawberries. His favorite. Then he remembered who he was supposed to be. He quickly pulled her away, bumping her back to the wall.

"Whoops, sorry." He released his hold and felt the loneliness. "You look devastated. What's happened?" He checked her over for injuries. No blood or cut clothing.

She didn't respond quickly enough for him. He frowned at her. Was she going to lie to him? He sniffed for it.

"Nothing. Well, two of my baby mice died." She paused then turned her head to the side. "The window fell. My lab was broken into again. I'm tired." He felt she held something back, but those reasons alone were enough to put her in the funk she was in. He'd get the rest later.

"Why don't you go home for the day? It's been a long week with all the break-ins. In fact, take tomorrow off. You have vacation time, right?"

She looked up at him. "You're the second person to tell me that today."

"Well, then." He smiled at her and brushed a non-existent strand of hair behind her ear. "That says to me you have no choice but to go home and open another bottle of wine."

Seeming in a slight daze, her hand raised to touch the place he brushed his fingers over. "That sounds like a very good idea. I need to clean up and get the vial—"

"Let me take care of everything. I'll make sure the mice are safely locked up in the other lab. Where's the best place to hide the serum? Your refrigerator is trashed."

"It's safe. I put it in the Virology guys' cold unit."

"Good. I'll talk with Kintu and tell him you're off until we can get you set up to work effectively again."

Her head tilted to the side. He caught her stare. "Why are you being so nice to me? You don't have to be."

He sighed. Man, he really wanted to tell her the truth about him, about who he was and who he worked for. He was tired of being undercover with her so close.

The urge to kiss her overwhelmed his senses. His animal wanted to make her happy, to make her smile again. He stepped closer to her. The mouse in the pen next to him screeched *at* him then ran to the far side of the pen.

Melinda said, "That was weird. It's never done that before."

Damn critter. It ruined the moment. If they weren't in an occupied building, he would've let his cat have a light snack. The cat rolled its mental eyes. *Don't waste my time.*

Hamel cleared his throat and headed to the other side of the table to get the mouse and put it in its cage for the night. Immediately, the mouse took off for the far corner where Melinda was. What the hell?

"Remember," she said, "they don't like you very much." She scooped up the mouse, gave it a treat, and set it in its cage. He recalled that, but how did the thing know he was coming to get it? Maybe it smelled his cat and just ran.

"If I leave," she started, "will you have something to do for the rest of today and tomorrow?"

"Oh, don't worry about me. I've got enough to keep me busy. Go ahead and go. I'll talk to Kintu to get the window patched, at least. Getting glass may take a few days."

She picked up the cage and turned to him. "Thank you for all you've done this week. You've gone over and above what most Oversight people ever would. Saturday's Halloween. Take it easy at the bars. You don't want to end up like you were this morning." She smiled.

He gave her a nod. "No worries. I'm not going anywhere near another bar. Have a good weekend."

She took the cage, got her purse, then walked out.

He let out a sigh and ran a hand over his head. Fuck, he was a mess inside. He knew what he needed to do, and then there was what he wanted to do, which was follow his mate to her bedroom.

He glanced at the non-operational cooling unit. There was no doubt in his mind the thief was after the vial. What happened when they discovered they still didn't have it? Would they come after her? How long did he have before that happened? A day or two?

Pulling a caveman and dragging her off was sounding better and better. It was hard to protect her when she couldn't know he was around. He was lucky last night and this morning. Nobody had attacked her while he was recuperating from the snakebite. That really did a number on him. He didn't remember a thing from the time he killed the snake until he woke on the grass outside the animal hospital.

He supposed she had taken him there, but why leave him outside the building? And how did the serum get into him? He'd felt it working. Thinking about it now, he vaguely remembered an old man talking to him while he was lying on the grass. But he couldn't recall what was said. Who knew? The old guy probably thought he'd found a panther and tried to scare the cat off.

He made his way to the door. He needed to speak with Kintu and get to Melinda's house before much time passed. He didn't like the thought of her being alone. Not for one second.

CHAPTER 19

Hamel padded through the woods from where he'd parked his car and stripped. The wooded area that extended to the water had come in handy. At first, he thought it would be a problem, blocking his view of her. Then he realized how his animal blended in perfectly.

It was late afternoon instead of being dark out, so he traveled deeper—closer to the water than usual. The last thing he wanted was kids following him to look at the pretty panther. He was a black jaguar, with spots, if one looked close enough.

Having moved south far enough, he cut in to find her balcony with the hammock chair and table. He'd have to try that chair. It looked really comfortable. He always fell off the hammocks strung between trees at the big resorts he'd vacationed at. His cat laughed at him to no end. Stupid human couldn't balance enough to lie on a hanging blanket.

A familiar smell reached his nose. Faint, but there. Melinda's bungalow came into view. The balcony doors barely stood, busted open. A spike of adrenaline shot him forward, over the rail, and onto the small patio. Fear. That was the smell. Just like in the lab not too long ago.

He sniffed at the doors. Absolutely no smell, meaning hunter's block had been used again. He stuck his head past the broken barrier to listen for movement. The only thing he heard was soft sobs.

Stepping in the two-room home, he surveyed the space. It looked like a trash dump with everything that had not been sitting on the floor now lying on the floor. Papers, books, computer, pens. Her mattress had been flipped up, even. Every pan, plate, and dish sat scattered. Cabinet doors stood open, boxed food and white powder covering the floor.

Letting his nose guide him, he found Melinda curled up in a corner next to the front door. She must've seen her devastated home as soon as she walked in and hadn't made it much farther.

Oh, god, his heart hurt for her. He wanted to shift and hold her in his arms, tell her everything would be all right now that he was here. He would protect her and never leave her side, except when she went to the bathroom, and then he'd stand outside the door. His overprotective streak was exhibiting itself again.

Her eyes widened when she saw him, and she inhaled to scream, no doubt. He fell to the floor, trying to tell her he wasn't going to hurt her. He meant her no harm. Of course, he had to land on top of a few forks and pointy kitchen utensils.

His eyes remained squeezed closed, waiting for the high-pitched yell to pierce his ears. Nothing came.

Opening one eye, he looked at her still crumpled in the corner. Her mouth gaped, but no fear was in her eyes. More like wonder. The thought to crawl forward was delayed as soon as the first fork tongs pressed against his stomach.

Well, shit. Now what? If he crouched just off the floor, it would look like he was going to pounce on her. If he got to his feet, she'd think the same. All normal options no longer being options, he rolled over, legs in the air, belly exposed, to flop onto his side. Not as graceful as he'd planned, but he was off the forks.

A small giggle floated to him. Was she breaking into fits of hysterical laughter, those that preceded a mental breakdown? He couldn't blame her. Having your home trashed by thieves felt like being assaulted. They'd invaded your supposedly safe home. She'd feel violated, dirty, even though none of it was her fault.

The smell in the air told him they were happy giggles. As he remained non-threating on his side, he glanced at her. Her eyes sparkled with unshed tears, and a hand partially covered a slight grin. Her line of sight was at his stomach.

He looked down to see his underside completely covered with white powder. Raisins, small nuts, and a fork were stuck to his belly. When he had rolled, he got white powder along his whole body. He didn't have to worry about looking scary anymore. Now he had to deal with being a laughingstock. He was so glad none of the other guys on the team were here.

As best he could with paws, he brushed off the unwanted tagalongs then rolled onto his belly. Head on his paws.

"Aww, aren't you so cute, big kitty." Joy filled him. His mate thought he was cute. Then his cat reminded him everyone thought kitties were cute. Dammit. Couldn't he soak in pride for just a second? No, his cat always had to keep him grounded.

She was no longer crying; that was good. He wondered how close he could get. On his stomach, he pushed forward with his back feet. She didn't cringe. Good sign. He repeated the action, coming within a couple feet of her.

No fear floated in the air, so he slowly inched toward her. She tentatively reached out and rubbed between his ears. That felt good. It'd been a long time since he'd been scratched with fingernails getting all the way to his skin.

He scooted closer, laying his head on her feet, her legs akimbo. With both hands, she scratched his scruff and neck, working farther down. Ahh, yeah. This was fucking great! He slid forward, resting his head on her thigh, then partially rolled to expose his stomach.

Her nails scraped along his tender skin. Fuck, yes! Shit, this felt better than sex, with anyone except his mate. She'd be incredible, if he ever got her there. But for now, this was it. Yeah, baby.

He couldn't stop his purring. Again, thank goodness his teammates weren't here to witness. Slowly, he came down from his high to realize she'd stopped her heavenly ministrations. He took stock of the situation.

His body lay splayed between her now straight legs, his upper back bent over her thigh. One paw sat on her shoulder and one foot wedged under her knee. His other foot dangled in the air, flashing his junk to the world. Whoa—he brought his leg down quickly. No need to impress with those. She'd appreciate the other form better.

He lifted off her leg, crawling back a bit. He parked his head between her knees and took a deep breath. Heaven.

Oh, shit. He looked up to see her expression. Did he just royally embarrass himself? Good thing animals didn't blush. She smiled down at him.

"You're my guardian cat, aren't you? I'm glad the snake venom didn't kill you. I would've felt terrible."

Yeah, him, too.

"You're so pretty and soft. I could pet you all night."

All in favor say "aye." Aye. *Aye*.

Melinda let out a heavy sigh and looked around her room. "What am I to do with this mess? I hate to say it, but I wish Hamel were here." He'd started to grow on her. She actually liked him. If she was honest, maybe she more than liked him. No, that wasn't possible.

She thought back to the hug he gave her not long ago in the lab. His incredibly strong arms had picked her up off the floor like she weighed as much as a piece of paper.

The feeling that went through her as he held her, pressing her against his chest—never had she sensed such safety, such peace than while she rested against him. And damn, he smelled so freaking good. She loved how his face shined when he smiled at her, and how his eyes lit up when he laughed. She loved how he took control when her mind was in a tailspin with what had happened. That seemed like a daily event lately. Right now, he could have all the control he wanted.

But he wasn't here. She laid her head on the wall. "I guess I shouldn't be that surprised about this. After all, I did take the serum home last night. I was lucky the guy went looking at the lab instead of here."

Her hands rubbed her eyes. "I am so tired of all this, kitty. All I want is to have it all go away." She'd never done anything to deserve this.

But what worried her most was that she still had the serum. Where and when would they strike next?

CHAPTER 20

Her house was trashed. She sat on the floor by the door, not wanting to go in any farther. But she had to eventually. So Melinda climbed to her feet and stretched her back. The jaguar was gone, and it was dark.

Dembe was right when she said Melinda should take a vacation. She needed it. But right now, her home was a war zone. A groan bubbled up her throat. She hated cleaning big messes. That's why she tidied up as she went when cooking or doing anything.

Still in her work clothes, she made her way to the bedroom, showered away the stress, and changed into stretchy pants and a T-shirt. She started cleaning the food and dishes from the floor. After a while her logic returned from overpowering fear.

Why would someone come after her personally? Perhaps it wasn't personal and they were just looking for the serum. That thought made her feel better. Whoever it was had done their homework. They knew where her laptop was locked away, knew a serum was made, knew which lab was hers. Did she know this person?

This all started two days ago, the same day Hamel fell into her lap. Good god, it seemed like weeks, not days. Was it too coincidental that Hamel arrived the same day as the first break-in? He had to have been vetted by Kintu. He was from the— She gasped. He wasn't from the CDC. In all that had happened after the phone call, she'd forgotten about that. He was a fraud. Holy frackin' shit. He had to be the bad guy.

It all made sense. His uncharacteristic Oversight temperament, the non-technical medical terminology. He was late this morning, but not from going to the bar. He was searching her house for the serum while she was at the lab. Perfect timing. He had as long as he wanted. When she had called him, he was probably at her place. That's exactly why he told her not to leave her lab. He couldn't take the chance she would leave and come home.

Should she call the authorities? This wasn't Atlanta, where the cops came in to bust the bad boys. The "cops" here walked around with machine guns strapped around their shoulders and grenades in their pockets. She understood why Mr. Kintu wanted to keep this whole thing under wraps. The advice was good and she'd follow it. She'd have to tell him first thing in the morning. That would work. Hamel thought she was taking the day off.

Wait. She'd told him where she hid the serum with the other department. He wouldn't wait until tomorrow when the guys were working. He'd take it tonight while everyone was gone. Five minutes had passed since she checked her watch last. If she left now, she could get to the lab well before then. She had to try, at least.

She slipped on her running shoes, grabbed her keys, and flew out the door. The food and destroyed house would have to wait. Nothing was more important than keeping the serum out of the wrong hands. What he would do with the virus, she had no clue. But he wanted it bad enough that the reason couldn't be good.

Traffic was light this late at night. Most traveled by moped or motor bike. The roads in town were paved, but narrow. The main road went from Entebbe airport at the southern tip of the peninsula, north to Kampala, the closest big city. Plus everything around the Uganda Virus Research Laboratory was much nicer than the rest of the town. Money went into the lab's surrounding area, housing scientists and visiting bigwigs.

She slowed when approaching the guard shack at the entrance gate. Rousing suspicions wouldn't be good. She handed her badge to the guard. He took several minutes, making two calls inside his hut. Security was probably extremely tight because of the break-ins. That made her feel safer, but right now, it just annoyed her.

The guard opened his door and handed back her badge. "Here a little late, Miss Caster?"

"I am, but I'm off for a few days starting tomorrow, so it all works out." The single-arm gate levered up. "Oh, has Dr. Hamel come through recently?"

"No, ma'am. I've been here several hours and I have not seen him."

That relieved her. She'd beaten him there, if he was truly coming back to steal her work. Should she say something about not letting him in? If she did then it would cause a big stir, and she didn't have time to answer a million questions from the security captain.

"Thank you." She waved and drove under the lifted gate arm, aiming for her building's parking area. Another guard stood at the entrance. He looked at her badge and radioed the gate guard. They confirmed with each other, then the guard let her into the building.

The interior felt strange at night with most of the lights off and nobody around. When she passed the lunchroom, through the windows, she saw Hamel coming from the side. Shit. He was already there. He was the one.

Wait. The guard said he hadn't seen Hamel come in. That solidified in her mind that he was the bad guy.

She had to hurry.

CHAPTER 21

Frantically, Melinda flipped through her ring of keys looking for the one that would let her into the Virology lab, hiding the set as best she could. The research scientists dealing with viruses and such shared keys in case they needed to get into another lab when working late at night. But that wasn't something they wanted everyone knowing about. Too many tempers had exploded when someone was not able to get something they needed in someone else's lab. The keys had come in handy for her several times.

The lock finally turned and she slipped inside. Her hand flipped up the light switch and she ran for the fridge unit. The tube with a rubber top sat exactly where she'd put it. She stuffed it into her pants' side pocket and ran for the door. She heard voices in the hallway, right outside the door. Hamel. Shit.

Her body slid behind the door as it opened. "Melinda?"

How the hell did he know she was here? He must have seen her. Dammit. How was she getting out of here? Would he kill her? Isn't that what all bad guys did? Kill witnesses?

A microscope sat on the counter next to her. She wrapped a hand around the main vertical support. Hamel came into room, stepping past the door. With all the strength she had, she whipped the scope off the countertop, and in a graceful arc, brought it down on his head. He went to the floor and she rounded the door, slamming it shut behind her.

Then she ran. If she could make it to the guard outside, she'd be safe.

"Melinda!"

Fuck! She was sure he'd be out for a couple minutes. Asshole had a thick skull.

She rounded the corner to the hall that ran past her lab.

"Melinda, stop!" He was getting closer. She hadn't even gotten to the lunchroom yet. No way she'd make it outside. She'd have to hide and hope for the best. Farther up the hall, the door to the smaller lab opened and a plastic trashcan the janitors used rolled out, followed by a man closing the door behind him.

"Wait," she called to him as loud as she dared. Within a second she was beside him. She recognized the man. "Walog. Thank god you're here." She pushed the trash barrel, and him, back into the room, closed the door, and turned the deadbolt lock.

A lamp shined on the counter not too far from them, so she could mostly see where she was going. Walog started to say something but she shushed him and pulled him and his cart toward the light.

"Melinda, it's okay. It's just me, Hamel," floated down the hall.

She snorted then whispered, "Right, just Hamel the thief and house destroyer." Walog looked at her with wide eyes.

"He break in your lab and stole things?"

She nodded. "He's after the last of the serum, but I got it safe with me." She patted her pocket. They rounded a table and hurried to the other side of the room, where Melinda switched off the lamp and crouched. She pulled Walog down and he finally let go of his trash cart.

Banging on the door startled her. What the hell? Did he have a tracking device on her? How could he know she was in there? The knob rattled, the deadbolt remaining in place. They should be safe. Hamel couldn't wait out there all night.

The distinct sound of metal against metal as a key slid into the lock surprised her. But it shouldn't have. Any good crook would have keys to everything, right?

Walog leaned against her heavily. Enough to where she almost fell over. She pushed back. Suddenly his hands were all over her body. What the hell? This was not the time nor place to cop a feel. Besides, he was married. "Walog, stop it." She blindly slapped him away, but he was a persistent bugger.

She felt the vial in her pant pocket slide out and Walog was gone. Melinda sprang to her feet and reached in the direction he was. Her fingers snagged material the same instant the lights came on. Walog grabbed her wrist and flung her toward his rolling trash cart. The impact wasn't as hard as she anticipated and she was able to keep from slamming into it by bracing her arms. Unfortunately, the trash barrel was on wheels and moved on contact.

Her hands gripped the top edge, her feet stumbling along, unable to get under her. She and the cart zipped between two tables until the wall ricocheted their advance backward and to the floor.

The door opened and Hamel started toward her. She jabbed a finger in Walog's direction. "He's got the last of the serum." Hamel stopped and whipped around to see the janitor halfway to the door. In a single leap, Hamel flew over tables toward the man. She sat on the floor in disbelief. Was he some super human? No one could do what he just did.

When Hamel tackled him, she saw the tube in the man's hand. "Don't break the glass vial," she screamed.

Hamel's hand wrapped around Walog's, protecting both from smashing against the floor. The doctor then punched the janitor in the face, but that didn't slow the thief. He twisted and landed a knee in Hamel's side, launching him away. But with his hand still around Walog's, he didn't go far.

Walog grabbed the doctor's wrist to jerk his hand away at the same time the doctor latched on to the glass tube. Hamel ended up with the prize and a very pissed-off janitor. Walog climbed to his feet, panting. His dark eyes now glowed red. Melinda screeched then slapped her hand over her mouth. Walog didn't look human or friendly. His mouth opened and a deep voice, not his, came out.

"Give the virus to me, and I will let you live."

Melinda heard the familiar squeak of one of her mice. She glanced inside the tipped trash container to see her mice's cage turned on its side. What the hell? She reached in and lifted it out, gently righting it. Momma mouse was fine, but the precog baby lay lifeless. She wasn't sure if the death was from a burned-out brain or rough handling. Either way, it didn't matter. It was gone. If the serum was destroyed, this little creature alive in the cage was their last sample. It had to be protected.

And why was the cage in Walog's trashcan?

Hamel's body flew backward through the air, crashing against the counter close to her. She scooted away in reaction to his violent landing. He simply shook his head then climbed to his feet. His arm reached out to her, the test tube dangling in his fingers. She snatched it from him and cradled it to herself, her wide eyes watching as the doctor stood.

Hamel asked the man, "Who are you?"

A growl came from the man's open mouth. Multiple voices sounded as one. "We are no one. Give us the serum and we'll be gone from this world."

Melinda sucked in a breath. Holy shit! She recognized this. Her parents had preached to her to no end about demons taking over human bodies. *The Exorcist* on steroids. This became more unbelievable by the second. Oh. My. God. Walog was going to vomit green shit and crawl on the ceiling.

"We need holy water! He needs an exorcism," she mumbled.

A destitute African villager, willing to do anything for his family, including giving up his soul, possessed by a demon in a country heavily into voodoo. Putting it like that, it sounded like an everyday occurrence. But she didn't believe in demons, did she? She watched Walog and decided that she most certainly did at that moment. She couldn't argue with what she was seeing with her own eyes.

Hamel asked her next question for her. "What would demons want with a virus that doesn't kill? Isn't that your purpose? To kill as many humans as you can and take over the world, or some deluded shit like that?"

Unearthly gurgles came from the gaping mouth. "Give us the virus and we'll let you live." A small centrifuge machine launched toward her. She ducked her head. She had the tube; she was the target again. Hamel must have thought the same. He lifted the trashcan, flipped it upside down, and put it over her.

Immediately, she pounded on the side. "Hamel, dammit, get this off me." She tried to get her fingers under the edge, but there was nothing to grip to pull up. When she reached up in her sitting position, her fingers grazed the top/bottom of the barrel. With the mouse cage in her lap, there was no way she could move.

Something heavy slammed against the plastic container she was under. Maybe it would be a good idea to stay put until Hamel said. Dammit, but she wanted to see what was going on with demon-possessed Walog and Hamel. This kind of stuff never happened to her. But it was probably dangerous, so she'd stay right where she was.

Outside her safe hidey-hole, a storm erupted. The sound of wind slashing around the room startled her. Other pieces of equipment sounded like they were smashed against hard surfaces. Howls and catlike growls and hisses cut the air. When did animals get into the room? Her poor momma mouse was probably traumatized.

The noise stopped. She held her breath, trying to hear the slightest sound. Footsteps came her way. "Melinda, you okay?" The trash barrel was lifted. Her eyes squinted against the bright light. As her pupils adjusted, the room came into focus. It resembled her lab from a couple days ago. Everything not previously bolted down was now on the floor.

Her heart raced. "What the hell happened? Why were his eyes red and why did a creepy-ass voice come from him?" Then she remembered Hamel was the thief. But wait. Why did Walog take the serum? And why was Walog possessed and wanting her research? She was so confused.

Hamel took the cage from her lap and set it on the counter. She scrambled to her feet. "Stay away from me, Hamel."

He looked at her with confusion on his face. "Melinda, I'm not the bad guy here. I'm sure Walog is."

No, she didn't want to believe that. Dembe knew Walog's family. They were honest people. Something had to be very wrong if he was the bad guy here. Even though things pointed to that. She must not have all the facts. "He's a hardworking man trying to make a living for his family." She looked around the room for him. Her pulsed doubled. "He's just into this Halloween thing really hard. Did you kill him?"

"No, just knocked him out. He's on the floor over there." He indicated the direction with a jerk of his head. She slid backward along the cabinet, keeping an eye on Hamel while looking for Walog. "And he's not into Halloween. That was not him talking to us before."

"If you're not the bad guy," Melinda asked, "then why are you here?"

"Here, as in this room? Or here, as in Uganda?"

"Both." The downed janitor came into her sight. She ran to him, sliding the vial down her shirt and bra, the only place she could think to put it. On her knees, she put fingers to the side of his neck. His pulse felt strong. Thank god, he wasn't dead—

Walog's eyes popped open. A red dot in the middle of each pupil focused on her. She pulled away, startled by the movement. His hand snapped up and grabbed her around the neck. Instantly, her air was cut off. "Give me the serum."

Ah, fuck! Maybe Hamel was right and Walog had more than a few things wrong with him. Hamel was beside her immediately. He slammed the man's head against the floor, knocking him out a second time. The hand fell away from her. She scrambled backward, bumping against an overturned table and other equipment on the floor. Hamel turned to her.

"Stay away from me, both of you." Her hands shook. She now understood why the mice's cage was in the trash barrel. Walog was mouse-napping them. She had told Walog earlier where she'd moved them. Same as she told Hamel where she'd hidden the serum. She really needed to learn to keep her secrets to herself.

Walog's mouth opened, yet his eyes remained closed. "He will not stop until the elixir and an army of demon mutants are under his control." A stream of vapor rose from his mouth, like a fire through a chimney. It hovered in the air below the ceiling, then vanished with a pop.

The prone body on the floor groaned. Hamel gently slid his hand under the man's head. "Walog, can you hear me?" The janitor's breath came shallow and fast. His tired eyes were back to human.

"Tell my wife, children, I love them." His eyelids began to droop. "I'm sorry for hurting you. He lied to me. Said he'd help my family. He lied . . ." Walog's body relaxed and he exhaled his last breath.

CHAPTER 22

⊸

Hamel gently laid Walog's head on the floor then stepped back. His brain was in a whirl from all that had happened in the previous five minutes. He needed to prioritize. His mate came first. He turned to see Melinda staring at Walog's body. Her eyes snapped to his. She backed away from him, fear in her eyes and in the air.

He raised his hands in supplication. "Melinda, please—"

"No." She snatched up a glass flask and wrapped her hand around the narrow neck. "Don't come any closer. I'll cut you with—" She banged the bottom of the flask against the countertop—not too hard, just to break off the end to have a jagged edge. When it didn't break, she did it again, harder. When it still refused to bust, she lifted it over her head, yelling, "Break, goddammit! Now that I want it to break, it won't!"

Hamel, using his supernatural speed, came up behind her to grab the flask and save her from hurting herself. From what he'd seen, Murphy's Law applied to her more than others. He set the flask on the countertop, then wrapped his hands around her waist and placed her on the cabinet. He snaked his way between her knees.

"Woman, will you calm down for just one second?" His exasperation showed. He couldn't remember the last time he'd felt this way. Maybe never. Great, she could drive him over the edge in minutes. That should make for an interesting life. He wrapped both her hands in one of his and laid them on her lap.

The back of his hand rested against the crease between her legs. The heat coming from that area was intense. The yoga pants she wore outlined everything quite nicely. A matching heat built in him. He'd been so close to her, watching her, for days, and not able to so much as hold her. His defenses were breaking down.

Now that the thief had been caught, this was over and he would seduce his little mate and take her with him. How could she resist someone like him?

But first he needed to call Kintu and get him to join them so she would chill out. After doing so and putting his phone back into his pocket, he focused on her.

"Okay, I know you have questions. Start asking."

She was taken aback for some reason. Her words stumbled and stuttered before she got a full sentence out. "You can't just *demand* I ask questions. I have questions." And those sentences didn't make much sense. She shook her head. "You know what I mean. H-how, I mean, y-you, and that." Her eyes went to where the demon's aura had hovered over Walog's body before disappearing.

"It's okay, sweetheart." Shit, where did that come from? He'd never called anyone that. Her disapproval shined clearly on her face.

"Do not call me 'darling,' 'sweetheart,' or 'honey' or I will turn you into a eunuch before you can even think to cover your balls."

His body involuntarily cringed away, mainly his midsection. "Warning noted," he said.

"Now let go of me and back away. I'm not going to do anything but wait for Mr. Kintu to get here." He released her hands regrettably and stepped back. His cat was scratching and telling him to get back in there. It was the closest they'd been since the all-over body scratch earlier.

At least Melinda didn't smell afraid, probably just confused. How much should he tell her? His cover was probably blown. Maybe it was better that way. He could get closer to her then. But that was sorta against policy, to screw your assignment. But she was his mate. That had to be different, right?

"Who are you really, Dr. Hamel? And if you say you're a doctor, you're well on your way to being a 'sweetheart.'"

He shoved his hands into his pockets and turned to her. "My name is Parish Hamel. I'm not a doctor, but a national security operative. I was sent here to protect you and the work you're doing."

"Protect me? Why? We just discovered the ESP virus a little over a week ago. How could you have known about it?"

He walked to the counter and hopped up to sit next to her. Really close. She frowned, but didn't say anything. "I don't get details like that, Melinda. I'm told to go, and I go. But I want you to know this assignment is more than a job to me. You're more important than that. I want to get to know you better."

"Know me better?" Unease floated in the air. "Why?"

"Because you've captivated me and I can't stop thinking about you."

She gave him a look of disbelief. "Right. And now you've completed your mission and want to just start seeing me and going on dates and stuff?"

"Yeah. I want to spend some time with you. Hang out at the beach, walk around town and see how much trouble we can cause."

She laughed. "I think trouble follows you. That's all I've had since you've been here." Her smile slipped a bit. "National security, huh? CIA, Homeland, Navy SEALs?"

She would get down to the nitty-gritty. "Our initials aren't well known. Let's just say we're a federal agency, sanctioned by the president. Will that work?"

Melinda leaned back and looked him over. He wondered what was going through that beautiful head of hers. She smelled so good. He shouldn't be sitting this close to her. Desire had burned low for several days and was ready to burst into a huge flame. He scooted his thigh over to touch hers. She noticed, but didn't move away. That was a good sign.

Fuck, how he wanted her. To make that dream they'd both been in a reality. To touch her and kiss her and make her his. He wanted no more lies or half-truths between them. Her scent called to his animal. They both wanted to mate with her. He struggled every second to not walk up to her and take her lips, press his body to her soft curves and finally have that skin-on-skin contact he craved.

"I guess that'll work. You haven't killed me or run off with the virus, so what can I say? I guess you're not the bad guy like I thought." She eyed him. "Maybe." The edge of her lip curved up. His heart flip-flopped. She was playing along, willing to let him get close.

"You could say that you'd like to go out with me this weekend. That'd be nice. Since I'm visiting and all. Show me around town?" Technically, he knew just about everything there was to know about the area, down to the closest fault lines. Part of his job was knowing the territory before going in. But he wanted to see it through her eyes.

Her laugh tinkled in his mind. "We'll see, big boy. Right now, I've got a lot to take care of. Starting with a dead janitor. Or whatever he was. Why were his eyes red?"

Boy, that was a good one. How did he answer that without her thinking he was loony? He heard noises in the hallway outside. Kintu walked through the door with a couple guards. Hamel pointed to Walog's body. Kintu gave orders to take the body to large cold storage and looked around the room.

"Let's go to my office," he said. "There're some things I need to tell you that you probably won't like."

CHAPTER 23

On the trio's trip down the hall to Mr. Kintu's office, Hamel rested his hand on the small of Melinda's back and whispered into her ear, "Are you okay?" He worried she would become overwhelmed with too much information in so short a time.

When they came to her lab room door, she said, "Hold on a second. I need to do something." Kintu continued on, but Hamel stayed with her.

"What do you need to do?"

She scoffed at him. "Nosy, aren't we? Just because you're here to protect me doesn't mean you get to know everything." She entered her lab and headed toward a cabinet. She opened the drawer, pulled out something small, then he heard the sound of a rubber topper pulled off.

All right. Enough of this being-secret crap, he wanted to know what she was doing. When he approached her from behind, he saw her hand tuck something into the center of her bra. He had to admit that was a great hiding place.

Melinda turned on her heel. "Okay, let's go. I'm done." He scowled at her and she laughed at him. "Don't be so grouchy, *Doctor*." As she walked away, he swore her hips swayed more than before.

* * *

Settled into chairs in front of Senior Principal Research Officer Kintu's desk, Hamel and Melinda sat staring at him, wondering what he'd tell them that they wouldn't like. Left to his own devices, Hamel could come up with some really bad shit he didn't like.

Mr. Kintu rested his elbows on his desk. "Dr. Hamel—"

"Excuse me," Hamel started, "but my cover is no longer in effect. Miss Caster knows my true identity."

"What should I call you?" the senior PRO asked.

Hamel shrugged. "Hamel would be fine."

"Okay, Hamel, tell me what evidence you've got against the janitor. Even in Uganda, they need a reason to put people in jail."

"He was stealing my mice. That's for sure," Melinda huffed. "I found the cage in the trash barrel he was pushing around. There was no trash in it, either. Plus, it was ten thirty. His shift ends at ten."

"First off, he didn't smell like anything," Hamel said.

Mr. Kintu's brows lowered. "What does that mean? He smelled like nothing?"

"Means he was wearing hunter's block to keep his smell out of the rooms," Hamel said. "Is it normal around here for janitors to wear block?"

"I wouldn't know why, so I'd say no." Mr. Kintu leaned back in his chair.

Hamel asked, "Do janitors have keys to all the labs?"

Mr. Kintu nodded. "Why would he take the mice?" He looked at Melinda. "Is there something I don't know about the mice?"

Melinda's face reddened. "I—I was going to write it up tonight. The extra brain nodes allow for mental abilities beyond normal. Telekinesis, precognition, clairvoyance. That's all we've found so far."

Mr. Kintu nodded again. "I was afraid of that. Go on; what else?"

Melinda answered a previous question. "When I was in Dembe's lab with one of the mice, I spilled a drink and he came in to clean it up. We probably said a lot of things we shouldn't have in front of a non-vetted person."

Mr. Kintu waved his hand in front of him. "That's neither here nor there. Did he . . . ?" Kintu sighed as if he didn't want to say what he had to. "Do you think Walog could've been possessed?"

Hamel and Melinda shared a look, silently telling the other to answer. Hamel caved to his mate with a sigh. "Fine. I'll say it. He had red eyes, a voice that didn't belong to him, and when he died, a vapor rose from his body then disappeared."

"I'd call that possessed. A witch doctor would, too," Kintu said. He wiped a hand over his face. "When I first started here at the lab in 1960, I was matched up with two guys who had been here a year. They were top notch with their research and procedures.

"During that year, word got to us that a farmer had seen strange things happening—stuff disappearing, things moved to different locations, and more. Then he found two dead, very young monkeys. Both bleeding from the ears. Since our threesome was at the bottom of the barrel, we were elected to visit this farmer to see what we could see.

"We brought the monkeys back, did normal workups. As you can imagine, our technology back then was nothing compared to today's. But the images did show unusually high synaptic connections. Since the animals were deceased, we had no idea what this meant.

"In the blood work, we found the virus. Since the animals had just died, the virus was still alive. From there, we made a serum for testing. When we discovered what the virus did, as you have, Melinda, we were ecstatic." Kintu swiveled his chair to look out the window behind him.

"Things get blurry here. I was sent on a fieldwork assignment, so this is what I've pieced together from others. One of the guy's grandfathers was a witch doctor or voodoo priest or whatever. The grandfather overhead the boy talking about this discovery. To gain favor from the 'other side,' he peddled it to a supernatural entity.

"That entity had the grandfather doing whatever he had to to get the serum. I have no idea why. But when the grandson refused to help him, the grandfather killed him and went about his own plan. Somehow he got in touch with my other team member. And all I know is he destroyed the serum, and he had quit before I returned.

"I've been here ever since, watching and waiting for this virus to pop up again. We knew it would sooner or later. It wasn't the kind of thing that just went away." He went quiet.

Melinda frowned. "So when you learned of the dead monkeys and that I'd found a virus, you suspected it was the same?"

He turned his chair to face them. "I looked at the brain scan you and Dembe took and put on the network for download. When I saw the additional synaptic connections, I knew it was. But even before that, I called a contact in the CIA and told him the basics and that we needed someone who could safeguard you and your work." Kintu looked to Hamel. "That was apparently you."

Hamel pulled the gate card and a key from his pockets and laid them on the desk. "Thanks for letting me use the back entrance. It's much quicker to get here. And your master key is next to the card."

Kintu's eyes got big and his face showed fear. "You're leaving? That's it? What about the serum and Melinda?"

He gave a calming smile. "Mr. Kintu, I feel sure the janitor was working alone—well, besides the demon inside him, which has been banished to where they go. I think the threat has been neutralized and there is no further threat, *if* Miss Caster destroys the remaining serum." His eyes slid to her.

She slapped a hand over her chest. "Me? You want me to get rid of the serum? I can't do that. Do you know what this serum can do?"

"Yes, Miss Caster," Kintu cut in. "I am fully aware what it can do, and the world isn't ready for that kind of power. It would be abused and used for evil purposes. The children with the abilities would be hunted down and killed, just like Frankenstein. Different isn't tolerated long among humans. If you like, I'll destroy the specimen."

She jerked in her chair. "NO." She looked to Hamel and back to Kintu, taking a calming breath. "It's my responsibility, my research—which is still missing, by the way. I'll take care of it."

"It'd be a good idea for you to take off tomorrow, Miss Caster," Kintu said. "It's late as it is, and without the virus, you're unassigned. Come back Monday all bouncy and cheery." He gave her a big smile.

Melinda rolled her eyes. "I'm never bouncy and cheery, Mr. Kintu. You know that."

"I do. That's why I said it." He stood from chair. "Let's go home. Except for the body, and buying you new equipment, Miss Caster, there isn't much else to do to erase all evidence. I appreciate your cooperation. Remember, it's vital this never gets out."

Hamel helped Melinda from her chair and walked her to the door, then turned back. "Mr. Kintu, what happened to your research partner after he quit?"

"I don't know. Never saw or heard from him again. He's probably passed away by now. He'd be fairly old as he was several years my senior at the time."

"Thank you, Mr. Kintu. Either I or someone from my team will be in touch." With that he walked Melinda out the door. He could tell she was tired. Her feet dragged and she slumped. He played with the idea of weaseling into her bed tonight. With one mission done, he could now focus on getting into his mate's pants. God, he was horrible.

She looked at Hamel. "Do you think it's really safe now?"

Not if he went by his jaguar. His animal prowled under the skin, aware and alert. "I'm not totally sure. Maybe I should stay at your house tonight. You know, just in case." He kept it light so she knew he was being playful.

Her eyes narrowed as she stared him down. "Rushing things a bit, aren't you? I haven't even agreed to go out with you."

He laughed. He loved that she could bring out his light side. He hadn't seen it enough lately. "Maybe a bit, but I was being serious about the threat. How about I come over in the morning and help you put your house back together."

Melinda groaned and dropped her head back. "I forgot about that. Shit. I'm so tired. It can wait, even the food stuff. I just want to go to bed." She quickly added, "Alone, for now."

For now?

He sobered his expression. "Of course it'll be alone. You are a modest, beautiful woman who doesn't need a big, bad ca—" *Fuck.* He almost said "cat." "Guy like me, cramping your style. I'll come over in the morning and help. With both of us, it'll get done faster. I can fix the balcony doors, too." He didn't voice all the other stuff he wanted to do to her tomorrow. "Are you okay to drive home?"

"Hamel, it's two miles. I could walk it."

"I know." He shrugged. "Just wanting you safe. That's all."

"That's very kind of you. But I'm good. You go back to your hotel, and I'll see you tomorrow morning around eight."

His heart lit up like a bonfire. "You got it. Not a minute later." He watched her walk to her car and get in. He lost sight of her after she passed the guard shack. Now it was time for his cat to take over while he "slept." They'd sit outside her balcony and keep a loving eye out.

CHAPTER 24

Tingles ran up Melinda's back as she waited for the security gate arm to rise in the lab parking lot. Being so close to that man drove her crazy. He smelled so good all she wanted was to lick him from forehead to feet. With a pause somewhere in the middle area. Her stomach lurched. Was that a scared or happy thing? Shit, she wasn't sure. Maybe both.

It'd been so long since she had physical human contact of any kind. That was no way to live. People needed touch as much as food and water. People needed sex, too, but thanks to her toy, she had been able to go without for two years. And now with the possibility so close and so good-looking, so tight, so hard, she really didn't want to say no. But good girls didn't do that kind of thing.

Good god. That was her parents talking—always telling her what good girls did. She was an adult. She could do anything she wanted. Who cared if she slept with someone? It wasn't like he was the twentieth person in two years; he would be the first. That had to count for something.

Decision made, maybe, a full body shake came on. Giddiness crept into her heart. One thing she was not was giddy. What was this man doing to her? She took a deep breath to get her emotions under control. He was doing nothing to her.

She couldn't allow her heart to get involved. For all she knew Hamel was like James Bond—a new girl each assignment. Never doing one twice.

It would just be sex. That's what she had to tell herself. He was going back to the States. There could be nothing between her and Hamel. But she felt so good in his arms, so secure.

She made it home and parked her car in its designated spot. She unlocked her front door, hoping all the mess was a dream; it was perfectly clean and nothing was wrong. The door popped open, and her heart fell. Still a complete disaster. Well, it could friggin' wait until tomorrow.

She dropped her purse on a chair and saw the balcony doors. They were off-kilter. How did he know? She had to have told him. God, she was losing it. Couldn't even remember what she said during the day.

She thought back to Walog. Demon-possessed. That's what it had to be, right? The man had red eyes, a weird set of voices—not like the one she'd heard from him before—and that smoke. Plus, he was old, skinny, and weak. So how had he shoved a big, buff Hamel across the room without batting an eye?

Her instinct told her there was more at play there than things she could understand with facts. Demons. Fuck. If she believed that then she might as well believe in the tooth fairy and vampires. She could hear Hamel in her head. *Stop trying to understand everything. Sometimes you need to just accept things.* Nope. Not unless she had further proof. And she needed to stop imagining his voice in her head. It was messing with her mind.

Propping a balcony door up and open, she let the soft breeze into the house. It felt so good to take a breath and relax. She wondered about her guardian jaguar. Was he out there, watching, keeping her safe?

Letting her guard down for a second, she opened herself to the night. Welcomed anything directed her way. Her conscience reached out, begging for what she desperately needed. And she found it, connected with it. She felt something inside her snap, and unknown peace and love flowed into her. It was so powerful, it brought her to her knees.

Where was this coming from? She had to have it. Her

emptiness inside was filling, slowly disappearing. Someone loved her with so much of themselves, they had enough to share. The small ache in the middle of her chest was gone. She hadn't even known it was there. It'd become a part of her waking hours.

Then she realized what she was doing. She was opening herself to ridicule and making herself vulnerable again. She'd spent so long closing off her feelings, determined to not let the past happen again. But the love felt so good. She'd forgotten how good. Who was gifting her with such compassion?

Only one new life, except Hamel who didn't count, had come into hers. The jaguar. Was it silly to think she could feel emotions from an animal? Maybe she wanted to be loved so badly that she projected onto the beautiful creature what she wanted most. Maybe she was giving herself permission to love again. Maybe she bonded with this animal. She sighed. Maybe she should just go to bed.

Mate.

Just like her sex dream with gorgeous Ham—Beach Man— she knew right away she was in a dream world.

She stood at the edge of a small village, a village so far from civilization they probably didn't know modern people existed. Several straw-and-mud huts laid out in a circle surrounded a barely flaming bonfire. No sounds reached her ears, which was weird. Usually crickets, critters, and birds were always chatting, mating, or calling to a mate. She felt like she was in an episode of *The Twilight Zone*. Creepy.

A thatched door to one of the huts opened by itself. Great, this was a nightmare. Like in every other horror movie she'd seen, she walked toward the hut with the intent of going inside. She could hear the audience screaming, "Don't go in there!"

She pulled the door open wider and peeked inside. She wasn't dumb enough to just walk in without looking. To her surprise, the space was large and like a snow lodge high in the mountains. What the hell?

From an entryway across the room, Buga the medical technician's grandfather walked in, holding a tray of food.

"Good afternoon, Melinda."

"Good afternoon to you, sir."

"Call me Sefu. Come in, come in. Close the door behind you." She did as told, but didn't move too far. "Melinda, this is a dream. You cannot be physically harmed in a dream. Please, have a seat." He gestured to a large saddle-brown leather chair. "We don't have much time."

"Time for what?" she found herself saying. Inching forward, her eyes darted to all corners, looking for anything dangerous.

"Your training, child. You must learn the chant."

"What chant?" Now she was curious to know what Sefu meant. He was dressed the same as he had been in the medical facility. A witch doctor didn't come to mind.

"And that's how I want it," he said. "'Witch doctor' has a bad connotation these days, and I wish to be no part of that. I work with white magic. But at times, that white dips to gray. That time comes soon. This is why you must learn quickly."

The tray he placed on the coffee table between the leather sofa and chair was filled with homemade chocolate-chip cookies. Her favorite. Her mouth watered. They smelled so good.

"Have some, child. Obviously they are meant for you. I don't eat such sweets."

"It's only a dream," Melinda said.

"It is," he said. "But the mind is a powerful tool. The brain controls the body's functions, but the *mind* controls reality. Your mind is saying those cookies are real. Your brain is telling you that you smell cookies. The part of your brain that controls smell is kicking in as you dream, even though no cookies are in your real surroundings."

"That's quite interesting. So I can't be physically harmed in this dream state because in 'real life,' my body is lying in bed. I'm totally in my head. Cool. But what has that got to do with this dream, though?" she asked.

"Patience, young one. Patience." He sat on the sofa catty-corner to her. She huffed at his scolding and grabbed several cookies, then sat back in her chair.

"I won't be talking down to you, as you put it. I will be teaching you what you need to survive where you are going."

"Where am I going?" Alarm-fueled adrenaline rushed through her. She didn't want to go anywhere. She was happy where she was.

"You don't have a choice. You will go as fate has dictated." Melinda noted he answered her unspoken words rather than her direct question. It was a dream; why not throw in mind reading?

The old man smiled. "Yes, now you are understanding."

"Understanding what?"

His smile turned to a frown and he shook his head. "Child, things are going to happen that will rock your little world. It's important you be accepting and take all at face value. Don't analyze it to death. Just believe."

Now she frowned. "I don't believe blindly. I get the facts then make a decision."

He raised his brows and stared at her deeply. "What do you do when there are no facts?"

"What do you mean? How can there be no facts about something?"

He sighed. "This will be most difficult for you. We do not have time to argue semantics. Close your eyes and listen. Learn." The old man began chanting. His voice was smooth, warm, comforting. It put her at ease. Her eyes closed and her body relaxed into the soft leather chair.

Huenda sisi kujiunga ukweli wetu kweli.

Kuziba ulimwengu huu milele kwa yake mwenyewe.

The phrase repeated over and over in her head. What it meant or what it was for, she didn't know. But it was her dream, so what the hell? A sharp sting burned on the underside of her wrist. She snapped her arm up and rubbed the area. Black lines emerged from under her skin as if coming to the surface.

When the pain stopped, a pretty curlicue design with intertwining vine-like lines decorated the skin below her hand. It reminded her of a tattoo. She rubbed her finger over it. Nothing smeared.

This would help trap the demons, she heard in her head.

CHAPTER 25

The next morning, Melinda woke with a sense of confusion. She lifted her wrist, twisted it over to stare at the underside. It looked normal. Why was she concerned?

She looked at her watch on the bedside table. Hamel would be there soon. She showered and was ready just before a knock sounded on her door. She opened it to see a breathtaking stud who made her knees and tongue not work.

He wore jeans that fit snugly in all the right places and a white T-shirt that was snug everywhere. She wondered if he did that on purpose. He had to have known the effect he had on her. Hell, probably on every woman. In his fingers he twirled a single wildflower. He flipped it up and nestled it behind her ear. Bringing himself closer in the process.

"A beautiful flower for my beautiful flower." He kissed her temple. "Did you get some sleep after getting home last night?"

She thought back to the dream with the old man and cookies. Those were the strangest theoretical, esoteric ideas she'd ever heard. It seemed like he was talking about out-of-body experiences. She had no idea what the hell her dreams meant. She was glad she normally didn't remember them. What a strange week. And last night was the worst of it. Sometimes she could be so dumb.

"Uh, Hamel, I want to apologize for last night." She held up a finger to stop him from interrupting. "I wasn't thinking clearly and jumped to conclusions when I accused you of the break-ins and stuff." He tried to say something again, but she stopped him with a second finger.

"There were just so many things that seem off with you. And they were off because you weren't who you said you were, but you weren't who I thought you were, either. So"— he opened his mouth and she raised another finger—"it wasn't all my fault, but it's all right now. And I expect some answers." She finished and looked at him. When he didn't move, she said, "You can talk now."

He fumbled with words, looked down for a second, then up at her. "What questions do you have? Let's talk and clean at the same time. You really are a messy person."

Her eyes popped wide. "I— This— My—" She wasn't a messy person. Really.

He laughed. "I'm playing with you, Melinda." He brushed his lips lightly over her cheek as he passed. That was several times since last night that he'd touched her. She loved his attention, loved how he looked at her, loved to stare at his ass as it passed by right now. Her fingers itched to squish them beanbags.

Hamel breathed deeply then stumbled over a bag of rice. She dove forward to catch him. "You okay, Hamel?"

He slapped his chest, coughing a bit. "Yeah, sorry. Didn't see the floor. I was distracted for a second."

He didn't see the floor? Distracted by what? She looked around at the disaster that used to be her kitchen. Maybe she could understand his distraction. He probably wondered what in the hell he'd volunteered for.

Melinda picked up the bag of rice he'd tripped over and asked him to put it on the second shelf of the cabinet. The next few hours flew by. She told him about her childhood and her parents. How she became interested in scientific research, but not about her past love and how he'd betrayed her. She didn't want to admit to being so naïve and running when things got rough.

She was afraid he'd see her as a loser. Someone who wasn't worth spending his time with, and she really wanted his time.

And more, as the day wore on. Every move he made rippled his muscles under his shirt and jeans. The way his biceps popped when he lifted something heavy to the way his ass bubbled when he stretched up on his toes. She had to check her chin several times for drool. That would be embarrassing.

Then when it came time for him to spill about his life, she couldn't tear her attention away for anything except to breathe. He made her laugh, made her smile. He was fascinating. She wanted to know everything. She wanted to be closer. She was on a slow burn.

After fixing her balcony doors a while later, he got to his feet and brushed his hands against his pants. "As good as new. Now you can sit in your hammock chair and drink all the wine you want."

She cocked her head at him. "How do you know I sit out here and drink wine?"

He fumbled with words until "You told me" came out. Something was up. This was the same way he'd acted when she talked medical jargon around him at the—

She never finished the thought as he leaned down and took her lips with his. When he pulled away, she grabbed a handful of his shirt and brought him back to her. She wanted him. He'd been teasing her, flashing his gorgeous body when he knew she was looking. He was doing it all on purpose, and she loved it.

Now she wasn't sure what to do to let him know she was interested in more. She was totally great with kissing, but much further than that and she was clueless. Not just clueless, but self-conscious.

He laid his forehead on hers and smiled. He was so gorgeous with the little crinkles radiating from his eyes and the dimple on his left cheek. "So, how about we call this place good enough and go into town for an early dinner?"

She couldn't help her huge smile. He wanted to spend time with her and not run away. "That would be fun."

He seemed to relax a bit. "Good. I want to change clothes first. How about I come back in thirty minutes and pick you up. Will that work?"

Since she was a little-makeup and no-fuss-hair person, thirty minutes worked perfectly. He kissed her again. Damn, he was really good with that tongue! He walked away, leaving her high on life. Then she remembered the danger she'd been in and realized she'd let her emotions overrule her brain and getting the answers she wanted about so many things. Maybe they could talk about those things tonight.

Later on, she picked a quiet eatery where she taught him about local cuisine and foods. He was surprised he liked so many dishes. Not sure of his palate, she was a bit hesitant to tell him what some of the meats she tried were, but he handled it well. No vomit on her shoes, anyway.

They walked the local market, talking and asking questions. He spoke the native language flawlessly. Since Uganda had adopted English as one of its national languages, she never really learned anything else. She was impressed with his brain as much as his body.

Past the market, close to the park, a soccer ball rolled toward them, escaped from the local kids' game. Not only did he professionally dribble it back, he shared tricks with the young ones. Foot, head, and knee bounces that amazed her.

As the sun set over the water, he took her hand and walked them along the trail toward a manicured beachfront. This day had been far better than any romance paperback she'd ever read. And it was happening to her. She wanted to cry she was so happy. But she couldn't let him know that. If he planned on being out of her life by the end of the weekend, she couldn't expose herself to such vulnerability.

He pulled her into his arms. "What's wrong, Melinda?"

How did he always know when she was feeling down? Was she that easy to read? "I was just thinking I didn't want this day to end. I've had a great time with you." That was safe to say.

"It's over only when you say it's over. You're on vacation tomorrow, remember? You can stay up all night and run around with the other drunken party animals starting Halloween tonight." He wrapped his hands around her waist and tossed her over his shoulder, then took off running toward the trees, imitating some of the younger couples. It was a strange custom, but she laughed the entire time.

When he set her down, he slid her down his front. She laughed at his boldness. Like she didn't know what he was doing. She wasn't that naïve. He backed her against a tree, then brushed a finger down her cheek.

"You're the most beautiful woman I've ever seen. The first second I saw you, I knew—" He stopped. If the light wasn't playing with the shadows, she thought he might be blushing.

"You knew what?" She held his face in her hands.

He was quiet for a moment before he said, "I knew I'd fall for you."

That was it. Game over. Hook, line, and sinker, she was his. She wanted him like no one else. She'd been celibate for two years, and fuck anyone who thought she was crazy for sleeping with a guy she'd known less than a week. She would have him tonight. This sexy stud was hers.

But she wasn't telling him yet.

CHAPTER 26

Melinda handed him a glass of wine, and he wrapped an arm around her waist and pulled her to him. On the balcony, the fresh lake air did little to cool his boiling need for her. She teased, touched, and kissed him into a tizzy of want.

The amazing thing was she wanted him as badly as he wanted her. She'd been so shy and distant that he thought his jaguar's *mate detector* could've been broken. His animal chuffed at him. *Idiot.*

Her nervousness scented the air. His attention was fully on her now. Something was going through her head. He had to figure it out before she backed away from him.

"Have I told you you're the most beautiful woman I've ever seen?"

She looked into his eyes, questioning at first, then determination set in. She smiled. "I'd like proof of that. Can you prove it?"

His cock went stiff at her throaty request.

"For you? Anything." He lifted a hand to cup her jaw, slipped his hand into her loose hair, and pulled her forward to press their lips together.

She licked the seam of his mouth, sucked his bottom lip,

and drove her tongue in. He slid her between the balcony doors, then closed each behind them, not once breaking their kiss.

Then things moved fast, each of them fully involved in undressing the other. With all items of clothing out of the way, he was able to see her as he had in their shared dream. Only now she was in the flesh and he could touch her with his hands and not just his mind. He led her to the bed, desire controlling his every move.

He laid her back with care, remembered her saying in their shared dream she'd been with no one in a long time so she might as well enjoy their time there. He'd make this perfect for her. He'd make it last even if it meant he ended up with blue balls.

His erection throbbed at the mewling sounds she made. He sucked her breasts, licking and biting her nipples before sliding his way between her thighs.

The scent of her honey called to him. She was slick and hot and so wet his mouth watered. One swipe of his tongue on her clit and she was shaking. Fuck! She was so responsive. So quick to moan and groan and call out to him.

A dip of his finger into her sex and she was moaning. Fucking her with his finger and sucking her swollen nubbin with his mouth brought the ultimate response. She gasped, gripped his hair in her hands, and rocked her pussy over his mouth.

"Oh, god! Oh, yes!"

He added a second finger into the mix while licking circles around her pleasure center.

"Dear god, that feels amazing."

He growled into her sex. She spasmed and dug her nails into his scalp. Her muscles tensed under his touch. He drove his fingers in and out of her pussy in tandem with the flicking of his tongue over her clit.

In thirty seconds she screamed and her pussy gripped his fingers with her orgasm. The sight of her coming was beautiful. Perspiration coated her smooth skin as she shook with her climax. He continued to draw out her pleasure by slowly rubbing his fingers in her channel in the shape of a hook.

One full-body shudder and she was still gasping for air. She tugged him up her body, curling a leg around his ass.

"So, my sexy CIA man." She licked his jaw and he slipped his cock into her wet heat. "I'd tell you to do me already, but . . ." She flipped them on the bed and he slid out of her in the shuffle. He was on his back and she straddled his thighs. "I think I'll do you instead."

She was sexy as hell in bed. "Works for me."

There was a millisecond of insecurity. Like she wasn't sure if her taking the lead was the right thing. So he did all he could to ensure she felt empowered.

"My cycle works like clockwork, and I'm on the pill, so don't worry about getting me pregnant."

He frowned. "Okay."

He'd give her time to get comfortable with him before discussing children. It was a good thing she knew her cycle, and that might keep her safe.

"That's it, beautiful. I want to watch you ride me."

She bit her lip and raked her nails on his chest. "Do you? I haven't done this before. I don't want to mess it up."

He grinned. "You couldn't mess it up if you tried. You're doing perfect. You're perfect."

A wide, self-assured smile covered her face. She caressed down his chest, flicking her nails on his nipples. "You have such a sexy body."

Passion and something else filled her gaze, something that made his stomach clench. Her soft laughter made the beast inside him calm. His mate was happy.

She placed the head of his cock at her entrance, met his gaze, and licked her lips. "I need you . . ."

She took him in and slid down, taking all of him in one fell swoop. Her pussy tightened around him in a silken hold. He groaned. He might die of pleasure, but what a way to go.

He gripped her hips and squeezed her ass. "Feel free to repay me this way for anything I ever do for you in the future."

She giggled and dropped again. And again. The heat built from the friction of their mating. She rocked over him, wiggling her hips and jerking his cock with her tight sheath.

"Fuck!"

Her rhythm increased in tempo. He helped her ride him. She laid her palms flat on his chest and thumbed his nipples. His cock was getting a serious sucking by her pussy.

She rocked harder, faster, faster, until she gasped and her body's grip on his dick tightened.

"Keep going, baby."

Her mouth dropped opened. She puffed in and out while gliding on his cock. He slipped a hand between her legs, rubbing a finger over her tight little nubbin.

One choked moan and her body turned stiff. He pinched her clit and she groaned. Her pussy rippled over his cock, sucking him deep with each contraction of her climax.

He lifted her by her waist and dropped her hard on his steely shaft while she was still coming down from her high. Pleasure blasted down his spine. He jerked inside her body, filling her with his seed.

She dropped on his chest. He stayed inside her, even after his dick softened for all of thirty seconds before he went hard again. She hugged him tightly while they each caught their breath.

CHAPTER 27

Hamel woke up completely in love and satisfied. Last night was the most amazing everything he'd ever had. All due to his beautiful mate. He lay on his back while she snuggled to his side, leg thrown over his. This is how he wanted to wake every morning for the rest of his life. Wouldn't that be fucking awesome? Man, the guys just didn't know what they were missing. Hopefully his friends and team members would find their mates and be as happy as he was.

Her arm over his chest moved. She started to pull away, but he'd have none of that. His arm wrapped around her back and pulled her closer. Her breast pressed against his side, making him harder than he already was. Morning wood was now a gift instead of a curse.

"Morning, beautiful," he said.

Her head tilted back to see his eyes. She smiled while her cheeks turned red, then buried her face into his shoulder. "Good morning to you, too."

He laughed and scooted to the side to bring her face into view again. She was a bit resistant, but gave in. "Are you embarrassed?" After she nodded, he smoothed her mussed hair back and kissed her. He wanted all his love to go into that kiss to tell her she needn't be shy around him. In fact, the bolder the better. With time she'd get there.

When he pulled back from her, she sighed and kept her eyes closed as if trying to hold on to the bliss. No worries there. Plenty more where that came from. She gave a little laugh. "I'm surprised you're still here. Most men would've been gone before the first hint of light."

"First off, I'm not most men. Secondly, I'm here to protect you. No place better than your bed to do that." He slid his finger along her smooth cheek and jaw. "Thirdly, I really like you, Melinda." His finger pushed her chin up so he could see her eyes. "I really, *really* like you, Melinda." Her eyes showed happiness, as did her smell. But what would she say?

She gave him a peck on the nose and rolled away before he could grab her. "I like you, too, Parish. I'm taking a quick shower. Alone, for right now."

He knew what that meant, hopefully.

He threw off the covers and dropped his legs over the side of the bed. It was nice to sleep in a bed. Luckily the cat enjoyed sleeping outside, or these past few nights would not have been very fun. His phone flashed a red light indicating he had a message waiting. Probably the office checking in. They needed updating after Thursday night's fiasco.

He listened to the voice mail then speed-dialed the boss.

"Hey, Tumbel. Got your message."

"Good. How's it going?"

"Thursday night we caught the thief and learned a lot of backstory that they neglected to share with the agency before we took this job. But it was still the right move to come down here."

"What kind of backstory?"

"Seems this same virus was first discovered forty years ago then quickly destroyed because of its effect on the human brain. Seems Kintu was part of the original story. He mentioned witch doctors and the 'other side.' I'm really hoping that doesn't mean some spooky shit. What do you think?"

Tumbel was quiet for a minute before responding. "I see."

Hamel didn't like the tone in his boss's voice. "You see what?"

A sigh met his ear. "We received more intel, but pretty much dismissed it as bogus because, at the time, it didn't fit with what we had." Hamel waited for the man to continue. "Lately, women and a few men have turned up missing after visiting or talking to *certain* people."

"Certain people as in witch doctors?"

"And voodoo priests, spiritual guides, anyone connected to what's on the other side."

"Is there really a complete 'other side'? Ghosts and shit don't just float around in our world waiting for some poor sap, there's actually a world of their own? I thought the full-blown monster world was all bullshit made up to scare kids into eating their broccoli."

Tumbel laughed. "That doesn't work anymore. You have to threaten to take their phone away, then they'll listen." Hamel needed to research how to raise kids. His would be coming soon. Once he mentioned to Melinda she was his mate. A sting touched his chest. Would she love him back? What if she didn't want him? What if she couldn't understand or accept the fact that he was different? That he was more than human. He was a shifter. And his animal wanted her love just as badly as he did.

"Hamel? Still there?"

He shook his head to clear his thoughts. "Yeah, here; sorry. Just thinking . . ." *About my mate.* But didn't say. He didn't want the boss thinking he wasn't doing his job.

Tumbel laughed heartily. "Goddamn, Hamel. Get your ass out of your mate's bed. Is she coming back with you?"

"Well, I, uh . . ."

Tumbel chuckled again. Hamel was starting to hate the sound. "Let me guess. You haven't told her yet."

He grumbled. "I'm working on it. You have to be gentle with this kind of thing."

Tumbel hooted and laughed on his side of the phone line. "Shit, Hamel, you crack me up. If you need to, take her to your home. Get her settled in, then call me. We'll see what's next. May be time to bring in a new recruit."

Hamel was speechless. He'd been on the ALFA team for so long, he didn't remember what civilian life was like. He'd saved enough money to retire with a cushy life, but he never really thought the day would come. It was sorta like dying. You knew it would happen, but didn't think about it.

"All right, sounds good," he finally said. "I'll work on getting us a flight out in a day or two."

Tumbel laughed again. "Better make it three or four days since you haven't told her that her life is about to totally change. I hope she's easygoing, for your sake, Hamel. Keep me updated." *Call ended* flashed on the screen.

Melinda was as far from easygoing as one could get. She was a research scientist with process and procedures drilled into her skull. He bet she hated change. He was so fucked. Living in Uganda wasn't a bad idea. The weather was great.

"I'm out of the shower, Hamel," Melinda hollered. "It's yours. I'll start breakfast."

"Sounds great. Thanks." He hopped into the small shower, still thinking about how he was going to break the news to his mate. Maybe he could do it the human way. Go out on a date a couple times, get engaged for a week, then married. That didn't seem bad. He could handle a week and a half. Two at the longest. But what would she do when she saw him shift into his cat? That was the question of the century.

A strange sound came from the other room. He stuck his head out of the shower. "Melinda? Everything okay?" When he didn't get an answer, he turned off the water and grabbed the towel she'd left out for him. "Melinda?"

As soon as he stepped out of the bathroom, the scent of fear bombarded him. She wasn't in the room. The balcony doors had been pushed apart. Melinda always had them fully opened or closed. He hurried through them. "Melinda!" His cat senses picked up her smell downwind and caught movement in the woods, not far off.

He leapt off the balcony, sliding down the hill to the flatter ground. With his first step, he was in jaguar form. He'd never changed that quickly in his life. And now was the time he needed it. Whoever was in front of him was fast. Faster than a human could move. That didn't sit well in his stomach.

His jag gained enough ground to hear Melinda fighting back. *Yes, that's it, baby. Fight as hard as you can.* The cat's nose scented blood, but not Mel's. Hopefully she could hold her own until he got there.

So much for thinking the threat was over. Who was this second person? Where did he come from? Why hadn't he or his animal picked up on a partner earlier?

He realized this other person had no scent. Was he using block also? How many people knew a shifter was there? Getting closer, he saw two people break from the trees into an open field. A man had Melinda over his shoulder, her fists pummeling his back, nails scratching at his skin. Even his tighty–whities had been pulled way up in the back.

Hamel shot out from the trees, sights set on taking down the douchebag without hurting his love. He'd have to go for the knees. Sideswipe.

Ahead of them, large stones resembling Stonehenge, but not as dramatic, sat barren with an altar in the middle. This guy was heading for that. Good; he'd pounce and rip the fucker's head off his body. Nobody touched his mate and lived.

The man didn't slow, still moving faster than a normal human. Hamel watched as Melinda's kidnapper leapt onto the altar, then turned and jumped off the back. But they never landed. Instead they disappeared. Gone. His mate was gone!

He came to a sliding stop, panting, not understanding what he saw. The cat smelled for their mate. She wasn't there. Her scent had completely vanished. How could that be? Anger and fear ripped through him. Shifting back into human form, he roared and systematically tore the rock structure to pieces. When he finished, only small boulders and rubble remained.

Bent over with hands on his knees, he sucked in breaths. Everything in him hurt. Not from breaking rock with his hands, but from his mate being gone. He couldn't feel her anymore. That could only happen if her soul was gone, if she were dead.

He fell to his knees and roared to the sky. Why did they take her from him?

Behind him a twig snapped. He turned to see the old man from the medical clinic. The one who was supposedly a witch doctor. Without thinking it through, he sprang to his feet and dove at the human. Death to all humans.

The witch doctor put his hand out and a lightning bolt came from his palm and connected with Hamel's forehead. Next, he found himself staring at the sky from flat on his back. The old man leaned into his sight. "You done?"

"Yeah," was all Hamel could think to say. His brain must've been fried with the strike. The man walked away. Hamel got to his feet and shook his head. That was intense. How did he do that? He jogged to catch up with the witch doctor.

"Wait up. I need your help. Do you know what happened back there, to my mate and whoever took her?"

The witch doctor nodded. "I do. And you're leaving to get her back."

CHAPTER 28

⟋

Emotions beat the shit out of Hamel. He felt like a pregnant lady—laughing and crying at the same time. The witch doctor kept a step ahead of him.

"Sefu," he said. "My name is Sefu, if you've forgotten. It means '*sword*.'"

Okay, nice to know. "I'm—"

"I know who you are, transformer. I see the cat in you. Glad you survived the venom. That woman of yours saved you. You know that, right? She's one of the reasons I'm doing this. Mates should never be separated."

"I totally agree. What's the second reason and what are you doing?"

"I will essentially kill you so you can bring her back. The second reason is what she carries should never get into the hands of the demon king."

Hamel grabbed his arm. "Whoa, wait a second. Listen, I will gladly die to bring her back, if that's what it takes. But this demon shit—" The conversation with his boss this morning flashed through his head. "I don't believe in it."

The witch doctor stepped into his face. Even though Hamel was six inches taller, he felt looked-down upon. "You listen to me, you little punk. I don't give a flying fuck what you believe. Just because you can't see or touch it, doesn't mean it doesn't exist. Can you grab and hold on to the wind? Can you put it in your evidence bag and carry it home? Yet it exists.

"Those magic tricks you see on TV, do you really think magic made the car disappear? No, you just couldn't see how they did it. Yet it's done. The eye is never fooled, huh? How do you ever expect her to believe that you are a transformer? That a cat lives in you and shares your spirit, when you doubt." He turned and continued walking.

Hamel thought about that as he followed. What the old man said was right. He couldn't touch the wind or see the sleight of hand of how magic tricks were done. And he needed Melinda to trust that he wasn't crazy when he explained he was a shifter. But still. He shouldn't believe everything people say.

Sefu growled as if he had an animal inside. "Child, I'm not telling you to believe everything you hear. There are many folks out there who lie and steal when they can. Don't get mixed up with them."

He curled his hands at his sides, trying to control his frustration. "How am I to know the difference between those who lie and those who don't?"

"Listen to your heart and brain. They will tell you true."

Right. Not good enough. He huffed out a curse. "But what if they're wrong?"

"Then you've been swindled out of some money."

"That's a lot of help." Hamel wanted to strangle the guy. "Tell me why they took Melinda. Why her?"

The old man walked quickly for someone his age.

"Today is the Day of the Dead, child. The veil is at its thinnest. That is why all the ghost and monster stories exist. This one day and night, they are able to move between realms with relative ease. The portal your mate disappeared into led directly into their realm."

"*Their* realm, meaning demons' realm." Fuck. He didn't want to believe in this shit. But if that was what it took to get Melinda back, he'd believe.

"Yes, child."

"But why her?" He growled.

"It is for what she knows, what she carries. It can never fall into demon hands. It would mean the end of our civilization as we know it." Sefu said the words quickly. Impatience tinged his tone.

Christ, what was he talking about? "What does Melinda know or carry?"

The man stopped and turned to him. "She carries the virus with her. Only she knows how to make more serum."

"Why the hell do demons want a virus that doesn't kill people?" His jaguar wanted to leap out of his skin and roar at the old man for talking in riddles.

The old man smiled. "That's for you to find out."

"Wait a minute. How do you know about the virus?" He prepared to take down the senior citizen twice over if he said the wrong thing. Was this a fucking conspiracy?

"No, child. It's a repeat of history because we didn't learn the first time."

Hamel froze in his tracks. "Ah, fuck! You were the other researcher with Mr. Kintu." Sefu stopped and turned to him. His face seemed sad, regretful.

Sefu turned back and continued. "Yes, I was. I've missed my dear friend many times through the years."

"But he works at the virus lab. He thinks you're dead. Go see him."

He shook his head. "No, child. That is not possible. It is best he think I am gone."

Frustration curled around his heart once again. "Why? I don't understand."

"Of course you don't, child. This happened before you were born."

The jaguar pushed at the skin, ready to ignore everything and look for a new way to find his mate. This shit was taking too damn long. "What happened?"

The witch doctor sighed, shoulders slumped. "Did Kintu tell you everything he knew? He was gone during most of it."

"He told us how you three worked together. One was killed by his grandfather. And you he never saw again."

Sefu wiped at his brow. "Good. That's all he needs to know. He's lived with heavy guilt for not being there when this all happened. The guilt is not his to bear. It is mine."

"Yours? What happened?" He scowled at the old man.

"Now is not the time or place to go into storytelling. Every second we hesitate is one lost before time runs out." The old man gave him an impatient stare.

"What do you mean, time runs out?" Frustration built within him. Bigger. He wanted answers and the man wasn't sharing. But if he had a limited period to find Melinda, then it would wait. The trees came to an end at a homesite with a beautiful log cabin and aluminum shed around back. One structure was large. They headed toward that one.

"Whoa, where are we? This is incredible." He'd watched enough *Amazing Cabins* to know this deserved a spot on TV. "So what are we doing here?"

The man looked over his shoulder and smiled. "This is where I kill you."

CHAPTER 29

Hamel sat on the dirt floor of the small shed behind the log cabin. In front of him, a campfire roared, smoke escaping through a hole in the roof. Sefu walked through the door with a huge knife in hand.

"Hey, there, man. I hate to admit it, but I *assumed* you meant to kill me figuratively." Then Hamel saw a chicken in Sefu's other hand. "Oh, man. You're not gonna—" Sefu laid the chicken's head on a log stump and hacked it off. "Oh, you are." Wasn't there some law against that? Where were those PETA people when you needed them? Oh, yeah. He was in the land of dark magic, where demons crossed over to steal people with viruses.

Hamel didn't want to watch what the doctor did next, but the shack was so small he had little choice. He noticed Sefu had been chanting the whole time. Hamel understood his language, but these mumbles he didn't recognize.

After setting a metal bowl of red liquid next to the fire, he spit several times into another bowl then dug up dirt from the floor and mixed it with the liquid into mud. If he needed water, he could've taken some from his sweat-drenched body. It was as hot as a sweat lodge. He was ready to die for Melinda, but that didn't mean he was looking forward to the pain.

Sefu set the container next to the other by the fire. A third bowl appeared in his hands. From a narrow table along the wall, he snapped off the leaf of an aloe vera plant and squeezed out its contents. He crushed a flower in his fingers and mixed them together.

With all three bowls next to the fire, he chanted over them, waving his hands. "Come here, transformer."

Hamel snapped his head up, then scooted around to the bowls. Had he fallen asleep?

Sefu dipped two fingers into the chicken blood and smeared it down Hamel's arms. "This sacrifice is to incite the favor of the gods who watch over this." He smeared mud across his forehead. "This is for the earth, and as we began as dirt, we will return."

The colorful aloe mixture went on his bare chest and heart. "May this be a reminder that time heals that which does not kill you. Your heart is strong, transformer. Let it guide you in your journey."

The witch doctor continued painting his body with items in the bowls. "There are certain things you must know before you travel. First and most importantly, you must return before the setting of their sun. The veil to the other side closes then, and if you remain in their land after the sun sets, you will never be able to leave.

"Secondly, never fear possession of your soul. With your animal, they will not be strong enough to take it. Never let them trick you into volunteering your body. Then they will enter and control you.

"Last, tell your mate to always mind whose reality she's in. Very important." He fell into soft chanting. Smooth and hypnotic. Almost like a song. Hamel let out a sigh and relaxed his shoulders.

Awaken.

Hamel popped up his head to come to a sitting position. Where the fuck was he? Did someone drop him in the middle of Death Valley? He climbed to his feet and brushed off his pants, which happened to be worn buckskin. Where the hell did that come from? His shoes were ankle high and formed to his feet as if barefoot. He had no shirt on. His bare chest rippled in the sun.

All that was fine and dandy, until he felt something on his back. He reached over his head, grabbed what felt like a handle, and pulled up. A sword, long and narrow, rested in his hand. Holy fucking shit. Was this for real? He was Conan the Barbarian. If a dragon showed up, he'd be the Dragon-slayer.

He gripped the sword with two hands and whipped it through the air. Great. Now he'd be able to kill some fucking demons and get his woman back. He lifted the sword above his head and tried to get it into the really narrow sheath. It was like putting thread through a needle. Fucking impossible.

Finally he gave up and decided just to carry the damn thing. Since he didn't have a better weapon, he'd keep it. He could practice his grip and swinging. No telling what he'd have to defend himself against. He wished he had a gun.

When he stepped, his foot kicked something. He looked down to see a handgun lying on the dirt. Where did that come from? He picked it up and checked the clip. Empty. Figured. He'd found his weapon, but with no ammo. He wished a full clip would've been included. Getting ready to toss the weapon, he glanced down and saw bullets shining in the sun. He couldn't believe it. How did he not see them when he picked up the gun?

He loaded the gun and slipped it between his backside and waistband.

He looked around. "Should I go the desolate way"—he spun around—"or that barren, desolate way? How about the barren, desolate way?" He turned to face the sun. It looked like Earth's sun. And it was fucking hotter than shit. He put the sun to his back and started his journey, as the witch doctor called it.

Then he remembered Sefu's instructions: He gathered several rocks and made a pile large enough to see from a distance. Sefu told him he had to come to this very spot to get back to Earth's side. With his sword, he drew a deep circle in the dirt indicating where to stand.

Breaking into a jog, sword still in hand, he focused on Melinda. He was here to save her or would die trying. He'd rather be dead if she wasn't in his life.

After some time of not seeing anything but dirt and rocks,

he questioned his choice of paths. Dammit. He wished he had a sign or something to guide him. That'd be nice.

He noticed movement far ahead of him. Far enough that it could've been a mirage tricking his eyes.

That dark mass ahead of him was getting closer, quickly. He stopped. His eyes and brain couldn't make sense of what he saw. No mirage, that's for sure.

With no warning, a shockwave of air almost pushed him to the ground. A black blob, floating six feet above the ground, headed directly toward him. Behind this mass was a solid line of the same creatures. Were those in the line chasing the first one? If it was a race, then one was definitely superior to the others. But that was not what his gut told him. His instincts told him to protect.

He leaned to the side to let the creature pass by without hitting him. It changed course to match his. That couldn't be good. He took off running to the side and the blob followed. Okay, he would listen to his heart and brain, like Sefu said. He stood straight then closed his eyes when the monster was too close to his face to avoid a collision. Then he felt a hand grab on to his neck. He never expected to die by strangulation.

CHAPTER 30

Hamel stood his ground while he waited for the creature to choke him to death. He should've been more careful. Who would save Melinda now?

The hand twisted around his throat as whatever attached to it spun in a circle around his head, twice, before coming to a stop against his back.

"What the fuck?" He hopped in a circle, trying to see what was holding on to him. Of course, he couldn't see much.

A tiny "Help me, please" rose to his ears.

Protect.

He snapped to attention and faced the oncoming horde, pulling his gun from his waistband. He fired shots, but he either missed or the bullets had no effect. He emptied the clip with no blob going down. As the mass was about to consume him, he wrapped both hands around the sword and slashed through the front line. Each mass popped and disappeared. His back swing took out the next line. Same result for them. Bodies popped and vanished.

From there, the blobs stopped their advance and floated motionlessly.

"Human, return our . . . friend to us." One of the blobs spoke, but he couldn't tell which one. They had no mouths or eyes. They looked like giant raisins the size of a tire.

Taking slower breaths and calming, he felt the blob on his back shiver. In fear?

Protect.

"No," he said. "He's with me now. I'll take care of him. You all be on your way." None of them moved. Hamel raised his sword.

The voice spoke again. "Who are you, human, to defy us demons?"

Ah, so that's who they were. Interesting. He expected horns, pointed tails, and ugly faces.

"I'm not human." The word Sefu always used to refer to him was "*transformer.*" Maybe that was what he should use, too. "I am a transformer." Hamel swore he heard gasps, and the group did float away a few feet.

A faint "Uh-oh" sounded behind him. Slowly, the blobs retreated to leave only one. Hamel imagined if it had a face, it'd be pissed-off looking.

"We will meet again, transformer."

Good god. That was what every bad guy said in the movies. They couldn't be original even in demon land? He let it go and watched as the demon floated away. When the group was out of sight, he said, "It's okay, uh . . ." What did he call this thing? "You can let go of me."

The pressure released from the base of his neck. He turned to see the demon close-up. It did look exactly like a raisin—on steroids.

"Why were they chasing you? Did you do something wrong?"

A weak "No" came from the demon. "They like to pick on me and hurt me. I am the weakest of everyone. Did you mean what you said, me being with you now? I would like if you do not kill me."

Great. What did he tell the little guy? No, and let him get beat up again, or yes, and who knew what?

The demon asked, "Why are you here?"

"I'm looking for someone brought here against her will."

"You talk of the woman who arrived today. I can help you. I know where she is." That came as a surprise. "Let me guide you." What choice did he have?

"If you take me to the woman, I won't kill you. How's that?"

"I like very much." The blob moved up, down, and around. If he had to guess, he'd say the thing was doing a happy dance. "This way. We go this way."

The direction was quite different than what he'd chosen. He looked around at the rocky desert ground. This land would kill anyone lost in it. Anyone like him.

What had he gotten himself into? Following a demon? He must be losing his fucking mind.

"So. What's your name, little guy?"

"Lamozierus."

"Ha. Yeah, I'm not remembering that. In honor of a great movie, how about I call you Wilson."

"Wil-son," the demon repeated. "I like that. Easier to say. Wilson."

Hamel squinted against the beating sun. "So, Wilson, I know nothing about this place. Tell me everything you can."

"There is a lot to know . . . What is your name?"

Used to living under code name or altered identity, he wasn't sure what name he should give. He'd used his real name with Melinda's job because he was supposed to be purely background protection, not talking with possible informants and bad guys. But now he was.

"Call me Clint." He recognized the name and jokingly mumbled, "Just Clint," in case the demon knew Clint Eastwood, his childhood idol.

"Clint, there is much to learn if you want to understand our world," the being said. The entity continued, "Perhaps it would be better if you asked specific questions."

Yeah, Twenty Questions time, Hamel thought. "Why do they want my mate?"

"What is 'mate'?" Wilson sounded confused.

He thought about that for a second. "A mate is the one person who can make you smile and laugh when you're feeling sad. They are the first person you want to see in the morning, and the last at night. You would do anything, even give your life, to keep your mate safe and happy. They are the only person who makes your life complete."

"That sounds like your word '*love*.' Is that right, Clint?"

That was surprising. "You are correct, Wilson. How do you know English so well?"

"The demon king says it is important to learn and study the enemy. You cannot beat them if you do not understand them."

Hamel stopped. "Hold on a second. You're saying I'm your enemy?"

"Yes, that is correct," he said assuredly.

Hamel frowned. This wasn't going well. "Then why are you here with me? Should you run away, or at least attack me?"

The demon spun around, his eyes red dots drilled through him. Oh, shit. What did he just do?

CHAPTER 31

Melinda's eyes opened. She stared at a nondescript white ceiling that covered plain white walls. She slowly sat up to see that she lay on a fancy cot on a gray concrete-like floor. Voices came from the other side of a door.

Quietly, she peeked out. Holy shit. A gaggle of women dressed in toga-like sheets lay around on beanbags and blankets. Food sat on trays mixed in among the bodies. The ladies laughed and talked like they were at the beach for the afternoon. No one looked threatening.

Melinda stepped out of the room, closing the door behind her. One of the women saw her. "Look, the new one is awake." All heads turned to her. She didn't like being the center of attention. One of the ladies hopped up from her seat and pulled another bag into the group.

"Come sit by me, young one. We have lots of questions for you. As I'm sure you do for us." The woman winked and smiled. Melinda put on a happy face, not wanting to appear threatening. Maybe she'd find out what was going on here. So far, so good. On her way to sit by the woman, a crashing sound on the other side of the room startled her. Four gorgeous men were gathered, one on the ground with a fallen table on him.

The woman who had called her waved a hand in the air.

"Don't worry about them. They're just fighting to see who gets to try to impregnate you first."

Melinda froze. "Excuse me? Impregnate me?"

Again, the woman waved her hand. "It's nothing. Come sit with us. We'll explain everything." Melinda wasn't sure she believed the nonchalance these women showed, but it did seem like no one cared about what the men were doing. She slid onto the cushy bag and looked around. Fruit sat on a tray next to her. It looked fresh and delicious, especially since she hadn't had breakfast.

"Please, help yourself. The food here is really good." Others paying attention agreed. She lifted a juicy slice and bit off the end. Wow, it really was good. Tasted like pineapple. She ate the slice then chose a different piece, which tasted like kiwi.

"So," the main woman started, "I am Kim, the head harem ho." The women laughed. "Not really a ho, but I've been here for a while and feel like the lady of the house when it comes to new recruits."

"New recruits?" Melinda didn't like the sound of that. "Recruits for what?"

Kim laughed. "Relax, dear. You're so uptight. Here you'll have nothing to do but sit back and enjoy life."

"What do you mean by nothing to do?" Melinda asked.

Another lady spoke up. "Just that. We do whatever we want, whenever we want. No job to go to, no bills to pay, no cooking or cleaning, no spouses to piss you off. But you do have hot men." The lady snapped her fingers in the air then pivoted her beanbag seat to put her back to them. One of the men came toward her, a smile on his face.

He bent over her, wrapped a hand around her neck aggressively, and kissed her. Going to his knees, he kissed down her neck and lower. Melinda couldn't see what was happening after his head dipped lower than the bean seat, but the lady flopped her head back and arms to the sides. Part of the sheet once covering her body draped her bent knees, opening her to him. Her sensual moan brought a deep blush to Melinda's cheeks.

Some of the others giggled. Kim leaned toward Melinda. "That's Deb. She definitely uses the provided accommodations often. We're guessing she had very little sex in her life before this. She can't get enough."

The women giggled again.

Kim sat up straight. "Now, tell us who you are and how you came to be with us in paradise."

Paradise? Hardly. "My name is Melinda and I was kidnapped by some man. I need help getting back home, I guess."

They all looked at one another.

"Why do you want to go back? You have everything here you could want. If not, just ask the king and he'll get it for you," a beautiful woman with long black hair said.

Whoa. King?

"What king would that be?" Melinda asked while Deb's moans became louder.

Kim patted her hand. "No worries. Cuzork is a generous ruler. He gives us everything we want, but he can be hard on the help. He's rather demanding and wants what he wants. Now. He likes material things. Seems the more he amasses, the happier he is. He's been a bit tense this past week, though."

Melinda wondered if that had anything to do with her and Hamel. "So this king, Cuzork, does he keep up with things in Uganda?" She assumed everyone here was from the area, too.

Kim's brows scrunched. "Uganda? That's in Earth's dimension. I don't know why anyone would want to pay attention to that plane. All us ladies want to stay here."

A shocked and excited burst of adrenaline shot through her. "You mean we're not on Earth? But a different dimension altogether?"

"That's what one of the help told me one time. I don't know if it's true or not, but going by some of the things I've seen happen, I'd believe it."

"Like what?" Melinda asked.

Kim leaned a little closer and lowered her voice. "I've seen things appear from thin air and disappear the same way. And a couple times when I was in forbidden areas, I've seen these ugly black blob-looking things floating around."

"I see," Melinda said with a nod. She had no doubt Kim was a few fries short of a Happy Meal. Melinda would probably have to find a way to escape on her own.

With an annoying scream, Deb sounded like the man had

finished her off. He sat back, wiped his mouth with the back of his hand, then grabbed her hips and turned her over the bag, stomach down. He crawled between her legs and slid an enormous cock into her.

Memories of last night with Hamel flashed in her brain. A tingle warmed her body. She had to find a way back to him. Life wouldn't be worth having without him. Did she just really think that? Analyzing her feelings at that moment, she realized she cared for him. Like, deeply cared. He was perfect in all the ways she wanted. Caring, nice, strong, hot, incredible at sex, and he liked her.

Of course, she had thought those things about her previous boyfriend, until he betrayed her. Melinda's stomach churned at the thought of what he'd done to her. She couldn't risk that again. Not yet, right?

Kim clapped her hands.

"Okay, everyone, time to eat soon. Freshen up in your room and be back in shortly." With the snap of her fingers, one of the men headed to them. He was a beautiful specimen, but nothing close to her Hamel. He offered a hand to help her up. "Please take her to the empty room next to Marian's."

He bowed. "With pleasure, Your Highness." A warm hand settled on Melinda's lower back and guided her toward the door. The hallway outside had the same plain white walls, ceiling, and floor that the other rooms did. No pictures, art, or decorations. Pretty bland.

After passing several doors, her guide opened the last door in the long aisle. She walked in and almost tripped over her own feet as a hand grabbed her wrist and yanked her against the wall.

CHAPTER 32

Hamel stared into the demonic eyes of the raisin-like blob in front of his face. This was what he got for asking personal questions. His cat's power filled his body, ready for fight or flight. His heart raced, muscles tightened. Shit, how much power did one of these things have?

Instead of attacking, the demon floated harmlessly. "I do not understand why you ask that question. You have given me no reason to run or hurt you, Clint. You are a nice transformer so far."

Yeah, he wondered how long that would last. He resumed walking with the demon. "Then I'm not your enemy. Not really."

Wilson seemed to ponder that. "I have to agree with you. Perhaps you are the demon king's enemy, but not mine. Even though he says all of mankind are our enemies."

"Who is this demon king?"

"He is the most powerful of us. Only he knows how to use the magic our home has."

"Is he a nice person, too?"

Wilson dropped a few feet to waist height. "I do not wish to answer that, Clint."

"Okay, by your reaction, I'm thinking he's a douchebag."

"I do not know the word—"

"Don't worry about that one, Wilson." He laughed. "Does this king have guards or demons that fight?"

"Yes, the King's Guard is the group who watches over the palace and disciplines the lower classes."

"Lower classes? What are those?"

"I am of such a class. I work in the palace to do as the king wants." Again, Wilson floated lower. Did he sound dejected? Hamel needed to listen carefully for Wilson's slight tone changes. The demon's feelings were not easy to guess. Wait a second. Demons had feelings? Weren't they just bad and wanting to kill everyone? Wilson wasn't what he expected in this realm. Maybe if he had a face, and not only red beady eyes, Hamel could tell more easily.

"Can you do something about how you look?"

"What do you mean? Do you not like how I appear?"

Shit, could he have been any more tactless? "Sorry, Wilson. What I mean is I am used to seeing eyes and a nose and mouth on others. Even our animals have a face."

"Would you like for me to have a face, Clint?"

"That would be nice, Wilson. Can you do that?"

"How about this?"

Hamel glanced over and saw the biggest bug eyes he'd ever seen. He stumbled to the side. "Maybe a bit smaller. Like mine. See how everything is in proportion to the area?"

"Yes, I do. How about this?"

Hamel was almost afraid to look. He turned and looked into a virtual mirror. "That's good, Wilson, but maybe not so much like mine. It's kinda creepy to look into my face every time I talk to you."

"There. Do you like this?" He'd made his eyes larger, his nose flatter, and his mouth longer.

"That's perfect. Much better. And don't forget to move your mouth when you talk." Wilson's lips separated then came back together. "And you never really answered the question on speaking our language. Do you know any others?"

"Only one. It is . . ." He seemed to be thinking, though it was hard to tell. "It is some form of Latin."

"Italian? That's based on Latin. Spanish, French, Romanian?"

"I remember. It is pig."

His brows pulled down. "What is pig?"

"The Latin I know. It is pig."

Hamel had a hard time keeping his laughter under control. "You know pig Latin?"

"Es-yay, I o-day."

Hamel rolled his eyes. Yes, that was pig Latin, but he'd rather not use something so childish. "That's a wonderful language, but—"

Wilson stopped and Hamel almost bumped his face into him. The first thing he noticed was the demon had no smell. Interesting.

"Was that sarcasm, Clint? I know the definition of the word, but not sure how it is used."

"You are correct, Wilson." Hamel sensed happiness from the demon. Could demons be happy? Seemed strange, but so did this whole thing.

"Pig Latin," Wilson explained, "is moving the first letter in the word to the end and add 'ay' to that letter. For example, your name would be lint-cay."

"I know how it works, Wilson, but how about we stick with English? I speak it faster."

"I agree, Clint."

Both fell quiet until more questions came to Hamel's mind. "Where I'm from, demons supposedly possess humans and are evil. Is that true?"

"That requires a long answer. Do you wish to hear the long or the short?"

He didn't have time for that. "Let's go with the short answer."

Wilson appeared to think before replying, "Yes."

Hamel waited for more and when Wilson didn't continue, he asked, "Yes, what?"

"The short answer is yes. Demons possess humans and can be evil."

Hamel wiped a hand over his glistening face. "Okay, let's go for a medium answer. That doesn't tell me enough."

"Medium answer. O-kay. Demons have some power in this realm. We can protect ourselves by manipulating the energy to shock others. Except for the powerful king, we cannot do much.

"In your realm, we have no powers. You cannot even see us as you see me here. If we are to have an effect, we need to have a way to do that. When possessing a body, we have to be stronger than the spirit already attached to it."

"If you're not, then you can't possess the body."

He nodded vigorously. "You are correct, Clint. But there are still other issues to overcome. Because of how the human brain works, taking control of the body is difficult. It is a learned process. The person's spirit has been with the body since birth and has learned how to move efficiently. A new spirit coming in has to learn it. That is where your zombies come from. They walk stiffly because the demon inside doesn't have good control."

"So zombies are real, too." Shit. Just what he needed to hear.

"It is what you call zombies in your myths and legends. Demons have learned much since we crossed realms. We don't let ourselves be known until we have more control over the body."

"That makes sense. You mentioned more than one issue."

"Yes. If the spirit voluntarily gives over the body, then we don't have to push the spirit to the side. It is shared control. We are able to immediately move like before possession. No one would notice a difference."

Hamel thought of the janitor at the lab. No one would've guessed he was possessed. But Walog didn't have a smell. He thought it was hunter's block. But perhaps it was from possession. Something to consider later. "Why would anyone voluntarily give their body to a demon?"

"Usually it is trickery or lies the demon uses to persuade the spirit. The promise of what the spirit longs for most. Humans will do much to get what they want."

"Like transformers who will do anything to protect their mates."

"I will warn you, Clint. Do not let others know your feelings for the woman. They will use that against you. Strangers are better than lovers."

"Warning taken. Thank you for telling me, Wilson." He wondered if he should ask another personal question. What the hell? Only live once. "Wilson, demons are known to be evil to the core. But you don't seem that way."

He floated lower. "No, I am not. I know what it feels like to be hurt and I do not wish that upon anyone. I do not want more than what I have. I have no need to feel the power like those who go to your realm. Only evil goes, so you only know the worst of us. Many are like me, but we keep it to ourselves."

"Ya know, buddy, I'm starting to think your realm needs an attitude adjustment. And I'm just the cat to give it to them."

CHAPTER 33

Hamel noticed how high the sun sat in the sky. Based on Earth's time, he estimated they had shorter days. Great, just what he needed. Next time he came over, which better be never, he'd have Sefu drop him a bit closer. Like ten miles closer.

"Wilson, how much farther? I'm running out of time. I only have until sunset."

Wilson turned to him. "You don't see it, Clint?"

Hamel turned in a full circle. "I don't see anything but dirt. No offense, but your planet isn't the most beautiful."

"It is not. I heard the land was once full of green plants and living creatures. But when the demons took over, it became this. It is truly sad."

"So, what am I supposed to see that I don't?" He squinted but only saw emptiness.

Wilson gasped. "The palace. You do not see the palace?"

"I'm going to say no to that."

"Ah, you must not be a believer. You cannot touch or see everything that exists with human hands and eyes, Clint. Sometimes, you must let yourself believe."

Hamel sighed. "You aren't the first to tell me that today. How do I . . . believe?"

"Close your eyes," Wilson instructed. "Now, open yourself to the world around you. Let everything in you reach out, and let all that is out, in. Only when allowing your sixth sense, the power of the mind, to roam freely will you *see* all that is there. By holding it in so tightly, so closed, you depend on your five human senses. Those are not enough for the truth."

Hamel did his best to do what Wilson said. He felt a little change in him, but nothing earth-shattering. Then his animal instincts took control and opened to the world his human self wouldn't see. His eyes opened, and he stumbled back and fell. Directly in front of him was a temple like only Hollywood could create. Marble walls rising fifty feet into the air. Sparkling floors with tall columns, statues, and stuff he'd never seen before.

"Holy hell. Where did that come from?"

"It has always been there, Clint. You just chose not to see it. Let us go to the throne room."

"Hold up." He lifted his sword, which had marked the trail to the return rock pile. "Help me put this in the leather thing on my back."

"It is called a sheath, Clint." Wilson floated behind him. Hamel poked the sword over his shoulder. "More to the left." He poked again. "Too far away, get closer to your body." He stabbed again. "Close, you almost made it." He jabbed again. "No, now you are too far right."

Frustration exploded in Hamel. "Wilson! Goddammit. Would you just put the fucking thing in?" He didn't know or care how Wilson slid the oversized knife into the sheath. Just as long as he did. "Okay, let's get going. Things to see, people to do."

Hamel followed Wilson, taking in the magnificence surrounding them. Who would've thought demons lived so well? Why in the world would they want to come to Earth?

A warm hand touched his back. He turned to see three very beautiful women dressed in white draping toga-like dresses. Gold glittered on their fingers, ears, feet. One hurried around him.

"Hello, ladies." The two giggled and stepped closer. Their fingers brushed down his arms and chest.

"We have never seen a man so well . . . taken care of."

"Yes, I try to eat right and work out when I can." The ladies circled him, fingernails leaving light trails across his skin. He felt a palm glide over his ass. That was going a bit too far. He was here to find his mate. Melinda's beautiful eyes flashed into his mind.

He turned back to Wilson to find the third lady pushing him through a door then closing it. She hurried back to the group and joined in the maul. Their voices were soothing, cajoling. They glided him toward a side room. Inside, plush pillows and blankets covered the floor. Food and gold wine goblets sat on tables. A delicious smell perfumed the air, but he didn't know what it was.

The women kept up their ministrations. Hamel relaxed, realizing they wouldn't hurt him. From somewhere, more women came in, all touching, loving him. Succulent grapes were offered from fingers painted fire-engine red on the tips. A cup was shoved into his hand. They encouraged him to drink, drink.

Hamel's head felt light, like he had nothing in the world to worry about. In fact, he couldn't remember why he was here. He drank more from the cup. When had the room become so hazy?

He was guided deeper into the room and rested on the pillows. So soft, so comfy. He could stay here all day. Hmmm, he felt so good. Lips caressed his skin. Succulent, sweet lips. So good.

Hands glided down his chest to his buckskin pants. Wonderful pressure surrounded his cock. Hot and moist. He could come quickly, feeling light and horny. Melinda's mouth was as good as her pussy felt. Melinda. His Melinda.

He opened his eyes to see a gaggle of naked women writhing around him and on one another. Tongues flicked plump clits, highly aroused. Mouths sucked in nipples, nipping and licking. Slender fingers pumped in and out of wet pussies, squelching. Moans filled the foggy air. What was he breathing? It made him giddy and hornier.

Melinda. Where was Melinda? A hot palm wrapped around his stone-hard cock. He was completely naked. Chills ran up his legs as more lips made their way along his skin. Goddamn, it felt so good. If he could just come with Melinda, he'd be perfect. Melinda.

The woman trying to put her mouth around his cock wasn't his love, wasn't his mate. He jerked away from the seductive orgy surrounding him. Fuck, if this wasn't a man's wet dream, he didn't know what was. But he wasn't into that anymore. He had a mate to find.

Yes, he was here to find Melinda, who they took. His head cleared enough to realize he'd been tricked by a harem of succubi. Hands reached for him, drawing him into the group. No fucking way. Not again. He tried to push away, sliding across the floor. Sunlight came from the corner of the room. He crawled toward it, hoping his mind wouldn't succumb further, because his body wanted him to stay. Fingers latched onto his legs. Ah, shit!

CHAPTER 34

Heat warmed his face, and he took in a deep breath of fresh air. He wasn't sure, but he felt he was lying on his back, his sword digging into his spine. Hamel opened his eyes to see Wilson hovering inches from his face, bug eyes wide and creepy, startling the shit out of him.

"Clint, are you well? You made it out of their grasp. You are safe here in the courtyard."

Hamel sat up, Wilson moving back. Fuck. He had the worst hangover he'd ever had. "Are they succubi?" He noted he was fully dressed with his pants and shoes. Was he ever really undressed?

"Yes, they trap males and sex them to death. You are lucky to escape."

"Maybe," Hamel said. "I know plenty of men who'd voluntarily die that way."

Wilson made a shocked face. "You humans are strange."

Hamel got to his feet. "You ever experience sex?"

"No, I am not sure if that is possible."

"Well, let me tell you, little friend, it's worth dying for if you're with the one you love."

Wilson remained quiet. Hamel glanced at the sun. It was on its way down.

"Shit. Wilson, come on, we're running out of time. Take me to the demon king or Melinda."

Wilson floated next to him. "I will take you to the king. I do not know where she is in the castle." Wilson zoomed away, leaving Hamel to run to catch up. They came to a set of twenty-foot-high doors with a guard on each side. "We wish to see the king," Wilson said.

One of the sentries replied, "He is not available. Come back later." Wilson turned away.

"Wait," Hamel said. "How do we know they are telling the truth?"

Wilson paused. "We do not know. Do you want to challenge them?"

Hamel wiped a hand over his face. "No, I just want to talk to the king and get out of this godforsaken realm." He faced the guard who had answered. "Is the king truly gone or are you saying that to make us go away? I am someone your king would want to speak to. I am a transformer." Both guards stiffened. The other sentinel grabbed the long gold handle and pulled the door open.

With no further words, Hamel and Wilson entered a grand room. The room was gaudy and over-the-top with precious items. Statues, paintings, busts, trinkets, artwork, and stuff packed the room. How could anyone live like this?

A voice boomed through the air. "Who dares to enter my presence without presentation?"

Hamel was not impressed. He hollered back as he and Wilson continued up a red carpet path, "I do. Come out and face me, demon." From a side entryway, a tall, skinny man dressed in a black-and-white-striped suit stomped in. Hamel whispered to Wilson, "Why is he in human form and you're not? I expected a bunch of big-ass raisins running around."

"I am a lowly demon. I am not allowed to change."

Well, didn't that just tickle him pink. He didn't think he'd like this king too much. The man sat on the throne and waved a hand, beckoning them closer. Hamel walked up to the steps in front of the golden chair.

Behind him, Wilson grabbed on to the thin leather straps draped over his shoulders that held his sword's sheath. Then he snuggled to Hamel's back and began trembling. A lot.

Hamel spoke over his shoulder. "W-Wilson, I—I c-ca-an't ta-alk wi-ith you sha-ak-ing so mu-uch."

A "*Sorry*" floated to his ear. The quaking on his shoulders stopped. He turned back to the king, then his lower back and hips started to vibrate. Wilson had moved down to his waist and held on. He could talk, but it felt weird with his commando-style freedom allowing his junk to shake in his buckskins.

"Lamozierus, where have you been? Consorting with out-siders, I see. Get back to work."

Wilson mumbled, "Yes, Your Highness," then zipped away almost too quickly for Hamel to see.

Hamel's jaguar wanted out. The animal didn't like this realm, and the demon king even less.

"I am here to return the woman taken this morning back to her realm." He tried to sound as intimidating as he could. Didn't seem to faze the demon king.

The king raised a bored brow. "I cannot let you do that. I need her."

"Need her for what?" Maybe he could finally get informa-tion to make sense of this fiasco.

"That is no business of yours, warrior. Is that all?"

Fuck. This wasn't going well. He had to think fast. "I've been paid to take her home. You don't think an honest warrior like myself would simply walk away, do you?"

The king's face scrunched up. "No. That would be no fun." A narrow grin sent chills down Hamel's back. But he refused to show any reaction to the douchebag. The king's eyes zeroed in on his, drilling deeply, diving into his soul. Hamel felt him, rooting around, as if searching for something.

Since Hamel cared little for the pompous ass sitting on the throne, he thought maybe a little scare would do the big shot some good. Hopefully make the demon more wary, make him think twice about jumping into his head again. Hamel spoke to his jaguar through their animal bond, which allowed mental communication. *Let's have a little fun. Time for you to chase some prey.* The jag liked that idea. Hamel created a scene in his mind for the king's brain to mentally interact with. Like a movie in his head, he watched it play out.

The king was surrounded by white clouds. His hands

pushed at the cottony air, getting it out of his way as if he were on a path, looking for something. The cat came up behind the king. Low to the ground, the jag took one stealthy step after another, never making a sound.

Agitation rolled from the demon. What did the guy want? Was he trying to possess him? Not gonna happen. The cat slithered to less than a foot from the demon. Its muscles tightened, prepared to jump and take down the intruder.

CHAPTER 35

Hamel stared into the demon king's eyes, both in a trance locked inside Hamel. But he had a foot up on the demon. It didn't know he was a transformer with a second soul that fought rougher than he did.

Flicking its tail, the feline sprang forward like a loosed rubber band. It tackled the king and rolled him on the ground. It wrapped its teeth around the demon's neck, but didn't bite down.

The demon came screeching out of Hamel, probably ready to shit his pants. The man on the throne recoiled a touch, barely noticeable if you weren't watching closely. Then his eyes narrowed.

"So, you're a transformer, dear guest. Why didn't you say that earlier?"

Hamel shrugged. "I didn't think it made a difference who I was, and you never asked. So . . ." He let his answer drift off like it didn't matter to him. The king broke into a smile, his body language shifting from superior to cautiously friendly. Hamel would do the same, but even more watchfully.

The demon steepled his fingers. "Let's make a deal, you and me, warrior."

"I'm always open to suggestions." Hamel listened very carefully for subterfuge or any trickery.

"I will pay you the equal amount of gold as those who paid you, to leave and tell the world the woman is dead."

Hamel thought on that. It seemed like a straightforward, fair deal. But since when would a demon be fair? The king could use this as a stalling tactic, but for what? To keep the woman here until after sunset. Then she couldn't return to Earth. That had to be it.

Now the question became whether he should accept the deal. If he did, that would keep him in the castle longer, hopefully long enough to find Melinda. But then there'd be more opportunity to ambush him. Fuck. He hated decisions like this.

He'd just have to stay on his toes. "I accept your offer, king."

"Please, call me Cuzork."

Hamel thought he'd just call him "Dork." "My name is Clint, Cuzork."

"Nice to meet you, Clint."

Hamel felt the demon's voice trying to seduce him, trying to put him under his control. "I am a transformer, Cuzork. Please don't try to spell me. I'd hate to have to kill you."

The king burst into laughter, but Hamel saw the red beat in his eyes. "I assure you, Clint. No tricks from me. I have nothing but respect for your kind." He stood from his throne and clapped his hands twice. "Let's eat to seal our deal, warrior. You must rest before you leave. It is a long journey into the desert and you just got here."

Well, fuck. This couldn't have worked out any better. The demon asking him to stay instead of him asking and seeming suspicious. "Yes, that would be welcome." Good god, could he sound any lamer? He felt like he was in a cheesy medieval movie playing the role of the rogue warrior assassin. All he needed were cheap scenery pieces and buxom maidens walking around with empty baskets.

When he blinked, the room turned from expensive, garish shit to a simple wooden table covered in cloth and with plush cushioned benches. The table was set with gold plates, eating utensils, and goblets similar to the ones the succubi had. Again, very lavish and over-the-top.

The demon gestured Hamel to the table to sit. Hamel took the bench on one side while the king sat opposite. "If you could wish for anything to eat, what would it be?"

This would be a story for the record books if he made it back to tell. "I'd wish for a big juicy steak, rare. I don't suppose you have cows here?"

"No need for earthen animals here. We work in magic." From a side door, a nearly naked woman walked in carrying a platter with the best-looking slab of meat he'd ever seen. And damn, it smelled divine. She set it on the table between the two. Hamel waited for the king to make the first move. He trusted the king as far as he could throw him. Actually, Hamel could probably throw him a good distance, so that cliché didn't really work.

The demon smiled. "Dig in, as humans say. What are you waiting for?"

"I was contemplating the reasons you would want to poison me. There are several. But I must say, if I don't return, an army of transformers much stronger than me will come looking. And your succubi can only take so many."

The demon king frowned. The red in his eyes flashed again. He waved a hand over the platter, but Hamel didn't see anything change. The demon must've removed whatever poison was there. He forked the meat onto his own plate and cut into it.

"Tell me. What is the relationship between you and the woman?"

Wilson's warning came screaming into his head. He shrugged. "I was hired to bring her back. She is no one to me." A commotion came from behind a door, but it didn't open.

The demon grinned. "Would you like to fuck her before you go? I *know* that is all earth men think about. She is pretty, yes?"

Hamel just about came out of his fucking chair and over the table, claws extended. No one talked about his mate like an object that meant nothing.

At his silence, the king added, "Perhaps one of the other ladies in the harem. They are all fabulous lovers. They could suck a nail out of a board."

"I think," Hamel said, trying to keep calm and play along,

"I'd like to take the woman. She would be a nice notch on my belt."

The king laughed. "You devil. Of course she would be. Fuck her brains out. Put your seed into her again and again."

Hamel looked at the steak on his plate. If he didn't divert his eyes from the bastard in front of him, he'd kill him. The amount of disrespect for the fairer sex was disgusting. It was probably the same toward humans in general. He needed to change the subject before he lost control of his cat. It couldn't take much more of this talk about their mate.

"Cuzork, I'm curious, how do demons possess humans? How's the whole process work?" He needed more information than what Wilson had provided if he was to find a weakness in the whole possession process. For shifters, they had animals to kick out the spirits, but if one tried to attack Melinda, how could he stop it?

The king appeared happy to have the question brought to him. "It's quite scientific, actually, besides for the spirit part. Demons are spirits just like what's in humans and those like you. We have power here, but in the other realms we have almost nothing. The only way to gain power is through the native species.

"We look for those who are weak, those whose spirits we can push aside, and take control of their brain. In humans, the brain controls everything. Once we get access to that, then it's like nothing happened to the person, except a change in personality." He smiled.

"So the trick is finding someone with a weak spirit."

"Yes, the number of weak humans grows exponentially. They don't treat each other with respect. They hurt each other, steal from and beat each other. Only a few places strengthen the spirit. As you can imagine, we despise these places."

Hamel asked, "Then why haven't you possessed all these weak humans?"

"That's where science comes in. The human brain is very complex, even for us to understand. It's taken hundreds of years to discover how to move the body through the motor skills. It takes practice, exactly like human infants learning how to walk. By the time we get everything under control, the body and brain give out."

The mystery was unfolding for him. "What if you possessed a baby? Their spirit is weak, right? Then you could grow with the child and learn all the motor skills as they age."

"Yes, we thought of this years ago. Where do you think your stories of possessed children come from? There is some fact to every myth, to every legend."

"Then why haven't you possessed all the babies?" Not that he wanted the children possessed. He was just wondering.

"Though the brain is powerful, it is fragile. The problem comes when we push the connections too hard to get all we want. We can't help it. The electro-chemical synapses overwork and burn out. Quite effective in killing the body, unfortunately."

Hamel nodded. "I would think so. Is there a way around it?"

"Currently, there isn't. Babies need stronger brains, more connections, for us to effectively control them for some time. We thought there was a solution several years ago, but . . . it didn't work out."

A bad vibe crept over Hamel.

CHAPTER 36

⤝

After stepping into her room, Melinda found her back against the wall and her escort's body plastered to hers. She felt his every muscle, including his hard cock poking at her stomach. She tried to push him away, but he didn't budge. In fact, his smile grew wider, wickeder.

"Now, precious one, don't be like that. I am here to grant your every desire." He ran his fingers down her arm, thumb rubbing over her sheet-covered nipple. "I bet you've never had a man tongue-fuck you before, have you?" His tongue flicked in and out of his mouth rapidly.

She turned her face away. "Get away from me. I'm not one of the harem whores you can screw at will."

He chuckled. "Why do you think you're dressed like one, in the room with them? And with no one in here to stop me, I can fuck you until you're pregnant."

That was twice being pregnant had been mentioned. "Why is it so important you get me pregnant?"

"Because"—he started unbuttoning his pants with one hand, the other holding her wrists above her head—"the king rewards us well when we do."

There were no children in the harem rooms. Were they

kept elsewhere? "Where are the children?" Maybe she needed to rescue them.

He shrugged. "Once they're born, we don't see them again. The king takes them."

Melinda pulled her arms, not finding any wiggle available. "What does he do with them?"

"Don't know, don't care." He slid his stiff dick free of his pants and lifted the bottom of her covering. She'd had enough.

"Well, I do." She smashed her heel onto his bare toes, then slammed her knee into his exposed crotch. He doubled over, releasing her hands. With the back of her elbow, she bashed the man's temple, sending him to the floor.

Melinda fled down the hall. Not sure if the harem ladies would help her, she ran the opposite direction of their rooms. Hearing a lot of commotion ahead, she slowed to a walk to pretend like she had every right to be there. When passing a large set of double doors, she glanced into the room to see a multitude of people working in a massive kitchen with appliances that looked to be from the 1950s.

With her short glimpse, she didn't get great detail, but when a woman came through a door, she thought she saw Hamel on the other side sitting at a table with someone wearing flashy clothes.

Was that really Hamel? Oh my god! He'd actually come for her. She was giddy with shock and excitement. Then fear for him flooded her veins. He'd found his way to rescue her and now she had to make sure they both got out of there alive and in one piece. But how, with all the people around? Melinda continued past the door, then flattened her back against the wall. She had to go through the kitchen to get to Hamel. Head held high, she started a purposeful but not too fast walk across the room. When she reached the door, it was slightly ajar. The stranger's voice floated to her.

"What is the relationship between you and the woman?"

With no emotion in his voice, Hamel said, "I was hired to bring her back. She is no one to me."

Behind her, someone dropped a pan or dish. It barely registered in her head as her mind reeled from what Hamel said. He couldn't possibly mean that, could he? Were all his pretty words just to get her in bed?

Her heart broke. She should've known better. Someone like him would never care for some geeky nerd like her. God, what was she thinking?

"Hey, you, harem bitch. What are you doing in here? Your food will be ready in a moment. Get out." Even though she didn't turn to the person yelling, she knew the admonishment was for her. She hurried out of the room and down the hall, paying no attention to anything except her aching soul.

When she looked up next, she was in her room, minus the asshole who had tried to force himself on her. She slammed the doors shut, locked them, then flung herself on the bed to plot ways of killing Hamel, for lying and using her, if she ever got out of this alive.

CHAPTER 37

—✁—

Hamel sat at the wooden table with the demon king sitting opposite. The intel the demon shared was too much to take in at once. Pieces. He needed to take it in pieces.

When the demon just mentioned "several years ago," Kintu and Sefu's story about the first discovery of the virus came to mind. This was all connected. This was what Sefu meant when he said Kintu didn't need to know what really happened.

Sefu engaged with the demons and beat them when destroying the first batch of serum. Now, Melinda had a second vial, a second chance for these bastards to carry out some horrific plan to possess humans.

"I have a feeling you're telling me this for a reason."

The king smiled. "You asked. But you are correct. I have another deal we could make."

"More money?" Hamel raised a brow, pretending that's all he cared about.

"Indeed, warrior. Much more money."

"What is it?"

The demon's smile turned sly. "The woman has something I want. We've been waiting for it a long time. She's hidden it and won't tell us where. I need you to get that information from her."

"Sure, but why would she tell me, a complete stranger?"

Scowling, the demon went quiet. He probably hadn't planned this far into his new scheme. A door opened and Wilson floated out, holding a pitcher of liquid. Wilson was shaking so hard from fear that he was splashing it everywhere.

The scared raisin poured/splashed drink into the goblet sitting next to his untouched steak.

"Lamozierus," the king yelled. "You incompetent, worthless fairy." The king hauled back his fist and punched forward. Before it struck the little guy, Hamel was out of his seat, sharp teeth descended, the king's fist in his clawed hand. Hamel squeezed the demon's fingers he caught.

He growled to the king. "You catch more flies with honey than vinegar, Cuzork. You earn the loyalty of your people through love, not fear. Fear will incite your downfall." His eyes locked onto the king's. Both refused to give ground. Hamel slowly released his grip.

Wilson snatched up the pitcher he'd dropped and glanced at Hamel with such grateful, sad eyes that Hamel would've shed a tear if he weren't a big bad transformer.

"Cuzork, thank you for your hospitality and food. I'd like Wil— Your servant here to give me a quick tour of your beautiful palace. I don't want to take any more of your precious time than I already have. Plus this will give me a private moment to consider all you've generously offered."

Whether the king had duties or not—probably not—he agreed and allowed Wilson to guide Hamel to another room. Once out of the previous room's range, Wilson plastered himself around Hamel's leg in a huge hug. No words needed to be said.

After a few seconds, Wilson floated ahead of Hamel as they passed through different areas. "Wilson, do you know where she is?"

The little dried-up grape spun around and put a "hand" over Hamel's mouth. "Shhh." Its eyes looked from one side of the room to the other. "She is in the arem-hay."

"The what?" Hamel tilted his head to hear better, even

though his supersonic animal ears could hear outside the building.

Wilson winked at him. "You know, the arem-hay."

Oh, fuck a duck. How did that pig Latin shit go again? First letter plus "ay" at end. So she's in the harem. "Okay, where is that?"

"On the ar-fay ide-say."

Chrissakes, Hamel wanted to kill him. But fuck him, if it didn't work. They were communicating. He translated in his head "far side." The harem was on the far side of the palace. They were quiet while he studied the artwork and paintings they passed. He noted the common elements of torture, death, and pain of humans in each. The demon king wasn't growing on him. In fact, he'd be happy to kill the bastard and give reign to someone else.

"Hey, Wilson, Cuzork said he has a plan. Do you know what it is?"

"O-nay—"

"Dammit, Wilson, just say no, will ya?"

"Sorry, no. But the arem-hay is getting much bigger."

That was interesting. Maybe the king was a horny bastard. "Wilson, do demons have sex?"

"Not in our natural forms. Only in human bodies do we feel the effects."

Okay, that tossed sex out the window for the harem. What else—?

The demon king hurried to them. "There you are." The two turned to the king. The man growled at Wilson. "Heel." Wilson lowered his eyes and floated to the floor behind the king's feet. He wouldn't look up at Hamel.

"As I was saying. I have an idea to get the woman to trust you."

"I'm listening."

"Tell her you love her. That seems to get men what they want in your realm."

Hamel thought if only that worked, he'd be a happy man. "That could work, Cuzork. Except I'm a stranger. She wouldn't believe me."

He frowned. "Even after you fuck her, she won't believe you?"

"Human women don't work that way. Trust me. I know. The man has to do something to show they love, they can't just say it."

"What can you do to show her love?"

"Usually men try with flowers, candy, taking them out—"

"That's it. Do that."

"Do what?" Hamel got lost somewhere in the conversation.

"Take her out. Pretend you are taking her home. Tell her you love her, then ask where the serum is."

Hamel slapped Cuzork on the shoulder. "My man, you have come up with the best plan creation has ever seen." The little bastard preened at his words. Hamel wanted to throw up. But he had a better idea for more authenticity. "For more gold coins, I'll get the serum and bring it to you."

The king laughed. "Yes, I like that. I'll give you two coins."

"Great," Hamel said. Could this demon be this gullible or does he have something up his sleeve? he wondered. "Tell me where she is, and I'll get started wooing her."

CHAPTER 38

Melinda was pissed enough to spit goddamn poisonous darts. At Hamel, preferably. How could that son of a bitch say those things? And he'd sounded like he meant every word.

How much money did he have to be paid before he willingly came to rescue her?

She is no one to me. That hurt the most. Brought tears to her eyes again. When she stumbled onto the room where Hamel and the king spoke, she knew Hamel had come to save her. But hearing those words just before she walked in stopped her.

When the other voice asked Hamel if he wanted to fuck her before he left, he didn't even answer. Was he so disgusted by her that he couldn't stand the thought of making love to her? What about the other night they shared in her bed? Was that all fake?

Then a horrible thought punched her in the stomach. If he was paid to rescue her, was he also paid to sleep with her, to pretend to be her friend? Her heart crumbled. She couldn't face him. She turned from the door and fled back to the harem, where she could hide among the beautiful women. No one would notice her when seeing all the gorgeous bodies and faces in the room.

Not long after returning to the harem, one of the women took her to a different room of the palace. It looked like a bedroom set for King Arthur. Whoever designed this castle must have watched every king and knight, demon and sword movie created. She thought it strange that some things were modern—post medieval times—while others weren't. It was a clusterfuck of grand proportions.

Tired of pacing, she plopped face-first onto the bed. Here was an example of old and new. The bed frame looked hand-carved. Something from long ago before machines. But the mattress and sheets were new. Didn't even look used.

She rolled over. What did she really care? Her heart was broken. And she was angry at letting herself fall again. Stupid, stupid, stupid. She pummeled her fists into the blankets with each word. With her jerky movements while laying back, the small plastic vial slipped out of her bra, onto her chest. Oh, shit. She sat up and stuffed it back in.

She was sure the virus was why she was here. The ladies in the harem had explained where she was, and she'd refused to believe them until they'd showed her demons floating by and the little magic they could do. Holy shit. That was enough to make a sane person crazy. There was no lying to herself anymore. No matter what science said, demons existed, and she was in another realm.

She told the women that when she was rescued, she'd come back for them. They told her no. They wanted to stay. They were living a dream life. All they did was lay around, relaxing, having food and drink brought to them. They were allowed to come and go as they pleased, but with nothing but desert for miles, the women never ventured out of the castle.

And if they were feeling sexually deprived, they were welcome to join the succubi in one of their orgies. That was highly recommended.

She sighed. All she wanted was to go home to her own bed and sulk. Then she'd go back to work Monday and forget any of this virus or Hamel stuff happened.

Suddenly, the doors rattled. "Melinda, it's me, Hamel."

She jumped off the bed and turned from the door. "What do you want? Go away."

"Melinda?" She heard the question in his voice.

"Yes, you heard me correctly. Go. Away." Her hands fisted. "What do you care? I'm no one to you! Can't even bring yourself to think about fucking me." Sobs choked her words. She slapped a hand over her mouth to keep them quiet. She leaned against the wall, looking out a glassless window, seeing a land as barren as her heart.

"No, Melinda," he pleaded. "You don't understand. I had to say those things."

She became disgusted with his lies. Her sobs returned. She was pathetic. Now she was angry at him and herself.

"Look, Melinda, let me in and we can battle it out after we get out of here. We're running out of time."

That caught her attention. "Time for what?"

"The witch doctor, Sefu, he sent me here to rescue you. He was the one with the serum all those years ago. We only have until sunset before we're stuck in this realm forever."

She only understood part of what he was saying. "Sefu? What does he have to do with the serum? He's a voodoo guy. What do you mean, stuck in this realm?"

He pounded on the door again. "Melinda, unlock these doors. We have to go."

Anger, frustration, heartbreak swirled in her heart. She wanted to scream, cry, and jump up and down like a three-year-old having a tantrum. Most of all, she wanted Hamel to hold her. But he didn't want her. "Why are you even here, Hamel? Did they pay you that much?"

She heard a sigh and the pounding stopped. "Melinda, please open the door and we can go. There's a place in the desert we have to be before sunset."

Her pride was taking a hit also. "Maybe I want to stay here. The ladies in the harem love it here. They say it's a dream come true to lie around and get fed all day."

"That sounds to me like they are being fattened up for the kill."

She gasped. Oh my god. Was that true? She had to get help. Her eyes darted around the room for some means of escape. Her room was thirty feet off the ground. She'd break her entire body if she jumped. The bed lay directly in her sight.

Hurrying over, she threw off the quilted overlay and snatched the sheets. Just like in prison movies, she tied them together. That made sixteen feet; adding pillowcases made it twenty. Then add her height, and she'd fall about five feet. That wasn't bad. She'd fallen off a slide in grade school that was higher than that. But it also had pea gravel, and she was a lot younger.

"Melinda, I'm going to rip these doors off in a second and it's going to scare you."

She tied the end of the sheets to the bed leg. "Humans cannot rip open a door like that, Hamel. Now go away. I'm saving myself." She threw her legs over the windowsill.

"You're what? Melinda, don't do anything to get hurt. I'll take care of you. I . . . I love you, Melinda."

Still sitting on the sill, she twisted around to look at the door. She shook her head and grabbed on to the first sheet. She didn't say it very loud; she couldn't muster the emotional strength. "No. No, you don't, Hamel."

CHAPTER 39

Hamel laid his head against the thick doors separating him from the love of his life. The last words she said tore at his heart. Yes, he did love her. He didn't give a shit about his job or his past anymore. All he was worried about was his future and having the one person he loved in it.

Grabbing hold of the steel rings attached to the door, he cleaved them open. Metal squealed and wood splintered. His eyes searched the room, seeing the white sheets trailing out the window. He rushed over and looked out. Melinda dangled dangerously many feet from the ground.

A growl escaped him. His cat said the distance to the ground was too great for them to risk a jump. They needed to get outside.

Hamel ran out of the room and down the hall. Why was there never a door when you needed one? Damn, he wished there was one now. The wall ahead turned blurry and fuzzy. When he reached the spot, a door sat slightly ajar.

He pushed it open, wondering what in the hell had happened a moment ago. Nothing about the door looked strange. In fact, it looked perfectly normal. He headed outside, heading back the way he came down the hallway. Coming around a corner, he saw Melinda hanging ten feet off the ground.

She wore thin white material wrapped toga-style around her. After seeing her in lab coats for so long, her being almost naked was breathtaking. She probably wore little to nothing underneath. As he stared, her hands slipped over a knot on the tied blankets, not slowing her descent. A shocked squeal escaped her.

Hamel's cat exploded through him and dashed toward her. He could shift when his faster cat reached her so human arms could catch her. But then she'd storm away, not wanting to see him as Hamel.

Staying as a cat, he ran under her. Reaching the last knot, Melinda hollered when it slipped through her hands. Hamel's cat slid along the ground, rolled belly up, and provided Melinda with a safe landing spot. Her knees slamming into his chest wasn't the best of feelings, and neither was not being able to breathe. But he got over it quickly and to his feet, growling for any demons to get away. There were none. Looked like Cuzork was keeping his word about letting them "escape."

"Jag," he heard Melinda say, and turned to her. She wrapped her arms around his neck. "I knew you were my protector. Sent to keep me safe. No man can compare to the true heart of an animal." He licked the tears on her cheek then pulled away. They needed to get going. Since they weren't sneaking out through the castle, hopefully they'd get a head start and be at the circle before Cuzork realized they'd gone.

In his cat form, Hamel set off away from the castle, around to where the trail led to their rendezvous point, Melinda following him. He kept them at a run not only to get them there quickly, but to keep the sadness at realizing that he'd failed his mate from obliterating his heart.

He couldn't seem to keep her from danger, couldn't make her love him. He didn't deserve her. If that didn't suck. All these years going on missions to save others and when the time came, he couldn't save his own mate. He'd get her back to their dimension, work with Sefu to destroy the serum and virus, then return to the States.

Maybe it was time to retire. Get new blood into ALFA. Young blood. He was old and tired. In his hometown, everyone was a shifter and knew everyone. There were other towns across the American continents that were shifter towns, but since they hadn't been discovered, they weren't "contracted" to work with the government.

Perhaps he should visit and see about living close to one of them. Maybe even find a suitable partner for companionship. He'd give her kids and love and protect them. But his heart would never be truly happy. It was apparent he didn't deserve that.

In the distance, his cat eyes spotted the pile of desert stones. Good thing. The sun was becoming alarmingly low on the horizon. Melinda panted behind him, never falling too far back. Even though she'd said she wanted to stay in the harem, she didn't. He must've really pissed her off for her to even think that, much less say it to him. More proof for him to go.

Then the next problem hit him. How did they get back to their side of the veil? Did they just stand in the circle and Sefu would zing them back? How would he know they were there? He blinked, then his pounding heart about blew from his chest. Fucking Cuzork was there.

The son of a bitch had an oasis image that would've been right at home in Elizabeth Taylor's *Cleopatra*. The bastard lounged on a golden chaise. Women in scant clothing waved large palm leaves over him while another female fed him grapes.

If he didn't know what the hell was going on, he'd swear this whole place was one movie set scene after another. Or duplicates of pictures in history books of how Egyptians and kings used to live. Then he realized everything here existed on Earth. For being in another dimension with creatures with magical powers, nothing was new or something he'd never seen before. He wasn't sure what that meant, if anything. But right now, he had an asshole to deal with.

Melinda walked by him, hands on her hips, breathing heavily. "How the hell did you get out here? You weren't here, then suddenly you were."

Cuzork looked at Hamel and he shifted back to his human form. "So, Clint, did you find where the serum is?"

Melinda's head cocked. "What the fuck are you talking about? Clint?" Hamel put a hand on the small of her back as he stepped beside her. She startled away with a screech, then stared at him, her eyes taking in his bare chest and buckskins. His eyes stayed on her, but he spoke to the demon king.

"I have an idea, but not the exact place. I'll have to search the area then bring it back. You can pay me then. That is if you're still planning to abide by our agreement."

The demon snorted and his eyes raked down her sweat-covered body, the thin white fabric transparent where touching her flesh. He licked his lips. "Of course, transformer. I'm abiding by our agreement. You get what I want and the female and I will wait in my rooms. I believe it's time to put my plan into action. Starting with her." The tented area of the demon's crotch became very evident.

CHAPTER 40

⤙

Melinda had never run so long or fast in her life. But if she didn't keep up with the black jag in front of her, she'd probably never get the chance to run, much less breathe, ever again. Something inside told her she was in serious trouble. Despite the weird-ass conversations with the ladies and the beautiful palace and gardens, something wasn't right. It seemed too perfect.

How could she forget the fact that they abducted her? They were probably trying to make her forget that. Make everything so nice that she'd want to stay. If she were to stay, she'd just be exchanging one lonely life for another. She was only really happy when Hamel was with her.

Well, not anymore, apparently. She was nothing to him. God, she was so glad she didn't tell him she loved him. Talk about the utmost humiliation. But he did say he loved her at the castle. Did he mean it? If so, he was lying to someone—her or the demon.

She felt bad leaving him behind. She wondered if the things he said Sefu mentioned were true. If she were here after sunset, would she be a permanent resident? The sun was getting rather low. She prayed her savior jag knew where he was going. She followed him blindly.

It was weird how she got the feeling that the big cat cared for her. Like someone determined to keep her safe, and keep her, period. She'd rejoice if she were a cat. The human side simply loved the animal back.

Squinting, she saw something low to the ground not far ahead. Looked like they were headed for that. Was it a portal between dimensions? That must be how her cat found her. As they approached, she saw a pile of rocks within a circle.

The wind gusted, blowing dust into her eyes. After she cleared the tears, Cuzork stood—well, lay—in front of her. She couldn't believe the mirage surrounding him. Something out of an old Egyptian movie. She moved closer to him. Why was he here?

The demon looked over her shoulder at the jag behind her. "So, Clint, did you find where the serum is?"

She cocked her head, giving him a confused stare. "What the fuck are you talking about? Clint?" A hand touched the small of her back and she startled away with a screech. Who the hell—?

Hamel stood beside her, but not only that—he was shirtless with tan pants that fit him tightly in all the right places. Holy shit. Drool-worthy. Not only did she love him, but he was damn fine to see half naked.

His eyes stayed on her, but he spoke to the demon king. "I have an idea, but not the exact place. I'll have to search the area then bring it back. You can pay me then. That is if you're still planning to abide by our agreement."

What were they talking about? Bring what back? Wait. Someone mentioned the serum a minute ago. The virus serum? This was all about the fucking tube resting between her boobs. She could fucking scream, she was so mad. Her head whipped around, looking for Jag. It was time to get out of here. Where did he go?

The demon snorted. "Of course, transformer—" There was that word again. No wires showed anywhere, so the word must mean something else. She turned to Cuzork as he continued talking. "I believe it's time to put my plan into action. Starting with her." Melinda startled again.

"Me? What plan?" All the pieces started coming together. He wanted her for the serum. And by the way his pants stood at attention, he wanted more than just that. Oh, fuck, she was going to puke. Her hand slapped over her mouth as her body shuddered.

Hamel ran his hands up and down her arms and whispered into her ear, "Don't worry, baby. I won't let him touch you." A breeze blew through the mirage, making her shiver again. He held her tighter, shielding her from Cuzork's hungry stare. "Are you cold? I wish I had a cloak to keep you warm while I kill the bastard in front of us."

Motion on the ground caught both of their attention. Before their eyes, a pile of material appeared from thin air. Melinda reached down and picked it up. It was a cloak. "Oh, fuck," Hamel said. "That's exactly what I imagined it looked like. Where did that come from?"

That was the question of the day. In her head, her dream with Sefu in his luxury hut flashed. She understood nothing of that dream. He kept talking about realities and weird concepts. She wondered . . . "Hamel, did Sefu say anything to you about reality or dreams?"

"Oh, yeah. He said to tell you to remember whose reality you're in. Whatever that means." It had to mean something. What? She replayed the dream in her head.

Cuzork sat up on his chaise. "What are you doing? I saw that."

She ignored the demon, putting more pieces of the puzzle together. The last piece clicked. *Oh, fuck.* She looked up at Hamel. "Wish for something again."

His brows drew down. "Wish for something?" His one brow raised. "I wish for a hamburger." Melinda rolled her eyes. If it wasn't sex, it was food for men. On the ground where the cloak appeared, a hamburger sat in the sand. Melinda dropped her head against Hamel's hard, warm chest. Sefu was right. She needed to pay attention to whose reality she was in. And holy shit, this was such a mind fuck. But she was in a parallel dimension.

"Hey!" A bolt of lightning from Cuzork's finger blasted the ground beside them. He stood and walked closer. "Hmm, seems you two do know each other. That or you get cozy really quickly, Clint."

Still wrapped in his arms, Melinda leaned back and looked up at Hamel. "Clint? Seriously?"

His cheeks reddened and he shrugged. "I had to think on my feet. Who else but my idol?"

Her brows scrunched. "Your idol is a movie star?"

He shushed her and pushed her behind his back. "Look, Cuzork. You cannot have Melinda. She belongs to me. If you release her, I will give you the serum."

He would what? Anger took over her fear. She'd had enough of this virus and serum shit. She pushed to Hamel's side, fighting his hands trying to keep her behind him.

"Clint has no idea where the serum is. Only I do. Tell me why you want this so much? It doesn't even kill people. What could you do with it?"

A smile spread on the demon's face. "Lowly earth female. You couldn't fathom what it is like living here—"

"Looks rather homey and nice from what I've seen," Hamel said.

The demon's face flooded red. "It is not! It's hell!" He stomped closer. "You will tell me where the serum is."

Melinda wouldn't back down. "Tell me why you want it."

The king fisted his hands and his body shook with anger. "Because I'm going to rule over you worthless, spineless, disgusting creatures."

Cool wind blew through the silence lingering between them. The bottom of the sun dipped below the horizon. Hamel took her into his arms, pulling her away from Cuzork, then said, "You told me that was almost impossible. Humans need stronger brains."

Cuzork clasped his hands behind his back. "I believe I said babies need stronger brains." Melinda gasped. The demon's smile brightened. "Do you finally see my genius?"

Hamel leaned down to her ear. "Help me out here. I'm not a doctor, remember?"

She wasn't sure she could think such horror. "The bastard plans to give the serum to women, then impregnate them and possess the babies when they're born."

"Fuck—possessed humans with supernatural abilities. That would be disastrous to mankind when they are old enough."

Cuzork laughed. "That's an understatement, transformer." His eyes locked on Melinda. "Now, tell me where the serum is or I will kill your lover."

CHAPTER 41

Hamel dropped his forehead onto Melinda's. Cuzork's words killed him. Not because of his own life, but what it was putting his mate through. She may not love him, but she wouldn't want him to die, no matter who he was. He needed to make this easy and guarantee her safety.

He raised his head. "I wish Melinda to return safely to Earth now."

She gripped her arms around him. "No! You can't do this." Her eyes filled with fear and . . . desperation?

He unwrapped her arms from him and brought her hands to his lips. "Yes, I can. I love you, Melinda, and want you safe. I don't understand how this wish stuff works—"

"Hamel, unwish what you just said. It works because we are in your dream world. Sefu sent your spirit here. Not your real body, like mine. This is my reality, not yours. In dreams, you can make anything happen. Wish me to stay here."

He kissed her fingers and shook his head. "No, my love. I want you safe. Destroy the serum. Have Sefu help you." Cuzork stormed toward them. These would be his last words to her. "Find someone who makes you happy."

Cuzork grabbed Melinda's arm. With no warning, he flew back as if yanked away, slamming onto the ground on his back.

Hamel no longer holding on to her, Melinda was dragged by an invisible force into the portal circle. A see-through wall of yellow light surrounded her. She banged against the solid air, her shouts not breaching the invisible barrier.

He wasn't sure his wish for her safety would happen. He didn't really understand what she'd said about him dreaming. Turning from his love, he saw Cuzork raise his hands, aimed at her. Even though she didn't love him, he would die for her. Hamel screamed to attract his attention and ran toward the downed demon, sword raised high, ready to strike.

The demon's head snapped toward him, hands readjusting then sending thick bolts of electricity into his body. Pure pain zapped every cell in his body. Fortunately, he died quickly.

Melinda beat her fists against the yellow light trapping her in the portal. "Hamel, no. Don't do this!" He turned from her, either ignoring or not hearing her pleas. He'd told her he loved her, and she believed him. His eyes said it all.

She should have repeated his words to him, but once again, the fucking fear overrode her heart. She so wanted to have control over her fear. Stop missing out on happiness because of one guy from the past who hurt her. But now she had to find a way out of this damn beam. Was she really going to give the serum to the demon king to save Hamel?

Yes, she was.

Her love ran at Cuzork on the ground. Before her eyes, she watched him die.

Everything in her stilled.

His body settled on the dusty ground, sword bouncing harmlessly away. A tiny white dot of light rose from his chest and floated just on the other side of her prison. Unconditional love and peace flowed through her. The same euphoria she'd had when she imagined bonding with her savior black cat the other day in her home.

She had no doubt this was Hamel's spirit sharing what he felt for her. It was so strong, so reassuring. Knowing how much he loved her, her fear of rejection was gone. With Hamel at her side, she realized they could conquer anything the world threw at them.

His last words floated in her mind: *Find someone who makes you happy.* She had.

Him.

The light zipped away, gone from her sight. She'd just lost who she knew would be her greatest love. Guilt, sadness, anger rose inside her, eating away the last of her energy. Extreme exhaustion overtook her consciousness.

In the darkness, she smelled the acidic bite of a campfire. She hadn't been camping since summer Bible camp as a child. The sweetness of flowers, the earthiness of mud, and the tang of blood quickly followed. A voice registered in her brain. The witch doctor. Maybe Sefu could save Hamel. She forced her eyes open.

She sucked in a breath. "Sefu?" Her vision was fuzzy in the low light. The chanting stopped. Melinda launched herself toward the man sitting next to the fire. "Please save him, Sefu. I was wrong. I love him and I'm not afraid anymore. I see how powerful real love is. We can make it."

The old man peeled her off him and held her at arm's length. He stared at her for a second then turned his head and looked to the side. Melinda followed his sight line and saw Hamel lying on the floor in the shadows. She dove toward him, letting her tears flow for all the stupid mistakes she'd made where it came to him and her feelings.

She laid her head on his chest and wrapped her arms under his neck. His heart beat strong under her ear. Wait. He was dead. She'd watched him die.

"No, child." Sefu gave a frustrated sigh. "He is alive. Nothing in this plane hurt his physical body, so he lives. Only his soul, his spirit, is gone. Why are you back without him?" Melinda scrambled back to the witch doctor.

"The demon king killed him when I was protected by the tractor beam in the portal."

His face scrunched. "The what beam?"

"Never mind," she said. She'd forgotten this man grew up without television or movies. "I saw and felt Hamel's spirit leave his body after Cuzork shot bolts of lightning at him."

Sefu jerked upon hearing the demon's name. "That piece of bug dung is doing all this?"

"Yes," Melinda said. "Can we save Hamel?"

"He is still alive. He was in a dream state, not reality. So his spirit lives on in the demon plane." He shook her shoulders to get her full attention. "Had the sun set before you left?"

She thought back to the last thing she remembered. "No, part of the sun was still up."

"Good." Sefu dragged three bowls toward him and dipped his fingers into each. "You have until the last ray of the sun to convince him to return to our plane. If you fail, his body will remain in a vegetative state on this side." He wiped fingers down her arms and cheeks. "Tell him how you feel, little one. Do not let your past control your future." He began his chanting.

Soothing, lyrical, intoxicating. With the heat in the room, Melinda relaxed and let her mind wander.

CHAPTER 42

—

Hamel floated freely along the desert environ. He didn't feel any different, but he knew he was no longer constrained to a body. That must be what happened when you died. He thought he'd turn into a speck of light and go somewhere, but he didn't have any thoughts about where. Most humans believed in heaven and hell. But his parents weren't religious, so he never was, either.

How long had he been dead? Time seemed to have no meaning. Or he just wasn't able to keep track of it like a human did. Either way, he was tired of looking at the same dead dirt ground and blowing dust and sand. He thought back to his home and the acreage his family lived on when he was a child. The land was filled with trees, fields of thick grass, and a gurgling creek not too far from the house. He really wished that were here.

The sound of a songbird stopped him. That was the first animal sound he'd heard since coming to this godforsaken place. A bird? There wasn't one tree for the critter to live in. He turned, even though he didn't have a body, per se, and saw the most beautiful landscape—his home, actually. Exactly how he saw it in his ethereal mind.

Wait a minute. How could that be? His mind thought back

to the gun that showed up out of nowhere, then the ammo. The door that appeared when he needed a way outside to get to Melinda sliding down the tied bedsheets. The cloak and hamburger he wished for. Everything he'd wished for or wanted, he magically got.

But he wasn't a demon; how had it happened? Melinda's words came back to him. *It works because we are in your dream world. In dreams, you can make anything happen.*

Was he really dreaming? Okay, he needed to think about this logically. He was dead, which meant no body, which meant he couldn't turn into his animal. "I wish to be in my jaguar form." Instantly, he found himself on ground level. He looked down at paws and black fur. So that was the trick. In dreams, you could have anything you wanted.

His animal ears perked up. A voice came on the wind. Melinda's. He honed in on the sound and took off in that direction. Was she back? Why? How? Then it dawned on him. Sefu sent her for something. Hamel wished to be by her side. When he blinked, she was in front of him. He could get used to this.

Melinda spun around. "Jag! You're here." She fell to her knees and wrapped her arms around his neck.

He inhaled deeply. She still smelled unbelievable. Wait. Was this real or just a wish?

She rubbed her face on his. "Oh my god. I thought I'd lost you, too."

His purr was automatic. She was here with him. This was all he wanted. But then she sat on her heels and cupped his animal's face in her hands.

"Jag"—she looked deeply into his eyes—"I need you to understand me." He nodded since he couldn't talk. Her eyes widened. Oh, shit. He just gave himself away. Her beautiful peepers about to pop out of her head, she continued, "Jag, you're creeping me out, but we'll worry about that later because I'm in a dream state, I hope."

Interesting. How in the hell would this work?

She swallowed hard. "Jag, I need to find Parish Hamel. He's . . ." She paused. "He's the love of my life, Jag. I don't want to live without him. I was so afraid of what would happen if I let myself be vulnerable with him. Last time I did, I was hurt beyond repair. So I thought.

"But Hamel fixed me. He showed me through his own actions what real love is. And to open up isn't being weak, but being strong enough to reveal your true self to another. I was such an idiot, Jag. But I didn't know." She breathed in a wobbly breath. "You haven't by chance seen a dot of white light floating around, have you?"

Before he could respond, Cuzork's voice cut through the air. "I knew you'd come back, female." The demon stood with a small army of demon guards who looked exactly like pictures he'd seen of China's first emperor's burial site of thousands of terra-cotta soldiers.

Fuck. Now he understood how everything in this place looked so familiar: the palace, the Death Valley desert, the guards, the food, the humanlike people. He'd seen all of it or something very similar before. This world was conjured from his brain, his memories.

It all made sense now. He'd never seen a demon, so the image of a demon was a blob of black material, nothing specific. He hadn't seen the palace until Wilson said it was there and he had to believe—wish—it was there. Everything he wished for was granted, based on what was in his head.

Cuzork raised a hand and a gust of wind knocked both him and Melinda out of the portal circle. "I've had enough of this." Demon eyes narrowed on his cat. "I see you have discovered the magic of this place, literally. So we have a change of plans for getting the serum."

His jag picked up the scent of anger from his mate. Melinda's hands fisted into balls. "I am so sick of you and this fucking serum." She slid her fingers between her breasts and pulled out a plastic vial. "Is this what you want, Cuzork?" She held it up and, with her thumb, popped up the cork top.

The demon's eyes turned into red dots. "You had it here all along." A wicked smile etched his face. "Clever woman. I don't give you enough credit. Seems your realm hasn't taught me enough about the female species. Your movies show women to be weak, dumb, and constantly talking. Seems I need to spend time in your dimension learning how current women have changed."

"Yes, you need to update yourself, demon, on more than just females. You'll find the human race is no longer scared of things that go bump in the night. We won't sit idly by and let others do what they want if it harms others."

Cuzork stalked toward her. "Shut up and give me the serum." Fear flashed in her eyes. She looked at the ground. "No, you don't, bitch." A solid slick surface instantly covered the ground. "Any drop you pour from that tube, I will easily gather. So just give it to me."

Hamel watched panic settle on her face. She didn't know what to do now. So she did the unthinkable.

CHAPTER 43

Melinda was just about to have a cow. She'd planned to empty the vial on the dust-covered ground, which would easily soak up the liquid. But this new floor the demon conjured looked the exact opposite of what she wanted.

Then she remembered she was in dream mode and made the decision. She brought the vial to her lips and tossed it back like a toddy on a cold night. Cuzork stopped in his tracks.

Melinda threw the small container to the side. "There you go, demon. No more serum. Kiss your plan good-bye."

The king turned slightly toward his army. "Lamo, heel."

From the men, Wilson floated to the king's foot, eyes lowered. "Yes, Your Highness."

"Lamo, my pet, kill the cat now. My men will bring the woman to the palace. She will now bear us children to possess until the day she dies. My plan will continue with only a slight delay."

Wilson floated in place, shaking in fright and staring at his cat. "Why me, Your Highness?"

The demon king slowly turned to the lesser entity. "Because I'm hoping the cat will kill you before you kill him. Then one of my pains in the ass will be gone without me lifting a finger."

The king turned and his army split in half to allow him a path through. Several made a beeline toward Melinda. She stiffened and spoke under her breath, "You will not touch him, Cuzork. I wish a sword in each hand and to be the best sword fighter this place has ever seen."

The next second, she ran toward their enemy, two long, narrow blades in her hands, a battle cry screaming from her lips. With a blur of hands, feet, and body, she mowed over the guards coming for her. Each direct strike popped a creature into oblivion. Just like taking a sewing needle into a field of balloons and jabbing at superhuman speed.

The rest of the military stared as if not knowing what to do. They wouldn't until their creator, Cuzork, told them. They were nothing but useless puppets until their leader put his hand up their asses.

The horde now charging, she noted her jag had extended his claws and taken up fighting. Shit, she hadn't anticipated that, but she should have. She yelled, "Jag, I wish your fur to be impenetrable like armor so no hit will hurt you." Her sword sliced through three men. Pop, pop, pop. She felt so badass right at that moment.

Melinda glanced at the cat to make sure he'd be all right. She couldn't be sure, but when the group of six men slashed at him at the same time, his body only jarred like being pushed, but nothing else. His paws swept the men's midsections, creating pop after pop.

Melinda heard footsteps behind her and spun. She kicked, punched, slashed, and body-slammed her way through the enemy. Behind the demons, over half of the sun was below the horizon. She had to end this and find Hamel.

She sliced a warrior in half while she was midair and landed in an attack stance. Her eyes met Cuzork's, swords lifted. In her peripheral view, she saw claws dig into dirt as Jag sprinted toward the king. Her eyes didn't move, giving away no hints of the coming attack. The jag leapt at the demon, taking the creature to the ground in a hard slam.

She watched as the cat morphed into Hamel, his arm wrapped around the demon's neck, securing him in a sleeper hold. His eyes sought hers. She stood, arms slack at her sides, swords dropped on the ground, mouth gaping at him.

With the king's capture, the remaining guards disappeared. Cuzork croaked, "Transform—" Hamel flexed his huge bicep, cutting off further words. Was the demon calling Hamel a transformer? When she realized what that word meant, she felt the blood drain from her face. Hamel transformed into her savior jaguar? But— How— He—

Worry coated his face. "Melinda, sweetheart, we'll talk when we get back. We don't have much time." Hamel looked around. "Wilson? Where are you? Get over here."

In a blink, a dark blob that resembled a huge raisin with eyes, nose, and a mouth appeared at Hamel's side. She snatched up her swords.

"No, Melinda. He's with me. He's okay." Hamel winked at her. "Watch what I figured out on my own." Her love turned to the floating raisin. "Wilson, close your eyes and picture something in your . . . well, I was going to say head, but I'm not sure that works for you." He cleared his throat. "Picture something you really want and make a wish that it was here."

The hovering blob stared at Hamel. "I do not understand, Clint." Melinda couldn't help the snort that escaped her, hearing his "name" again. Hamel scowled at her but continued with the blob.

"Wilson, haven't you ever wanted something you didn't have?"

"No, Clint. I have all I want thanks to the king. He has granted us the needs to survive."

Melinda realized how simple this demon's life must be. He didn't seem like a bad guy, but humble.

Hamel rolled his eyes, the king still trapped in his arms. "Let's go about this a different way, Wilson. If you could have anything you don't have, what would that be? Close your eyes and say 'I wish' whatever."

Wilson's eyes slowly looked at the king's then looked down. "I—I do not—"

Hamel sighed. "Wilson—"

"Okay. I wish to have a human body." Suddenly standing in front of her was an image of Zac Efron. That was interesting. The floating creature seemed to be surprised. "I have been told I could not have a humanlike image because I was too worthless, too nothing." The new person examined his body, smile wide, eyes shining. "Is this body pleasing, Clint? I saw a picture of this person when the children where learning pig Latin."

Pig Latin? She looked at Clint— Hamel. He nodded. "Yes, Wilson. From what I understand, that is a very appealing image. What else would you like to have?"

From nowhere, a black upright piano materialized. Hamel and Melinda looked at Wilson. The demon said, "I heard it one time. It has beautiful sounds." Then a few chickens popped into existence. "These creatures made me feel happy when watching them. They are fun and intriguing. The way the white ball that comes out of their—"

"Got it, Wilson," Hamel said. "Do you understand how the king's magic works now? It didn't belong to only the king, but to everyone. He simply refused to tell others how to use it because he wanted the power all to himself.

"Now only the four of us know, Wilson. And soon it will be only you and Cuzork here. Do you want me to kill this son of a bitch?"

Wilson stared at the king, fear no longer shivering his body. "No, I wish that he floats among the universes, never finding a home, never returning here, and never again able to wield the magic of this realm again."

Cuzork's eyes widened and panic crossed his face before he popped out of sight. Hamel climbed to his feet and put a hand on Wilson's shoulder. "Wilson, with your ex-king banished, you are now the only one who knows how to use the magic. It's up to you how you create your world.

"It seems Cuzork spent a lot of time on Earth becoming familiar with our way of life and came back here to re-create it. He saw the same pictures and movies I saw as a child. You can keep it or change it."

Wilson looked deep in thought. "I will gather many who are knowledgeable and we will make a decision."

Melinda smiled. "Wilson, I think you're going to make a great leader. The lowly will inherit the land." She stepped forward and the sun shined in her eyes. Just a sliver remained. "Hamel, we have to go now."

He grabbed her hand and they hurried to the circle. Wilson waved. They waved back and Hamel said, "I wish for us to return to our realm." Nothing happened. The two looked at each other. Hamel repeated, "I wish us to go back to Sefu's shed." Again nothing. Wilson still stood waving at them, with a goofy smile on his face.

"Hamel, why isn't it working?" Her eyes glanced at the vanishing sun.

"I don't know."

"What do we do?"

The sun would be gone in seconds. The underside of her wrist burned. She hissed and lifted her arm to see what stung her. From under the skin, an image came to the surface. It was the same as the tattoo she'd received in one of her recent dreams. Sefu's chant in the dream filled her ears.

Huenda sisi kujiunga ukweli wetu kweli.

Kuziba ulimwengu huu milele kwa yake mwenyewe.

Her eyes closed and the foreign words took over her mind. She repeated them over and over. She held up her hand to let the sigil shine upon the land. Just as the last ray of sun gave out, complete exhaustion once again overtook her mind.

CHAPTER 44

—✂—

Melinda opened her eyes to see the handsomest man she'd ever seen staring at her. Lying next to her, his hand brushed down her cheek. She leaned forward and kissed him. It was better than any dream. Though her Beach Man was really damn hot.

"Ah," came an old, scratchy voice. "You both return this time. Good. The veil is closed. Time to go home." Sefu stood and headed for the door.

Melinda and Hamel looked at each other then turned to the old man. "Wait," they both said.

The witch doctor sighed. "What?"

Melinda didn't know where to begin with questions. "What just happened?"

"You haven't figured it out, young one?" Sefu asked.

"What if the demons come back?" Melinda asked.

The witch doctor shook his head. "No worry. You closed the portal."

"I did? When?"

Sefu sighed again. "Your spell."

Hamel joined in. "It was the words you mumbled to bring us back here, when my wish didn't work." He looked up at Sefu. "Why didn't my wish work to bring us back?"

The old man leaned against the doorframe, thinking. "I would say the magic chose not to work."

"The magic has a conscience?" Melinda asked.

Sefu laughed. "Of course. Magic is as alive as you and me. It chooses when to obey and when to do something else. A good witch doctor learns to keep magic happy. Always happy."

She looked at Hamel sitting next to her by the fire. "So the magic decided I should do a spell instead of letting Hamel wish us back? What did the spell do?"

"Listen to the translation and see for yourself: *May we join our true reality. Sealing this realm forever to its own.*"

"That's it?" Melinda said. "All those words to bring us here and seal the portal closed." Sefu gave a nod. "One more thing, Sefu." She pulled out the plastic tube with the serum. "We need to destroy this now. I wanted to wait until Monday, but I've changed my mind."

"Wait," Hamel said. "I saw you drink that. How is it here?"

Melinda rolled her eyes. "Hamel, my body was here with yours. When I came back, I was in the dream world. What you saw is what I wished you to see. It was to trick the demon into thinking there was no serum. I'd hoped he'd give up his plan and go away. It didn't quite happen that way, but he believes it's gone, which is all that's needed."

Sefu came around the fire to her and took the vial. He opened the top and chanted over it. He then poured the liquid into the fire. "It is done." His chin rested on his chest. "This old man is tired." He shuffled toward the door again. "Take her home, cat, and bind her to you. She is the one. Mate." Once out the door, he walked away, not looking back.

Alone with Hamel, she smiled and took his hand. "Have I mentioned that I love you?"

He brought her hand to his lip for a kiss. "I've prayed to hear those words for a long time, my love. I love you more than you know."

She couldn't help the grin creeping onto her face. His brow rose. "What's in that devious head of yours, love?"

"Shift for me, transformer."

He laughed. "I can't. I have to take my clothes off so I won't tear them."

"But in the other realm," she started, "you had clothes on when you shifted."

"Magic, my love. I didn't want my junk hanging out for everyone to see."

She nodded. "I see. So go ahead and shift."

"But, darlin', I'd have to strip."

Melinda licked her lips. "Yeah, that's the whole idea."

Hamel jumped to his feet and held a hand out to her. "If that's the case, then I know of a great little bungalow that has a great bed." He pulled her into his arms from her sitting position. She loved being wrapped in him, safe and loved. She tipped her head up and his hot, wet lips bore down on hers. God, she loved this even more.

She had a ton of questions about shifters, but that all could wait. Like Sefu said, she wanted to mate. Being bound to this man was the best thing that could ever happen to her.

Nothing would hold her back.

CHAPTER 45

Inside her two-room love shack, the air was hotter than the middle of summer. After the last several hours of insaneness, being held in Hamel's arms was the most sensible feeling known.

She took a deep breath and let out her feelings. "I love you."

Finally. She was able to express to him how she felt. If only he could see inside her. Her words had an incredible effect. He was on her, kissing her hard, branding her. He pushed her back on the bed, caressing every inch of her body. He cupped her face and allowed her to see the same things she felt mirrored in his eyes.

"I love you, too."

To hear him say the words made her heart flip. Emotion clogged her throat. She threw her arms around him and kissed his neck. She inhaled the scent of her man and the passion burning between them.

"Bite me, Hamel. Bite me, my love," she whispered.

He growled and dropped to seal their lips together. She widened her thighs to allow him easy entrance into her body.

He didn't enter her, much to her disappointment. Instead, he kissed her neck. Then he slowly licked his way down her chest, circling first one nipple, nipping the little bud with his teeth and sucking so hard her pussy quivered. Then he moved on to the other and did the same until she writhed under him, whimpering for more.

She gripped his hair in her fists, squeezing and loosening her hold depending on how his lips moved over her.

He growled into her belly, licking his way around the indentation of her belly button. Her sex grasped at nothing. She needed him inside or she'd lose her mind.

He glanced up from between her legs. Her breath reeled. Sandpaper clung to the inside of her throat. He inhaled and licked his lips, and she almost came.

"Melinda?"

"Hmm?" She couldn't speak past the knot in her throat. His look was so hot and possessive she felt melted onto the bed.

"I love how you smell." He licked a cool, wet trail from clit to slit.

Her body wound into a ball of tension with the feel of his tongue swiping at her entrance. He slid two fingers on either side of her clit, massaging her. Dear god, he was amazing.

The two fingers speared her sex and curved to rub her upper walls and G-spot. Her knees shook. She sucked air hard and moaned. He flicked his tongue into a quick motion that made her promise him the world. A sharp, husky gasp later and her whole world exploded.

She half lifted off the bed and slammed back down, hitting the mattress hard. Electric currents racked her body. Wave after wave of pleasure filled each of her brain cells. It took a while before she stopped shaking.

A lone thought filled her mind: pleasing him. She lifted to her knees and grasped his cock. She could do this. This was her man. Her love. She wanted to make him as crazy as he did her.

"No, baby. As much as I'd love that, it can wait," he groaned.

She ignored him and moved into a position where her shoulder brushed his thigh and lowered her head to lick the beads of moisture dripping from his slit. She sucked his cock into her mouth, twirling her tongue a full circle over the head. She was new at this but she wanted to make it good for him. Fuck good, she wanted it to be incredible.

After a few slow sucks, she pumped his shaft in her hand.

The combination of saliva and precum allowed for easy gliding between her fingers. He was so smooth. So hot.

"That . . . feels . . . amazing."

She grinned and sucked him into her mouth fully, relaxing the back of her throat to allow him a deeper slide, until she couldn't take him any farther.

"Fuck!"

She whimpered with his cock in her mouth. She increased the pressure on her grip and hollowed her cheeks to massage him better.

Soaring heat lanced at her pussy. Her arousal turned into desperation. Her bobbing increased in speed. Faster and faster until his cock was hot steel in her mouth. She groaned and slid him out of her mouth.

"Hamel," she whispered breathlessly. "Please . . . make me come!"

"Oh, I will make you come, baby. I'll fuck you raw, but first, let's make you my mate." His voice was so deep and rough she shivered. "Get on your knees and lean forward on the bed."

She didn't know she had it in her to move so fast. All talk of orgasms would get him anything. She flipped over to her stomach, lifted her ass high in the air and waited.

The broad head of his dick was slipped past her entrance and filled her. Her nerves stretched so taut she swore something inside her was going to snap at any moment. He propelled back and slammed back in with a groan. She whimpered and gripped the sheets in her fists. Holy shit! Now this, this was paradise.

"God, yes!"

Heat spread through her pussy, traveled up her body, and licked at her veins. The continuous skin-slapping drove up the bar on her pleasure.

He dropped on all fours, caging her with his body. Passion thickened between them like a warm blanket of need. With each powerful thrust her body slipped closer to the edge of the cliff she knew so well, the one that would bring her limitless pleasure. She was close. So damn close.

His breaths puffed by her ear. Each one a soft growl that made her bones melt. Her nipples grazed the bedding with each slide of his body into hers.

"Melinda," he growled by her neck, "you're mine, sweet-heart." He twisted his hips and his cock slammed into differ-ent pleasure cells. "Only mine."

"Hamel . . ."

"No, baby. I'm never letting you go."

Her orgasm took her by surprise. The knot inside her snapped. She gasped, and energy bloomed and washed through her. He struck, biting deeply into her shoulder. The sharp pain intensified her pleasure. She screamed. Another snap and she was riding the wave again. A breath later he was jerking into her, filling her with his cum, his claws digging into her hips and leaving deep scratches where he held her tightly to him.

Her lungs constricted. Hell, her entire body shook as mini aftershocks took hold. He kissed and licked at her bite wound. Each swipe of his tongue felt like a new bond between them. A new link she never thought she'd have with another person.

"Oh my god."

He dropped beside her on the bed, pulled her into his sweaty embrace.

"Are you okay?"

"Yes," she mumbled.

"Mel, I need you to listen to me for a second. I know this is all new to you and you might have doubts about where we are going."

She frowned. She did have doubts. Hell, who didn't? But unlike her past relationships, she was willing to give this man a chance. He'd gone to hell for her and she was okay with seeing how things went. "It is going to be a bit difficult for the scientist in me to see things I have sworn my entire life are not real, but you know what? It's okay. I can live with it."

"Are you sure?" he asked, his voice a low, gruff tone.

She slid up his body, brought her face close to his, and gave him a kiss.

"Yes. I'm sure. Things might be weird and we will surely have differences of opinion, but the point is that this isn't just any other relationship. I believe in us. I know it sounds strange, but I do. Something inside me is pushing me to trust us. I won't fight it."

He sighed and hugged her hard. "Thank god! I couldn't image trying to figure out how to live in two different places."

She chuckled. "We'll adjust. Because we love each other, we'll make it work."

"I'll do anything for you. Anything."

He loved her. She knew he did, but hearing him say that just calmed the tiny worry in her mind. No other words were needed. The feelings bombarded her heart, coming through their mate link. It would take time to understand this, but knowing Hamel loved her as much as she'd come to love him made any issue seem insignificant. Everything was going to be fine.

"I love you, my Mel. My beautiful mate."

"I love you, my sexy transformer."

MATING
NEEDS

CHAPTER 1

"Do you know who I am?" Amerella Capone stomped her foot on the floor of the First National Bank of Las Vegas. Several people standing in line for a teller looked at her. A few pointed and laughed. She lifted her chin and ignored them.

The bank attendant's face paled. She was not waiting any longer to get into her safe deposit box. "I am the great-great-grandniece of Alphonse Capone. You know? Al Capone." Even though Al hadn't taken much interest in Vegas, some of the Capone family did, moving down when other Mob families began paying attention to the city.

"Y-yes, Ms. Capone. I'm s-sorry, Ms. Capone." The poor kid sweated bullets. He couldn't be a day over twenty. "I'm sure the senator will be done talking with the manager any second now, and he will let you into the vault. In fact, let me go check." The young man dashed away as quickly as he could without drawing attention to himself.

Amerella plopped onto a hard wooden chair in front of a desk next to the side door that led to the room with the safe deposit boxes. It was already six o'clock and she hadn't done any shopping yet. She hated that she had to go to the bank every time she dipped into her personal savings. Being a trust fund baby wasn't all it seemed to be. She had a chain tightly wrapped around her neck, controlled by her guardian, Uncle Giuseppe. Soon, when she turned twenty-six, she would come into her inheritance and do whatever she wanted.

Like buy an island on the equator and disappear.

The glass doors in the lobby swung open and several men wearing ski masks ran in. The first robber fired machine-gun ammo at the ceiling.

"All right. Everyone on the floor, now!"

On the floor? Was he shitting her? She was in a snug short skirt and high heels. She'd never get up if she got down. With full breasts, hips, and thighs, she had a lot to get back up. Luckily, being so far to the side of the tellers' central location, she was hard to see from the lobby. Maybe she could just scoot farther to the side.

She slowly rose from the chair and turned to quietly shuffle toward the door. Right behind her came a squeaky voice. "He said everyone on the floor, lady." A very familiar squeaky voice. She swiveled on the ball of her foot to face the robber behind her. The robber's eyes grew large. Hers narrowed.

"Joseph Albert Lanzia. I'm so telling your mother."

The slim young robber lowered his handgun. "No, you can't, Aunt Amerella. She'd be so mad at me."

"And so she should be." Amerella slapped her fists on her hips, careful not to mess up the mani/pedi she had before this. "What do you think you're doing, Joey, robbing a bank?" she whispered. "Do you know how much trouble you can get into?" Even though Joey wasn't her biological nephew, she'd spent so much of his childhood with him that he'd grown up calling her "Aunt."

Joey glanced over his shoulder then back to his aunt. "I know, Aunt Amerella. But I didn't have much choice."

"What do you mean?"

The leader screamed more commands and handed bags to the tellers behind the booth. Joey moved in front of her so she couldn't see what was going on. Or to keep the others from seeing her.

"I don't mean nothing, Aunt Amerella. Just stay hidden—" Joey was younger than the attendant who tried to calm her a few minutes ago. Oy vey. Kids these days. Ha, listen to her—

thinking like an old woman when she was practically a kid herself. She'd grown up fast in the last four years.

The main robber's voice rang in her head. She gasped. "No. Is that Cousin Tony?"

Joey's released a sigh and his narrow shoulders slumped. "You can't tell anyone. He'll kill you if he sees you."

She harrumphed. "I'll show him kill when I tell his father. Uncle Giuseppe is not going to like this. Not one bit, I tell you." Her uncle, Las Vegas's Mafia king, took everything his family did personally. It wasn't a good idea to piss off Uncle Giuseppe. And a simple thing like a bank robbery would shame him. Now, the three-million-dollar jewel heist last year by another cousin, that he was proud of.

Tony's loud voice echoed to their side of the lobby. "Little Dick, everything okay over there?"

Amerella's eyes widened. "He calls you Little Dick? How dare he insult you like that." She took a step toward Joey. He put his hand up.

"No, Aunt Amerella. You can't."

"Joey, he's being a big dick. I won't put up with big dicks."

The voice came over again. "Little Dick?"

"Yeah, Big Dick. I mean, Big Dog," he stammered.

Amerella rolled her eyes. "Big Dog? Seriously?" Joey shushed her from further replying.

Joey continued louder. "Everything's fine. Just keeping the crowd quiet over here."

Fine. She'd stand there until she could think of something to do. Amerella could not believe her only "nephew" had gone to the dark side. His momma had raised him right. She would know. Even though she was only six years older than he was, she'd partially raised the boy, babysitting for free while his momma worked two jobs on the Vegas Strip.

On the other side of the tellers' stations, the side door opened. Out walked a distinguished-looking man in a suit and tie followed by the bank manager. Surprise registered on both their faces.

"What is going on—?"

Two shots echoed and the man fell out of her sight. Shouts of "Senator" and "Call an ambulance" were almost drowned out by more automatic gunfire. Sirens finally sounded in the distance. The leader backed away, only a gun in his hand. Tony wasn't taking any money? What kind of idiot robbed a bank and didn't take the money? Joey moved to follow him.

"No, Joey," she called out. "Stay with me."

Her pseudo-nephew turned to her. His eyes, the only part of his face showing, reflected a torn soul: a kid trying to fit in and be accepted versus doing the right thing. He glanced back at Cousin Tony watching him. She read Tony's look. His instant recognition of her was obvious. As was the emanating hate. His eyes glowed red, then he pointed his gun at her and fired.

Her shock at his garish action stunned her, keeping her brain from reacting. Then Joey spun his body between her and the shooter. He jerked twice. Once from firing a bullet and a second from being hit in the chest.

Then Joey was gone from her sight, and her vision locked on a bloody splotch on the glass entrance door. Cradling one arm against his chest, Cousin Tony dragged himself through the door.

Amerella's eyes drifted down to the body crumpled at her feet. Blood flowed onto the shiny white tile floor. Barely registering her actions, she fell to her knees and ripped the mask off Joey's face. His face was beyond pale.

"Oh my god, Joey." She scooped his head into her lap. "Hang on, baby. I got you." She smoothed back hair from his face. "Aunt Amerella won't let you go."

The boy's eyes rolled to her wet gaze on him. "I want . . . right thing . . ." he breathed out. She shushed him, telling him to save his energy, tears falling on his baby face. But he went on. "Promise me . . . you . . . stop him."

She pulled him closer, rocking him. "I swear to you, Joey. I will do everything in my power to make sure he gets what he deserves."

"He's . . . demo . . ." Joey breathed out. No breath raised his chest. Demo what? Democrat? No, she couldn't see that.

Amerella didn't know how long she sat holding her beloved friend's son in her arms. At some point, paramedics pried the boy from her. Through the glass door, she glimpsed

Cousin Tony placed on an ambulance gurney. The emotional turmoil spinning through her rocketed her out the door.

She slipped off one high-heel shoe and chased after the rolling bed, her body bobbing up and down depending which foot she was on.

"You goddamned, motherfucking, piece-of-shit, shit-headed, gangrene-infested, coke-whore bastard!" She reached around the dumbfounded paramedic pushing the gurney and repeatedly beat Cousin Tony upside the head with her shoe.

But that still wasn't enough for her. No. Joey was gone because of him, and she wouldn't be happy until the same was done to him.

Tony shielded himself the best he could with his arm in a sling. "Somebody get this crazy bitch away from me!"

The EMT grabbed at her flinging arm, but she slapped him with her purse hooked over her arm. "Don't even think it, buddy. He's my family and I can beat him to death if I want to." Onlookers gathering on the other side of the parked police cars laughed and pointed at her. She didn't care. Over the past three, almost four years now, she lived for two purposes: to show how much she loved her son and how much she hated her family.

With renewed vigor, she swung at the bastard strapped to the gurney, but someone stopped her arm. "Ms. Capone, please." An older, rougher voice came from over her head. She looked up and back to see who the hell stopped her rampage.

His face was familiar. He needed a shave, though. The beard seemed to be the rage lately for men. Her opinion of men with hairy faces was they shouldn't mind women with hairy legs. She was all in favor of the sexy five-o'clock shadow, but the scraggly pubic-looking hair on the chin she could do without.

He snatched the shoe from her hand and dropped it next to her foot.

"Hey, these shoes cost six hundred dollars. Don't scuff them."

"Then keep them on your feet, Ms. Capone," he said.

She frowned and slipped her foot into the shoe, now standing at the same height on both legs. The paramedics quickly took away their patient while she was distracted. She turned and yelled toward the ambulance, "I hope they get stuck in traffic and you die, bastard." Cousin Tony flipped her off. She returned two birds to him.

"Can't do that, can you, crip asshole," she hollered.

The man beside her sighed. "Ms. Capone, please."

Irritated, she pivoted. "Who the hell are you, and why are you bothering me?"

That drew an unhappy face from him. "I'm Detective Freeman with the Las Vegas PD."

"Oh," she said. "Sorry."

"Ms. Capone," he asked, "were you witness to the bank robbery and shootings inside?"

"Front and center," she said. "Well, more like back and side, but I did see it all. Well, most of it. I know it was Tony who shot the senator."

"Tony shot Senator Sherman?"

"Good god, Detective. He's the only senator I know. The man came out a side door in the bank and Tony shot him. Then the dipshit started backing out—"

"Which dipshit?" he asked.

"My cousin Tony. That dipshit was going to leave without any money."

"Was your cousin there to rob a bank or shoot the senator?" he asked.

That was a very good question. One she didn't care about at the moment as the bank door opened and another gurney, this one carrying a black zipped body bag, rolled out. After all the years in a Mafia family, black body bags seemed almost a cliché. What other family kept a stock of them in the closet at home?

A hand touched her shoulder. "Ms. Capone?"

She turned to the detective. "Yes."

"Are you willing to testify as an eyewitness?" Detective Freeman asked. She noted a smile in his eyes. Taking down the son of the local Mafia boss would be a dream of any law enforcement official. This was his chance.

Amerella looked around at the growing crowd, roaming officers in dark blue uniforms, and what looked to be reporters trying to get past the uniforms. Would she testify against her family? She thought back to a few years ago, right when she was about to graduate college, and remembered what her uncle made her do. Her decision was made.

"In a heartbeat."

CHAPTER 2

It was dark when Amerella parked her Lexus in the round drive out front of the house. She climbed the wide steps to the ornate glass door, exhausted and ready to go to bed. Hopefully Maria had something to eat waiting. She could so go for a veggie burger and a huge cranberry-and-apple salad sprinkled with sugared pecans. Her stomach growled. Then chocolate pudding for a chaser. Yum.

The door opened to a worried Maria. Her hands were waving through the air, punctuating words flying from her mouth. Amerella had no clue what they meant. Amerella walked in and closed the door behind her.

"You think your day was rough," she said to Maria. "Just wait 'til you hear mine. OH MY FREAKIN' GOD. I was almost killed, Maria." She laid the back of her hand on her forehead. "Shot down in the prime of my life. Can you imagine?" Amerella leaned against her companion. "Help me to the kitchen, Maria. I feel weak."

Maria wrapped an arm around her shoulders. "You poor bebé. Maria is here now. She take good care of Ms. Amie and all her drama." They shuffled to the kitchen, where Maria deposited her into a chair at the small round table. "I have a veggie burger and salad ready for you, Ms. Amie. Are you hungry?"

She sighed. "I don't know if I can eat with all the distress I'm in, but I'll try." Maria set a plate and bowl filled with food in front of her.

"That's a good girl. You must keep up your strength for the young one."

Amerella's spirits instantly rose. There was only thing that made her happy these past three, almost four years, and she thanked god every day for her son. The sound of small feet thumping on tile grew louder.

"Mommy, you're home, finawy." Her young man stood with tiny fists on his hips in the doorway from the hall. "Where have you been, young wady?" With her feigned-surprise look, he giggled and ran to her. She opened her arms and he wrapped himself around her. She lifted him into her lap and inhaled his sweet scent.

"I missed you, French fry."

He rolled his eyes. "I been right here with Mawia for hours, Mommy." She laughed at his over dramatics he'd picked up from her. He was so smart. Like his father. Just as handsome, too. Maria set a Thomas the Tank Engine plastic plate with cut-up pieces of rare steak in front of him. He gobbled them up like they were cookies, which he never touched. She hadn't figured out his strange diet, but his dad only ate meat, too. Like father like son in more ways than one, apparently.

Amerella reached out and slid her iPad closer and pushed the button at the bottom to bring the screen alive. After entering the passcode, her son's birth date and year, the homepage popped up with the latest news. Across the top flashed *Senator Killed in Bank Robbery*. That didn't take long to get out.

She skimmed the article to get the highlights, mainly to see if she or Joey were mentioned. The reporter noted only the facts and the recent bill the senator was trying to push through that would revitalize parts of Vegas by tearing down the old and putting up new attractions and buildings.

She knew more about that bill than she cared to. At the last several Monday night dinners, when all the cousins and family in the area were required to eat at Uncle Giuseppe's, the main point of conversation had been about how the senator wanted to knock down the old Mafia gambling holdings but didn't want to bring them in on the new stuff. Effectively shutting off the Mob's source of income.

A shiver crawled down her back. She refused to acknowledge what her brain wanted to piece together. If she thought too much about it, she'd hide away in deep depression like she did four years ago. And this time she might not come out of it. No, that wasn't true. She had a son to protect. And she would with her very life.

With her finger, she tapped the back button and saw Capone in a smaller headline. Her heart hiccupped. Seemed one of the reporters outside the bank heard her and Detective Freeman's conversation. The headline read *Capone Niece to Testify Against Mob Family*. Fuck. This scared the shit out of her. What if her uncle read it?

"Mommy," her son said.

"Yes, love."

"Bobby's daddy picked him up from daycare today."

"Did you meet his daddy?" she asked.

"Yeah, he's nice, I guess . . ." She heard a question in his voice and despaired at what was coming. "Mommy, why don't I have a daddy wike everyone else?"

Her heart squeezed. Maria glanced at her with sad eyes, excused herself, and left the room. The subject of his father has been skirted for a while, but now with his exposure to the world as he grew, she knew the questions would come. But today really wasn't the best day. She'd rehearsed the line she would say to him.

"You do have a daddy like everyone else," she said.

His small body rotated in her lap. "Why isn't he here, then?"

Amerella looked him square in the eye. "He's lost." Good god, that sounded pathetically lame out loud. Fortunately a three-year-old didn't understand lies.

"Wost?" he said. "Where is he?"

She rolled her eyes and harrumphed. "If I knew where he was, he wouldn't be lost, would he, silly?" She tickled his tummy and he burst into laughs, wiggling in her lap. Maria stood in the kitchen entrance.

"Time for your bath, young man, then to bed," the woman said.

"Awww, Mawia," Amerella's son whined. "Mommy just got home." Amerella slid him off her lap and patted his bottom.

"You know Maria is the boss around here. I'll come up and tuck you into bed. I love you."

"Okay, Mommy." He trotted to the woman Amerella never would've made it without and grabbed her fingers. "Can we have bubbles tonight, Mawia?" His sweet voice faded as they headed down the hall. She hoped Maria saw the thankfulness in her eyes for the distraction from talking about the boy's father.

She couldn't handle the emotions the conversation would bring. Not enough time had passed to take the raw edge off the event. Maybe in fifty years, but certainly not four. She fought the tears burning in her eyes.

Amerella gathered the dishes from her dinner and carried them to the sink. She stared out the window into the lot's manicured backyard. Like all the other rich people in her 'hood, she had the new-fangled playsets for her child, the perfect flower garden for fresh floral displays year round, and a lush, green, fertilized lawn in a place that averaged fewer than five inches of rain each year.

This life was expected of her. This was what she had to do to keep her son safe. But with the Internet article she just read, she worried how secure it was anymore. She walked up the balustrade stairs to her son's room, where Maria was drying off the child from his bath. He tore from her and ran across the room as naked as the day he was born. This was their nightly game.

"Can't catch me tonight, Mommy. I'm getting faster." And he was. His speed for a child his age, even for an adult, was more to the superhuman side of things. That was only the tip of the spookiness going on.

Amerella pulled out a pair of Captain America skivvies from the dresser and tossed them on the bed. A whine started in her son's throat.

"No complaining," she said. "Our agreement was you didn't have to wear pj's to bed, but undies are a must."

He huffed and sighed. "Fine, Mommy." He snatched the underwear off the Marvel Comics comforter and slid them on. "But when I get older, I don't want to wear anything to bed."

Curiosity won her over tonight. "Tell me why you don't like wearing clothes, French fry."

His eyes glanced at Maria then her. She looked over her shoulder to see the woman standing with the towel in her hands. She turned back to her son. Behind her, Maria went into the bathroom to leave them alone.

Amerella brushed wet hair from his cheeks. "Is it because of the . . ." She never knew how to address the problem. "The changing issue?"

He nodded, tears forming in his eyes. His lower lip trembled. She leaned forward and kissed his forehead. "It's okay, baby. I'm sure you'll grow out of it. Everybody has something different about their body."

"But, Mommy. None of my friends can make cat claws come from their fingers or hear and smell things wike I do."

Amerella sat up quickly. "You're not showing your friends your fingers, are you?"

He shook his head, a wet drop rolling over his cheek. "I don't want to scare them."

She wiped the tear. "That's a good boy. We don't want anyone to know. Especially Uncle Giuseppe or Cousin Tony, right?" He nodded again.

Her heart ached for the pain she knew he felt at being different and hiding his true self. She understood what it took to hide who you really were. She'd been doing that for four years now.

"How would you like to stay with Grandpa and Nana Running Wind for a while?" she asked.

His eyes lit up. "Can I? Please, Mommy, please. I'll be good, wike I always am."

She laughed at his use of persuasion. But he was always a good child. When Amerella met the Native American couple on a field trip for her sociology course in college, she never thought they would play such a big role in her and her son's lives. And even though the Running Winds weren't biologically his grandparents, they loved the child and gave him something she couldn't: belief in the unbelievable.

The Mojave people, like many Native Americans, had a religion steeped in nature and the supernatural. She just couldn't accept aliens, gods, and animals that changed into people as part of her world. Like everyone else, she liked things backed by science and facts.

"I'll give them a call and see if they can get you tomorrow morning. How does that sound?"

"That would be great, Mommy." Her Francis sat up and hugged her. "You're the greatest." That was new. She hadn't heard him say that before. He must've picked it up at daycare.

"You know I love you, right?" she said.

"I wuv you, too." He snuggled in his covers. She tucked the blankets around him.

"Now go to sleep and the morning will be here before you know it, okay?"

He closed his eyes. "Okay. Goodnight."

"Goodnight, French fry." She flipped the light off and pulled the door to. Downstairs, searching in her purse, she dug out her phone, which was leaning against the business card Detective Freeman had given her and Joey's face mask and gun from the crime scene. He died for her and she would do whatever she could to protect his name in death. Just like she would protect her own son.

CHAPTER 3

F rank Dubois breathed in the cool early morning air. He
loved jogging this time of day. Everything was fresh, quiet.
The world was just waking up. And being in his hometown
for the first time in years made it that much more special.

Coming around the corner into town, his feline's extra-
sensitive nose caught a whiff of juicy red meat, raw. He hadn't
had breakfast yet and his cat decided now was time to eat.
François noted how his cat had been getting rather bossy
these past several months. He hoped a trip home would chill
the pussy out. It'd only been eight hours since his flight got
in, so maybe it'd take a bit.

Whatever, his cat said. It didn't matter where in creation
they stayed. They weren't with their mate. It'd been long
enough, almost four years, and it was time to get his ass in
gear and find her.

He asked, Where would you like to start looking on a
globe that has a total surface area of about 197 million square
miles? His cat was quiet to that. Yeah, that's what he thought.

Ahead, François saw their alpha, Butch, the town butcher,
unloading a truck full of chilled meat. He thought he'd lend
a hand, or a paw. Butch glanced up when he approached.

"Franky. How ya doing, boy?" The big lion held out a thick hand to shake his. "I heard your mom say you were visiting for a while. Good to see you."

"Yeah, great to see you, too, Alpha." François never thought about it until now, but if Butch was a nickname because of his profession, he had no idea what Butch's real name was. It's funny how those kinds of things occur when visiting home after being gone a long time. Things that seemed so normal and everyday when young looked different with older, wiser eyes.

Butch scowled at him. "François, you know we don't go by titles here. Everyone is free to do as they wish as long as they don't hurt others. I don't like telling shifters what they have to do."

François nodded. "I know, Butch. Just showing you my respect for how you help everyone and make sure the town is safe." Specifically, keeping watch over his single mother. François worried about her all the time. Hopefully one day, she'd remarry. He lifted a heavy chunk of meat. "Anyway. It's good to be back. Besides being a bit older, everything looks the same here." He followed the butcher into the back of the store.

"Yeah, the outside changes slower than the inside it seems nowadays," Butch replied.

"What do you mean by that?" François laid his package on the shelf next to a rack of ribs. Those looked really good, too, his cat mentioned.

Heading back out, the lion shifter took a rag from his back pocket and wiped his forehead. "Oh, you know," he said, leaning against the meat truck, "time moves on. People get old and out of touch with the world. The young ones get out of town as soon as they can and have families hundreds of miles away."

Butch yanked on a box of sausages from the back of the truck. "When I was young, the few shifter towns like ours were the only places we could peacefully live. But that doesn't seem to be the case anymore. The town is dying, falling apart at the seams."

François looked at the buildings lining the main street.

Really looked. The structures were built almost a hundred years ago, and time had taken its toll. Bricks crumbled, paint peeled, wood deteriorated. The post office resembled something out of an old Western movie. The abandoned buildings looked like fire hazards ready to happen.

"The place does look a bit rough," François said.

"Yeah, but it's more than that. If I didn't have the store, I wouldn't have a clue what was going on with anyone. Our last town social was thirty years ago. Shifters come and go, some causing problem before they do go. We're down to two restaurants, one hair place for the ladies, and one clothing store for everyone."

"Seems like the town needs some life. Someone to create events and restoration projects, bring people together."

Butch closed up the truck and the back of the store, then headed for the front. "If you find someone who can do all that, bring him in. We can't pay him a dime, but we'd appreciate his time."

François laughed. "I'll keep my eyes open for someone like that."

Butch slapped him on the back and handed him a pack of ribs. "Give these to your mother. I saw her eyein' them pretty heavy the other day. I know she'll love 'em." He unlocked the front door for François. "Great seeing you again, kid. Glad you found time to come back and see your ma."

François waved bye and continued his jog toward his mom's house with the package in hand. Now he noticed the downturn in the town's details that his eyes had glazed over before. But wasn't that what happened to every town? It expanded in all directions, leaving the original, older areas behind to decay while other new spaces become the "it" places to be? Then eventually, investors come in, buy up the old, cheap stuff, and make it new again?

Maybe some things were meant to dry up and disappear alongside the dust in the wind. He really liked his hometown, though. After living in Washington, DC, for years, being in rural areas was a godsend. Who would have thought California had such forested mountain areas? Nowhere in DC could his cat roam wild and free. He had to hike the mountains west in Virginia for any privacy. Here, he could walk naked out his back door and be in the forest. His parents knew what they were doing when they settled here.

After hurdling the decorative fence, François ran through his mom's yard to the back porch and up the stairs to the kitchen door. Aromas of cooking meat riled his thankful, hungry cat.

Inside, he handed the ribs to his mother, who stood over the stove flipping bacon.

"Where did these come from?"

"Butch said to give them to you. I saw him unloading while I was out."

His mom's cheeks turned red. What was that about?

"I'll have to thank him the next time I'm down there." She turned the stove off and forked several pieces of bacon onto a paper towel–covered plate. "You ready to eat now?"

"You bet. The cat hasn't thought about anything else since we came around the corner to the meat market." His mom placed plates filled with ham, sausage, bacon, and steak on the table. Heaven. If he ate like this every morning, he'd get back from vacation ten pounds heavier.

Mom sat across the table from him. "So, what all did you and Butch talk about?"

He gave a single shoulder shrug. "Nothing, really. Just about the town getting older and people leaving. I hadn't noticed how downhill the buildings in town had gone."

His mom nodded. "I have to agree. People are definitely moving away. You left the first chance you got."

"I went to school then got a job, Mom. You make it sound like I abandoned the place." In all honesty, he did want to leave. But everyone knew there were no opportunities in the dying town.

"You seem pretty set now, living in DC and all. When you going to find a nice cougar or human and settle down? I'm not getting younger and I expect cubs, like, last year."

He smelled the humor in her words. Thank god. This conversation would get awkward quickly. His thoughts rarely veered toward the opposite sex. His cougar on the other hand . . .

"I'm not ready to find somebody yet," he said.

"What about that girl from college? You really liked her."

François tried to control his intense emotions that always erupted when thinking about that time.

"Oh, I'm sorry, François," Mom said. "I didn't mean to bring up painful memories."

"It's okay. And I can say the same for you, Mom. It's been years since Dad died. Why haven't you hooked up with anyone?"

His mom laughed. "I see I taught you well. The art of changing the subject flows rather smoothly from you."

He smiled. "I did learn from the best. But seriously, maybe you should get into the new century and leave the 1950s behind. The avocado-and-harvest-gold-colored appliances are really outdated."

She sighed. "I know. It's just such a daunting task and I don't even know how to start." Mom pushed ham around her plate. "Maybe one day."

"Would you please pass the sausage?" Mom handed over the plate and François borrowed his cat's claw and speared a link.

She rolled her eyes. "I see your table manners are out the window."

He bit into the sausage and chewed with a smile. "Nah. I just like tormenting you. It's been years." Plus, he didn't like when she got down about her life without Dad.

"Speaking of years, how's the job going? Fourth year soon, right? Are you glad you volunteered right out of college instead of waiting like your father?"

His father, and grandfather before him, spent time working with the U.S. government. Shifters had kept their general anonymity for hundreds of years until one of the military officials decided to tap into the abilities shifters had that humans didn't.

An agreement was written between the two groups that said the government would deny shifters' existence and do everything in their power to keep the species unknown to the public. In exchange, shifters would keep a group of men available on a moment's notice to do whatever they were called to do by the government.

The men were specially trained in espionage, hand-to-hand

combat, martial arts, and supernatural intelligence humans couldn't know. They were the shifter equivalent to the Navy SEALs and Special Ops.

The group was called the Alpha League Federal Agency: ALFA.

Unlike him, his father mated his mother and started a family before volunteering for the agency. The job was well paid and usually not overly dangerous. Most of the time, they were bodyguards for someone the government deemed important.

But not too long ago, fellow agent Parish Hamel was dragged into the demon world to save his mate he was protecting. The stories Hamel relayed were beyond incredible. He truly hoped he'd never have to deal with things like that. He wasn't sure how he would react if a demon kidnapped his mate to take for his own. Hamel was a great agent and friend.

"Yeah," he started, "I'm glad I hired in after graduating. It was the right thing for me at the time."

"At the time?" His mom's brow raised. "Are you saying the time isn't right anymore?"

"No, I'm not saying that exactly. I just need a break. That's why I'm on vacation for a week." Not to mention the fifteenth anniversary of his father's death was in a few days. He wanted to be with his mom during that time. Make sure she was okay.

His cell phone rang in the back pocket of his running pants. He pulled it out and read the ID on the screen. "Come on. No way." He tapped the green icon and immediately put the phone to his ear. "I'm on vacation, remember?"

"Yeah. But you know with Hamel on his honeymoon, we're a man short. I need you," his boss, Director Josh Tumbel, said.

François rubbed the bridge of his nose. This really was a bad week for his vacation, but he'd had it planned for a while. Hamel finding his mate was a surprise, and he couldn't deny the man getting married.

"Besides," his boss continued, "this is an easy gig. You're babysitting a Mafia prima donna who the police want to keep alive. They're worried she has a hit out on her, even though her uncle is the Mafia boss."

"Huh," François said, "that's a fucked-up family." Realizing who else was in the room, his eyes widened. "Sorry, Mom." She gathered empty dishes and carried them to the sink. "All right, Director, send the details and I'll get on it. When do I leave?"

"Tomorrow morning."

CHAPTER 4

François stretched his legs as he sauntered along the side-walk of the Las Vegas Strip. He hated cramped plane seats. When he sat, his knees dug into the back of the seat in front of him. Usually the exit row was larger and he chose those seats, but being that he booked last minute, those spots were already taken.

He had some time to kill before his meeting with Detective Freeman, so he thought he'd take advantage of the liberty to roam.

Not much had changed since his college years. In his second semester freshman year, a group of new friends from his campus dormitory just outside of Las Vegas wanted to "have a little fun." He joined in, figuring it would be interesting with the dolts he roomed with.

In town, he met another college freshman, Amie Truman. His beautiful, vibrant, sexy mate.

The second he saw her across Caesars arboretum, he knew he'd found his other half. It was total luck. She lived off campus at the time, driving in for classes. He might have never met her. The next three years were the happiest— Stop. He didn't want to go any further with those memories. He needed to move on. His mom was right. Almost four years had passed. Time to grow up.

A light breeze blew into his face as he stared down the street. He noted a black Hummer sitting at the stoplight. He thought about buying one of those, but could hardly justify the cost given DC's nicely paved streets and living alone.

His cat poked him. There was a delicious smell floating in the air. He sucked in a deep breath. Damn, it was good. And familiar.

He hurried along the concrete walkway, searching for the source. A shopping mall was ahead. Prada, Gucci, and other very high-end store logos graced the sign out front. Behind him, a large vehicle rumbled up the street. The black Hummer passed him, then in front of the Prada entrance, it jumped the curb and skidded to a stop on the sidewalk.

Automatic gunshots rattled over the area, shattering one of the glass doors. People screamed and ran in every direction. The Hummer's backseat window slid down and the end of a grenade launcher poked out, aimed toward a bench to the side of the mall entrance.

Assault training and shifter instincts kicked in, and François was at the truck in a heartbeat. He grabbed the launcher, snatched it partially out the window, then rammed it back in to smash the shooter's face. Hopefully dishing out a broken nose. The truck tore away, leaving him with the RPG launcher in his hands.

François surveyed the area, looking for the most damage and greatest number of injuries. Sirens sounded in the distance. And that wonderful smell. He followed his nose to the bench and concrete planter the RPG had been aimed at.

Behind the seat, a woman was curled into a ball on the ground. He stared at her ass. Damn, if that wasn't the most perfect ass he'd ever seen. He could see she was curvy and not scrawny like most women in this place of sex and sin.

He caught her scent. It was . . . his mate?

He stood frozen as the woman unwound herself and peeked through the bench slats. Her hands shook. He wanted to hold them in his and assure her everything was okay now. But his body wasn't receiving the message, or was playing stupid, because his cat told him he hadn't moved toward their mate yet.

More noise and confusion erupted behind him, but he couldn't worry about that. He had a mate to help. She turned and met his gaze. Her fear and shock floated in the air. Eyes widening, her jaw dropped open. Then her look moved to focus behind him, then at the grenade launcher still in his hand. Shit. He'd forgotten he had it.

Next thing he knew, he was facedown on the concrete, surrounded by a dozen cops pointing guns at him. His mate took the opportunity to scream and run. Shit. This was not good.

ALFA rules said that when in a situation where being arrested by local police, the agent would follow commands and allow himself to be taken into custody. When the agent reached a more secure location, the agent would contact the DC office. In no case should the agent reveal his true identity or shift. So guess where he was going.

He complied with officer demands and was cuffed and shoved into a police cruiser. Well, now he wouldn't have to pay for a taxi to take him to the station for his meeting with Freeman. That was the only good thing in the past several hours.

Sometimes he loved fate. It led him to her years ago.

Sometimes he hated fate. It led him to her once again. And she ran. Again.

Fuck. Trying to keep his cat focused on their job would be nearly impossible now. The animal inside agreed. They needed to find their other half and convince her to mate. No, that wasn't happening. They had a job to do. Screw the job. Nothing is more important than mate.

He almost agreed to that. Almost.

"Officer, would you please call ahead and tell Detective Freeman I'll be early for our meeting?" The cop eyed him with a frown. A few minutes later, he picked up the radio's mic, hopefully passing along the info.

The police car pulled into the station parking lot and, with little consideration, François was hauled inside the building. The place was busy for morning hours, but in a city that didn't sleep, neither did the police.

A partially bald guy with deep lines etched around his eyes leaned against the wall. His sport jacket looked as worn as he did.

"Thanks, Marshall," he said, pulling keys from his pants'

pocket. "I got him from here." The man removed the cuffs and held out a hand to François. "I'm Max Freeman."

François accepted his hand. "Nice to meet you. François Dubois." The man opened a door next to him and motioned for François to precede him. The cougar shifter wasn't keen on having a potential threat at his back. And that's why the detective made him go first. This was a test for the detective to see his reaction: team player or rabble-rouser.

"Second door on right."

He kept his cool and chose team player. No reason to cause problems. Yet.

"Seems you got caught up in some gang action at the mall," Freeman said.

"Got caught up in something," François said. "But didn't feel like gang. How many around here carry RPGs?"

The detective's brow raised. "Really? At a shopping mall?"

"Yeah, a bit overkill, I'd think." But what did he know about the Las Vegas underground? Zilch. He entered the second office on the right. He'd heard once that the longer a person lived in one place, the more they accumulate and nest. Freeman was well nested with stacks of folders on every flat surface, photos taped to the walls, and an empty pizza box sitting on top of the black mesh trashcan.

"How'd you end up with the launcher?" Freeman asked.

"I took it from the person in the backseat of a black Hummer, after smashing his face for my warm welcome to your city."

Freeman laughed. "At least you're alive still." He pulled a file from several sitting on the side of his desk. "Did you by chance catch the number on the tags?"

"I did," François said. "They had a paper plate like those on new cars, which I'm sure was faked."

Freeman sighed. The tired office chair creaked when he leaned back and laid his twined fingers on his hairless crown. "Goddamn Mafia boys."

"Yeah, about that," François replied. "I thought the Mafia was history in Vegas. How strong are they now?"

"Not very," Freeman replied. "Their influence has been cut way back, but they are still here. Most have corporations to hide their names and illegal activities. Giuseppe Ragusa is the power right now."

"Why would the Mafia want to blow up the front of Prada?"

"Who knows what the fuck they want," Freeman said. "If I had a clue, I would've busted Ragusa's ass long ago and retired when I was young enough to enjoy it." He rocked his chair forward to put his arms on the crowded desk. "All of which brings us to you."

"Ah." The first puzzle piece locked into place for him. "The Mob boss's niece you want to keep alive."

"You got it. I don't know if you know much about the Mafia in Las Vegas, but they've been here since the beginning. They owned several of the first casinos and gambling hangouts. As I mentioned, the current head of the family is Giuseppe Ragusa, and he's a real son of a bitch.

"But his son, Tony, apparently didn't get the shitload of brains his father has. Robbed a bank yesterday, killing a senator and a kid in the process—and didn't even take the money bags when trying to leave. Someone shot Tony on his way through the door, so he was an easy catch. But who wielded the gun and where that gun has gone is a mystery. We're getting bank surveillance footage shortly.

"Anyway, Ragusa's niece was inside the bank and agreed to testify. But I'm hoping she's the foot in the door we need to get in and bring down Ragusa. She's important, Dubois." A hidden phone rang. Freeman reached into his jacket's pocket and pulled out a beat-up cell phone. He glanced at the ID on the screen. "Hmm. This could be interesting."

He answered, and a high-pitched voice that sounded scared shitless floated to François. Whatever it was didn't concern him. His attention turned to the surroundings. The cat inside paced, was agitated. It needed to chill out. Maybe later they would search for their mate and find out why she left him four years ago without even a good-bye.

Freeman launched from his chair. "Come on. Got someone you need to meet."

CHAPTER 5

＜

Amerella crouched in the corner of the far stall in the women's fitting rooms inside Prada. Her mind was in such a spin she didn't know whether to be scared by the attempted hit on her or the fact that her past boyfriend, her only love, saw her. Each held consequences not in her favor.

How could fate be so cruel? Meeting Frank on the Vegas Strip while in college, realizing they were both attending the same university, giving way to three years of the happiest times of her life, then never seeing again until now.

Her heart ached like it had four years ago when she left him. But she had no choice. Still had no choice. Not if she wanted to keep her son alive. Tears from her helplessness at the situation stung. If only she could find a way to keep everyone alive.

Speaking of staying alive, if not for her keys, she'd be dead. When she dropped them in her purse, they caught on the edge and fell onto the concrete. As she bent to scoop them up, gunfire rang out and a bullet hit the palm tree where her head would've been if not bent over. She'd dived behind a bench, which provided only mediocre coverage.

Then Frank appeared, holding a grenade launcher. She

thought about that image. There would be no reason for her Frank to have such a weapon on the Strip. Her mind had been under such stress and fear, maybe her eyes pretended to see the only person she ever felt safe with. Yeah, that was it. Her mind fricking playing tricks on her. She'd never been so scared in her damn pathetic life.

Her heart started to slow and her breathing became deeper and longer. She swore she was going to hyperventilate. Oh my god, she would've been so dead. Who would've taken care of her son? Her heart froze, thinking of Uncle Giuseppe getting his hands on her son. She couldn't let that happen. She wished the police would put him in prison.

Wait. She opened her purse and pulled out the business card Detective Freeman gave her yesterday. After the third try to dial with her shaking hands, she heard his voice.

"Detective Freeman, I was shot at. Uncle Giuseppe's men are trying to kill me. Oh my god. What do I do?" He calmed her and asked where she was. She told him and he said he'd be right over. Her courage to leave the stall was non-existent. Anyone out there looking like a normal shopper could be an assassin.

After several minutes, a knock sounded on the fitting room door. She startled but remained quiet.

"Amerella, it's Detective Freeman. Are you in there?"

His voice was familiar, so it was probably him. She had to be fast to be sneaky. With one hand, she opened the door several inches, and with the other, she grabbed his arm and jerked him inside. Quickly, she closed and locked the door. Her body slumped against the wall. He placed a hand on her shoulder.

"Amerella, are you okay?"

Tears she would not cry burned her eyes, but she would not cry. Here in the small room, she didn't have to be "on." She could be herself.

"I'm better, but scared to go outside. What if they are waiting for me out there?"

Freeman shook his head. "First, tell me: Are you sure this is your family, not just coincidence?"

She snorted. "What do you think? Nobody testifies against

the Mafia and lives. Oh my god, I'm going to die." She whipped around and pressed him against the wall with her hands. "Swear to me that you'll put my son in Witness Protection if I'm gone."

Freeman scowled. "I didn't even know you had a son. Where is he now?"

She took her hands off him and paced a step forward to the door, turned, paced another step to the back wall, then turned and paced to the door again. She was getting dizzy. Maybe pacing wasn't such a good idea.

"Look," Freeman said, "let me take you home, then you can relax. I have somebody I'd like you to meet. He's a bodyguard of sorts. His job is to keep you alive."

She stopped and looked at him. "Really? Is he cute?" He gave a deer-in-the-headlights look. She held up a hand. "Sorry, never mind. I don't expect you to answer that." She leaned against the wall. "I have my car. I'm just worried about getting to the parking lot."

"This bodyguard is really good with detecting things. I'll have him tail us to see if anyone follows. I'll walk you to your car and we'll follow right behind you all the way to your house."

She chewed her lip. "That would probably work. But first I need you to bring me the biggest scarf the store has and a lightweight cover-up." She opened the door and shoved him out.

"Wait. What's a cover-up?" he asked.

"Ask the saleslady. She'll help. Hurry up."

François casually walked out of Prada, avoiding the shattered glass door wrapped in plastic and duct tape. He took a seat on a large concrete planter holding a young palm tree. From his pocket, he pulled out his phone and pretended to be occupied with it.

He took a deep breath, smelling for anxiety, anger, or anything that clued him in to a bad guy. Besides the urine, shit, puke, and trash, all smelled fine. Then he surveyed the area for a sniper or shooter. He texted Freeman the okay to come out.

François continued sniffing and carefully eyeing each person who walked along the sidewalk. A group of people including a curvy, delicious woman with large sunglasses and blue wrap around her head came out the opened door. Not too far behind came Freeman. Shit, was a person in the group the one they were protecting? He should've asked for a picture or physical description at least. He didn't expect her to hide with others.

Then he smelled it. His mate. She was close. One of the women coming up or down the sidewalk was her.

Frantic, he searched both directions looking for her long dark curls. Which direction was the wind blowing? He headed into the breeze, following the group that just left the store. No one had the right hair or body.

Wait. Could the woman with the blue scarf be her? She wasn't with the group anymore. He turned back, looking for her. No, he reminded his cat. They were there on a job. He pivoted around and looked for the group of women. One of them had to be their girl. But which one? Where the hell was Freeman?

His eyes caught a flash of blue, the same as the scarf the woman wore, hurrying through a parking lot. His cat went wild, coming close to stripping away his control. Mate! Feet rooted, he couldn't move one way or the other. Fuck!

A car came to a screeching stop beside him on the street. Freeman leaned over the seat and opened the door. "Get in, Dubois." François looked over his shoulder at the parking lot. She was gone. His cat screamed. He tried to control his wince to the pain, seeing as he was the only one hearing it. Somehow, he got in the car and Freeman took off.

Freeman glanced at him. "You all right, man? You don't look good."

François rubbed his temple. "Just got a headache coming on. Must be the dry air messing with my sinuses. Nothing to worry about. Which car is hers?"

"The Lexus a couple cars up," Freeman said. François kept his eyes roaming, memorizing other vehicles around them, studying the drivers' faces for signs of something different. Within a few minutes, they'd left the Strip behind and entered residential areas. They pulled up to a security gate and it opened immediately. She must've told the guard they were with her.

Freeman caught up with the Lexus and parked behind her in a circular drive.

"Nice place," François said, opening the passenger-side door. But he wouldn't have expected anything less. The Lexus's car door closed. He turned to finally get a look at the prima donna.

The most beautiful women he'd ever seen approached Detective Freeman. François's cat spazzed and broke into a happy dance. They'd found her, and she was their charge. Good times ahead. François reminded his cat that they had to remain professional throughout the entire job. The cat snorted. Guess it didn't believe him.

Amie shook Freeman's hand, then the detective motioned to François on the other side of the car, and her beautiful eyes turned to him. Their sparkle quickly died, along with his heart. He'd hoped that her disappearance was some kind of fluke. Something beyond her control that made her stay away from him.

That little bubble of hope that he'd lived in for four years popped.

Even the cat was pissed. How could their mate not want them? Was that even possible? Did Mother Nature screw up? Didn't matter right now. They had a job to do and that took precedence over everything else, he thought.

Amie hurried around the front of her car, away from him, and up the steps to the front door. He wasn't letting her get away that easily this time. He caught her arm before she slid the key into the lock. Holding her so closely after so many years, he couldn't think of what to say. There were a book's worth of questions he had, but the cover to that tome didn't open.

Amie jerked her arm from his grip, but he held fast. He wasn't sure he would ever be able to let go. Her sad eyes met his. He smelled her love for him and heartbreaking dismay. He didn't understand what that was about. He'd have to ask her. Duh, his cat said. Shut up, cat.

The tang of chemicals hit his nose. The same chemicals he spent a lot of time learning in his ALFA training.

Amie turned away and slid her key into the lock and twisted the deadbolt. François and his cat jumped at the same time, taking Amie to the ground, covering her body with his as the front door and windows exploded.

CHAPTER 6

Amerella sat in the front seat of Detective Freeman's sedan, blanket draping her shoulders, but her body still shook uncontrollably. The only thing running through her mind was that she would've been dead. She should've been dead. The love of her life saved her. Of course he did. Who was the last person in the world she wanted to see? The one walking toward her with broad shoulders, well-fitting T-shirt showing off his narrow waist, faded jeans that cupped in the right places, and worn leather boots.

Fuck. She could spontaneously combust right this second, just from watching the man walk. God, how could she have forgotten how sexy he was? The same way she tried to forget everything about him: pharmaceutically induced suppression. She took so many pills she was sure she'd put a couple sales reps' children through college.

Pills for manic depression, bipolar depression. Pills to let her sleep, pills to wake her up. Pills for high blood pressure the other pills were causing. God, she was such a fucking mess.

The car door opened and Frank looked at her with his amazing smile and happy eyes. She melted on the spot. He took in a deep breath, then held out his hand. "Let me help you out. Everything is safe." She placed her hand in his and savored the feel of his callus-roughened hands.

She remembered how those hands had slid over her body, caressing every part of her. Every part. Shit. Her undies were wet now. Frank's grip on her hand tightened as he inhaled. He couldn't smell that, could he? No, humans weren't able to do that.

He pulled her out of the car and into his arms. Oh, god. How she'd missed this. Missed his touch, his smell, his body pressed against hers. Nowhere else had she ever felt so protected, so safe.

His chest vibrated against her ear, kind of like a cat purring while its back was being scratched. The sound had always calmed her when agitated.

"Dubois," said Freeman, skirting the driveway. She pulled away and for the first time noticed the people who roamed her drive and front porch. Police, an ambulance, people in hazmat gear, a guy snapping pictures, and more police. Then there was everyone lining the fence, gaping at her blown-up front entrance.

Detective Freeman hurried toward her and Frank. "Did you find anything else?"

Frank shook his head. "Everything is clean except for the kitchen door, which had two desert people and a family member here not too long ago."

What the fuck . . . "How the hell did you know that?" she asked. She was concerned about someone knowing her son's whereabouts more than if someone was spying on her.

His gorgeous smile reappeared. "There were two sets of footprints that had sand particles that had fallen from their shoes or clothing."

Seriously? How did he notice something so minute? A person just didn't see sandy footprints. Wait a minute. She snapped her head around to him. "Detective Freeman said you were here as my bodyguard. Are you . . . you . . ." She looked his body up and down. "A security person?"

Freeman stepped forward. "Let's go around to the kitchen and talk there." He glanced at the crowded fence. "Too many spectators for my taste."

She let Frank guide her along the side of the brick house

to the back porch. Frank pulled her keys from his pocket. "Any of these open the door?"

She picked out one with a key cap designed like a hot pink cupcake. She loved those tiny desserts. She could eat one or three with each meal. Before she twisted the lock, she looked back at Frank. He grinned and gave her an approving nod. She continued to unlock the door and went inside.

Her heart jumped into her throat when thinking about Maria being injured. Then she remembered that with her son staying with the Running Winds, Maria took the day to visit her elderly mom. Thank god.

Frank put his arm around her shoulders. "Something wrong?"

She grinned at her memories. Frank always could read her like a very open book. He knew when she was sad, worried, or needed a hug. He was either the most perceptive man she ever met or her face screamed everything she felt. She also noted how no one since him had cared about her feelings. No one gave a shit if she was alive or dead.

No. She couldn't let her feelings for him resurface. It took so long to push them down just to keep alive with such heartache. She was angry for a second, thinking how Frank never came looking for her. Then she remembered who she was in college—not Amerella Capone, great-great-grandniece of the infamous gangster. She was Amie Truman—normal girl from Nevada. There was no way he could've found her even if he tried. She wondered if he had.

No, no, no. For everyone's sake, she had to stop this. She shrugged off his arm from around her shoulders.

"I'm fine. Everything is peachy." She sat on a wooden chair at the breakfast table and put her head in her hands. This was a complete nightmare. Now was not the time for this man to come back into her life.

A cup of coffee slid under her nose. Her favorite roast with a hint of cinnamon. Yum. One of the other chairs squeaked as it was pulled back from the table. Detective Freeman sat while Frank popped another pod into the coffee machine.

Freeman cleared his throat. "Amerella, besides the obvious, is everything okay? Something we should know about?" She shook her head and sipped from her mug. "Do you have a place you can hide out until the judge decides if there is enough evidence to go to trial?"

She thought about the Mojave, where her son was hiding. That wasn't an option. If she went there and they found her, her son's safety would be jeopardized. "No. This is the only place I've been."

"What about a summer home your family owns?" Freeman asked.

Again, she shook her head. "Everything like that belongs to Uncle Giuseppe."

"Whoa, whoa, whoa." Frank nearly dropped his coffee cup on the table. He leaned both hands on the wood. His eyes slowly rolled to her. "You're tied to the Mafia? You're family to the Mob?"

She glanced at Detective Freeman then back to him. "Uh, yeah. Haven't you figured that out already? I guess we're not all on the same page."

Frank raised a hand. "No, we are. It just sank in. I was"—he looked at her with narrowed eyes—"preoccupied with unforeseen circumstances until now."

Oh, god. He must've realized everything she told him about herself was a lie. Flat-out, premeditated lie. Everything except her feelings for him. Those were as real as the sun and moon. He seemed to be debating whether he was going to sit or leave. Please sit. Please sit.

He pulled out a chair and slid his gorgeous backside onto the seat. He whipped his head toward her with a deep breath. His look was filled with anger and disappointment, nearly breaking her. She stared into her coffee.

Freeman sat back in his chair and crossed his arms over his chest. "Am I missing something, or do you two know each other?"

She would let Frank answer. She didn't know what to say.

As usual, Frank stepped up. "Yeah, we were in college at the same time. Long time ago."

Freeman snorted. "Can't be that long ago. Both of you are still kids compared to me." The detective looked between her and Frank. "Is there going to be a problem with this? Should I call Director Tumbel and get another agent?"

She said no the same time Frank did. She didn't plan to

be around him much. She'd hide in her room while he guarded the house. That would work, right? Then she remembered the RPG launcher. Shit. The bad guys could be two neighbors over and fire one of those into any window. Shit, shit, shit. This was getting worse by the second. Where could she go where the Mafia wouldn't find her?

Frank sighed. "Getting back to the situation, the only place I can think of that would be safe for her would be my home."

What the fuck? She replied, "I don't think so."

CHAPTER 7

"What in hell did you pack in these, woman?" With three large rolling suitcases, two medium-sized, and a duffel around his neck choking him, Frank struggled through the rent-a-car lot to their assigned vehicle.

"Don't chastise me, Frank. I had fifteen minutes to pack up my entire life and move out. I didn't have time to think about it," Amie said.

"So you packed your entire closet and bathroom?"

"Don't be silly. That's not even a quarter of my closet." Amie adjusted the two bags she'd carried on the plane. "I don't know how long I'll be staying. I hope the dry-cleaner in this town we're going to isn't too busy." Frank bust out a laugh. She was in for a big surprise.

She refused to go to DC, where he had an apartment. So the decision was made that she'd go to his hometown, which very few people knew about. He hated the idea of dumping this woman on his mom, but she could handle it. Plus, he'd still be somewhat on vacation.

"Why are you laughing? What aren't you telling me, Frank?"

With a sigh, he said, "Nothing, Amie. Or should I call you Amerella now?" Her chin dropped to her chest. Aww, shit.

He smelled her shame and the guilt she felt. But he was pissed, dammit. She lied to him about who she was, her perfect family, and her normal life. Did she lie to him about her feelings for him, too? Was it all some kind of charade?

No. That was true. She really loved him when they were together. He saw it in her eyes and smile. And of course, her smell. But now it was different. She was different. She was a prima donna who spoke her mind whether the other person wanted to hear it or not.

He clicked the key fob to open the car's trunk. After stuffing it, he ended up putting some bags in the backseat. He'd never seen someone with so much luggage for one trip. Granted, he didn't know how long she'd stay. Maybe he should tell her about a new-fangled appliance they called a washing machine.

Finally settled behind the steering wheel, he took a deep breath and relaxed. Well, as relaxed as he could be with his mate, but not his mate, sitting a couple feet from him. The entire drive, Amie stared out the window. Which he was glad for. He didn't know what to say to her. He had so many questions he didn't know where to begin.

Then there was the issue of her living in Spotted Creek. During their time together, he'd never told her he was a shifter. He would've told her before they married, but the day after he proposed to her, he never saw her again. Maybe his mom would tell her. Women knew how to talk with other women. Men only messed up things when trying to talk.

A green road sign marked five miles to his hometown. "We're almost there." His training kicked in and he felt more sure of himself. "Remember, you have to keep a low profile. The more people who know you are here, the more likely something could get out. You shouldn't walk around town, but you can hang out in Mom's backyard. It's private and really nice. You'll like it."

He slowed the car and turned onto the main street.

Amie's eyes widened. "Is this it?"

"Yes," he grumped. "Something wrong with it?"

"No. It's just . . . quaint."

"I know it could use some sprucing up. The folks here are a bit stuck in the past, but they're all great people." He eyed the battered-looking beauty salon and falling-down warehouse next to it. The butcher's shop could use painting. Yeah, the town could use a shitload of sprucing up.

He pulled onto the pebbled driveway alongside the house and stopped in front of a garage that no longer had room for a car. Maybe he and his mom could go through all the crap in there and toss out most of it. A lot of his dad's things were in there. Things his mom couldn't deal with at the time.

Mom met them at the back porch. Fortunately, he was able to call her ahead of time to warn her about what was going on. Of course, his mom was thrilled with the idea of having another lady friend around. He got the feeling that she might be getting lonely. When he was younger, his parents socialized with others in town, but after Dad's death, Mom didn't go outside much.

"Remember," he said to Amie as she opened her car door, "keep a low profile."

"Yes," Amie said. "I got it the first time."

His mom stood next to the car, waiting for him to get on with introductions. After stepping out of the car, he gave his mom the obligatory hug, then turned to Amie. "Mom, this is Amie Truman. She's the one I told you about who I need to keep safe for a while."

His mom stepped forward and gave her a hug. Amie looked at him over his mom's shoulder with a *what do I do?* look. Like he had a clue. He made a silent gesture waving his hands around, then headed for the trunk.

Mom leaned back but kept her hands on Amie's upper arms. "I'm so glad to meet you, Amie. François didn't mention how pretty you are. Or young. Right at his age, aren't you?" Mom looped her arm around Amie's and started for the porch. "Are you married, Amie?"

Oh, god. Maybe this wasn't a good idea. He leaned his head against the lifted trunk lid. What had he gotten himself into?

After hauling the suitcases out of the trunk, into the house, up the stairs, and down the hall, he left Amie to unpack. He pointed out the one bathroom that both bedrooms upstairs shared. He, of course, slept in the room on the other side of the bath.

This really was a bad idea. His cat loved it. He reminded

the feline that it had no say in how this was going down. It yawned then stretched out to enjoy the show.

In the kitchen with his mom, he spoke in whispers. "Mom," he started, "don't start playing matchmaker between Amie and me."

Mom slapped a hand on her chest. "Me? Play matchmaker to get grandcubs? I would never!" She grinned.

He rolled his eyes at her playfulness. He didn't want to tell her how he and Amie knew each other. Because he never told Amie about him being a shifter, he never told his mom he met his mate. Knowing his mother, she'd make sure Amie spit out a cub exactly nine months to the day after meeting her. But he had to tell her something.

"Mom, Amie and I knew each other in school."

She clapped her hands together. "Even better! You already know each other's pasts."

"No, Mom. She has no idea who we are or what we can do. And I'm not sure she should know." He worried about others in town shifting in front of her. The town's general rule was not to shift in public in case a human was in town. What was he going to do? Go around and tell every resident they couldn't shift for who knows how long? Not practical.

"She's in a shifter town, son. How do you expect her to not figure it out?"

He wiped a hand over his sweat-covered forehead. "I don't know, Mom. I hadn't really thought the whole thing through yet. Just keep everything a secret as long as you can. Okay?"

"All right. I'll do my best. Would you like me to chain her to the bedroom wall so she doesn't go outside?"

He sighed. "Mom, you're not helping." He had to push away the images of Amie chained to the bed, naked and wet for him. One hint of desire and his mom would be all over him. "I need to let my cat out. Can you watch her for a bit?"

"Sure, son." Her smile worried him. "I got this."

Oh, god. This was a really, really bad idea.

CHAPTER 8

In her heels, Amie carefully stepped on each tread of the stairs. She figured back when this older house was built, they didn't have many big-boned women who wore four-inch-high shoes. Maybe she could go shoeless. At least she wasn't pregnant. Been there, done that.

Before leaving her guest bedroom, she'd called Maria and told her what happened at the house and to stay with her mother until everything settled. Last thing she wanted was for Maria to walk into some ambush and get hurt.

Then the thought of her son being hurt sent fear straight to her heart. She'd talked to Grandpa Running Wind and he told her to not worry about her "cub." He would make sure the child was well taken care of. He told her to take care of herself first, then she would be ready to take care of her son. She hoped he was right.

The scent of cooking steak wafted in from the other room. She realized how hungry she was. With everything going on in Vegas, they hadn't stopped to eat. Not too long from now, the sun would be setting.

"Amie? That you?" Frank's mom said.

How could the woman possibly know she was standing on the stairs? Frank's mom popped her head around the corner. "I forgot to mention to be careful of the sixth step. Occasionally it gets loose. When it creaks like it does now, usually means I need to take a hammer to it again."

Amie looked back at the steps. She hadn't even noticed the sound, she was so focused on not falling. But that explained how Frank's mom knew she was coming down.

"Come on in." The woman gestured with a tilt of her head toward the kitchen. "I'm making something to eat. Bet you all haven't had anything in a while with all your carrying on."

Amie followed her into the kitchen. The room was . . . cute. In a fifties kind of way. Frank's mom blended in perfectly. Her dark hair was pulled back in a bun at the nape of her neck. The housedress she wore was gray with small white flowers. She wore no makeup or jewelry. Yet she looked timeless.

"François mentioned you know each other from college. What did you major in?" Oh, she hadn't thought about what she'd tell his mom. Apparently, Frank hadn't told her everything, so she wouldn't, either. She'd gotten good at selective fact-giving—not outright lying, but carefully choosing what to divulge—over the past several years after college. If she could fool Uncle Giuseppe, Frank's mom would be a cinch.

"We did know each other. I saw him around campus and we had some mutual friends, too. My degree was in art and artistic design. He was much more into math and science."

"Oh, how nice," his mom said. "There's something to be said about opposites attracting."

Hold the phone. If she didn't know better, that sounded like Frank's mom wouldn't mind if they hooked up. Not happening. Amie thought back to his sculpted body and the muscular valleys she used to run her tongue along. Her body shivered.

His mom turned to her with a wide grin. "I hope you like steak. That's all I have right now. Need to go to the butcher's tomorrow to pick up more red meat for the rest of this week. Maybe you could come with me."

At least she'd be able to get out of the house, Amie thought. "That would be great, Mrs. Dubois."

"Oh, no, no, no. That just won't do," the woman said. "I insist you call me 'Mom' just like François does. If you must, Mom Dubois would be fine also."

"Thank you, Mom." Maybe this place wasn't going to be all that bad. It was Frank's family, who he seldom talked about. She hadn't talked about hers, either, but she was hiding the fact that she was related to the Mafia. What could a perfect guy like François have to hide?

Frank came through the kitchen door in different clothes. Now he sported a tight white T-shirt and sweatshorts that hung low on his hips. Damn, the man could be wrapped in a rug and look sexy.

"Uh, I need to change. Be right back." With that he was gone. His mom watched him go with a gleam in her eye. What did that mean?

"Amie," Mom said, "would you mind pulling out three dinner plates and setting them on the table, please?"

She jumped from her chair. Finally, something she could do besides sitting with her thumb stuck up her ass. "Absolutely." She opened a cabinet to the largest dinner plates she had ever seen. They were more like serving dishes. She could fit several veggie burgers and salads on one.

After setting the table with plates, silverware, kick-ass steak knives, and cups, she wondered if anything needed to come from the fridge. The only thing cooking was steak. No beans or corn, no lettuce salad or fruit. She opened the fridge to see what was there and stared in disbelief. The only thing besides milk—skim at that—was meat: chicken, pork, ground beef, a couple steaks, bacon, sausages, sliced deli meats—a package of Colby jack cheese; woo-hoo—shoulder roast, and brisket.

No wonder Frank only ate meat when at school. That's all his mom cooked. Well, she'd always wondered if the Atkins diet worked. She was about to find out.

CHAPTER 9

After a somewhat quiet dinner, Frank sat on the back porch in one of the old rocking chairs from his youth. These exact wooden rockers had been there as long as he could remember. Most nights after supper, his dad would come out and sit and rock for hours. Occasionally, he smoked a cherry-flavored cigar that gave the yard a fruity smell while kids chased fireflies in the night air.

Tonight, it was his turn to contemplate the universe or whatever his dad thought about all those long hours. His cat had no interest in the universe unless their mate was out there. And she wasn't. She was on the other side of the door, watching him.

He tilted his head and caught her peeking behind the door's curtain. She smiled and looked down. His heart warmed. Her smile used to light up his day, no matter what shit was happening in his life. He missed that.

The door slowly opened, revealing a shy Amie. The Amie he knew. Not the flashy, attention-seeking woman she had become.

"Can I join you?" she asked.

He sat up in the chair. "Yes, I'd like you to." She quickly opened the door wider, stepped out, and scuttled to the rocking chair on the other side of the door. They remained quiet, rocking, staring out over the yard. He couldn't smell her emotions with the wind blowing the wrong way, which put him at a disadvantage. Of all the times to not know how a woman felt . . .

"Your mom is really nice. She's a great cook. I don't think I've had a better steak anywhere in Vegas."

"Yeah, she's pretty good," he replied. "She's been cooking them a long time." An awkward silence lingered again.

"I noticed you hadn't told your mom about us. I guess you never mentioned me to her while we were dating, either."

Oh, fuck. He didn't need to smell to know what she implied. How did he tell her that would've been a bad idea at the time? He didn't.

"You haven't mentioned your dad. Where is he?"

His stomach rolled. He didn't talk about his dad for a reason: The emotions that grabbed him when talking about his dad were too tough to fight. He glanced at the curtains on the kitchen door.

"Your mom went upstairs if that's what you're wondering." He had always been amazed by how she knew what he was thinking at times.

That's what mates do, dumbass. Shut it, cat. They weren't really mated. He'd never bitten her hard enough to qualify. Though there were times he came dangerously close. Why he didn't, he wasn't sure. Maybe he thought they were too young or not ready yet. Maybe he didn't want to strap her to someone she didn't want to spend her life with. Which happened to be the case.

"Frank?"

"Yeah. My dad, right." He realized Amie couldn't scent him. Perhaps it would be all right to tell her, since no one else was around. "My dad worked for the same organization I do, right now. He used to come home and astound me and the local kids with wild stories that had to be exaggerations, if not outright made up, to entertain the young ones.

"He spoke of demons and witches, and warlocks that flew on giant dragons. He told of other dimensions where beings were different from us, but had the same issues humans do. But mostly, my dad protected celebrities from all over. A couple movie stars who received death threats when they said something stupid in public. Senators and government officials when they went to other countries. An occasional Mob member who needed to hide out in nowheresville." He got a smile out of her for that.

"He was my idol. I wanted so badly to be just as great as he was. Of course, as a kid, you never heard about the bad stuff. So in my mind, he was a god."

Amie sat forward in the chair. "What happened?"

"He was on a special ops mission with a group of SEALs outside the country. The government didn't tell mom or me much; it was all classified. But we pieced together what we could from those who survived and were willing to talk with us.

"They were sent to infiltrate North Korea to verify if rumors about the country having nuclear missile capabilities were right. They were true, as the whole world knows now. On the way out, they came across a Korean militia group roaming the land for whatever they could pillage. At that moment, they were attacking a small village of helpless people. They had mud huts and dirt floors, for fuck's sake. Yet the military had to have what was there.

"The SEAL leader told his men to ignore the conflict and get to the pickup location. We were told that Dad refused to let the villagers be murdered in such a way. He stepped in and single-handedly took out most of the marauders.

"Then supposedly he was shot by one of the remaining soldiers fleeing into the jungle. But some of the men on the mission question the sequence of events. I don't think anyone knew what really happened. They brought his body home. Gave Mom a U.S. flag in a triangle box and said good-bye after the burial."

"Oh my god, Frank. That's horrible, not knowing exactly what happened."

There was more to it, but he couldn't tell her about his dad shifting, then being mistakenly shot by friendly fire. But that was beside the point. His father died and there was nothing anyone could do about it. And now he worked for the same people who got his father killed.

"So you work for the military?" she asked. "In some secret organization?"

"Not the military, but yes, a secret group. What do you do now? Anything with art design?"

Amie laughed. "Are you joking? If you consider attending stupid high-society functions, charity balls where little goes to the charity, and shopping at overpriced stores as art, then yes. I'm using my art degree very much."

He laughed this time. Her cheeks blushed. "Stop laughing at me. I know how dumb I seem."

"Especially if you consider the time you got trapped in a garbage container while Dumpster-diving our junior year."

"Oh my god," she squealed. "I forgot about that." She rocked back and laughed. "Holy shit. I didn't think I'd ever get the smell of rotting food out of my hair. Remember the time when you and your roommate got caught hanging underwear on the mascot statue in the quads?" She laughed harder. "I thought I was going to die when they made you wear tighty–whities on your head for an entire day."

Shit. He'd forgotten about that. Talk about embarrassed. He and his roommate had to wear the undies with their eyes showing through the leg holes and their noses sticking out the center slit. Luckily, they were able to wear brand-new pairs and not used ones.

"That was so humiliating," he started. "At least it kept me from getting nervous about that night."

"That night?" Amie replied. "What did you do that night?"

His heart hurt a little from her not remembering, but it was four years ago. "I asked you to marry me." Her guilt and shame filled the night air. Shit. He'd done it again. He wanted to kick himself.

His cat interrupted. Here, let me. It scraped claws down the inside of his brain. Fuck! He winced at the pain.

As he expected, she remained quiet. He should apologize, but for what? Remembering that she walked out on him with no explanation, no reason? Remembering his pain and worry that something had happened to her until getting a simple text several days later that said *I'm fine. I can't see you ever again.*

Amie stood and opened the door to the kitchen. She looked over her shoulder at him. "Frank, I'm sorry how it ended up. And despite all that, you still decided to help me now."

"Don't get too excited. It's my job."

"Maybe, but Detective Freeman could've called and requested someone else. But you stuck beside me."

Yeah, he did. What did that say about him? He was a hopeless fuck overrun with weakness when it came to protecting his mate? That's what mates do, dumbass. Shut it, cat.

"Anyway," she said, "I can't thank you enough for taking me in." She stepped inside and quietly closed the door. He heard her climb the stairs as the sixth step squeaked. He should find the hammer and take care of that before leaving.

He sat back in the old rocking chair and stared at the million points of light overhead. In the city, he never got this view. Always too many damn lights. Only when he let his cougar out in the mountains did he get this sight.

He took a deep breath then let it out slowly. The comfort of home spread through him. Where he was loved and accepted. Not having to hide who or what he was.

His mate filled his mind. He would protect her with his life despite anything he said. He still loved her and always would. No other woman was for him. No other woman would even interest him enough to say hi.

Actually, what was stopping him from trying to rekindle the spark between them? The absolute terror of being rejected again. But she still felt something for him. He'd smelled her desire a few times already. Maybe it was just sex she wanted. That could be a start. Remind her how he drove her crazy, her crying out his name as she came hard around his cock.

Shit, now he was getting hard. He adjusted to sit on one ass cheek.

Yes, maybe that would be a good start. Bring back how good it used to be between them and then never let her go, no matter what she said. They were meant to be together. He had to find out what was getting in the way and end it.

Feeling better with a plan, he went into the living room and lay on the couch. He knew he'd never be able to sleep knowing his mate was on the other side of the bathroom in bed without him. Fuck!

CHAPTER 10

～

Amerella woke earlier than normal. She knew when she opened her eyes. The sun was usually much brighter when she peeled the sleeping mask from her face. Thinking back to last night, she didn't remember waking once, which was extremely unusual for her. Guess feeling safe and cared for worked better than meds. She'd forgotten to take them after talking with Frank on the back porch.

Frank.

She couldn't believe she was in his mother's home. After their three years together and four apart, never once did she think she'd be here. She wondered if Frank was still asleep. Quietly, she slid through the door on her side of the shared bathroom and opened the door to his room just enough to peek in.

His bed was messy, but nobody was under the covers. Darn.

No, no, no. She couldn't think that way. Her options were clear—she had none. She couldn't let herself open to him. Not if she wanted to keep him alive.

After a quick shower, she dressed in a casual pantsuit and heels then headed downstairs. Everything was so quiet here. No cars zipping along the road. No siren or people shouting. No blaring music from the pain-in-the-ass neighbor kids. It was nice, but a little spooky. Like in a Twilight Zone episode where everyone on the planet disappeared but her.

"Hello? Mom Dubois?" The kitchen door closed, startling her.

Mom looked her up and down. "Good morning, Amie. I didn't expect you up so early." Amie eyed Mom's housecoat and flip-flops. Mom's cheeks reddened a bit. "Oh, don't mind this old thing." She gestured at her garb. "I was out for a run in the woods. It's a beautiful morning."

"A run?" Amie asked. "In flip-flops?"

Mom looked down at her feet and remained quiet for a second, then looked up. "I'm going to change. How about you pull out some things for breakfast and I'll be right back."

Amie watched her leave and wondered what that was all about. Who ran in the woods in flip-flops? She could barely walk in the damn things without stumbling over her own feet. She brushed it off to living in a small community, and headed for the fridge. She was hungry.

As soon as she opened the refrigerator door, her memory of the contents from the night before came back. Meat, meat, and more meat. Except only half of what was there last night remained. Had Frank eaten already? Was he even here? Could she eat a steak for breakfast? The thought turned her stomach.

She closed the fridge. Hopefully they had cereal. Her favorite was cinnamon Life. That shit was so good, she could go through a box in two sittings. But seeing as there wasn't much fiber in it, she had the occasional bowl of tree bark doused in sugar. And that shit was never good. No matter how much sugar was added to cardboard, it still tasted like cardboard.

On the counter sat a couple of paper grocery bags. She peeked inside to see normal food. Thank god. Wheat bread, eggs, a stalk of romaine lettuce, veggies, fruit, sliced chicken, mayo, and other things she'd gladly eat were stuffed inside. She thought about unpacking the bags, but then wondered if they were meant for someone else.

Mom came back into the room wearing another dress Beaver Cleaver's mom would wear on a bad day. If that's what she liked, who was she to criticize?

Mom said, "Looks like François did some shopping this

morning. Let's see what he got." She pulled items out of the bag like she'd never seen such things before. She shook her head, rolled her eyes, and said, "Of course, how silly of me." She carried items to the fridge. "I forget that our little town has its quirks and when visitors come we need to be prepared. Not that my son gave either of us much time to prepare, huh?"

Amie remembered her own dash through the closet and bath to pack things before Frank pushed her onto a plane to BFE. "I agree. Not much time. But I'm not picky when it comes to food." She gestured to herself. "As you can see."

Mom looked at her. "I can see what?"

Amie raised a brow. "I'm a big girl, Mom Dubois. Nothing like you."

Crossing her arms, Mom leaned against the counter. "Dear, you are stunning. Every man in town will kiss your feet when you walk by. Now, don't get me wrong, sweetie. In our town, you're beautiful. But even if you were skinny, you'd still be welcomed. We'd just feed you a lot so you'd look healthy."

Tears stung Amie's eyes. No one had ever made such a fuss telling her she was beautiful, except Frank. He'd loved her body even though there was more of her than other girls he could've had. He always called them scrawny with pointy knees and elbows. He liked her softness against him, not bones. And he had shown her almost every night how much he loved her softness by pounding into her again and again. A shudder crept down her back.

Mom took a deep breath and relaxed her shoulders. "François is in town talking with the police chief. I think he wants to let them know you're here and to keep an eye out for anything unusual."

She stiffened. "Do you think there will be any problems?"

"No, there never is. Because the single road here is somewhat hidden in the trees and hard to find, usually only the people who live here come this way. I don't even think Google has us on their map. Maybe the satellite view, but not the ground view. When we heard the vehicle with the video recorder was in the area, several of us disguised the turn-off as a camp road that dead-ended quickly. They drove right on by."

Amie laughed. "That would be an accomplishment. Google has everybody's number."

"It seems that way. Now, how about eggs, toast, and bacon for breakfast? That's normal, isn't it?"

That was strange. Was it not normal for them? "Yes, that would be very normal. Thank you."

After a couple attempts at the eggs—the first set burnt to a crisp while the two ladies searched for the toaster, which they never found—several slices of bacon cooked to perfection, and fruit, Amie was once again full. Maria's cooking was great. But seldom did Maria create a meal for her. Usually, it was just tacos, burritos, veggie burgers, pizza. But both she and Maria made certain their little Francis had all the food groups, even though he barely touched anything but meat.

Mom stood at the open refrigerator. "Well, seems we're low on red meat. Would you like to go into town with me to the butcher's?"

"Sure, it'd be great to walk around and see the place."

Mom clasped her hands together. "Great. I'll be right back."

Amie found her purse by a chair in the living room and noted the blanket and pillow on the sofa. She wondered if Frank slept there last night. Did he despise her so much that he couldn't even be on the same floor as her? Her heart broke a little. She hurried out of the room, mad at herself for letting her walls down.

She nearly collided with Mom in the kitchen. "What's wrong, dear?" Mom asked.

"Nothing. Let's go." Amie hurried outside.

Mom was right about it being a great day. The late-morning sun was shining, but it wasn't too hot with the fresh, cool breeze in their faces. As they walked along the crumbling sidewalk toward the shops, Amie noticed the lack of people around. In Vegas residential areas, others were always out walking dogs, working in flower beds, washing cars. Games of pick-up basketball were almost continuous with the kids.

The single court they passed here had more weeds than asphalt and the one hoop still up didn't look like it would be that way much longer. "I guess you all don't have many children around here?"

Mom looked at the court also. "We do, but I guess they do other things."

"All you need to do is put salt in the cracks with the weeds to kill them without using chemicals, then put a coating over the top of the asphalt, and you'd have a clean surface again. Wouldn't cost more than a couple hundred dollars."

"Really?" Mom said. "That doesn't seem too hard."

"It's not. And if basketball doesn't work, you can stretch a rope across the middle with mosquito netting hanging over it for tennis or volleyball. Badminton, too."

"That's a great idea. I will bring that up at the next community meeting. Thank you."

Pride swelled in Amie's heart knowing she contributed something important and someone cared about her ideas. She was starting to like this place more and more.

They crossed the street toward a building that could use a couple layers of paint. The sign out front read Butch's Butchery. Catchy name. Mom stopped at a window outside a vacant store and picked at her hair. Amie then noticed Mom wore a touch of lipstick—wrong color for her skin tone, but she tried. This was interesting.

Mom opened the door and walked into the cool butcher-shop air. A few people milled about, each stopping to take a good look at Amie as she walked in. She felt a bit overdressed with her flashy jewelry and high heels. One old lady in particular sneered at her. Amie hurried to catch up with Mom.

Mom whispered to her, "Don't worry about old Mrs. Hagerty. She doesn't like strangers. Or locals, for that matter." Amie covered a smile with her hand and caught the old woman's narrowed eyes again.

"Good morning, Mrs. Hagerty. It's nice to meet you," Amie said, figuring she'd agitate the woman more than anything. She was right. The old bitty turned her nose up and walked out the door. Then Amie felt bad for the lady. Living a life disliking everyone. The lady probably seldom came out of her home and probably didn't attend any social functions. Amie could see herself turning into Mrs. Hagerty in twenty years.

Mom Dubois smiled with a shy look toward the man behind the counter. "Good morning, Butch."

The man spun around and his face lit up. "Good morning

to you, Jean. You're looking stunning his morning." His eyes twinkled.

Oh my god. Did Amie see what she thought she was seeing? Mom Dubois was flirting with the town butcher? Holy shit. Did Frank know his mom had the hots for the meat man? Was that why there was so much meat in the fridge at home? The meat man giving Mom the meat. Geesh, she could be so dumb. She needed sex. Badly.

Mom gave a coy wave of the hand. "I bet you say that to all the single ladies who come in."

Butch winked at Mom. "Maybe. But with you, my darling"—he leaned over the counter closer to Mom—"I ain't lying." Or did he say lion?

As Amie watched, the butcher's face contorted to form a furry snout, large eyes and mouth, and a light brown Mohawk down the back of his head. Amie sucked in a breath then screamed louder than she thought possible and ran out the door. She ran straight across the street, lucky no cars were driving by. She didn't even slow down to look before flying off the sidewalk. The image of the man with the lion face filled her chest with horror. She couldn't breathe.

She ran past another store before noticing two wolf pups and a cougar or mountain lion cub sitting back on their haunches, watching her barrel down the sidewalk, yelling her fool head off. One of the wolves shifted into a small boy, then opened his mouth to say something. Amie sucked in another breath, screamed, spun around, then slammed into a glass door that had been opened by someone peeking outside to see what all the commotion was about.

Amie felt a sharp pain in her nose, then her world went black.

CHAPTER 11

A mie heard voices. Her head was about to split and her nose
ached. Shushed whispers abounded and everything si-
lenced. "Amie," came Mom's voice, "are you okay, sweetie?"

She forced her eyes open and looked at an aged and
cracked concrete ceiling. Mom leaned into view. "Amie, darling. You hit your head. How do you feel?"

She slowly sat up on the plastic vinyl sofa and glanced at
her surroundings. Barbershop chairs sat in front of mirrors
with people staring at her wide-eyed. Many females had rollers
in their hair and some looked to have pieces of aluminum foil
wrapped in. Then Amie realized she was in a beauty salon.

Her head pounded. "Except for my nose and headache,
I'm fine. What happened?"

Each person looked at another. Mom said, "I think you
saw Butch play one of his practical jokes and it scared you.
You ran out screaming."

The ladies nodded and agreed.

"Yes, that had to be it."

"That ol' Butch. Always joking around."

"Yup, Butch is a jokester, all right."

Yeah, okay. She got it. A lady with big blond hair handed
her a Dixie cup of water. "Here, sugar. Drink this."

She did as instructed and the women backed away, giving her breathing room. Amie remembered being in the meat shop and meeting Mrs. Hagerty, then it went blurry.

"Well, I don't feel one bit sorry for her." Amie turned to the voice that sounded like a mad nun in Catholic school scolding a student. Who else? Mrs. Hagerty. "Look at the shoes she's wearing. Can't nobody walk in those. And all that fandangled glitz she's wearing will blind anyone in the street."

The woman turned to Mom Dubois. "Whoever your guest is, Jean, she doesn't belong here. I can tell she's trouble. She'll bring riffraff here." The old woman walked out the door. "Trouble, I tell you. Mark my words."

One of the ladies in the shop waved off the old woman. "Don't worry about her. She's a bitch."

"Oh," Amie cut in, "please don't call her that on my behalf. I am a bit difficult."

The lady smiled. "No, honey. She is a bitch. A wolf—"

"Amie, dear"—Mom Dubois stepped in front of her—"use this cold cloth to dab your face. It might help."

"Thank you." Amie wiped her forehead. "I'm sorry, everyone, for causing such commotion. I don't know what came over me." A young teen in one of the beauty chairs giggled. Someone, her mom maybe, gave her a look and she quieted.

"No, you're fine, dear," the big blonde said. "What's your name?"

Amie put her hand out. "I'm Amie. I'm staying with Frank and his mom for a bit."

The blonde shook Amie's hand then hauled her up into a hug. "We're glad you're here, Amie. I'm Sherri Wolfe, beautician and owner of this here shop." Sherri went on to rattle off the names of several other ladies Amie probably wouldn't remember for a while.

The teen in the chair looked at Amie in the mirror. "You're not from around here, are you?"

Amie raised a brow. "What gave that away?" She smiled to soften the harshness she didn't intend.

Sherri turned to Mom Dubois. "Why don't you two hang out for a bit? It's been a while since we've seen each other."

Mom looked at Amie. "Works for me."

"Great," Sherri said. One of the other ladies asked Mom

a question while Sherri twirled the teen in the chair. "Okay, missy, what'll we have this time?" The beautician brushed her fingers through the wild curly dark hair.

The girl said, "Something different. Something up to date in the cities—"

"Nothing too wild," a different woman who looked a lot like the girl said. Probably her mom. "Your father will be upset if he has a purple-headed cub." Cub? Was that what they called the kids here? Just like Grandpa Running Wind. She did a mental shrug. To each their own.

"Amie," the teen called, "what do you think would look good?" Amie looked around for another Amie in the room. Someone wouldn't possibly want her opinion. Sherri and the girl's mom stared at her.

Amie cleared her throat and walked to the chair. She focused on the young visage in the mirror. "Well, your face shape lends well to short or long styles, so that's good." Amie lifted a handful to see how heavy it was. It was thick like animal fur. Had to be hot. "Most kids your age like long straight hair. If you want to be that group, then feather the sides with spikes around your face, let the rest fall behind your shoulders."

They discussed it. Sherri pulled tendrils forward to get an idea. Didn't look bad. "But," Amie continued, "if you want to stand out and get noticed, I'd go with straight-cut bangs to the brows and the back really short to have it bob under at the ears. Tuck the sides behind the ears."

Now the group stared at the teen with wide eyes. "Oh, one more thing," Amie said. "It's a bit old, but I still love it—have a strand on each side of the bangs that's really long and white-blond. They would hang down to curve under your chin."

The teen smiled. "I can see. Mom, can I?"

The mom chewed her lower lip. "Well, it doesn't seem outlandish. It's just a cut. If we don't like it much it will grow out in a year." She sighed. "Go for it."

The teen squealed and gyrated in her chair. Sherri swiveled her around. "Okay, here we go."

Over her shoulder, Sherri called Mom Dubois. "Hey, Jean. I have a spot open since Mrs. Hagerty left. You want a trim . . . or a city do?" She winked at Amie.

Jean slowly walked to the empty chair in front of the mirror. She let down the tight bun, revealing thick waves. Everyone in the shop stopped what they were doing to watch. Amie got the feeling this was a momentous event.

Mom stared into the mirror, finger-combing strands that hung below her waist. "My husband once told me that he loved my long hair. Gave him something to hold on to since I'm so scrawny." Her cheeks reddened with that private detail. "I told myself I would never cut it. Keep it long just for him." Mom paused, not moving, eyes locked on mirror. "But he's been gone for so long. So long now."

My god, Amie thought. Never had she seen such love or devotion for someone who'd been gone for so long. That was the kind of love she wanted. Someone she could love so much, even after death, she'd love no one else. Could Frank have been that man for her? If she hadn't run from him, would he have loved her as much as his mom loved his dad?

Mom sighed. "But I'm sure he doesn't care right now, so let's chop it."

Amie startled at the complete flip in tone while everyone else cheered. Never mind everything she just thought. Mom sat in the chair and one of the ladies swung a cape over her. Amie slinked back to the torn vinyl sofa. What had she done? Frank's dad's ghost would haunt her for life.

Letting the women do their thing, Amie looked at the layout of the shop. "Sherri, you have a great little space here."

"Little is right," Sherri said. "I don't have any room to add any more spots, so some of my customers have to wait awhile to get in. Even though the building next door is empty."

Amie thought about what she'd just said. "Do you share a wall with the empty space next door?"

"We do. I looked into buying some of the space, but the price was just too much. I'd need a sudden infusion of cash to make that happen. And with only a few customers each day, that won't be happening."

Amie nodded. "I see the problem."

"Hey, city girl," an older lady in the last slot called to her. "Come here, child." The beautician removed the cape and shook off the hair. The lady had incredibly beautiful facial bone structure. Very Angelina Jolie–ish. She reached out a slightly withered hand and grabbed Amie's arm with more strength than she thought possible for someone the lady's age.

"What can I do for you, ma'am?" Amie asked.

The woman sat back in the chair and looked directly at Amie via the mirror. "Tell me what you think."

Oh, shit. She was in trouble now. If she offended one of the older generation, who probably held a lot of influence in town, she'd be kicked out for being a bitch. Or a wolf, like the other lady called Hagerty.

Amie studied the woman's face, the high cheekbones, arched but faded brows, full upper lip but thin lower one, large almond eyes. "Hey," Amie started, "anybody got blush or an eye pencil on them?" Each of the ladies, except Mom Dubois, pulled out enough makeup to look like the cosmetic counter at Estée Lauder.

Amie chose a dark brown eyeliner and brow pencil. Two different shades of blush for the cheeks. Chocolate and leather eyeshadows went well with the natural liner and pencil. Lipstick she chose to balance out the eyes, extending the bottom lip to give it a fuller look.

Then she stood back, between the mirror and the woman, and studied what she'd done. Almost there, but one more thing. She unbuttoned her cardigan sweater, slid it off, then helped the lady put it on. Amie than pulled off her gold earrings and thick necklace and put them on the woman in front of her. Her fingers brushed bangs to the side, creating a lift at one spot.

Amie stood back and let the woman see herself. And the woman stared at herself. And stared, and stared. With no expression, Amie knew she hated it. She burst forward. "I'm so sorry. I'll wipe it—" The woman grabbed her arm, tears in her eyes. Amie cringed, waiting for the tongue thrashing.

"Child," the woman started, "all my long life, I've been a plain ugly duckling. A long time ago I gave up trying to be pretty like all the younger generations wearing the crazy black raccoon eyes and too-white faces, too-red on their lips.

"But what you've done has made me feel beautiful." She turned to the mirror. "I see the changes. I know the makeup is there. But it looks so natural. Feels natural. I'm pretty for the first time in my life."

Amie was a bit stunned by the opposite reaction; she'd expected to be yelled at. "That's a good thing, right?" She needed to make sure she'd heard correctly.

Tears rolled down the elder's cheeks. Amie grabbed a tissue from a nearby box. "No, no, no. You can't cry. You'll mess up the liner." She dabbed at the woman's tears as her own threatened. The lady laughed.

"Don't worry, child. You've given me something no one else ever has. Confidence." She started to take the cardigan off.

"No," Amie said, pulling the sweater back onto the lady's shoulders, "you keep all that. I don't need it. Frank will be happy it's one less thing to pack when I head home." The elder held her hand and patted it. And Amie wanted the woman to never forget something. "One more thing, ma'am. Makeup or not, you are beautiful. I know by the way the people here relate to you that you're a great person. That makes you good inside, which is far better than anything outside." Then she added, "Plus, no one here has called you a 'wolf,' so you gotta be okay, then."

The lady laughed. "Of course they wouldn't call me a wolf. I'm a cougar."

"Oh," Amie said. Then it dawned on her. Cougar as in older woman, younger guy. "Oooooh." The lady walked out the door with everyone still watching, speechless.

The woman on the far end of the aisle leaned forward. "Can you do that to me?"

A chorus of Me toos rang out. Amie laughed, her heart full of belonging and being wanted.

"I can run home and get all my stuff and we can have a fashion and makeup party," Amie said.

Mom Dubois turned in her seat. "Sherri, do you still shut down for lunch?"

"Sure do," Sherri replied. "No appointments between eleven thirty and twelve thirty. Gotta eat sometime."

Amie looked at her watch: 11:35 a.m. Her excitement drained.

"Perfect," Mom said. "Let's finish up here, then we can tell everyone to come to my house at noon and we can have the party there."

Sherri pulled her cell phone out. "Telling everyone will

be a cinch. I have every woman's number in this town in my phone. Mass text going out in thirty seconds. Oh, since it's lunchtime, I'll tell everyone to bring food to share with those who are taking their lunch break to attend."

Amie couldn't believe this was happening. People were coming to see her for advice. Never since college had anyone given a shit about her. She just played her part and acted like Uncle Giuseppe thought correct. These people truly wanted to share their lives with her. She didn't have words to express the feelings in her heart.

Maybe she'd stay here forever.

CHAPTER 12

~

Frank rubbed the back of his neck. He'd spent all morning at the town's small police house going over exit strategies, talking with the sheriff about the situation with Amie, and updating ALFA headquarters.

He thought about calling Detective Freeman in Vegas, but he was hungry and wanted to chill in a comfy chair with peace and quiet. Mom's place was always perfect. As he got closer to the house, he noted more and more cars lining the street. After parking behind the cars in the driveway, he wondered what in the hell was going on.

Since there were no ambulance or police in the area, it seemed that nobody was injured. As he got out of the car, his shifter hearing picked up female laughter and voices inside the house. Lots of females. He wasn't sure if this was a good thing or not.

He hurried up the front steps to the door and laid his ear against it. Suddenly, the door opened and he stumbled inside, tripping over a stack of books but catching himself on the windowpane. In awe, he looked around the room. Women were everywhere.

One spot in the room had several ladies putting makeup on other ladies. Another place had nail polish galore. In the back, he saw fancy, colorful clothes strewn on the stairs, chairs, table, even a lamp. His fourth grade teacher displayed a sexy evening outfit. He slapped a hand over his eyes. He couldn't think of one of his teachers as being sexy. Just not right. No Mrs. Robinson here.

A squeal came from somewhere in the room, then his beautiful mate had her arms around his neck, planting a kiss on his cheek. "Isn't this great!" she said.

"Uh . . ." He wasn't sure what to say. "Define great."

She slapped at him playfully. "Oh, stop that. This is fabulous." She turned and leaned against him as she eyed the room.

"So," he started, "I take it this is your doing?"

"Well, sorta. Mom invited everyone over. I just help if there're questions."

He pulled away and spun his mate around to face him. "My mother invited everyone?"

"Well, technically, she told me to call her 'Mom,' too, but yes, the woman who spit you out of her womb is playing hostess. Quite well, I would say."

If he wasn't there in person to witness it, he would've never believed it. Then he saw his mom making her way to them.

"Isn't this great!" she said.

Amie clasped her hands. "That's what I said." They laughed. At what, Frank didn't know. Didn't want to.

His mom sighed and surveyed the room. "It's been such a long time since I've seen a lot of friends even though they live in the same town. Sometimes it's a shame how caught up we get in our own worlds that we forget there is another outside the door." Mom turned to him. "Are you home for the rest of the day?"

"No" came from his mouth faster than he thought possible. "I mean, we'll see. And why are you wearing a handkerchief on your head?"

She nervously adjusted it on her head. "We'll talk about it later. But Mae didn't call it a handkerchief; she called it a do-mop."

Mae's voice carried over the den. "Do-rag, Jean. Not a do-mop."

"Yeah, whatever," Mom said. She stepped away and filtered through the crowd, smiling, waving, even giving a thumbs-up to a group walking around with books on their heads.

"What are they doing?" He couldn't fathom a reason for balancing a book on the noggin.

"Really?" Amie rolled her eyes at him then lifted her foot in a spiked-heel shoe. "Do you think it's easy to walk in these correctly?"

He raised a brow. "Hadn't ever thought about it. I only know one way to walk." He smiled at her irritation. She was always adorable when flustered.

"And that's why all you men sound like a herd of cattle on a stampede when you walk." She turned and hollered across the room, "Evelyn, toss me a pair of your heels." Seconds later, two hot pink shoes flew through the air, Amie catching both.

She poked him in the ribs with her elbow. "Take your shoes and socks off."

Fear burst through him. "What?"

"I said take your shoes and socks off. I'm teaching you something to expand your horizons."

He stepped back. "Yeah, I don't think so." He wasn't sure what she had in mind, but he didn't think he'd like it.

By the scent in the air, his mate didn't like that answer. Several of the nearby ladies took deep breaths and turned to look at him, eyes narrowed. Oh, fuck. Maybe he should reconsider. Shit. Fine. He shed his footwear quickly.

"Good," she said. "Now put these on." She dropped the hot pink heels by his feet.

"Come on, Amie. What did I do to deserve this?"

One of the ladies said, "You're a male and were born. That's what you did." She then laughed with one of the other ladies.

"Mrs. Holcomb," he replied, "I can solidly blame my mother for that." He looked down at the shoes. "How can they possibly make ladies' shoes so big?"

"Ladies aren't the only ones who wear them, Franky," Mrs. Holcomb said.

He groaned and shoved his feet in the stupid things. He put a hand on the wall to keep his balance. "All right. Let's get this show on the road."

Several of the ladies had stopped what they were doing to

watch. "And a show it will be, won't it, ladies?" one of them called out.

He had a choice to make. He could either be a pussy and fight this all the way, or he could man up and give them something to watch. The twinkle in his mate's eyes made his decision. God, he still loved her.

"Okay, then." Amie turned her backside to him. This was getting better already. "This is the proper way to walk in heels." She took a step forward, lifting her knee and setting her foot flat on the floor—toes and heel hitting at same time. "The biggest thing with walking is make it look like you're gliding. You don't want your body parts flopping all over the place. Which means you don't slam your heel into the ground when you step. You place it flat on the outside of the foot then roll to the inside to push off your big toe.

"Then while you're coming forward and rolling, you bring your other knee forward and place that foot on the outer edge to roll when you move forward. Watch." Amie slid across the floor effortlessly. And damn she looked good doing it. Some of ladies whistled at her sexy strut. On the other side of the door, she completed a perfect one-step turn, resting a hand on her hip. Damn, he wanted to see those curvy hips do that again.

"See how I lead with the knee, step down with heel and ball touching at the same time, quietly. Then swivel to the inside of my foot while I lead again with the other knee." She glided toward him and he thoroughly loved the exhibition. He couldn't help but lick his lips. She caught his movement and gave back a smoldering look. A chill took him, but he couldn't let his dick get hard. That would not be good at the moment.

She came to a stop beside him. "Your turn, stud muffin."

He loosened his tie and unbuttoned his sport coat. The ladies cheered like he was going to take it all off. He mentally snorted. He had this.

His knee came forward and he placed his hairy foot flat on the floor. Thank god the room was carpeted so he wouldn't make noise even if he did it wrong. Which he did. But that wasn't the point anymore. Catcalls followed his balanced trod to the other side of the door where Amie did some kind of turn.

He placed the ball of his foot on the floor and spun. Being his first time in ladies' shoes, he forgot he had to raise his heel even higher. The shoe's spike caught on the carpet, sending him flailing into an upholstered chair, causing the women sitting in it to scream, and all three tipped over, crashing into a side table and lamp.

Amie rushed over to pick them up. Others helped while laughing hilariously at his antics. Yeah, he knew he was a ladies' man. Gladly slipping the shoes off, he stood on flat feet and breathed a sigh of relief. The ladies cheered again.

"Thank you," he said. "Next show is in thirty minutes."

Amie hugged him like old times. She felt so good against him. Her hair had the same apple scent, her skin soft and supple. He nuzzled her neck and, without thinking, placed a kiss on her neck beneath her ear. She melted against him, then must've realized her actions and pulled away.

Not so fast. He grabbed her hand and led her around the outer part of the room, through the kitchen, and out the back door, which he closed securely behind him. He pressed Amie's back against the wood exterior and took her lips with his.

She tasted so good. Like sweet tea and cake. Her lips were lush and soft on his and for once he gave in to the craving. The desire. Amie was his and he didn't need to worry that this was a dream. This time, she was really there. This was really happening and he wouldn't wake up to her gone. To them being apart and his missing the one woman he knew owned his heart. He'd loved her from the moment he'd laid eyes on her and that love had only grown with time.

CHAPTER 13

It was well past three o'clock before Frank, his mate, and Mom had the house back to normal. He hadn't seen his mom so happy in a long time. But he'd noticed that she didn't participate in any of the groups who were learning things. She'd flitted about serving finger foods and drinks and talking to everyone. Goes to show that some things don't change, even though you try.

"Mom," he hollered. "Are there any of those little food thingies left? I'm starving."

"Now that you mention it, I'm hungry, too," Amie said.

Mom came out of the kitchen looking exhausted. "No, those were gone halfway through. I can make us an early dinner."

Amie bumped his arm and raised her brows at him. He thought back to their college years, trying to remember if they had a secret code for raised brows or something. After another second without a response from him, she dug her elbow into his ribs and whispered, "Tell Mom you'll take us out to eat, dammit."

Of course. His cat hit him upside the head. Dumbass. Go out and drag a deer home by the neck. Take care of the females. He reminded it they had modern things called restaurants so people didn't have to hunt anymore. Oh, yay. Let's chase down a plate of filet mignon set right in front of us. That's damn exciting.

Frank sighed. "Mom, let me take us out to a restaurant tonight. You've been going nonstop for hours. Take a break and let's go eat."

"Sounds wonderful."

All three walked down the sidewalk of the shopping district, which consisted of two places to eat, one clothing store, and the beauty salon and butcher's shop. Everything was exactly the same as he remembered. As long as he didn't look too closely.

"Hmm," Amie said, staring down at the crumbling concrete foundation and faded material decorating the front. "Place needs a bit of TLC. But I know how tight money can be." He watched as Amie studied everything around her. He knew the wheels churning in the wonderful, highly creative brain of hers. Her willingness to help and give freely of herself had not changed in the years they'd been apart. A hint of heartache came with the thought.

Mom said, "It could definitely use a remodel, but the dinner entrées are divine. I can't even make a steak as tender as the chef here."

They walked in to seat themselves. For being mid-afternoon, there were several tables occupied. The aroma of red meat smelled fabulous. No place in DC even came close to down-home shifter cooking. When passing each table, he glanced to see what each person was having. All of the dishes made his mouth water. His mom picked a booth along the wall and sat on the outer part of one bench, forcing him and Amie to sit together. He eyed his mom, knowing what she was doing. Her look was just daring him to call her out. He kept his mouth closed.

The waitress was quick to come by with menus. She introduced herself and took their drink orders. Next to him, Amie thumbed through the menu, turned to the back, then flipped it over to the front.

"Is this everything?" He looked down at her menu. It was the same as his.

"Yeah, why?"

She shrugged. "Didn't see anything but . . . Never mind. I think I know what I want."

The waitress returned with their drinks. Mom asked her, "Didn't you used to work at the other restaurant?"

The girl nodded and smiled. "I did. I thought tips might be better here since they do more dinner business. Bob's place does mainly breakfast and lunch. This restaurant is owned by his ex-wife. You knew that, right?"

Both Mom and Frank nodded.

"I love Dorothy to death. And I'd do anything for Bob, so . . . I don't know. I like sleeping in. Dorothy doesn't even open until one o'clock."

"If Bob and Dorothy would work together, they could combine their places and have one awesome place all day long instead of two rents and two sets of employees. They could save a ton of money," Amie tossed out.

The waitress snorted. "That's the problem. I think Dorothy would kill Bob within ten minutes if they were in the same room."

"Oh," Amie replied, "they don't get along at all?"

The waitress rolled her eyes. "Are you kidding? Bob's a dog, according to her. And Dorothy's pussy just can't take all of him."

Everyone had placed their orders when the front door opened and another couple walked in. "I'll be back in a minute with your meals."

Frank and his mom caught the whiff at the same time. Intense, unadulterated embarrassment. They looked at Amie. Her face was beet-red, mouth hanging open, eyes ready to pop out.

Mom got a worried look on her face. "What's wrong, dear?"

Amie stuttered and couldn't put a sentence together. Finally she spit out, "She was talking about her boss's hoo-ha like it was no big deal."

"What's a hoo-ha, dear?" Mom asked.

Amie's face turned redder. "You know. A woman's . . ." She looked around then pointed to her lap under the table.

"Oh!" Mom said, understanding. Frank kept his mouth shut. This was way too dangerous a territory for him to tread. "No, sweetie." Mom put her hand on his mate's. "She was talking about her cat. Oh, wait." Mom looked at Frank.

He put his hands up. "Don't drag me in on this. I don't talk about pussy in public." Mom slapped his arm and Amie laughed. Amie pushed on his arm to let her out and she headed to the restroom.

"Son," Mom whispered, "you've got to tell her what you are."

"No, we don't. She's doing fine. Were there any problems with the ladies at your house today?"

Mom sighed. "No, but she went freakazoid when Butch shifted his lion's head in the store this morning."

"What?" He almost came out of his seat. "Why did he do that?" A few customers glanced at him.

"Keep your voice down. He didn't know she didn't know. She went screaming from the store and hit her head on the salon's door and knocked herself out for a couple minutes."

"She what? Oh my god, is she hurt?" He stood ready to run into the restroom and check his mate head to toe for injuries.

"Sit down." Mom yanked on his jacket. "She's fine. But doesn't remember the seconds before she passed out. And we should leave it at that. But, François, you have to tell her."

He ran nervous fingers through his hair. "Fine, Mom. I'll tell her when the time is right."

"Good." Mom sipped tea from her glass and set it down. "Now, tell me about you two in school, because by the amount of pheromones floating in the living room earlier, you two know each other much better than you're letting on, François. Any more scent floating around and we would've had a full-blown orgy going on."

"Mom!" He ducked his head and looked around, praying no one was listening in. "You can't say those things in public."

"Sorry, son. I just don't like not knowing the whole story."

He wiped a sweaty hand down his face. "I met Amie at school. She's my true mate—" His mom gasped. "I know,

Mom. Let me finish. I never said anything to you because I didn't know how to tell her about shifters. If I brought her home and she found out, I was afraid she'd leave me. But it really didn't matter because she left me anyway right before graduation.

"She went home for the weekend while I stayed to study for my last exam. I never saw her after that. She sent me a text saying she couldn't see me again."

"She couldn't see you again?" Mom replied. "What the hell does that mean? You don't just up and leave your mate—"

"Mom, calm down," he said. "I know. Something was going on at her home that stopped her from wanting to see me. That's the feeling I got. Like she had no choice in the matter." He pulled that story out of his ass. He hoped she didn't smell his uneasiness.

"Why didn't you go to her home and ask her?"

Oh, fuck. He didn't want to get into all the Mafia stuff and Amie's real name and why he didn't know about either back then. He sighed. "At the time, it wasn't possible."

"What—"

"Just take my word for it, Mom. I couldn't."

His mom was quiet for a moment. "That's why you joined ALFA so quickly. To get away from the pain you and your cougar were suffering." He nodded. "That makes sense now." She laid a hand on his arm. "Why didn't you tell me?"

He wiggled in his seat, uncomfortable with his mom's scrutiny. "Mom, I'm not good with that kind of stuff. I didn't want to come home with my tail dragging on the ground."

She smiled and patted his hand. "Your father was the same way. He wouldn't say a single mushy word or sentiment unless it was pulled out of him with giant pliers. You know, he didn't ask me to marry him." That surprised him. They were married, right? "He simply told me to make wedding plans and tell him when and where and he'd be there." They both laughed.

Amie walked out from the hallway, talking to a familiar woman. He then recognized the woman as the owner of the restaurant. They talked and looked around the place. Amie pointed at something and Dorothy nodded.

His eye caught old Mrs. Hagerty staring at the two ladies.

And the look didn't appear nice. It looked rather hateful. He didn't like that. No one threatened his mate. He started to stand, then Amie shook hands with Dorothy and came toward them. He moved to let her slide in, then sat beside her. When he looked back at Hagerty, she was gone. Crazy old woman, he thought.

"What were you and Dorothy talking about?" Mom asked.

"Oh"—Amie shrugged—"I had some low-cost decorating ideas she might be interested in. Just simple things, really. But they could have a big impact."

Not too far from their table, a baby cried out. Two parents sat at a table with eight children. The kids looked identical, except in age, all with white fluffy hair and under twelve. Ah, yes, he remembered the rabbit family.

Mom said, "That's Roger's family. I think he was a couple years older than you. I can't remember; he has so many siblings." She stifled a giggle.

The waitress set a tray on a holder next to their table. She saw them looking at the rabbit family. Amie said, "There sure are a lot of them. I've never seen such fluffy, curly hair. Wow. How does she do it?"

The waitress waved a hand. "And that's not even all their children. That's normal for rabbits. You know the saying." She handed over a plate with a steak taking up the entire area.

Amie motioned to the mother with the crying baby. "She has salad and carrots and veggies. I didn't see that on the menu."

"Good thing she's a rabbit, then." The waitress laughed. Frank, horror racing through him, glanced wide-eyed at Mom.

Amie said. "You mean she eats like a rabbit. Yeah, she does."

"That's because she is! But I love them to death." The server laughed, picked up her empty tray, and headed to the kitchen. Amie looked at him, but he cut into his steak, pretending that the strange conversation hadn't come from down the rabbit hole.

Amie asked Mom what the mother's name was. Mom said, "Alice, I think. Alice and Roger—"

"Rabbit," Amie finished.

His mom smiled. "Actually, it's Angora. Roger and Alice

Angora." He hoped his mom didn't go on to tell Amie that Angora was a breed of rabbit.

The three went about quietly eating. He wanted to get back to the house as soon as he could. Not only to get away from the whole shifter debacle, but he had plans for his guest this evening. His mother sniffed and looked at him. Fuck. Being in a shifter town sucked when you had your mate with you and you hadn't had sex except with Mr. Hand for a couple years.

The main door opened and Mom's breath caught. He noted a scent he never expected, nor wanted, to smell from his mother. Thinking about your parents having sex is one thing. Smelling when they wanted it was another.

He turned in his seat to see who had walked in. It was just Butch. Amie tapped his arm. Even she noticed Mom's reaction. Huh, his mom had something for the meat man. At least she picked a guy who could keep her fed.

He'd think about matchmaking his mom later. Right now, he had his own libido to think about.

CHAPTER 14

B lanket thrown over one arm and an old basket with a couple water bottles and beef jerky sticks in the other, Frank led Amie out of the backyard and into the woods.

"Where are we going?" she asked.

"It's a surprise. You'll love it. Just wait." Seeing that they had an early dinner, the sun was just now settling over the tops of the trees. The breeze was cool, which was good because his skin was already hot.

He stopped and looked over his shoulder at his mate. "Hurry up, slowpoke. We're here." She came up beside him and her eyes widened. "You like it?" The old hollow hadn't changed much in the years he'd been gone. Overgrown a bit. He could take care of that before he left. He wanted to keep it clean and easy to access.

"It's beautiful, Frank." A small rocky stream meandered through the woods, flowing over worn-smooth stones into a shallow pool. The tinkling of the mini waterfall was calming and serene. The perfect place to talk and . . . whatever.

Frank spread the blanket over a flat spot by the peaceful pool and helped Amie sit. He settled next to her, not expecting the butterflies in his stomach. Since when had he been shy or nervous around anyone? That was what she did to him.

"Frank—"

"No, let me say something first," he said. "I have questions about things that happened in the past, but I'd rather let them go if we can begin again."

"Begin again?" she asked.

"Yeah, you tell me about you. I tell you about me." Her eyes were on her fingers pulling at a thread in the blanket.

"Have you been with a lot of other women?" she asked, catching him off guard with something so personal.

"No," he said. "I went on a date once, but it was a disaster. She talked about her ex, and I talked about you. At the end of the date, she gave me the number to her shrink and left. How about you?"

"My uncle has paid for escorts to take me to functions he wanted me to attend, but I arrived and left by myself. I had no interest in anyone."

He nodded, feeling very relieved. His cat would've pushed him to find and skin these "escorts" if they would've touched her. "Your uncle the Mafia boss?"

She sighed. "Yeah, him. Giuseppe Ragusa."

"I never thought—"

Amie grabbed him around the shirt and pulled his lips to hers. Her mouth was hot and tasted of filet mignon from dinner. He wanted more of her. Needed more of her.

She pushed him back just far enough to talk. "Frank, don't ask any questions, don't expect any answers, don't hope for any future. But tonight, hold me the way you did before I had to go away. Make me believe we were never apart. Love me tonight."

He leaned down, intent on giving her exactly what she asked for. What she didn't know was that he planned on keeping her. He would find out what made her "go away" and put an end to it. But for now, he would love her with everything he had.

Amie loved the feel of his lips on hers. If she'd had any doubt about wanting him, it had gone out the window at that point. The feral way his gaze swept her face made her shiver in need.

"I'm going to take what's mine, Amie. You." His words skyrocketed her need out of this planet. Desire and lust pushed her at this point. He took her clothes off in a quick, tense rush. Then his lips were all over her. Not nearly as fast as she wanted, but driving her slowly insane with their perfect caresses.

He bit down on her belly. His downward travels stopped when he reached her bare pussy. He licked her inner thigh and she groaned. "I've been dreaming of having a taste of you again, Amie. So badly."

She bit her lip. Words stuck in her throat. Any will to say no had evaporated and been replaced with her need for him. To give in and to get her man. She'd missed him so much and it was time to stop waiting for him. Her legs spread wider as if to give him the hint. His lip curled in a fuck-a-licious grin.

"Know what I want?" He licked closer to her pussy but not close enough. God, that was nowhere near close enough and she might lose her mind if he didn't hurry it up. She almost yelled at him. Did he fucking need a map? He was bent on torturing her.

Jesus, how she needed to come. Her legs already shook from her lack of control over her muscles. He was going to kill her from sexual frustration. She lifted her hands to her nipples and pinched, the bite of pain adding to the ever-growing need in her body.

"I want to feel your pussy soaking my face."

Oh. My. God.

A sharp electric current shot down right to her clit, making it twitch. Her body trembled and all he'd done was have a few licks around her pussy. At this rate she'd never make it another five minutes.

He licked at the crease between her pussy and her leg. So close but still so far.

"Please, Frank," she moaned. She let go of her nipples and gripped clumps of his short hair.

"Ah, fuck, baby." He licked over her pussy lips. "Wiggle those hips and show me how much you like my tongue on your clit."

She whimpered, pressed closer to his mouth—if that were possible—and waited. If he didn't do more, she'd be the first woman she knew to come with words alone.

"You are so fucking gorgeous, Amie. I'm so hard seeing you slick, hot, and wet," he groaned. He rubbed his face on her slick folds. "You smell delicious, like an amazing memory. Only you're real and this won't be a dream that goes away when I wake up. You'll be mine. All mine."

The ragged sounds of her breaths filled her ears. She couldn't think. All she could do was hope he'd lick her again. Soon.

She spread her legs even wider. "Frank . . ."

His gaze caught hers at the moment he flattened his tongue and licked a slow trail up to her clit. It ended with an agonizing suck of her tiny hard nub.

"Yesss."

Her nipples puckered so damn tight. She hadn't had sex since the last time she'd been with Frank. He'd killed her desire to be with anyone else. Now here he was again, touching her, taking her. Everything was perfect as long as he was doing those wonderful things to her body.

Frank licked her clit in quick hard swipes. One after another, they left her breathless and begging. Her body tensed so fast it caught her off guard.

"Oh . . . oh . . . my . . ." She choked the words out.

Frank reached his hands up to cup her breasts and tweak her nipples. The feel of his callused fingers added a new dimension of painful pleasure. Desire flowed through her in waves of heat and fire, and a storm raged in her core, pushing her closer to the edge. She rocked her hips, rolling them back and forth on his face.

"That's it," he muttered between licks and sucks. "Ride my face."

She liked the sound of his voice. Liked the way he encouraged her to be naughty. Not that any encouragement was necessary. She was one lick away from coming on his face and that thought alone made her even hotter.

"Come, baby." He pushed his tongue into her sex. She almost came on the spot. "Once you do, I promise to lick up every bit of your sweetness."

She wanted that oh so badly. Her body vibrated with the need to ride the orgasm wave. She was at the peak; a little push and she'd go over.

Frank's actions got more aggressive. He pressed his tongue over her clit and then sucked her harder. Her body trembled with his low growl over her sensitive flesh. That definitely caught her off guard and pushed her into the abyss.

She screamed. Her back bowed. Her head thrashed with the eruption of pleasure rushing her body. Her breath reeled, pumping hard into her lungs. She kept coming, her orgasms pushing each other until she was spent and almost falling asleep from the amount of energy she'd expended. She'd missed this. She'd missed the intimacy between her and Frank. He pulled her into his arms and held her close.

"Tell me what you want now, beautiful."

She rolled him onto his back and placed a leg on either side of him and slid his cock into her entrance. "You. I want you. Deep."

She rode him hard, her body gliding up and down and tensing with every slide down. He was hot and thick, pulsing deep inside her. He gripped her hips with every single slam down.

"Do it, baby. Ride me. Suck my cum into your hot wet pussy."

She wiggled more. He helped her, biting his fingers into her hips and lifting and dropping her on his cock.

With every slam down, she moaned and whimpered his name. He grunted, telling her how much he loved her curves. How gorgeous her body was. Then she was going faster and faster, her body slick with perspiration and the tension inside her ready to snap.

She slammed down a final time, taking him as deep as she could. Pleasure flowed as tension snapped. He growled, lifting his hips up and driving deeper into her. His cock felt harder, hotter, and bigger inside her. Then he was spilling his seed into her. She took large gulps of air while her pussy contracted around his cock. Her body sucked his cum into her channel.

"That's it, baby. Take it. Take me." He yanked her head down and met her lips for a ferocious kiss. "We're just beginning, gorgeous. I plan on having you every way possible." He met her gaze. "Every way."

CHAPTER 15

Even though it was early morning, she called her son. The Running Winds were up with the sun, so she knew her little one would be awake. She missed him so much. His cute way of talking, puppy-dog eyes, innocent baby-toothed smile, and great big heart. That he'd definitely gotten from his father. She loved thinking of the conversations with her son. He was adorable and if she could hug him every day of her life and never let go, she would.

"Hi, Mommy!"

"Hi, baby. I miss you so much! How are you?"

"'Kay. I eat eggs," he said in a muffled voice.

"That's really good, French fry. Are you having fun?"

"Mm-hm. We feed the chickens. I miss you, Mommy. When you coming?"

"Soon, baby. Really soon. I just wanted to tell you that I love you, okay? You know how much I love you?"

He giggled. "A cow?"

"Nuh-uh. Try again."

"A chair?"

"Bigger, baby. Think really big."

"A pwanet?"

She snorted at the awe in his voice. "Even bigger."

"The sun?"

"I love you more than all the biggest things. You're my heart."

"You my hart, too, Mommy."

Now in her robe, Amie stepped off the sixth stair and heard the creak, switching her weight to the next step. She was a bit sore this morning after years of no action. But it was the sweetest pain, for her heart's happiness far outweighed the ache.

Frying bacon and ham smelled great to her growling stomach.

She came around the kitchen's corner to find Frank standing at the stove and Mom sitting at the table with a newspaper in front of her. "Good morning, early riser," Mom said. "No need to send the cat up to get you."

Frank glanced over his shoulder at them.

Amie didn't know what Mom meant. "What cat?"

Mom waved her hand around. "It's just a saying we have." Mom grinned and her brow rose. "Ask Frank about it. He'll explain." Frank frowned and flipped the ham. Mom snapped the paper in her hands.

"Oh," Mom said, "did you hear about the senator killed in Las Vegas? They think the Mafia used a bank robbery as a cover to kill the man. Kinda strange. Not sure why they wanted to cover it up like that. Why not just shoot him? That's how they usually do it, right?"

"Mom," Frank said.

"You know what I mean. It's the Mafia, for crying out loud. Since when did they care if they were thought to have killed someone? Honestly, though, I didn't know the Mafia really existed anymore."

Amie peeked at the newspaper in Mom's hands. "Does it say why they killed the senator?"

"It doesn't come right out and say it, but the latest thing the senator was working on was rebuilding the old parts of town to make them family-oriented: parks, playgrounds, residential housing."

"Oh," Amie said. "So he wanted to cut off their income.

That's smart." Which is exactly what Uncle Giuseppe complained about. She wondered if there was a way that she could do something to get her uncle out of her life. Frank laid a plate of bacon in the center of the table.

"Oh, my," Mom said after Amie plucked a bacon slice from the plate, "did you know Al Capone still has relatives alive?"

Amie choked on her bite of food and coughed. "Really?"

"Yeah, it says Amerella Capone, Al's great-great-grandniece—her home was damaged in an explosion and she has disappeared." Nonchalantly Mom turned the page. "Lots going on in Vegas this week. Glad we have none of that nonsense in this town."

Amie kept her eyes to herself. She felt Mom gauging her Frank's and reactions. Did Mom know something? Was Mom telling her and Frank they weren't welcome if they had anything to do with the Mafia or Vegas? If Mom kicked them out, where would she go?

Frank brushed a hand across her shoulders as he passed behind her, setting the ham on the table. "How about I show you around town later this morning?"

"That would be great." She turned to Mom. "Any plans for today?"

"Not that I know of. Not unless we have another impromptu party this afternoon."

"I don't have any clothes left," Amie said, laughing. "We'd have to do something else."

Frank looked at her. "Why don't you have any clothes?"

Mom gave him a funny look. "She gave them all away yesterday, silly. Didn't you see all the women had something nice when they left? All the blink."

"Bling, Mom," Amie said. "It's bling."

"All these new words you kids bring home. I feel like I'm learning another language."

Frank beamed at Amie. She felt a bit embarrassed by his attention. Had she gotten so wrapped up in herself and material objects that she came across as spoiled or snooty? What had happened to her over the past four years? She almost didn't like the person she'd become. In college, she didn't care about such things.

Last night with Frank at the stream was magical. She was happy again. Her heart opened without fear of reprisal. No one knew they were there. No one knew she was here. As long as she was here, she could have him. She could love like she'd always wanted to. When it came time to go back, she'd deal with it then. But for now, she could love him. Tears burned her eyes. She blinked them away before embarrassing herself.

Frank's mom sighed. "I think you kids spending the day out would be great. Maybe we can do lunch at Bob's. He's got a great lunch menu. But first, Frank, take her shopping at Marianne's."

Frank snorted. "Like there is another place to shop for clothes, Mom."

She brushed him off. "Yeah, yeah. Keep that East Coast attitude to yourself, young man." She winked and carried her dishes to the sink. "Frank, think about what we discussed at dinner last night. I think it's time." Then she left.

Amie looked at Frank. "What's she talking about?"

He frowned and turned away. "Nothing. I'll tell you later. How about you put on something to go shopping and I'll clean up so we can go."

The walk into town was exhilarating. The clean air had humidity and felt great. They were only a few hours from Vegas and the desert, but she was amazed how different the weather was. Her hair was a constant frizz of curls.

Frank opened the door to Marianne's Clothes Stop and ushered her inside. Amie froze in her tracks. No wonder Mom and everyone in town dressed like they lived in the past. That's all they had to choose from. She thought about the Prada store she was in less than a week ago. Night and day.

Bright side was she'd now blend in and not stick out.

A lady stepped from behind a curtained-off area by the counter at the back. "Hello, can I help—" Recognition lit the lady's face. "Amie and Frank. How good to see you again." Marianne hugged them both. "I have to say, Amie, you and Jean throw a wonderful spontaneous party. I loved every bit of it. And I didn't even hog the clothes. But look here." Marianne flipped her earrings.

They were a pair with pearl centers and gold petals around them. Frank didn't remember ever seeing those on Amie. But he remembered her saying that when packing, she'd just dumped handfuls of stuff in the suitcase.

"They look fabulous on you," Amie said. And they did.

"Let me guess . . ." Marianne said. "You need to buy clothes because you gave away everything yesterday." Her laughter rang through the customer-free store. "Frank, your mate is one of the nicest ladies I have ever met."

Amie's eyes widened. "Oh, we're not—"

"Not here to replace everything she gave away," Frank cut in. "And she is the best, isn't she?" He kissed her on the top of her head and swatted her ass. She squeaked and jumped a bit.

Marianne's smile drooped a bit as she looked around. "Well, I'm afraid I don't have much that will suit your taste. As you can see, the only things most women in town buy are unfashionable and way out of style. I've tried updating the clothing, but it just doesn't sell."

"Let Frank and me look around for a minute and maybe an idea will pop up based on what we learned yesterday with the ladies. It might be the right time for an upgrade."

Marianne's hands crossed over her heart. "That would be so wonderful. Go, look around. Tell me what comes to mind. I'll be by the counter."

Frank felt lost, not having the slightest clue about anything. Some of the clothing his mom would like. But he really couldn't see his mate wearing any of it.

Amie found a section with a variety of options that were more like her, he thought. Conservative, but more modern.

Frank cozied himself behind her, his hard dick settling between her ass cheeks. Hidden among the myriad of clothes, he slid his hands around Amie, under the waist of her pants. She quietly hissed as his fingers separated her pussy folds and found their way inside her. He took her weight as she leaned back.

Fucking damn. Wetness nearly poured from her, slickening his fingers. God, how he wished his dick was inside her. He rubbed up and down her ass, wanting to come hard inside her.

She snatched a few items from the metal rods and hurried

toward the fitting room. "Marianne, I'll be in the fitting room for a while," Amie called.

"Holler if you need any help," the owner replied.

She stepped into the stall at the far end and dragged him in with her. He closed the door and pressed her back against it.

CHAPTER 16

Frank smiled and cupped her breasts in his hands. She was so fucking beautiful. "We don't have time to play," Amie mumbled, but continued stripping off his T-shirt.

"We don't?" He chuckled.

"No," she groaned, sliding her hand up and down his chest, then down into the waistband of his jeans. She undid his zipper, her hands pushing the offensive material down and off his body.

"Then we better make this quick," he whispered, his gaze locked onto hers. Her eyes filled with love and he knew what she wasn't saying. That she loved him just as much as he loved her. She was his. In every primal way possible.

Her clothes came off in a rush. She spread her legs open for him, giving him access to her moist heat. He loved the scent of her arousal. Like the sweetest cream, she drew him in for a taste. He planted small kisses on his way down her body. When he reached her belly, he rubbed his cheek on her abdomen before moving down to her sex.

"You smell fucking delicious," he groaned. Curling his arms around her full, sexy thighs, he pushed her legs back and rubbed his nose over her clit.

"Frank!" She clung to the metal hanger rods.

Knock.
Knock.
Knock.

"Are you okay in there?" Marianne asked. "I heard a scream."

"Yeah, uh, we're"—she groaned—"good."

Marianne gasped. "Oh my god," she mumbled before her they heard her heels tapping on the wood floor as she rushed away.

Frank chuckled at Amie's groan. "She must be imagining the worst," Amie said.

"Relax," he whispered and placed a kiss at the center of her gleaming sex.

He licked at her pussy in circles over her tender, slick flesh. Her scent drove his animal wild. There was a clear need and desperate urging on with every word she spoke. She gripped his hair tight in her fists, pushing her pussy to his lips.

She moaned louder at each twirl of his tongue on her clit. Her channel flexed around his tongue, sucking him deep. He wanted to feel her doing that to his cock. Feel her pussy squeeze tight on him with every glide into her fluttering walls.

The tiny bundle of nerves peeking between her pussy lips made his mouth water. He flicked his tongue over the hard little nub. He loved her body. Loved touching and tasting her. He'd die a happy man if he could do this forever. She gasped, legs locking tight. With another lick and the grazing of his teeth, she screamed as her body shook. He inhaled her scent, caressing her quivering sex with his lips.

A tugging on his hair caused him to glance up. Her smile and sleepy eyes brought back that satisfied feeling from before. He didn't know why she'd left before, but this, them, they were fucking perfect together.

"Come here," she whispered with a wide smile on her swollen lips.

He stood up, ignoring the aching hard-on and the desperate need to ram into her. He'd been thinking of this, her and him inside her for way too long. It never left his mind. With one hand on his cock, she pumped him hard from root to tip.

Lord, that felt so fucking amazing. He clenched his teeth to keep from begging her to do it again, and watched her smile widen.

"I love that."

"What?" he asked with a crazy rough quality to his voice. One he couldn't help since his animal lay right below the surface.

"That brightness in your eyes."

"You like it? Why?"

She pumped him in her grip again. "I can see you're fighting your control and losing," she mumbled. "Are you losing your control over me?"

"Baby, I'm this close to fucking your brains into the next stall," he said, his voice deeper and harder due to how turned-on he was.

"Do it." She licked her lips. "I feel empty without you."

Fuck, this wasn't what he'd expected her to say. Another time and he'd have tried to take it easy. Taken it slow. Not today. He wanted her too much. Her scent called out the beast within. In a single thrust, he drove deep. Her pussy rippled around his cock.

"Oh, god!"

Her whimper of satisfaction did him in. They locked lips and kissed while the urge to fill her with his seed overpowered all his thinking abilities.

Fuck her. Take her. Mate her.

Thrusts turned frenzied, his movements uncoordinated. She dug her nails deep into his shoulders. The bite of pain only pushed his feral side to the open. A growl rumbled in his chest, blending with the sound of her enjoyment. Her nails raked his scalp and she yanked his hair back, pulling his face from hers. She chose that moment to squeeze her pelvic muscles around his cock.

"Hell!" he choked out.

"Make. Me. Come," she ordered breathlessly.

He rammed her repeatedly. Their gazes locked. The link between them thickened with each thrust, until there was nothing but the two of them. Nothing else existed in their passion bubble. Sliding a hand between them, he rubbed on her slick center and watched her go over.

Pleasure filled her features, and she choked back a scream. His muscles burned from exertion. His beast turned his body stiff as he closed in on his own release. Fire crackled down his spine, shooting through his cock and releasing into her channel, filling her with his scent. Marking her as his from inside.

He jerked into her greedily, groaning at each suck her pussy did on his dick. With every spasm of her sex, he jerked again. It went like that for long moments.

"Wow, Frank. I've never had this type of experience in a fitting room, but damn. This is a much better way to go shopping."

He chuckled and kissed her, holding her still-shaking body in a tight embrace. She was his. No matter what she said, she was his.

Amie straightened the new outfit she finally got to try on and decided she'd wear it now. She made her way to the counter while Frank slipped outside. That was a good thing. If he was anywhere near her, she'd never cool down.

She laid the tags and garments on the counter for Marianne to ring up. The owner's cheeks blushed a bit. "May I ask you a question, Ms. Truman?" she asked.

"Only if you call me Amie," she replied with a smile.

"How did you become so self-confident and powerful?"

Powerful? Amie never thought of herself as powerful. In fact, she felt like she was under the thumb of her uncle. But she put herself in Marianne's place in this small town. Thinking that way, Amie could see how she looked bigger than life with all the flashy clothes and jewelry.

"Truthfully, Marianne, I live by a motto: Fake it 'til you make it. You can't be confident if you don't see yourself that way."

"How can I possibly see myself like you?"

Oh, god. If Marianne only knew how pathetic Amie felt sometimes, but had to be strong for her son. What could she tell this woman that would help her?

"Well, the first thing you have to do is take control of your life. Write down how you want to be and work on doing just that. For example, if a woman wants to feel sexy, she needs to wear what she feels sexy in. The place to start is with lingerie."

Marianne giggled. "Crotchless undies and stuff? Should I add that to my lingerie inventory?"

"Not necessarily to that extreme. Granted, granny underwear doesn't usually make someone feel sexy, but maybe a high-cut bikini with slick material. Just by changing from cotton to silk, you feel a difference against your skin and in how it makes you feel."

Marianne seemed to be taking everything in.

Amie chewed her lip, wondering if she wanted to broach this subject or not. What the hell? "Have you ever been properly fitted for a bra?"

The woman looked at her. "I don't even know what that means."

Amie realized what she was about to share with the store owner could change the woman's life. "This, Marianne, is how you are going to change this town and make it better than it has ever been for women. To feel confident, you need to wear what makes you feel that way and wear it correctly." Amie looked around for other customers. The store was empty.

"Come with me." She grabbed Marianne's hand and led her to the fitting room. "You're a big gal like me. And sometimes clothes have to be adjusted a bit." Amie took the lady to the mirrors then turned to Marianne. "Unbutton your blouse, and I'll show you what you need to teach each woman and maturing girl when they come for their first bras."

Marianne blushed a bit, but she seemed eager to learn.

"Okay, let's start here." Amie pointed to the bottom front of the cups. "The underwire or band across the chest needs to lay against your ribcage right under the breast. No gaps of too far down or on the breast itself. Right now, see the gap at the bottom? The wire is not flush against your chest." Marianne ran a finger over the bottom of the bra smashed against the underneath of her large breast.

"Hmm." More than just the verbal discussion was needed

here. "Don't move," Amie continued, "I'll be right back." She headed toward the undergarments section at the back of the store. Needed to do something about that, too. People couldn't buy what they couldn't see. Lingerie is a spontaneous buy.

She pulled out a size 36DD. Some women suffered all day long just because they wanted to say they wore the same size they did in high school. They are doing more harm to their bodies than good.

"Put this on," Amie said, handing over the brassiere, "in the stall, then let me know how it feels." While Marianne changed, Amie thought it best to talk about the other side of the coin. "There's the opposite case, where the underwire is too low, which allows the ladies to sag in the cup. We all know sagging is not good. So if the wire is on the ribs, exactly where the breast ends and chest begins, then there shouldn't be drooping."

The stall opened and the store owner stepped out. "This is so much better. I hate that it's a size bigger, but it feels so much better."

Amie leaned forward. "Now, bend over a bit to have the ladies dangle, then reach in and lift one as high as it will go." When Marianne did so, the bra's underwire rested against her ribs. "Do the same for the other lady. Lift the breast so the bottom strap sits on ribs. Now stand straight."

Marianne's expression told Amie she'd done good. "Oh my goodness. I feel so much lighter. I don't feel as smashed."

"Exactly," Amie said. "By lifting and letting your ladies settle, the underwire is doing its job of holding up instead of letting the breast hang with nothing underneath. You want your ladies looking up and not down, if you get my meaning." Both laughed as Marianne stared at her correct support.

"Of course, the rest of the fit is to make sure it's not too tight or too loose. Needs to be comfortable. And the cup needs to be big enough to hold the entire breast in the front. If your bra smashes your ladies and they fall out of the cup's sides, then get a bigger size. Plus, the wider the straps, the better the support also. Women like us really shouldn't wear elastic spaghetti straps with a one-eye hook in the back for long periods of time."

"I know," Marianne said. "You'd be a walking time bomb, ready to explode. Literally." They giggled. Amie buttoned up her friend's blouse then stood back and looked in the mirror.

"If you start feeling heavy during the day, step away from others' eyes, then bend forward and give the straps a little shake to get the ladies up again. Now it's your responsibility to teach correct support to others." Amie hooked an arm through one of Marianne's. "I also think you can bring in modern styles. But the trick is showing the other ladies in town how to wear the new stuff.

"Maybe every spring and fall, have a fun little fashion show here at the store and have some of the ladies model outfits. Show everyone how to wear the right jewelry, even how a scarf can change a look. Show them how to wrap and tie a scarf, and the ladies will more than likely buy what they know how to use."

At the store's entrance, Marianne stopped Amie in her tracks. "Oh my god. You're right. That's the problem. The women don't know how to wear the new fancy stuff. They don't know how to match leggings to the right sweaters or tops. Or how to use a belt around the sweater to make it a manicured look."

"Yes," Amie said. "You got it! Exactly."

Tears came to the store owner's eyes. Oh, shit. What did she do wrong? "You okay, Marianne?"

"I'm fine. It's just that for the first time, I see this store being what I've always wanted it to be. It'll be a dream come true to give women self-assurance through wearing what makes them feel good. Like you." Marianne gave her a hug. "Thank you so much for the ideas and confidence to finally do this."

"You'll do great. Let me know if you ever want someone to bounce ideas off. I make a great sounding board." Amie sighed with happiness, knowing she was able to help someone and made a new friend for life. Frank opened the door and stepped in.

"We ready to go to the park—" Frank looked her up and down.

"Something wrong?" Amie asked.

"No, just admiring my lady like I remember her. No flashy stuff. Just you." Both she and Marianne melted on the spot.

"Wow," Marianne said, "you got yourself a good one, Amie."

Amie slipped her arm around Frank's waist. "Yes, I do."

.

CHAPTER 17

Frank held on to a shopping bag with a couple outfits Marianne had handed him before they left the store. The park they strolled had more people milling around than he was used to seeing. Moms sat on benches, talking while the kids played on the playground. So much for her keeping a low profile. The entire town knew her already.

"So," Frank said, "did you mean it when you agreed on me being a great guy? Which I am, you know." He tugged on his shirt, lifting his chin.

"Please," Amie retorted, "don't make me puke." She laughed when he feigned being emotionally hurt. His heart hurt, but for a different reason.

A couple ladies on a bench waved. "Hi, Amie, Frank."

Susan gave them a conspiratorial wink. "We know it's not our business, and not to pressure you guys, but are you planning on dating soon?"

Cheryl elbowed Susan. "I think they already are. You two make such a cute couple. Thanks for the party yesterday. It was great."

Amie waved back. "Thanks, Susan and Cheryl. I'll see what I can come up with for an encore."

He mustered the courage to ask what he really wanted to

know. "So, what do I need to know about Amerella Capone that's different from Amie Truman?" Her fear and shame floated in the air. But he stood strong. He wanted her to answer him. Answers were important.

She chewed her lip. "Amerella and Amie are the same. I never lied to you. I just gave selective answers."

"Selective answers?" he asked. "What's that?"

"You know the saying that men have 'selective hearing.' I was offering selective answers. Things that I knew wouldn't scare you or make you leave me." He couldn't believe she thought her family would scare him off. She never gave him a chance to show her. As he readied to make a retort, Amie held up a hand.

"Hi, Amie. Hi, Frank. Loved the party, Amie. Tell Jean thanks for hosting."

"You're welcome, Scarlet. We'll be sure to tell her." Amie took a deep breath. "Let me finish, then you can tear into me. My mom and dad died in a car wreck when I was young. I told you that. Uncle Giuseppe became my guardian and I lived in his mansion until I escaped to college."

"Did he treat you badly?" Frank would skin the man alive if he so much as laid one hand on her.

"He did his duty giving me food and shelter. But the emotional stuff he wasn't good at. I spent a lot of time babysitting for the child of a friend, who was more a mom to me than anything." Amie looked away and wiped at her eyes. He sensed a sadness roll through and waited for her to explain. But when she didn't, he wasn't going to push.

"Is the woman and her child the reason you came back to Vegas after school?" He was hoping to wheedle out an answer for why she left him.

"Not really. By then Joey was old enough to take care of himself." She snorted. "I thought so, anyway. But actually my uncle is still my legal guardian until I turn twenty-six next month and my trust fund becomes mine. Until then, he has control of it along with my dad's attorneys."

Instant fear ran through him. In his experience, large sums of money and giving up control of it never worked out well.

"What happens to your fund if . . ." He couldn't say the words. The thought was too horrible for him.

"If I'm dead?" Amie finished. "It goes to a very close family member before my uncle could get to it."

Frank let out a whoosh of air. "That makes me feel better."

Amie laughed. "Dad knew what he was doing when it came to money and security for Mom and me." Overwhelming sadness poured from her, almost sending Frank to his knees. His cat told him to change the subject, or it would.

Amie stopped and shoved at his arm. "You're a big-time super-secret agent now. Show me some moves."

"What moves? I'm an agent, not a dancer," he replied. "Although, I rocked in those women's shoes yesterday." He strode forward, pretending to walk like he did in the high heels.

"Yeah," Amie began, "until you wiped out the chair, the ladies in the chair, and table and lamp."

"That was part of the show."

She shoved him again. "You are so lying. Now show me some self-defense moves."

That was a great idea. Even though he planned to never be away from her side for her to use them. "There are some basic moves that are really easy." He lined himself in front of her.

"Let's say you're walking in the park like this. The first thing you do if someone starts to get close to you is to turn and look them in the eye. The bad guy is wanting to use the element of surprise to get you off balance. But if you confront them, that's gone. Hopefully, they will get flustered and run."

He reached out and wrapped a hand around her forearm. "But perhaps he doesn't run and grabs on to your arm. What's your initial instinct?"

Amie stepped back and pulled her arm. "I want to get out of his grip."

"That's what you want to do. But when you stepped back and yanked your arm, all you did was drag me toward you. You did nothing to my grip. My hand is still on your arm."

Scarlet hurried toward them from where she was sitting closer to the kids. "Frank, are you showing Amie self-defense moves?"

He felt a little dumb now for doing something so publicly. Amie replied, "Yeah, do want to learn, too? You never know when you might need help and it's not there." Scarlet took Amie's hand and led her closer to the playground.

"Yes, all the women in town need to learn this stuff. I've

been trying to get someone to hold a class, but nobody around the area knows how to do anything." Scarlet leaned closer to Amie. "My mom was attacked when she went to the city. Luckily she got away because she had a brick in her purse and beat him over the head until he ran."

"A heavy purse is a good defense if you have nothing else, I'd think," Amie said.

"Well, Mom had a real brick. She was in the city to find paint to match her and Dad's house." Scarlet called out to the other ladies. "Come on, Susan and Cheryl. Get over here." Amie gave Frank a look. He didn't need to read her mind to know what she was thinking. What were they getting into?

In a group, they stood at the edge of the playground, not far from the kids. "Okay," Scarlet said to Frank, "you had a hold of Amie's arm."

"Right." He once again put his hand on her soft skin. He thought back to last night and all the touching he did then.

"Hey," Scarlet said after an inhale, "keep all that stuff for later. No sexy smells in self-defense."

His face instantly heated. Living among humans for so long had made him forgetful of his own kind. The thoughts fled his mind from embarrassment more than discipline. He cleared his throat and glanced at Amie's smiling face. She was so beautiful.

"Yeah, I was showing her how to get out of a hold if someone grabbed her arm. Instead of tugging back like your first instinct says to do, you want to bend your arm at the elbow and snap your hand in the direction where his fingers and thumb meet. By doing this, you're taking advantage of the weakest part of the hand—the ability of the thumb to hold down. Same thing if you're grabbed by the upper arm. Try to move your arm so it lifts at the thumb."

"What if you're grabbed from behind?" Susan asked. "How do you get out of that?"

He stepped behind his mate for demo purposes. "There are several things, but what I think would be the easiest is to . . ." Well, shit. He should've thought this one through before enacting it. "Uh, is to grab his, uh . . ."

"Balls," the ladies said at the same time and laughed. Not only was his face hot again, but sweat broke out.

"Scrotum," him interjected. "Please, ladies. Let's keep this scientific, shall we?" That earned a round of laughs. He wrapped his arms around his mate's upper arms. "A guy is more than likely going to grab up here and not at the waist. So that leaves your lower body free to move side to side." Taking care to follow instructions, his mate gladly rubbed her ass against him side to side. Almost instantly making him hard. Fuck. This was so not good in front of a bunch of near-stranger ladies.

He cleared his throat and whispered into Amie's ear. "Love, you keep that up and we'll show them more than defensive moves." Of course, with shifter hearing the ladies heard every word. A little whoopin' and hollerin' followed.

"Okay, back to seriousness. All the woman needs to do is bend forward, slide her hips to the side, and swing her fist back to—"

"Rack him in the cojones," Scarlet said. "For those who don't speak Spanish, that would be 'scrotum,' scientifically." With no warning, Amie tore from his arms and ran toward the playground. One of the little ones was about to fall head-first from the top of the slide.

CHAPTER 18

———✂———

Held in Frank's secure embrace, Amie glanced at the children on the playground equipment. One of the dark-haired boys resembled her son. It had been several days since she'd seen her François. She missed him. He was more than delighted to stay longer with his "adopted" grandparents. With them, he got to play outside with others his age and do fun things all day.

Not to mention, his "issue" with fur erupting from his skin and claws growing from his fingers didn't bother the Natives. They treated him as special. As hard as she tried, she couldn't help but worry how being different would affect his socializing and making friends.

She hoped the strange incidents would just go away. If she had to take him to a specialist, she wouldn't know where to begin. What if some scientist wanted to experiment on her child and took him away from her? Grandpa and Nana Running Wind assured her that her son was fine. It was normal for someone like him. Her brain refused to believe humans could turn into an animal. No matter what her eyes told her.

The boy on the playground reached the top of the slide, but his foot slid off the step and he lost his balance. She saw what was coming. She tore from Frank in a headlong race against time and gravity. If she could soften his landing in any way, she might save the child's life.

Skidding on the sandy ground, she was able to stretch far enough to grab an arm, turning the headfirst plunge into a smack down on the child's side. The boy wailed instantly from being hurt and scared from the fall.

On the ground, Amie reached out to carefully check him for broken bones. She saw his little hand change into claws exactly like she'd seen on her son. The claws swiped toward her face, ready to gouge out skin and eyes. Amie's hand snapped up, catching the child's flailing arm like she had to with her boy.

A second later, Scarlet was there, scooping the boy into her arms, quieting him. The child's hand had returned to normal. But she knew she saw it. Knew it was exactly like her son's. Stunned by the realization, she remained on the ground, watching mom and child, until Frank picked her up and set her on a bench.

He brushed hair from her forehead. "Are you okay? You scared me, diving like that at a steel ladder."

Her eyes settled on his calm face. "Did you see his hand? Did you see it change into claws? I know I saw it." She grabbed on to his shirt. "Tell me you saw it."

Frank frowned and looked over his shoulder at the ladies gathering around. "Frank," Susan said, "does she not know about us? Have you seriously not told her what you are?"

Amie whipped her head around to the woman speaking. "What do you mean what he is?" Did he lie about being a special agent? She didn't understand.

Frank wiped a hand down his face. "Uh, Amie. There's been something I've been meaning to tell you."

Her heart raced. What was wrong with him? Did he have cancer and was dying? Was he married? What the hell was going on? Cheryl sat on the bench next to Amie, laying a hand on hers. "It's all right. Really. Just something that takes getting used to, and everything will be fine. You two can mate and—"

"Mate? As in sex?" Amie said. Made it sound like something animals did to procreate and that was it. Wham-bam-thank-you-four-legged-creature. Eww.

Susan plopped next to her on the other side of the bench.

"Don't listen to her. She's into the wild side of it all. We are what you call shifters. We change into animals." Amie jumped up. The two ladies pulled her down to be seated. "There's more."

"You all are crazy. People can't do that."

Susan lifted her hand and it changed into a bear paw with lots of brown fur. Amie gasped. Cheryl's forearm was covered with shiny black fur ending in a catlike paw. "Oh my god," Amie said. "I'm crazy, too."

Scarlet walked up to them with a sniffling young head on her shoulder. He held his hand out and it turned into golden fur with claws—exactly like her son's.

Oh my god. It was real. These people could really do what Grandpa Running Wind had said. Oh my god. She gasped. Her son was normal for their kind. Oh my god. Frank was a shifter. She looked at him.

"I'm a cougar. So is Mom." The last time she'd heard that word flashed in her mind. The older lady at the beauty salon said she was a cougar. A laughed ripped from her stomach. That was the funniest thing she'd ever thought.

Between bouts of laughing, she said, "Sherri is a wolf, right? And Alice—" She slapped her knee and leaned back laughing. "She is a rabbit. Oh my god. This is great."

But the best part was that her son was fine. He had no strange disease that would kill him at a young age or eat his mind until he was comatose. Her son was going to be all right. Oh, shit, though. What was considered all right in their world? She had a lot to learn. Better yet, she and her son needed to live here so they were surrounded by his own kind. But what would Frank think if he knew he had a son? Did he even want children? Would he leave her if he knew?

Would he run, screaming, saying he wasn't ready for this kind of commitment? His job kept him busy all days and hours of the week. Would he ever be home?

By the look on Frank's face, he was more than worried. She was just told the sky was green and she believed it. Maybe something inside her hoped so much that her son was okay that if this was how that was going to happen, then by golly, shifters would be more real than people.

She searched the faces around her and said the only thing she knew would make everyone happy. "Let's eat."

CHAPTER 19

———✂———

Frank took his seat at the long table in Bob's restaurant while the moms seated their rabble in booster seats and high chairs. His mate smiled and squeezed his hand. She was so beautiful. Over the four years, he had suppressed how much he missed her, or his cat would've gone psycho not having its mate. The animal was crazy enough as it was. I heard that.

He'd worried how she'd react to discovering he was pretty much an alien as far as she was concerned. But she took it well. Like she already knew. Her smell wasn't overwhelming fear, but relief, and dare he say, happiness.

Or maybe she hadn't really accepted the idea since he hadn't fully shifted in front of her. Like telling someone about being in a car crash is nothing like actually being in one. She seemed fine, wasn't running away, and that was all that really mattered right now.

A couple of young waitresses came over and took drink orders. The children were all still in play mode with wriggling bodies and rather loud screaming. Did all girls shriek like that? He could maybe handle a boy. The girls scared him.

Amie opened the worn menu. He already knew what he wanted. "Oh my god," Amie said.

"What? What's wrong, love?" Frank was in protection mode red. Lots of stuff going on within his confined space.

Amie replied, "Nothing is wrong. Just the menu has eggs and toast and pancakes. Dorothy's menu was a choice of meat, meat, or steak."

The women laughed. Cheryl said, "That's one thing about shifters. They love their meat."

"That answers one question I've always had," Amie said. He didn't like the sound of that. If she had questions, why didn't she ask him? Duh, his cat said. Like you would've answered honestly back then? Dumbass. Shut it, feline. One more dumbass comment and we'll see who doesn't get to scratch their dumb ass for a long time.

"Hey, Franky." A big guy wearing a greasy white apron lumbered around the busy tables toward them. "I heard you were in town visitin' for a bit. And this must be your lovely mate." Bob held his hand out. "Nice to meet you. I'm Bob, owner-operator of this fine dining establishment."

Amie smiled. "I'm Amie. Glad to meet you, too."

"Whatcha been doin' while in town?" he asked. "Not a lot going on in the past thirty years or so. I sure miss the summer picnics the town used to have. I always won the best potato salad contest. Not that anyone ever orders it." He sighed. Bob hadn't changed much over the years. Still talked up a storm. Frank thought that might've been a problem between his ex-wife, Dorothy, and him. She never got a word in edgewise.

Frank took the second Bob needed to breathe to talk. "We haven't done much. Stayed close to the house. We were in the park a bit and met up with everyone here." He gestured toward the rest of the table.

Bob laughed. "Franky, boy, you were always the one to catch the ladies' eyes. I, on the other hand, couldn't catch the two eyes my mate had. That woman just took my best waitress the other day. Burns my tail, I'll tell ya." He leaned closer to Frank and Amie. "Just between us, I'm gettin' kinda tired of the continuous battle over prices and customers. Breakfast and lunch are great, but dinner is mostly nonexistent."

Frank remembered having this conversation last night with

the waitress at the other restaurant. He wondered if Amie would give him the same advice she gave Dorothy.

"You know, Bob," Amie said, "if you and Dorothy shared one eating place, you controlling the breakfast and lunch, then Dorothy taking care of dinnertime, I'd bet you'd both make out a lot better."

"Me? In the same room as that woman?" He looked away sheepishly. Even though his words said one thing, his smell said something else. All shifters knew it was impossible to ignore your mate. Nature put them together for a reason: They were perfect for each other. "Well, gotta get back to the kitchen." Bob slapped Frank on the back. "Nice meeting you, Amie." He gave her a wave and disappeared behind the swinging door to the back.

The waitress had returned and was taking food orders. Frank ordered his steak and his mate ordered a tall stack of pancakes and potato salad. The server looked over her writing pad at Amie then shrugged a shoulder. "You got it."

A lady came up to their table. He recognized her from the party at his mom's house yesterday afternoon. She and Amie whispered together, and with the kids making so much noise, he couldn't pick up enough words to makes sense of the conversation, so he stopped trying. They were probably talking shoes and clothes anyway.

Then his memory latched on to their time in the fitting room earlier that morning. Fuck. He was getting hard and it hadn't even gone completely through his mind yet. He adjusted his sitting position and glanced down the table to see each woman staring at him with a *you're busted* grin. Oh, shit. He was so busted. Damn shifter noses.

After the lady left, another came to the table and the ladies all leaned together again, whispering. Now he was really curious what they were talking about. A few of the ladies had blushed and giggled.

Sherri, who used to cut his hair when he was a kid, walked in. Amie waved her over and she pulled a chair up and everyone scooted to fit her in. Thankfully the food came out and several servers placed plates and baskets of fried something or the other in front of the kids. The table went instantly quiet. Ah, the power of food.

Amie leaned toward him. "Who is that guy over there?" She nodded toward a good-looking guy, impeccably dressed, sitting at a table by himself.

"Never seen him before. Ask the ladies." Amie leaned to the other side and asked.

"He's new. His name is Jeffry," Scarlet said. "Moved here a month or so ago. He lost his male partner recently. That's what I've been told, but I haven't met him yet. He keeps to himself and doesn't come out much."

Amie nodded and went back to her pancakes, which she seemed to be overly enjoying. He could make pancakes. Maybe. Just add water to Bisquick and flip, right?

Toward the end of the meal, the kids started getting restless. Must be naptime soon. A lady he didn't recognize came to their table to say hi to Amie and thanked her for the party. Then they went into private whisper-mode again.

Amie sat back in her chair. "What is wrong with you people? Didn't you learn all that before . . . you know?" She waved a hand in the air.

"Not really," Susan answered, looking around the room. "Shifters don't date much because their animal doesn't want to waste time on anyone but their true mates. So until they meet, it's pretty much nothing."

Amie slapped a hand over her eyes. "God help the horny teens around here." She leaned forward over the table. "Here's what we gonna do. We need a place to hold another class." The ladies squealed and bunched together.

"We can use my place," Cheryl offered.

"Great. Sherri, send out another text to all the ladies inviting them. Tell them not to worry about lunch this time. I've got that handled. Oh, and tell them to bring any toys, which by the sound of it, many won't have. See y'all shortly."

The ladies scattered and Frank wasn't sure what was going on. "Obviously, you're having another party, but you said you didn't have any clothes to give away."

She kissed him solidly. "What we're learning today doesn't require clothing. In fact, the less clothing, the better this is."

Amie got up and sat down at the table with the new gay

shifter and shook his hand. Her last statement about the less clothing bothered him. He had a bad feeling about all this.

After a few minutes, the guy got up and hugged Amie then hurried out the door, not giving his cat the time to get jealous. But if he ever touched his mate again . . . Dumbass, his cat said.

CHAPTER 20

After a quick trip to the butcher's and setup in the kitchen, Amie joined the group in the living room. Their guest speaker, Jeffry, had everyone's complete attention. He laid furry handcuffs on the table beside him and picked up a scarf.

"But you don't have to buy something new, though Marianne would love that you do." He smiled and Marianne wholeheartedly agreed. "You can use items at home. I have a scarf here, but a tie would work. Also, if you're in the heat of the moment and don't want to step away, here's another idea.

"Have your man lying down, then push his shirt over his head, but keep it on his upper arms. That way his arms are trapped." Several of the ladies ooh and aahed. "If you lean his head forward and push the shirt lower on his arms behind his head, then he can't even bring his arms down." Many of the women liked that idea.

Jeffry looked up at Amie and Cheryl and Amie gave him a nod.

"The hostess asked me to give our upcoming lesson because for many you, your mate was your first and only sexual partner. Because of that, many of you may not know certain things gained with experience. It's very important in every relationship to have a healthy and happy sex life."

Amie hurried into the kitchen and helped Cheryl with the hot serving dishes and paper plates. In the living room, they passed the containers, plates, and napkins to everyone.

"Everyone take a sausage for class, but don't eat it yet." Some of the ladies understood right away and laughed loudly. "And for those of you with human males for mates, there are regular-sized hot dogs." The rest of the room joined in the joke and laughter.

Jeffry started. "Unlike Sherri's blow jobs, which turn out very beautiful—"

"Thank you very much," Sherri interjected. "Today walk-ins need to come here until we're done." Amie laughed at the silliness. "Sorry, Jeffry. Please continue."

"Thank you, my sweet lady. Okay, unlike the name blow job, this requires you to suck. This is also called giving head, fellatio, BJ, going down on, oral sex, sixty-nine, blow me, suck chrome off a tail pipe, deep throat, get head, Lewinski, play the skin flute, suck dick, suck a nail from a board. You and your mate may even have a special name like 'ice cream sundae.'

"Now, women, I know you cannot fathom how men can like this, but trust me, they do." He put his sausage in his hand. "Now, everyone take your sausage, and for the unlucky ones, their hot dog, and wrap your hand around it, making sure your pinky rests against his skin. This is called the base. Make sure your thumb is on the underside."

A lady raised her hand. "How tightly do we squeeze?"

"Your mate will need to tell what feels good, but it will probably be tighter than you'd think. Now, on a real penis, the top is called the head and it has a delicate ring around it. Running your tongue around it or flicking it with your tongue will drive him crazy." Jeffry shivered. "So good." The women laughed at his actions.

"It's important to know, ladies, that you don't have to put the penis in your mouth to make it good. But if you can, then you have more leveraging power to get what you want later." He winked.

"Next thing is to lick like you have an ice cream cone, all the way up the sides. You can also run your lips up and down." Amie looked around, watching everyone lick their sausages.

Some things should never be done in public. Licking hot dogs sexily would be one of those. Cheryl nudged her arm.

"Where is Frank?"

"His boss called, so he said he'd be here later."

"Is everything all right?"

"I'm sure it's fine. He just needs to check in for updates on stuff."

Cheryl nodded. "I'd always wondered where he went after school. I figured he'd go into the ALFA program since his father did, but I didn't think he'd go that soon. From what I see, you two are an official couple. I'm glad he found you so early. You'll have pretty babies."

Amie felt her face heat. Yes, her little Francis was very adorable. She turned her gaze to the group to see them all with sausages in their mouths, Jeffry still giving instructions.

"Make sure to hollow your cheeks. Suck those things in as much as you can. Ladies, you have no idea what a difference there is between cheeks and no cheeks. All right, everybody together. Suck it into your mouth as far as you can go."

From the front door, two knocks sounded and the door opened, revealing Frank taking a step inside. All the women turned to him. He let his eyes skim the ladies with sausages half in their mouths. Without saying a word, he stepped backward and closed the door quietly.

Amie hadn't laughed so hard in years. She worried about peeing her pants. Her poor Frank. She hadn't warned him what the sausages were to be used for except for the group to eat for lunch along with other finger foods. She wondered if Frank would believe her if she told him they were just eating that second he walked in. Probably not.

Her phone buzzed. The text read *I'll see you at home. F*

"Okay," Jeffry said. "That's how to give a blow job." He glanced at his watch. "We still have a few minutes, so I'll show you the most popular toy for women: the Rabbit." He looked up and paused. "Sorry, Alice."

"No problem," came Alice's high-pitched voice. "I already got my rabbit and he's way better than a toy." Her cheeks reddened while the ladies laughed.

Cheryl leaned closer to Amie. "You know, I think Jean has the hots for Butch."

"The meat man?" Amie asked.

"I heard that, Cheryl, and I don't have hots for the man. He just happens to smell good."

"Yeah," Cheryl said. "Like meat." She tilted back to Amie. "You all should go on a double date."

"Amie," Mom called from the group, "don't listen to that woman. Obviously, she's insane." They laughed.

"Jean, you're just being stubborn," Mrs. Holcomb hollered across the room. "We've all seen how he looks at you. Like you smell like meat."

Amie wondered . . . "I'm guessing this obsession with meat is because of being a shifter."

Mom looked up. "I'm so glad you're aware of what's going on."

Scarlet said, "Yeah, little Tommy shifted a paw when he fell off the slide. Cat was out of the bag, literally."

"Did he tell you all the things we can do?" Mom turned to Amie. "Did Frank tell you we can smell emotions? He knows when someone is lying. That's why shifters make such good spies and police people. We have super-hearing, too."

"Don't forget being possessive and protective," one of the ladies call out.

Alice added, "And you have to tell them to breathe deeply while you stand right in front of them to notice you're pregnant. I know that one."

Cheryl looked concerned. "Does this mean Frank hasn't mated or bitten you?"

"If he bit me," Amie started, "I'd kick his ass out of bed. Some BDSM is okay, but I draw the line with pain." Judging by the laughter in the room, she had no doubt she'd said something dumb. "What did I say?"

"Honey"—Cheryl laid a hand on her shoulder—"getting a bite during sex is like tying the knot. You're hitched for life."

"So, Jean," a lady said, "should we buy gifts for a mating party at your home soon?"

No way in hell was Amie letting anyone watch her and Frank have sex. She'd stay single forever, or maybe a really long engagement. "No wedding gifts, please. Just buy me a sausage for my birthday later this month."

Jeffry spoke up, "I have one last thing to add, then I have

to leave, ladies." When he had everyone's attention, he continued. "Remember that sex is a healthy part of being alive. But don't forget that romance is also important. If your mate is a knob-head, then take charge. Have a picnic in the park or just lay under the stars while the kids play. Playground equipment is a great free babysitter. I hope to see everyone around town. It's nice to meet everyone."

Amie watched as the females in the room embraced Jeffry in more ways than just a hug. Hopefully he would be able to heal from losing his mate with a great support group around him. Her phone vibrated in her pocket. The text from Frank read *Let me know when it's safe to come out*. She laughed and texted back: *Mom and I will be home soon*.

"Amie," Mom said, "can we stop by the butcher's for a moment? I need to get meatballs for dinner."

"Sure, Mom"—Amie winked—"meatballs. Is that shifter code for something I don't want to know?"

CHAPTER 21

After cleaning up Cheryl's home and giving out the rest of the remaining sausage, Amie found herself standing next to Butch. She thought back to the last time she was there and she remembered what had happened. He'd partially shifted and she ran, screaming, from the building.

"Oh my god, Butch. I'm so sorry how I reacted to you the other day. I just learned about shifters a few hours ago."

"Not a problem, girly. I probably would've scared myself if I had a mirror."

Amie smiled to show her appreciation. Then she looked around for Mom on the other side of the store. "Say, Butch, ever think about asking Jean out on a date?"

He froze in his tracks. "I—I don't know if she'd go with me."

"Oh," Amie said, "I'm pretty sure she would say yes."

"You think?" Butch looked at her with wide eyes.

"Yup, but you have to ask her or she won't. You can do that, right?"

Color drained from the lion's face. "What do I say?"

Amie rubbed a hand over her forehead. These townies where just too much fun. "Just say, 'Jean, would you like to go out?' It's easy."

Butch straightened up, indicating the woman of topic was coming. Amie stepped behind Mom as she laid meatballs on the counter.

"Good afternoon, Butch. How are you?"

Amie looked over Mom's head at him. She nodded, giving him encouragement.

"Jean. Would. You. Like. To. Go. Out." This was probably the first lion who ever turned robot when asking out a girl. Mom stood staring at him, and he stared at her. Dear god.

Amie waved her arms to get his attention. She pointed to her watch, mouthing, *Six tomorrow*. He looked at his watch.

He said, "At six tonight."

Tonight? No, no, no. Amie shook her head. *Tomorrow*, she mouthed again.

Then Mom said, "Six o'clock tonight would be great."

Amie dropped her head into her hands. This could be very bad. Mom waved and walked away. Amie grabbed the bag with the meatballs, which was still on the counter. She gave him a thumbs-up.

Outside, Mom grabbed her arms. "Butch just asked me out."

"Yeah, isn't that great?"

"No! That's not great. What am I going to wear? I don't know how to fix my hair. Oh my god. What am I going to do?"

"Mom. It's going to be okay. I'll help you."

"Oh, thank you. We have to get home." In a blink, Mom was gone.

Amie looked around. "Mom?" She turned. "You just did not disappear on me. This has to be a shifter thing."

"I'm sorry, dear."

Amie startled and whipped around. "Mom! Where did you go? What happened?"

"Shifters have the ability to move so quickly, humans can't track the action. Now let's go."

Frank sat in the rocking chair on the back porch. His mom and mate had kicked him out when they'd walked in. From what he could figure out, Mom was going somewhere. He thought he heard she was going on a date. But he knew that couldn't be right. Though he did tell her the other day that she needed to get out more.

He didn't have time at the moment to worry about his mom. More serious things had come to light. His conversation with his boss was filled with good and bad intel. Good in that Giuseppe Ragusa had been under police scrutiny for a long time, bad in that several officers doing the watching had mysteriously disappeared over the years.

Ragusa's history was as full of death as any other popular gangster from old. True to modern Mafia, Ragusa was associated with several corporations. Frank was sure that was where the family's money came from. He told his boss about the connection with the senator's killing being covered by the bank robbery, his bill, Ragusa's companies, and the money flow.

What Frank found interesting was that Ragusa didn't bail his son out of jail. His kid had to post his own money today. Guess Giuseppe didn't want to fork out the $1.3 million needed to get his son out. Was there a reason besides the money that Ragusa let his son stay in jail? Nice family dynamics. No wonder Amie wanted out as soon as possible.

Now the question was: How safe was Amie in his hometown?

In the driveway, a car pulled up and stopped. A strange sight getting out of the car met his eye. If he was seeing correctly, Butch was dressed in a clean suit and tie. He'd never seen that in his life. He didn't even think Butch owned such attire.

Butch waved, opened the gate to the side of the house, and joined him on the porch. The smell of worry and slight fear followed in his path.

"How you doing, Butch?"

"Good, yeah, good. Haven't done this kinda thing since school. Even then, not very much."

"Done what, exactly, Butch?" All types of things went through his mind. His protective shifter side woke.

"Date, son. Somehow I asked your mother on a date. I barely remember doing it." He wiped a hand over his brow. Frank let out breath of relief and laughed.

"Come on inside." He stood and opened the kitchen door.

"I have meatballs simmering in sauce. Barely finished before getting kicked out by the women folk."

Butch grunted. "I hear that, man."

Inside, Amie poked her head from around the corner. "Hey, guys. Sit in the living room so Mom can make her entrance." She smiled and gave him a wink. Oh shit, what did she do to his mom?

Now as worried as Butch, Frank led their visitor into the other room. They sat in chairs opposite each other. Frank asked, "Where you all going?"

"I thought I'd take her to the movies in Columbus."

Frank nodded. "I don't have to tell you to behave yourselves, do I? No drinking or fooling around."

"No, I'm good. I'm not drinking anything but water." Butch's foot bounced up and down.

"What time do you think you'll be back?" Frank asked.

"I'm figuring by eleven."

"That's good. We'll be waiting up."

Butch nodded his understanding.

"You know," Frank started, "my mom is priceless, and I hope you treat her like that. Don't get into any dangerous situations, and if you need help, call me right away. Okay?"

"Got it. Yeah. Thanks." Both men turned when the ladies came into the room. Frank almost asked Amie who the hot woman with her was. Then he realized the "hot" woman was his mom. Oh, shit. He knew his mom got a haircut yesterday but he hadn't seen it and hadn't really made much of an effort to try. She'd been wearing a scarf on her head after going to the salon. His mom's hair was short, pixie-like. Looked great on her. Her eyes were lined with color and she had cheekbones. And apparently, Amie had one more dress she hadn't given away, because he couldn't see his mom buying it. It was stylish and modest. Perfect for her.

"Wow, Jean," Butch said. "You look amazing. Well, you always look amazing, I just mean more amazing than normal—"

"Yeah, Butch, we get it," Frank said. "Remember what we talked about. And no sex on the first date."

"Frank," Mom admonished. He shrugged.

The couple left through the front door. Frank joined Amie,

standing in front of the window. "They move on so quickly."
Amie gave a sigh. "One minute they're sucking a sausage,
and suddenly, they're going on a date."

"Yeah, we have to learn to let go," Frank added. "So"—
Frank looked at her and licked his lips—"would you like
meatballs or a sausage first, milady?"

"How about you hold the sausage for a bit and let's go for
a walk?"

CHAPTER 22

Amie knew that asking to go on a walk was probably the last thing Frank wanted, but she'd had so limited time just him and her. And she really wanted to talk to him about their son. He needed to know.

"Sure," he said and left her at the front door before coming back a few moments later.

She glanced at the blanket under his arm and smiled. "A blanket?"

He shrugged. "I figured we could watch the stars or something."

God. Frank was such a good man. She'd loved him from the very moment she'd laid eyes on him, and now here he was, being that amazing man all over again.

They walked down to the park. He laid out the blanket and for a little while they lay there and just stared up at the sky.

"I stopped doing this after you left me," he admitted.

She hated that. Hated that she'd stopped him from doing something he'd taught her to love. "Why?"

"It felt wrong to do it without you. This was our thing, remember?"

She sighed, letting the cool breeze run over her skin.

"Yeah. You used to tell me all about the stars and I'd sit there acting like I understood."

He chuckled. "I used to wonder how I got you to be quiet for so long."

"Smart-ass! I've seen some really active children running around here." She laughed. "It's a wonder how any parent gets anything done in this town."

Frank was quiet for a moment. "I don't know. I guess they like their kids."

"Oh, and you don't? What, don't you want kids of your own?" Her heart tripped at the base of her throat. She'd tried to throw the question in casually so she could re-direct the conversation to their son.

"No, not really." His answer caught her off guard. He didn't want kids. No children meant she didn't even need to discuss French fry with him just yet. Not when Frank was clearly not open to the idea of kids. Maybe she could work him into changing his mind.

"Frank, I have to tell you something—"

"Hey, guys," someone called out to them.

They flipped onto their stomachs and glanced up at the some of the ladies from the party.

"How's it going?" Frank asked.

"Great! Frank," Cheryl said with a smile, "we are just loving the changes Amie has brought to our town."

"She really has given the town a new, updated outlook." Sherri grinned. "We love having her here."

Amie was left speechless. No one had ever spoken like that of her, to anyone. She smiled and waved as the women left, her mind busy with the wonderful things they'd said.

"Ready to go back?"

She met Frank's gaze and realized it was time to stop hiding behind her uncle. He wasn't going to control her any longer. She wanted Frank and she'd have him. They'd figure something out about their son. Not like her baby boy was going anywhere now. He was her heart and Frank would learn to love their son or she'd have to go on as she was, without him in her life again.

They raced back to the house, rushing up the stairs to his room and tossing the door closed behind them.

He kissed her. Deep. Hard. Hungry. Every brush of his lips melted more of her willpower and any thoughts of stopping. Clothes came off in the time it took her to take a breath, and then his body was over hers on the bed, his lips branding her as his.

That all-consuming kiss lasted but a short moment before he moved to her chest. Her gasp of pleasure as his mouth encased her nipple was loud. She didn't care. She could only feel at that point. Feel his tongue flicking back and forth over her hard little tip while his hand molded the flesh of her other breast in his grasp.

When he sucked hard on her nipple, she swore lights exploded behind her lids. Her body shook. She couldn't stop the rocking of her hips, searching for his cock to enter her. To fill her. Another full-body shiver, and his dick slipped to the entrance of her sex. That didn't last.

With every moan out of her lips, he moved farther down her body, until he was lying between her thighs. She dug her nails into the bedding and glanced down, past her quivering belly to meet his golden stare.

"You and me, babe." His look turned possessive. She groaned. "There's no going back after this."

"God, yes!"

He licked at her clit, slowly, lazily. A harsh whimper tore from her throat. "Frank . . . I really need to talk to you about something."

"Just give me a sec, love."

Another slow lick and she groaned, gripped his short hair in her fists, and pushed him into her crotch. Maybe later. "You need to get a move on. If you don't hurry up I'm going to start giving orders."

He gave a soft growl that sounded like a chuckle. "So what are you telling me?"

"Make me come. Do it now, do it fast, and please don't make me wait any longer."

He licked at her clit in quick flicks. Her muscles tensed in expectation.

"Oh, god!" she choked out.

His hot breath caressed her folds as he swiped his tongue repeatedly over her pussy and drove it into her channel. It was unlike anything she'd felt before. She rocked repeatedly, wiggling her hips over his lips. Her blood burned, firing each of her cells.

She couldn't form a coherent sentence if her life depended on it. In a second or two, Frank would lick her to the point that she'd scream and come and then she'd lose herself in the moment. She needed that so badly.

He shoved his face in her pussy, burying his tongue in her. "Oh, fuck!"

He fucked her pussy with his tongue. Every single thrust was a dream, slick, erotic, hot. Harsh breaths pounded out of her lips. She came apart with a single one of his growls. Tension snapped inside her, rushing air out of her lungs and leaving her breathless. A quick explosion of bliss and her body filled with joy as she rode the pleasure wave.

She screamed his name. Oh, so loud. She shook down to her core. Her legs felt liquefied and oxygen fought its way into her lungs. She tried hard to stay aware of what was happening but it was hard. Especially when she knew there was more coming. A lot more. He crawled up her body, kissing her with lips that still held the taste of her own climax.

He slipped into her pussy in a quick, hard drive. A rush of pleasure tore a scream from her lips. He felt so good inside her. So perfect. She dug her nails into his slick shoulders and panted. She tugged his head down for a kiss, raking her nails into his short hair and clutching the strands at the back of his head.

The world ceased to exist. She curled her legs around his waist, crossing her ankles at the small of his back. His body turned into a fine-tuned machine bent on breaking her and pulling every last orgasm from her body. She clung to him, letting him own her with each thrust. Her body no longer hers but his now.

They kissed in a fiery blaze that heated her already scorching flesh. Nothing but the feel of his tongue delving deep into her mouth at the same time he filled her with his cock. He slipped a hand between their sweaty bodies and rubbed circles over her swollen clit. She tore away from the kiss with a moan.

"Christ, Frank!"

He swiped his cool wet tongue over her neck, rubbing over her harsh beating pulse. "Let go, baby."

One tap on her clit and she came apart. A scream flew from her lips as her back arched off the bed. Her body vibrated with each new wave of pleasure flooding her core.

Taking choppy breaths, she opened her eyes to meet his bright ones. With his cock still rock hard, he pulled out of her. In the moment it took her to gasp, she was on her stomach with him lifting her ass high in the air. She glanced over her shoulder to see him clenching his jaw.

"Stay this way, baby," he said with his voice low, rough. "I need inside you."

God, she needed him inside her, too. Again. Again. She'd never tire of him being in her, filling her. Digging her nails into the sheets, she leaned down and waited. He slid his hands down her back, kissed her cheeks, and a moment later pushed the head of his cock into her pussy. His thick shaft stretched her as he took her in a quick thrust.

"Oh!" She whimpered low. Tension wound into a tight ball of need in her core. It shocked her how quickly she was ready to come. He drove forth and pulled back. Each slide slickening her pussy. His fingers bit into her hips, holding her in place. Another thrust. Harder now.

"Yes! God, that feels good."

Her words seemed to propel him into increasing his speed. All she could do was enjoy the ride. His cock rubbed her pussy walls in a friction she'd pay to feel forever. A shiver raced down her spine, sparking never-used pleasure cells to life. She squeezed her pussy muscles around his cock.

"Fuck!"

He dropped to all fours behind her, not once missing a beat. He continued in a rapid pace that increased the sizzle in her blood with each glide. She was lost to the sensations. Lost to how close she was to flying.

Then he rubbed her super-sensitized clit in quick flicks and sent her soaring.

"Oh. My. God!"

She became lost in the moment. In the fire and the waves of joy. Adrenaline filled her veins and gave her an almost giddy sensation she couldn't push away. It grew with every contraction around his cock. His teeth scraped the back of her shoulder in a bite that only enhanced her orgasm. His thrusts stopped suddenly, his body tensed, and then he growled. His hand bit into her hip, his nails digging into her flesh hard enough to leave wounds.

"You're mine, Amie. There was never any doubt. Always mine."

His orgasm shook him hard enough that she felt it when he plastered his chest to her back. The bite turned painful enough to make her scream louder as he filled her with his seed. For long moments she continued to have aftershocks of mini orgasms. To her pleasure, he continued to jerk in her channel. Her pussy squeezed at his cock, not willing to give up a single drop of his cum.

CHAPTER 23

Amie couldn't imagine ever giving this up again. To be wrapped in Frank's arms, under warm blankets, snuggled up to his powerful body was heaven. She couldn't think about it coming to end. That was too hard to accept.

Frank kissed her shoulder. "I hear Mom downstairs. I think she's going for a run. I'm going to join her. You stay in bed; it's still really early."

She slid her hand down his chest. "Are you sure you don't want to do something else while she's gone?"

"Hmm. When you put it that way . . ." Frank scooted back under the blanket. Then Amie realized she was being selfish. No mate of hers was going to neglect his mother. She smacked his ass.

"Go with your mother. I'll be here when you get back. There's something I need to talk to you about. Later, with more time." Frank kissed her forehead and hurried toward the door. "And don't grill your mother on her date. She has a right to her privacy, regardless of what you may think."

"Yeah, yeah," he said as he exited the room and went down the stairs. Not long after that the kitchen door opened and closed. She sighed and rolled onto his pillow, taking a deep breath of him. For the first time in a long time, she was happy.

* * *

Her eyes snapped opened. She must've fallen asleep and something woke her. Were Frank and his mom back? There wasn't a clock in his bedroom, but by the sun's brightness, she knew a bit of time had passed.

Then she heard the sixth step on the stairs squeak. Someone was on the second floor. She waited for the door to open and Frank to walk in, but when that didn't happen after a few seconds, she got up and put a robe around her.

She opened the door to peek out and saw a man she didn't recognize. When his eyes turned to slits and long canine teeth descended, she screamed and slammed the door closed. Running through the joining bathroom, she made her way into her room and locked her door.

Next, her hands slid under the mattress, searching for Joey's gun she'd stashed when she unpacked upon first arriving. Weapon in hand, she waited to see the man's next move—whether that be continuing to beat on Frank's bedroom door or coming to hers. Either way, she didn't have much time.

Her only escape would be the window overlooking the backyard. She pulled the window frame up and bent over the ledge. Nothing but siding between her and the ground. Yeah, not happening. How did she call for help? Her phone wasn't in here. She spun around and yelled out the window for Frank. Mom said they had super-hearing. Let's hope it was really super.

The banging on Frank's door stopped and then her bedroom door nearly popped its hinges. She dove for the closet, fear not caring if it was the first place the man would look. It was the only place to go. The bedroom door busted open. She tried to hold her breath to keep quiet, but her lungs and pounding heart demanded oxygen.

"I smell you, Ms. Amerella Capone. Don't think for one second that you have everyone in this town fooled." His voice drew closer to the closet. "Now, you come out of there real nice-like and we'll take a trip to Vegas to visit your family. I'm sure they'll be glad to see you. Glad enough to hand over some money as a nice reward." He was at the closet. Her time was up. Frank must not have heard her or was too far away to get home in time.

Amie lifted the gun in front of her, arms straight out. She'd die before she went back to her uncle. The closet door swung open and the man's face twisted into an ugly snarl, teeth dripping saliva, a growl escaping his throat. His clawed hand reached for her throat.

She squeezed the trigger several times, knocking the man away and onto his back, landing in front of the window. Amie scurried out of the closet, gun still in front of her. The next thing she knew, another snarling creature with golden fur, teeth, and claws flew through the window. She fell backward, screaming and shooting again.

The animal lurched to the side, crashed onto the wood floor, then skidded through the door and down the stairs. That was when she realized that must've been Frank in his cougar form. Shit!

"Frank!" She skipped down the stairs to where his human body lay at the bottom, facedown, not moving. "Frank! Oh my god. Please say I didn't kill you."

He groaned when she laid a hand on his back. "I haven't fallen down those stairs since I was a toddler. They hurt more than I remember."

Frank's mom, slipping on a robe, came around the corner. "Amie, we heard gunshots. What happened?"

Amie scanned Frank for his bullet wound, too concerned over him to think about what Mom had asked. "Frank, did I miss shooting you? You're not injured."

"Oh," Mom said, "another shifter trait. Unless you hit a shifter in the head or heart, it's difficult to kill one. When injured, we just need to shift to repair any structural or physical damage. Then good as new."

The man upstairs had to be a shifter. Did she hit him in the heart or head? She had no clue. To say her mind had been preoccupied with staying alive at the time would be an understatement.

Amie walked back up the stairs and into her bedroom, Frank pushing ahead of her. Mom leaned over the intruder. There was a hole right in the middle of his forehead. "I've seen him before," Mom said. "I think he's a wolf. He probably saw the same news article I did and made a lucky guess."

"Yes," Amie said. "When he shifted his hand, it looked like a furry paw. "

"Let's take it downstairs and I'll put it on the back porch until the police arrive," Frank said.

"Ewww," both ladies said together.

"Would you rather me leave it here?"

"No," Mom said. "Back porch would be perfect."

Amie sat at the kitchen table sipping tea after the breakfast Mom made for them. Perfect thing for right now. She could drink to stall the investigator's answers, to make sure all she recalled was correct and not made up from fear or seeing things.

Frank paced the porch with his phone stuck to his ear—had been for the last thirty minutes. The police chief came down the stairs. "Thank you, Mrs. Dubois and Ms. Capone, for your patience. We've got everything we need forensic-wise. No charges will be filed."

"Thank you, Chief, for coming out this morning."

"Never a problem, Mrs. Dubois. Good to see you again." He stepped toward the back door, then stopped and turned back. "Also, I'd like to thank both of you for everything you've shown my wife. She's happier than she's been in a long time and socializing more. That's good for us and the town." He gave a nod and walked out the door.

Frank hung up the phone and spoke to the chief for a few minutes before coming inside. "Well, I talked with others in DC. They ran prints on our guy and he's just a local who has a long record of arrests and prosecutions."

"A long what?" Mom asked.

"Rap sheet," Frank explained. "Just like they say on TV. R-A-P sheet."

"Anything else on him?" Amie asked. "Maybe Mafia related?"

He shook his head. "They didn't find any connections."

"So are we safe to stay?"

"Probably," Frank said.

That wasn't good enough for Amie. She couldn't let her uncle come to this town and hurt her friends while trying to find her. No, that wouldn't be acceptable. Several hours had passed since the break-in this morning. She glanced at the clock. Surprisingly, it was almost time for lunch. Since Mom cooked breakfast, the least she could do was take them out to lunch before she and Frank left.

"How about we change and I buy lunch?" she said. "We can figure out a plan and go from there." They agreed.

In her room, Amie decided to take Joey's gun with her. She wasn't taking anything for granted anymore. When she reached inside the luggage pocket where she had stashed the weapon, her fingers grazed an envelope. She pulled it out and looked at it. She'd penned Frank's name on the front. Inside was a letter telling him about their son and how to find him in Mojave with his adopted grandparents. When she wrote it the other day, she wasn't sure if or when she should give it to him. But if something happened to her, someone needed to know about him and keep him safe from her uncle. She couldn't let the boy fall into his hands.

She put the letter and envelope back into the pocket and pulled out the gun. Downstairs, the small group gathered to head out, when an explosion rocked the house.

CHAPTER 24

Frank glanced at the women then tore out of the house, heading downtown, where the explosion seemed to have come from. Taking a few steps then shifting into his cougar form, he sprinted down the sidewalk.

Acrid smoke met his nose, leaving a tang in his mouth he could do without. What in the hell was going on? Was there a gas explosion in one of the buildings? What could account for shaking his mom's house at that distance?

He slowed to a fast trot after passing the park. Flames hurdled high into the air from the vacant building on the far end of town down by the corner.

In the middle of the street sat three black Hummers. The same he'd seen at the Prada store in Vegas. Fuck. How could they have possibly have found his mate here?

A back window of one of the Hummers rolled down and an RPG launched into the beauty salon, blowing it to shambles. He had to stop this now. He shifted and walked down the middle of the street toward the unwelcome visitors. At the moment, he didn't give a shit if they saw him shift. Maybe it would freak them out enough to get the hell out of his town.

"What do you want, Ragusa? You should turn around, the

way you came, and leave before the opportunity to escape is gone."

Laughing came from loudspeakers mounted on the hood of the front vehicle. "And who might you be, little naked man? You speak for everyone here?"

His cat became pissed at that. It was ready to tear into the asshole hiding in the truck.

"I do speak for everyone here. And this little man, as you call me, would love to see you face-to-face. Or are you too afraid to come out?" The front truck rocked on its axle, the speaker making a loud squelch. Then a different voice came over the megaphone.

"We are here to collect Amerella Capone. Send her out here and we will leave."

Frank noticed wolves slinking along the shadows. A couple black panthers crossed the street behind the vehicles. Butch's fluffy gold mane filled his door window. The town was getting riled. They were backing Amie, not giving her up. A pride he had never felt for his home bubbled inside him.

She may not have been one of them several days ago, but she was now, and they'd fight for her. Butch shifted back to his human form and joined Frank on the street. Solidarity.

"Who says this Capone woman is here?" Butch asked, standing proudly as his junk dangled.

A sigh sounded over the speaker. "We have it on good authority that she's here. Apparently, not everyone wants her around. Now, hand her over or we'll blow up another building of your precious town."

Butch turned to Frank. "You gotta get back to the house and get Amie out of here now."

"How do I do that without looking suspicious?" Frank asked.

"Easy." Butch grabbed Frank around the neck and punched him in the face. At the last second, he pulled it. But it was still enough to snap Frank's head back. Then the meat man grabbed him around the waist with his hands and launched him toward Dorothy's restaurant.

"And stay gone, you flea-bitten piece-of-shit pussy!"

Dorothy, standing at her restaurant's door, helped Frank inside. "What the hell is wrong with Butch? Has he gone crazy?"

Frank stumbled through the kitchen toward the back door. He laughed. "Believe it or not, the man is a genius when it comes to being sneaky." He opened the door and stepped out. "Dorothy, come outside. Don't go back in. Those RPGs are too close for comfort. Don't need you going anywhere. You need to feed us still." He smiled as he shifted and ran down the alley toward the park and his mom's house.

Amie and Mom cringed at the third explosion. With her shifter abilities, Mom was able to relay what she heard to Amie as they stood in the park, out of sight. Amie was horrified. All this destruction and possible death because of her. No, it had to stop.

She turned to face Frank's mother. "Mom Dubois, I have to go—"

"No! You can't go with those people. They want you, don't they?"

"They do. And I'm going." She quieted Mom with a hug.

Amie hurried across the park toward the street just in time to run into a gorgeous cougar. Oh, shit. How did she explain this to Frank? The cat shifted into human form and she was captivated and freaked at the same time. That was her first time seeing the full change. It didn't look like a comfortable process. But she didn't have time to think about that right now.

"Where do you think you're going, young lady?" Frank wasn't happy with her.

"Frank, listen to me—"

"You are not going with them. It is my responsibility to keep you safe—"

"Hold on there one second," Amie fired back. "Your responsibility is not to keep me safe. That's mine. I've done a damn good job of protecting my"—she almost said "son"—"self my entire life and I will continue to do so—"

"No, Amie. I love you and won't let you go again."

He loved her? She loved him so much. Her heart broke a little.

"Frank, there's something I've been trying to tell you, but"—she gulped and shoved her hands in her pockets—"I've been too scared of what you might say. Too scared of how you'd react."

He frowned, holding her by her arms and looking deep into her eyes. "You can tell me anything, love."

"It's probably easier if you just go back to the house and upstairs to my suitcase. There's a letter there, addressed to you." She bit her bottom lip to keep it from shaking. "Will you read it?"

"Of course. Anything you want, sweetheart. But, Amie, nothing you say in that letter will change how much I love you."

She wanted to believe him so bad, but she knew keeping their child a secret had been a mistake. She'd had a reason that felt valid at the time, but now it felt wrong. "I hope that's true."

She threw her arms around him and pulled back quickly. No sense in dragging this out. It was so much easier to sacrifice when there wasn't anyone else getting hurt in the process. But she had to suck it up. The town was being destroyed because of her.

"Frank, this is how this is going down. I'm getting in the truck and they will take me to Uncle Giuseppe's in Vegas. He lives a few houses down from mine. Detective Freeman knows the address. You get with him and pull together a force to get me out of there.

"My uncle won't hurt me. If the rest of the family discovered he killed me, they would riot and overthrow him from power. He isn't risking that. He has around fifteen guards and security people, and cameras all around the exterior and interior of the house. Freeman probably knows all about those, too. Get with him. He's made it his life's mission to take down my uncle. Help him." She looked over her shoulder. The Hummers waited for her.

"I have to go."

Frank grasped her in a hard hug. "Don't leave me again."

Her heart broke all the way. She hadn't wanted to leave him the first time, but like now, she had no choice. Someone else's life was on the line.

"I love you, Frank. I never stopped loving you." She pulled

away from him. "Now, come get me from my uncle's house. And if you have to kill him in the process, you'll get extra sausage licks." She backed away, then turn and ran.

She made a vow right then. No matter what it took or what sacrifice she'd have to make, she would bring her uncle down.

CHAPTER 25

＞━

Worn out and tired from the long ride to Vegas, Amie's hot head had cooled. She sat behind Tony, who glared at her in the rearview mirror the entire drive. What was his fucking problem? She wasn't responsible for his fucked-up life. She'd stayed away from him as much as she could growing up.

Her stomach knotted worrying if Frank had read her letter. He'd know by now that they had a child. Little Francis was his daddy through and through. How would Frank take it? Would he hate her? What if he didn't want to meet their baby? She rubbed a hand over her brow. Wondering the what-ifs wasn't going to make anything better.

If Frank learned to love their son, there would be a future for them. She didn't dare think about what would happen if he rejected Francis. She already knew that she'd leave him. Her son came before everyone.

"Tony, what the fuck is wrong with you? What have I done to you that makes you fucking scowl at me all the time?" His eyes glowed red, just like they had the moment he saw her in the bank before shooting Joey. What the hell? That wasn't natural. A chill ran up her back. Tony looked almost demonic.

Wait. Before Joey died, he said "demo." At the time, she'd thought he meant something like "democrat" or "demolition person." But did he mean "demon"? Oh, god. So there were shifters and demons? What else was out there waiting?

The Hummer skidded to a stop in the middle lane of the interstate, and Tony turned in his seat to fully face her.

"You want to know why I hate you?" He could've breathed fire.

Amie grabbed the door handle to her right and gripped the chair cushion on her left. Her heart thundered in her chest from the frantic stop. The guy was insane. They could have been in a crazy accident and both be dead. "'Hate' is a bit strong, don't you think? I am family, unfortunately."

Tony's hand snapped out to grab her throat. She squeezed back into the corner of the seat, barely out of his reach. She hadn't feared him before. But right now, he could kill her. The red in his eyes pulsed.

"That's one reason I prefer you dead. You never appreciated the power your name gave you. You pissed it away, spending time on those who only took from you. There was so much you could've done empowering the family."

"The family?" Amie screamed back. "The family is worthless. Stealing money to survive? How fucking pathetic is that? Someone who can't even support themselves, but has to take from others.

"And killing those who get in their way," she continued. "Instead of negotiating and figuring out a way to work things out like grown-ups, you just off them. Talk about being a pussy." Tony lunged toward her as the Hummer shook on its wheels while a semi-truck blew by blaring its horn within feet of her door.

"Unless you want to join your dead ancestors, I suggest you get us moving." Amie fought to keep his hands off her.

He grinned at her. "I'm ready to die. Are you? What about your son?"

She reached out and slapped him. "Don't talk about my son, seeing as you have no idea what a real son should be like."

He laughed, turned around, and pushed the Hummer to over one hundred miles an hour. Amie felt sure it was to intimidate her. There was nothing she could do about it, and her son would be taken care of, so whatever happened to her now didn't matter.

* * *

Amie stood in front of Uncle Giuseppe's desk in his study, staring the man in the eye. "I have to say you are the most pathetic creature—let me edit that—second most pathetic creature on this earth."

Her uncle's brow raised. "Who, may I ask, am I second to?"

"Really?" Amie rolled her eyes. "You have to ask? Who's fucking stupid enough to blow up a town to get one person?"

He chuckled. "My dear niece, if that is the worst you have to say to me, then I will accept it."

"It's not the worst by far, but I don't care to stoop to your gutter level of intelligence to tell you how I really feel."

"Amerella"—her uncle sighed—"you have always been a step higher than the rest of us."

"What do you mean?" That almost sounded like a good thing, but coming from him, it couldn't be.

"My sister—your mother—always thought she was better than I was. She had it in her head that the lesser intelligent made their living stealing and killing—"

"Like mother, like daughter," Amie added.

Uncle Giuseppe chuckled again. That frightened her. He never laughed or even smiled when she was growing up. "What you and your mother believe no longer concerns me. I have found a way to show the world the Ragusa family was meant to shine. And you, my dear, are a vital part of that process."

A side door to the office opened and a stunning blonde in a slinky dress strutted in. She eyed Amie and slowly made a circle around her, looking her up and down. Then she sat on the corner of the desk.

"She'll do perfectly, Giuseppe."

Amie's eyes narrowed. "I see you're back to fucking whores for fun, Uncle. She'd do perfectly, too, looks like."

The woman returned her glare. "Be careful, bitch. I'll turn you into a frog, which wouldn't be a far cry from what you look like already."

Oh, shit. Magic was real, too? Wonderful. Shifters, demons, and witches, oh my. Wait a minute. "If you're a witch, and not fucking him, why are you here?"

A grin slowly spread across the witch's face and an evil

spark flashed in her eyes. "You'll find out soon." She hopped off the desk and slithered toward the double doors leading into the ballroom at the far end of the study. "Good thing you found her in time, Giuseppe. Otherwise, we'd have to wait a month. And I'd rather spend a month in hell than in this place with you." The witch turned to the guards hovering around the edges of the room. "Take Miss Priss to the room, then I need all of you in the ballroom with me."

CHAPTER 26

Amie paced the bedroom on the second floor. What was going on? Why would her uncle have a witch here? And how was she personally involved? No matter how she tried to look at it, it was all bad.

She stood in front of the barred window. Bars on a bedroom window. She really shouldn't be surprised. And to think that all the years she lived here growing up, she never came into this room. The second floor was always off-limits to the kids. She never questioned it; same with so many other things. Just accepting what she was told. Not finding answers on her own.

The sun brushed the top of the trees. Soon it would be dark. Would Frank be able to get with Detective Freeman in time to gather a posse and rescue her from this place? She didn't think her uncle would hurt her, but she doubted that anyone who threatened to testify against a Ragusa would go unpunished.

She had to get out of here on her own. If Frank came through, great. If not, she was on her own, like she'd been the previous four years.

Slipping off her shoe, she headed for the door. After studying the hinges, she hit the bottom of one, making a nasty noise. She dumped a pillow on the bed from its case and padded the bottom of the hinge and struck again. Much quieter. After all three pins were removed, she pried the back side of the door off the hinge.

Hurrying back to her purse, she pulled out Joey's gun, then tiptoed down the hall toward the stairs. No one was around, which was strange. Then she remembered the witch wanted the men to help her with something in the ballroom. The woman couldn't possibly be having a party, could she?

Heart pounding, she rushed through the downstairs hall toward the kitchen at the back of the mansion. If she could get out the back door, she might have a chance at getting out of there.

"Miss Amerella?" She jumped and almost peed her pants.

"Chef Louis," she said, slamming a hand on her chest, "you scared the crap out of me."

"So sorry, mademoiselle. I did not know you vould be joining us for dinner."

"No worry, Chef Louis. I just dropped by. Don't plan on staying long." She kept the gun behind her back to not frighten the man. He did notice her feet, though.

"Vere are your shoes, girl? You cannot valk around vithout shoes."

Amerella wiggled her toes. "Uh, I left them outside and am going to get them right now." She stepped toward the door leading outside. "Thank you, Louis. See you later." She slid out to the man's shaking head. He rattled off in Italian like he always did when going on about kids nowadays. She loved the man. His good cooking was most of the reason for her curvy body. The man had a way with a spatula.

Outside, she stepped through the grass to the back corner of the rectangular house and peeked around the side. The sun shone on the other side of the yard, putting her in darkening shadows.

Rubbing her body along the shrubs, she hoped to put her smell where Frank would find it and follow. When she got to the tall ballroom windows, she ducked before someone saw her. Security guys were carrying in boxes, a few tables, chopped wood, candles, and all kinds of weird shit.

Two men leaned the tallest ladder she had ever seen against the wall with the fifteen-foot windows. Behind them, three more men carried in a long black roll of material. They laid it at the foot of the ladder, then one of the guys grabbed a corner and walked it up the ladder.

After he fiddled with the material at top of the window, she realized he was hanging a curtain. A fifteen-foot-tall velvet blackout curtain. No wonder it took five men to hang the thing. It had to weigh fifty pounds.

Squatting under the windowsill, she dragged her hand along the wall, leaving more scent. From here, she could see the side gate mostly hidden in overgrown shrubbery. She'd have to make a run for it. Careful to wrap her hand around the gun's handle, away from the trigger, she stepped away from the building.

Her movement drew the attention of the valet, who hollered to a guard. Goddammit. She took off as fast as she could across the yard. Quicker than she thought possible, arms wrapped around her upper body. She leaned forward and shifted her hips to the side, then swung her arm down, grabbed his balls, and squeezed. Just like Frank showed her in the park. And it worked like a charm.

The guy dropped her and clutched his groin, rolling on the ground. Unfortunately, other guards were behind him. She sprinted for the iron-bar gate. Breathing hard, she reached out and snagged a bar, then yanked. It was locked or stuck. Repositioning the gun in her hands, she fired two shots at the locking mechanism. Something popped and the gate loosened from its hold.

Pain tore through her scalp as her head snapped back. One of the men had grabbed her hair and kept her at arm's length. He must've seen what she'd done to the other guy. One of the others snatched the gun from her hands.

Amerella screamed in frustration. She was so fucking close. They once again marched her back to the house and into her uncle's study. He looked up from his desk when she was pushed through the doorway.

With a disapproving arched brow, he scanned her up and down. She was hot, sweaty, barefoot, and dirty from crawling under the ballroom window.

"What are you doing, child?"

She crossed her arms over her chest. "Since when am I

not allowed to walk around in the yard on my own?" A man laid her gun on her uncle's desk.

He eyed the gun and pulled a piece of material from the top desk drawer. "Wipe your prints off the gun. I have no idea where it's been. I don't need one of my guards associated with it." The guy did as instructed.

Giuseppe turned his attention back to her. "You have not been free to roam the grounds ever since I put you in a room with bars on the window. There was a reason behind that."

This scared the shit out of her, but she wouldn't show it. Never before had he locked her in a room. She must've really pissed him off. Well, he'd really pissed her off, too.

Behind her, the ballroom doors opened and the witch slinked in, all smiles. "The sun is down. We are ready to begin."

Giuseppe rose from his chair behind the desk. "Fabulous."

"Begin what?" Amerella asked.

Her uncle looked her squarely in the eyes. "Your sacrifice for the family."

CHAPTER 27

Amerella's body tensed. That did not sound good. She didn't feel like being a martyr for anything right now. She looked around the study at the three guards. None were by the exit door, but two were close to her.

Uncle Giuseppe stood behind his desk, scowling at her. Nothing new there. If she was to make a break for it, now would be a good time. She turned toward the door to the hallway and casually stepped forward. A guard grabbed her wrist. She bent her elbow and pulled back her forearm, lifting his thumb. Holy shit. That worked, too.

The other guard approached. She kicked the first guard in the balls and pushed him into the second man. The second shoved the first out of his way and lunged for her. Her fingers wrapped around a small lamp on a table and she bashed it against her attacker's head. He fell sideways, taking the table down with him.

A gunshot echoed in the room, loud enough to hurt her ears. Everyone in the study froze. "All right, no more of this nonsense, Amerella. Get into the ballroom."

"Fuck you. Get someone else to be your lamb to the slaughter," she said, chest heaving for air.

"I'm sure your son would make an acceptable blood sacrifice." He smiled at her. He knew he had her. Bastard. At least her boy was safely hidden. "Oh," he continued, "don't worry about getting him. Tony can drive down to Mojave and pick him up."

Her heart stopped, but her face turned to stone. "Don't you lay one finger on my son, or I will kill you." How dare he threaten a helpless child? Did he say "blood sacrifice"?

He waved the gun toward the double doors. "Into the ballroom, Amerella. I'm tired of waiting. Tony turned out fine. I want mine."

The witch opened the doors to reveal an eerie scene. Amerella had never seen the room so dark. The blackout curtains covered the entire glass wall, keeping out all ambient light. If the witch hadn't said the sun had set, she wouldn't have known. In the center of the room was a collection of stuff that begged more questions than answers. The strangest bit being a mini bonfire inside a metal container. Why in the hell couldn't they put it in the fireplace? It wasn't like it was overused in the middle of the desert.

A hand between her shoulder blades pushed her into the room. "Get on the table, bitch."

Amerella spun around and slammed the woman in the face. "Watch who you're calling a bitch, witch. I'm family."

The woman's face turned a red Amerella had never seen. The witch's hands snapped into the air, fingers wiggling. Uncle Giuseppe grabbed both wrists and held them down. "We need her, remember. If you ruin this, I will kill you unpleasantly. I want my demon."

"Sorry, what?" Amerella asked. She knew she heard wrong. The door from the hall opened and her bastard cousin Tony walked in. His eyes glowed red.

"And it's about damn time. We've waited too long already. I want to get out of this fucking desert." Tony lifted Amerella off the floor, carried her to the table, and dropped her on it.

"Ow, you dick." She rubbed the hip she landed on. Tomorrow there would be a bruise. "You really are a piece of shit, aren't you?" His red pupils flared and he burst into laughter— deep laughs that carried a nonhuman resonance. He shoved her to lie back and wrapped Velcro around her wrists, holding them to the table. "What the fuck are you doing?"

"Sit back and enjoy the show. It's the last you'll ever see."

She yanked on the binds. "What do you mean? Uncle Giuseppe, what are you doing?"

Her uncle stopped at the table, next to her head. "I'm sorry, child." He brushed hair from her forehead. "But the ritual calls for family blood. And since you're supposedly missing, then we might as well keep it that way."

Tony pulled a sheath from his pocket and slid an athame from it. The knife was beautiful, but looked deadly as hell. She swallowed hard. This looked really bad for her. If Frank wanted to rescue her, now would be a great time.

Giuseppe turned to Tony and took the knife from him. "Anything I should be prepared for before we start this?" Giuseppe asked his son.

Tony's head cocked to the side and he stared at nothing. "Not really. There was a learning curve between me and the human's motor skills. But that is to be expected since your son fought me. You must let the demon take control without fighting it. Your son was not happy with me taking over."

"He had no say in the matter. The pissant was pathetic. I would've preferred my niece over him."

Amerella couldn't remain quiet anymore. "Hold on just a second. What the fuck are you talking about? Both of you sound batshit crazy."

The men laughed. Uncle Giuseppe patted her restrained hand. "Julia here is a powerful witch who summons demons. These demons make humans stronger, smarter, and slightly magical."

Amerella shook her head. "Let me get this straight. You're letting demons—evil spirits who care about nothing except themselves—take over your body. Had it ever occurred to you that humans don't usually do that for a reason?"

Julia smacked Amerella across the face. "Shut up, bitch. No one asked your opinion. You have no idea what you're talking about." Blood seeped into Amerella's mouth. Try doing that when her hands were untied and they'd see who bled.

"Julia, please," Uncle said. "Let's get this started. Re-runs of *The Sopranos* are on TV tonight. I don't care that the show ended in 2007. I still love it." He handed the ritual knife to the witch, then took a seat in a chair next to where Amerella lay.

The witch rang a bell, chanted, and lit four blue candles encircling their area, stopping at four places around the circle to kneel. *"In nomine dei nostri . . ."*

Amerella assumed the language was Latin. Shit. She was hoping the witch was a fraud, or at least a freak. But then again, Tony's red eyes looked pretty damn real.

Julia came toward her with the fancy knife in hand. Amerella pulled on her bound hands. "Stay away from me, lady. I have a mate that will be really pissed if you kill me."

The woman stopped, and her eyes narrowed. "Why did you use the word 'mate'?" she asked.

"Because that's what shifters call the other half of their souls. And my mate is rather damn possessive. He'll tear you to shreds."

Uncle Giuseppe sucked in a sharp breath. "How do you know about those creatures? Are they in Vegas? Can we capture one?"

"Fuck, no, you're not capturing one," Amerella shouted. Shit, she should've kept her mouth closed. Now she might've endangered Frank.

The witch placed a small silver bowl-shaped container at Amerella's neck and one by her feet, into which she crumpled a lot of strong incense. Knife in hand, Julia returned to the first bowl, still chanting, and slit the side of Amerella's throat. Amie tried to turn away, but her head wouldn't move. The witch must've spelled her. She felt her blood flow into the bowl.

After a few seconds, the witch carried the blood-filled container to the fire and poured the liquid into it. Shit went crazy from there.

A wind swept through the room, circling the perimeter, almost tearing down the blackout curtains. Then it cut to the center of the room and swirled around the fire, creating a tornado of flame. Julia shouted her words to be heard above the howling chaos.

Amerella felt warm wetness under her head, soaking her hair. Her blood still trickled out, spilling on the table.

From the whirling fire, a humanoid form stepped forward. Julia bowed and stepped behind the table. "Oh, powerful one. Thank you for blessing us with your presence," the witch said.

"What the fuck?" Tony yelled. "This isn't a powerful demon! What are you doing here, Lamozierus?"

"Ashol? I wondered what happened to you," said the demon in front of the fire. His voice was so guttural that it made Amerella think of wild animals.

Did the demon just call Tony "asshole"? If she weren't so tired, she would've laughed. The demon hit that right on the nose.

"Where is the king?" Ashol/Tony asked.

"He is no more," the demon said.

"What the fuck, Lamozierus?" Ashol/Tony replied. "What does that mean?"

"You're no longer in the underworld," Lamozierus said. "It's no longer your business what happens there."

"I don't understand what's going on. We're calling a demon to take possession of the man in the chair," Julia said.

"Oh." The demon shook his head. "Out of the question."

"What do you mean?" Julia sounded panicked. Amerella felt gratified. Maybe the demon would kick her ass. Stupid bitch. Amerella would do it herself, except her body felt tired. She'd just lay there a bit longer.

The demon tried to make himself bigger again, more intimidating. The whole thing had turned into a mess. "I said no. No one will possess the human."

"I don't understand. Since when did demons stop doing possessions?"

"There are still those that do, a group of rebels, but not on my watch," the demon said. "You called on me and I won't allow a possession."

"What is happening in the underworld?" Ashol/Tony asked.

"Everyone has powers the former king had kept to himself." Ashol/Tony frowned. "How can that be?"

The demon gave him a serious look. "We've had a lot happen recently."

"Can I come back?" Ashol asked. "Wait. What about the plan?"

The demon turned to Julia.

"Don't ask me," she spit out.

"What plan are you talking about?" the demon asked, his eyes focusing on Ashol/Tony.

"The ultimate plan the king had to take over this realm and rule the planet."

The demon's red eyes brightened. "Not at this time."

"What?" the witch asked, surprise clear in her voice.

Amerella couldn't believe how stupid the woman was. Whatever the hell was happening in the underworld, the witch wasn't getting a possession. A chill rushed her body. Did someone open a window? It was really cold suddenly. Maybe it was just the blood leaving her body. Hello, Frank. Anyone home?

"I'm going back to the underworld," Ashol/Tony said.

Uncle Giuseppe jumped from his chair. "Tony!" Uncle knelt and held a finger to his son's throat, obviously checking for his pulse frantically. Amie couldn't stay awake any longer. Her lids felt so heavy. Her eyes closed and she felt her last breath escape her chest.

CHAPTER 28

A merella knew she had just died. Her heart stopped pumping, her lungs stopped expanding. But the oxygen in her
brain would hang around for a couple of minutes. Then she'd
go. Her dead heart ached to see her baby, Francis, one more
time. To see Frank. Tell them how much she loved them both.
She wanted them to know.

Thankfully she'd gotten a chance to tell Frank about the
letter. She would be able to rest in peace knowing her son
would be with others like him, who would love and teach
him. She felt horrible about the town being destroyed because
of her.

Dorothy's restaurant could've been really cute with the
décor ideas they'd shared. And Sherri's beauty shop may have
been small, but it was really nice. Did shifters insure their
property like humans do? Probably not. They most likely
dealt as little as they could with the human world. Then again,
couldn't there be shifter insurance salespeople?

Was she brain-babbling? This had to be what happened
when waiting for the brain to die with the rest of the body. It
wasn't like there was much to do but lie there.

Her life flashing before her eyes didn't happen. Did she
regret anything? Yeah, not taking down Uncle Giuseppe. The

world would be a better place without him. She wondered if she could become a ghost and haunt the man until he shit his pants, and put that on Facebook. Public humiliation would be the worst for him. Making the family look bad.

Hopefully Detective Freeman would have his goal of seeing the end of the Mafia boss before he retired.

Getting justice for Joey would've been good. But Tony did seem dead when the demon left his body. He never said anything or stood after that. She also regretted not telling Frank about their baby sooner.

She felt a cold pressure on her neck, then the worst pain she'd ever experienced. Her brain screamed as fire consumed her body from her neck down. It surged through her veins like stinging spears. This was what final death throes felt like? Dear god, she hoped she died quickly.

A shock jolted her body, like touching an electric fence. Her heart started beating. Holy shit! What was happening?

"No!" the witch screamed. "What's happening?"

"You sacrificed her but there will be no possession. She stays alive," she heard the raspy demon's voice say near her ear.

Amerella's eyes popped open.

The bindings over her wrists loosened to the point where she could free her hands.

"Stop it!" the witch yelled. "You're ruining everything!"

"There shall be no sacrifice," the demon repeated, his gaze meeting hers. Then, he turned to the witch. "Unless you want to offer yourself?"

Trying not to move too much, she looked around the room. Tony was a lump on the floor while Uncle Giuseppe and Julia stood back several feet from the table she lay on. The demon walked to the bonfire.

"N-no," Julia stammered, the anger vanishing from her voice.

"Don't open another portal," the demon said to the witch. "Or I will come back for you. And I won't be alone." He stepped backward into the fire to disappear. Immediately, the fire died to cold embers.

"Where did he go?" Uncle Giuseppe asked. "Does that mean I'm not going to be all-powerful?"

Julia gulped. "I don't know what just happened. How can a demon not want to do a possession?"

Giuseppe hit the witch. "Are you listening to me, bitch? I want the demon you promised me." God, if her uncle didn't sound as whiny as Tony had a few minutes ago.

Julia turned to him, rubbing her arm. "Are you deaf, old man? Or just dumb? The demon said they are no longer into possessions. They have a better deal elsewhere." She walked toward the door.

"Stop," her uncle ordered. "Get back here and get my demon." Didn't affect Julia.

You go, girl. Stand up to her bastard uncle. A gunshot rang out and the witch dropped. On second thought, bad advice. Could be hazardous to your health. Her uncle turned the gun on Amerella, who was still lying on the table. Oh, fuck.

"How is it that you were the only one supposed to die, but you end up the only one alive?" Her uncle's eyes didn't look right. They creeped her out. Guessing that had been a rhetorical question, she kept quiet. Didn't want to make the man any more irritated than he already was. He stepped toward her. Well, shit. Did she come back to life just to die again?

"Mr. Ragusa, Detective Freeman is here to see you," a guard poking his head through the doorway said. Her uncle froze, not answering the unasked question. Was he losing his mind? "Sir?"

He spun around. "Yes. I'm coming. Get all the guards in here to watch the ballroom doors. I don't want anyone going inside, unless they want to die. Am I clear?"

"Yes, sir." The guard straightened and opened the door wider. "Do you want the security monitors up here also?"

"Yes," her uncle replied. "I need their guns right now, not their eyes watching TVs." Did her uncle intend to kill Freeman? Oh my god. She had to stop that from happening. "Also," he continued, "make sure Freeman leaves his gun in the lobby or he doesn't come in."

"Yes, sir."

The doors closed and silence encompassed the room. Laying there quietly in the dim candlelight, she felt the life pumping through her body again. Now that she knew what it felt like to be dead, being alive was freakin' great. Now to get to Freeman.

She pulled her arms from the semi-wrapped ties, swung her body to sit up, and hopped to the floor. Immediately, vertigo swept her away. Her vision spun, eyes darting side to side relentlessly. Her body stumbled sideways and she did her best to stay on her feet until she slammed into a wall.

Grabbing at whatever her hands could find to keep her from falling, her fingers dug into soft, velvety material. The blackout curtains? She let the curtain hold her weight. Then she heard a tearing sound from directly overhead.

She remembered the strange wind that blew through the room earlier had nearly ripped the material from the wall. It seemed that her body would be the means to finish what the wind started. Her ass smacked onto the floor. She ducked her head and rolled against the wall as fifteen feet of heavy curtain folded up on top of her.

CHAPTER 29

＜

Frank paced in front of Ragusa's house. "I'm telling you, Freeman, I have a really bad feeling. We need to go in guns blazing and sweep the house. Something is happening."

He had to see Amie. He needed to know more about their son. He needed to see both of them. Make sure they were okay and take them home where he could protect them. His family. His stomach knotted. He'd never imagined having children with anyone else, but once Amie left him, he didn't think he'd ever have a family at all.

In her letter, she'd given him a bigger reason to fight. Not just for her love, but for their child. The little boy who he already loved with all his heart but had yet to meet.

He would do whatever necessary to get his son and his mate to safety. He had a family and he would protect them with his life.

"Calm down, Dubois." Detective Freeman pushed the doorbell button again to make sure they didn't forget they were there. "Let's see what's going on before killing whoever steps into sight. Unlike you, I'm accountable for my actions."

Frank was in his face in a heartbeat. "What do you mean by that? You think I'm not responsible for my actions? That I'm reckless and kill for no reason?"

"No." Freeman put his hands on Frank's shoulders and pushed him to arm's length. "What I'm saying is that you are in a spot where the public can't know you exist, which leaves me making up a story to explain the superhuman, kick-ass heroism I showed cleaning up the Mafia on my own."

Frank snorted and sighed. "Yeah, yeah. I get it. It's just . . . Amie's in there. I don't know what he's doing to her."

"We're going to find out." Freeman clicked the end of an audio recorder disguised as a ballpoint pen in his chest pocket just before the door opened.

"Leave your weapons here or you don't come in," a guard said. Frank shucked his gun, setting it on the table. After a quick pat-down, they were escorted into the study. Ragusa sat behind his desk, supposedly working. He stood when they entered.

"Ah, Detective Freeman. Always a joy."

"For you, maybe, Ragusa. I'm sick of looking at your ugly mug."

Ragusa laughed, but it was forced. The man smelled funny to Frank. Like a bunch of things normal humans shouldn't encounter. Incense was strong—very strong. If he weren't so close to the Mafia boss, he probably wouldn't have smelled anything but stale sweat from his pores, along with fear and anger. It was too old to be from him and Freeman arriving. What had the man been doing before they got there?

Ragusa's face showed no expression. "Please, gentlemen, have a seat." He motioned to the chairs in front of his desk.

"We'd rather not," Freeman said. "I have a warrant to search this house for a missing Amerella Capone. Her last known location was her home, down the street. We need to know if you are harboring someone who was at a homicide scene."

Frank knew that was a bunch of bullshit talking, but Freeman had to keep Ragusa talking until he smelled or noted something. He needed to find Amie.

"Homicide scene?" Ragusa said, brows raised high. "Never heard that one."

"We haven't had this situation come up with you before. Usually it's the body—post homicide—that you hide. And for some reason, judges don't believe you would keep a body in your sparkling mansion."

"Of course they wouldn't," Ragusa replied. "I pay them enough to be confident of that."

Freeman held his tongue. Frank was ready to rip into the guy. But since he couldn't do that yet, he surveyed the surrounding area, looking for anything suspicious. Several guards where in the room: two stationed at the door they came in through and two more at a set of double doors behind them. He needed to nonchalantly move about the room to catch what smells he could. The incense was overpowering next to Ragusa.

Freeman leaned on the expensive desk. "I bet you're so proud of that, aren't you? Knowing you have to pay off so many people to keep them in your pocket. That's why you have to extort and skim money from your corporation, isn't it?"

"It appears I don't have you in my pocket, Detective."

"I'm about the only one," Freeman said.

"Don't be ridiculous, man. The senator wasn't in my pocket."

"He's dead," the detective shot back.

"Unfortunately, he is. Too bad, really. He was a good man for the public. Just very bad for us."

"So you had your son kill him, making it look like a co-incidental killing at a bank robbery?" Freeman laughed. "I really hope you didn't come up with that idea. You'd be slipping if you did."

Frank had moved around the room. The closer he came to the double doors, the stronger the smell of campfire. Not the soft smell of a fireplace, but hard woodsy burning.

"What my son does is of his own accord. You have no proof of my involvement, and you won't find any now that he's dead."

Frank froze and Freeman stepped back. "Dead? How did he die? Where is the body?" Frank turned toward the doors and took a deep breath. Death. Two people in there were dead. Neither were his mate.

"Fine, Detective," Ragusa said. "Would you like to start your search upstairs in the guest rooms or down in the dungeon?"

Frank asked, "How about in there?" He headed toward the ballroom.

Ragusa laughed. "I'd say that was a brilliant idea, but it wasn't an idea but a smell—wasn't it, shifter?" Once again, Ragusa had caught him off guard. "I don't need introductions now. I know who you are. Amerella's mate."

Frank spun on the man, ready to tear him a new asshole. Ragusa had his gun pointed at Freeman and fired. Frank's cat said it was time to get his ass moving on four legs. His shift came quickly, freaking out the men guarding the double doors, allowing him to bust them open.

With his cat being in the room, he smelled Amie's blood. There had been lots of it, but his eyes didn't see any sticky liquid in the candlelit room. The guards from the study fired shots at him. He ran for the only cover available: the table and bonfire remains. He would've loved to get the download of what went on here. He'd expected to see sticks with wieners and marshmallows for roasting. Instead, he found two bodies, both of which were toast.

And Amie had been in the room.

More guns fired at him. Men opened other doors and joined the first two guards. As he ran, the trailing bullets blasted through the windows, dissolving into the night air. When scouting the area outside just before he and Freeman knocked on the front door, he'd picked up his mate's scent by a side gate and followed it to a room with large windows and curtains. The material was on the floor, but this had to be the room. If not, they could be screwed.

CHAPTER 30

⤙⤙

Amerella lay on the floor under the pile of curtains. Damn, that shit was heavy. She could barely move, but for the moment, that was fine. If she did move, she'd probably throw up until her vertigo settled down.

What was she thinking, getting up so quickly like that? She'd donated blood in the past and they always say to sit up slowly—that was with a few pints taken out. She was bled dry then had all the blood shoved back into her by the demon. That was something she did not want to repeat.

Voices came from the other room. She remembered Detective Freeman was there. She knew her uncle would kill him if the man came alone. Something was off with her uncle. He'd looked strange before he left room. Did he lose his mind when his only son died? The whole family seemed off their rockers.

Enough lying around. She had to get out of here. Warn Freeman, if she could get to him in time. Then escape, find Frank, and kick his ass for not saving her. Damn pussycat. Where the hell was he?

She tried lifting to her hands and knees, but her limbs weren't strong enough yet to overcome the curtain's weight. Good fucking god—who had ever gotten stuck under curtains before? This was damn embarrassing and pathetic. Then gun-shot reverberations came from the other room. Okay, maybe being stuck was all right for now.

One of the doors to the room crashed open, followed by other doors, and then more guns went off. People were in her room shooting. Anything aimed her way would hit the windows, causing them to—she felt the dull impact of hundreds of shards as they sliced through the air on the way to her body. She prayed the curtains' thickness repelled razor-sharp glass as well as it did light.

From where she hid, it sounded like an army of men were standing next to her. Each yelling and shooting. Then one of them roared like a lion. The floor vibrated with impact, as if people were stomping. Torrents of bullets were loosed. A stampede of feet clomped. Growls and howls and roars scared the shit out of her. What was going on out there? She tucked closer to the wall.

Men's screams were cut off in wet, tearing rips of material and flesh. Gunshots became more sporadic. She felt the curtains tug and shift around her. Had the men found her? She was about to scream, when something soft and fluffy rubbed against her arm. What the hell? She pushed her hand out to lift a bit of the curtain in front of her face, and a little critter scooted closer to her. A bunny? A little bunny had found her under the ton of material.

She latched on to it and squeezed it to her chest as the battle raged. Poor bunny was just as scared as she was. No wonder it was trying to find a place to hide.

The noise quieted. No shots rang through the air. Even though she was human, she smelled the bloodbath. Her stomach rolled. But she didn't want to puke on the bunny, so she quelled the bloody image in her head.

Sirens sounded in the distance. One of the neighbors must've called 911. She would've, too, if World War III was being fought in her neighbor's house.

Then the floor shook again with the stamping of a hundred animals. They came toward her, then suddenly stopped. Wait a minute. Were people jumping through the broken windows, back into the night? But she thought she heard animals. Oh, god. She'd gone crazy, just like her uncle.

She clutched the bunny closer, if there really was a bunny. She surmised she could be imagining the creature to comfort her in this darkest hour of her life.

"Amie, I smell you. Where are you?" The curtain was again tugged.

"Frank? You're here?" She pushed her body up, making a hump in the mound. "I'm over here." The weight started to lift and she scooped the bunny to her so it wouldn't accidentally be tossed with the fabric. She was feeling better about the bunny being real, though she wasn't going to think about how it got in the room and to her. That leaned toward the crazy side of things.

The curtains were lifted off her and she took a deep breath. She hadn't realized how hot and oxygen-deprived her little pocket of air had become. Frank scooped her up and pushed her face against his shoulder. "Keep your eyes closed, sweetheart. You don't need to see anything in here."

"Oh my god, Frank," she murmured. "Did you read my letter? You know about—"

Glass crunched under his feet for a few steps, then all was silent.

"Yes, I know about our son. We'll talk about it later. When you're safe."

She realized Frank didn't have a shirt on. With one of her hands, she skimmed her fingers over his chest and up to his neck. "Frank, why don't you have a shirt on? Can I look now?"

He set her on a divan in the foyer of the mansion. "You can open your eyes, sweetheart."

She saw he was completely naked. "Not that I'm complaining," she said with a grin, "but now, of all times, to get naked and busy?"

He laughed. "I'll explain later. We never really went into all the aspects of shifting." He looked at the critter in her arms. "I see Alice found you."

Amie glanced around the area, looking for her white-headed friend. The front door was open, but no one was there. Then it clicked. Alice was a rabbit. The thought freaked her out less than it should've, but shit, she'd been dead, come back to life, met a demon, nearly died under a heavy-ass curtain, and now she held a creature that was a good friend.

Alice jumped from her hold and headed out the front door. After a couple panting breaths, Amie laughed at herself. And she laughed. Frank lifted her, then sat with her in his lap. Her laughter turned to tears and he stroked her head while she de-stressed from her ordeal.

She let out a deep breath. "It's over now, right? I'm safe."

"A bunch of men are dead, but I don't know specifically about your uncle. We should get out of here in case he's still alive somewhere." He helped her to stand and they moved forward.

"Wait," Amie said. "Detective Freeman was here. Did you see him? Is he okay?"

Frank frowned. "I don't know where he is, either. Last I saw him, he was in the study. Your uncle shot him. I'm sorry, Amie."

She shook her head. She'd worry about it later. She wanted out of the house.

Two gunshots blasted through the foyer, almost deafening her. She covered her ears, but Frank's falling body dragged her to the ground. "Frank?" She wiggled to sit up and saw her uncle, bloody and limping slightly, aiming Joey's gun at them.

He looked insane. "Yes, Amerella. I am sorry. Sorry that I didn't kill you when I killed your pathetic parents. You've been more of a thorn in my side than anyone except Freeman. But I've finally taken care of the bastard."

"Wait," Amerella said, "you killed my parents in a car wreck? Why? They were no threat to you. And Mom was your sister. What kind of person could kill his own good-hearted sister?"

"After she married that Capone, she became all high and mighty, always wanting to do the right thing. She acted as if his family hadn't been worse than ours. The Capones, for fuck's sake."

"That didn't mean you had to kill them," Amerella shouted. "You could've sent them back to Chicago."

He laughed. "And let your mother tell them all our secrets?

Where all our hidden cache is? What our corporations are? No. I didn't trust her or that husband of hers. They were planning to take over the family. Your mother was second in line after me to rule the family, until Tony came of age. I couldn't have her running things. So I offed them before they offed me. Fair is fair."

Amerella wanted to pull her hair out. Anger roared through her. This man had ruined so many lives. He didn't deserve to live.

She glanced down at Frank beside her. He hadn't moved and she wondered why. The two bullet wounds in his back were streaming blood. She gasped and ripped her shirt off, using it to press down on the wounds. Why weren't they healing? Didn't he say shifters healed? The memory flashed in her head. They healed mostly when they shifted. Frank needed to shift or he'd bleed to death.

Her uncle limped toward her, gun lifted. "Now I will kill you and put you with the other bodies, and no one will know the difference. I will have your trust fund and be set for the rest of my life."

That caught her off guard. Her trust fund? Where the hell had that come from? "The rules say if I'm dead on my twenty-sixth birthday, you get nothing. Guess my dad didn't trust you, either."

He chuckled. "Wise man. But you forget the law, dear niece. What you have goes to your son . . . and his guardian. I so dearly loved you, taking you into my house when my sister tragically died. The courts will grant me custody of the child and all that is his. Just like they did you."

If she weren't trying to keep Frank from bleeding to death, she'd punch the fucker standing in front of her in his saggy, old balls.

"You will never get your hands on my son. He is protected now." Well, by a grandmother shifter if his father died here in her arms.

"Child, don't be dense. Your Mojave friends are outed. Phone records are the easiest things to track. You should've had a burner phone for them instead of your normal mobile. You would've made such a bad goodfella, niece."

"Fuck you, Uncle. So would you," Amerella retorted.

He chuckled and put Joey's gun against her forehead. She closed her eyes. She'd be joining Joey shortly. This time dying would be quick, with no waiting around for the brain to die.

The gunshot rang in her ears again and she cringed, waiting to fall over lifelessly.

CHAPTER 31

She continued to wait. Then she popped open an eye. Either heaven looked exactly like her uncle's foyer, or hell did. But her uncle lay sprawled on the floor in front of her, blood pouring from the side of his ruined head.

"Finally."

Amerella whirled around to see Detective Freeman leaning against a doorframe.

"You okay, Amerella?" he asked. He stumbled forward, his arm and shirt covered in his own blood. She jumped up to help him sit on a chair.

"I'm fine, but you and Frank aren't. I heard sirens and thought they were coming here. Maybe they got stuck at the guard gate." She went back to Frank and continued pressure on his back. The blood didn't seem to slow. Did he have to shift for being shot twice? How did she get him to do that?

"Amie!" Mom Dubois came through the front door, dressed in a robe and flip-flops. "Oh my god. Frank!"

"He was shot twice and I think he needs to shift." Amerella said the words so quickly she was breathless at the end. "Make him shift, Mom, now."

"I—I can't."

"You're his mother. You can make him do anything!" Panic rose in her voice. She was going to lose the only man she ever loved. After he did finally save her. She leaned over his body. "Frank, you have to shift or you're going to die. Do you hear me? Shift. You have to do it for me. For our son!"

Mom got to her feet and ran to the door. "Butch, Butch! We need you inside."

Amerella then noticed that half of Frank's hometown stood outside the front door, all dressed in robes and house-coats. Why? Then she remembered Frank's mom in a robe after shifting. Had everyone in the town shifted? Wait. All the animals she heard in the ballroom, all the roars and howls. They were from the townsfolk shifting and fighting to save her.

These people she'd befriended a few days ago put their lives in danger to save hers. Another wave of emotion rolled over her. She could barely deal with the fact that she was losing Frank. She needed a very tall margarita. Make it three.

Mom came back, Butch in tow. "He needs to shift to heal, Butch. Only you can make him do that while he's uncon-scious."

The meat man paled. "I haven't done any alpha commands in a long time, my love. But I'll try." The man knelt and laid a huge hand on Frank's head. "François Dubois, I command you to shift." Nothing happened. Amie shrank away, feeling the sheer power of an alpha. She'd never felt raw power ema-nate from someone. It was like standing next to a wire with electricity coursing through it. The hair on her arms stood. Mom gathered her into her arms.

Butch cleared his throat. "I won't say this again, boy. As your alpha, I demand you shift into your cougar"—he leaned down to Frank's ear—"now!"

Frank's motionless body shuddered. Bones cracked and skin stretched. Butch continued mumbling in the cat's ear, hopefully encouraging Frank's subconscious to heal his body. So much happened in so short a time that Amie couldn't comprehend all she witnessed of his body changing. She blinked, and a bare Frank lay on the floor, breathing and with no gaping wounds. Her son still had a father.

* * *

The next day, Amie had the Running Winds bring Francis to her house. She couldn't wait any longer to have the two men who owned her heart meet each other. She missed her son dearly. And as much as she wanted Frank to meet him from the moment he'd taken her to his home, it had been best if she'd kept him hidden until things settled with the family. Today, she'd have her baby home.

She rushed out to the back, where some of the townsfolk had stayed behind to keep them company for a few days—just to make sure everything cleared up without Frank needing backup. They gathered for a barbecue in Amie's backyard.

Movement made her look down.

"Mommy, Mommy!" a high-pitched voice called to her. Her heart filled with joy to see her son after being away from him. Her baby jumped into her arms and she hugged him like she was never letting go. "I missed you so much, Mommy. But Grandpa and Nana and me did so much stuff. I have to teach you to put worm on hook to catch a fish. You get your pwetty fingernaiws dirty, but it wash off, right, Nana?"

The two Running Winds walked closer, with Mom Dubois at their side.

"Yes, French fry, dirt will wash off," Nana said, hugging Amie and her son in her arms.

Frank stared at the boy, saying nothing.

Amie sighed, nerves making it hard to say anything. "French fry, I'd like you to meet someone." She turned to face Frank, still staring wide-eyed. "This is Frank. Say hi to him?" The boy buried his head in her shoulder. She laughed. "Since when have you been shy when meeting someone?"

Her son put his tiny arms around her neck and whispered into her ear, "Mommy, he has the same thing in him that's in me." At first she didn't understand, but then it clicked. Of course; that made sense.

Frank snapped out of his daze. "Hey, little guy. How old are you?"

Partially turning from her neck, her son held up three fingers. "I free," he said.

Frank laughed. "Free, huh?" The boy nodded and dove back into her shoulder.

Amie smiled and quietly whispered to her son, "Remember when I told you your daddy was lost and I couldn't find him?" Her son nodded, his head down. "Well, I found him."

The boy gasped and sprang back with such power that he broke her hold on him. Before the child fell, Frank reached out and snagged him, bringing the boy to his chest, arm under his bottom. Both sets of identical male eyes met and went wide with surprise at the sudden change.

Amie lifted her hands to her chest, wringing them with worry. This could be the last time she ever saw both her loves together.

"Frank," she said, "I'd like you to meet your son, Francis Capone Dubois. French fry, this is your daddy."

Francis's mouth dropped open to join his still-wide eyes. "You're my daddy?" His little face scowled and his fists popped onto his hips. "Where have you been, young man? Mommy's been wooking for you a wong time. Me, too."

Frank hugged the little guy to him and laughed at the reprimand. "Just like your mom."

Mom Dubois raised her hands in the air. "Woo-hoo! I have a grandchild!"

Several at the barbecue clapped and cheered.

Amie pulled her son from his father. "How about hanging out with Gram Jean for a minute while I talk to your daddy?"

"Okay, Mommy. But just a minute. I have wots of quesions to aks." She couldn't help but laugh at the tot's serious face. Gram Jean and the others headed toward the food on the main picnic table.

Amie tentatively glanced at Frank. Was he ready to run screaming?

"Tell me now. How did this not come to light when we were in school?"

"Yeah, about that," she said. "After you proposed in college, you stayed at school to finish exams and I went home to tell Uncle Giuseppe we were getting married, and that I was pregnant. I was going to surprise you when we were together next.

"But Uncle didn't react like I thought he would." She paused for a breath and courage. "He said if I married you or ever saw you again, he would kill our son." She broke down in tears. Her heart hurt so much remembering what she went through having to text him that she could no longer see him.

Frank took her into his arms. "Fuck, Amie. Don't cry. I understand how hard that must have been. I would've agreed with your decision. But why would he do that?"

She sniffled. "He wanted control of my trust fund."

"Money. It's always money, it seems." He kissed her forehead. "We can start fresh, love. I love you and our son."

EPILOGUE

"That's a great idea, Ms. Capone," the senator from New Mexico said on the phone. "I don't think you'll have any problem naming the restored opera house after the deceased senator. If anything needs to be passed here in DC, then I'll make sure it goes through quickly."

"Thank you so much, Senator," Amerella said. "I can't thank you enough for your help with this. Our senator started the bill, and I felt it important to Las Vegas to complete the renewal. I'll get the paperwork started and let you know if I hit any snags. Have a great morning, Senator."

Amerella hung up and breathed a sigh relief. The past couple of weeks had been packed with problems that had to be solved immediately. The other townsfolk had gone home and left her, Frank, and their son to get better acquainted and become a real family. She'd never been this happy in her life. Having both of the people she loved most living in the same home with her had filled her heart with joy on a daily basis.

Even better was watching Frank with their baby. He'd turned out to be an amazing father. More than she could have ever expected him to be.

Her cousins and rest of Uncle's family had no complaints

about her taking charge of the business after Giuseppe's and Tony's deaths.

She told the family that her plans included shutting down illegal activities and switching to legal businesses and charity works. They groaned when she told them they would have to live more frugally. No more renting yachts for a month to party away the time. She gave them the option of finding a job, and that shut them up quickly.

She needed to talk with Detective Freeman to close any files still open. He was finally ready to retire, having taken down the Mafia boss. Even though the boss was dead, Freeman had all the evidence he needed to prove his obsession had been worth the while.

The gun in Ragusa's hand—which he'd used to almost kill Frank and her, and did use to kill the witch—touted the Mafia boss's guilt. Joey got his justice in the end. If not for his gun being easily picked up off the desk, things could've been different.

The door to the study opened and Frank struggled to get through. Seemed the balloons he held weren't cooperating, trying their best to stay outside the door. Amerella sat back and smiled. He was such a great guy.

"Don't peek yet," he said, wrestling the flowers now falling from the bouquet. "This is a surprise."

Amie laughed at his antics. She loved him. Never stopped, really. Things would be very different now. Frank set flowers, a box of chocolate tied to balloons, and a card on the desk. "Happy birthday, my love." He pulled her out of her chair and kissed like there was no tomorrow. Damn, she wanted to go back upstairs after that.

"Are you ready to go?" Frank asked. She looked around the desk at the piles of shit needing attention, then grabbed the box of chocolate. "Let's hit the road." She untied the balloons and took Frank's hand.

With time being short, they flew up and rented a car to drive into town. Mom Dubois had invited them to a luncheon to celebrate Amie's twenty-sixth birthday. She couldn't believe how quickly the past few weeks had zipped by. Seemed only a few days ago when she'd first arrived at the town.

The closer they got, the more nervous she became. Only

looking over her shoulder and seeing their sleeping toddler calmed her down.

Frank took her hand. "What's wrong, sweetheart?"

Amie rolled her eyes. She'd never get used to him smelling her moods. "I feel really bad about what Tony did to destroy the town just to get me. There are people who worked their entire lives to make a living, and in five seconds it's all gone. Do you think the town will hate me? Should I duck down in the seat when we drive through?" She started scooting beneath her seat belt.

Frank laughed. "Don't be so worried. If they hated you, my love, they wouldn't have saved you that night. Or stayed after and made sure we were safe."

She remembered back to that night when she was meant to be a sacrifice for a demon. Several from town rallied and flew down with Frank to meet up with Detective Freeman. When they got to the property, Amie's scent was easily detected on the iron gate hidden off to the side. Her trail led to the tall windows, which were covered with curtains.

Frank had told them to wait there and be ready to charge the front door when he called. As it turned out, the curtains came down (because she grabbed them, taking the fabric down with her), and they saw the ritual getup. When Frank bounded through the double doors in his cougar form, the windows were shot out behind him, and all the shifters simply jumped into the ballroom from there.

She was thankful Frank had kept her from seeing the nightmare and bloodbath the room held. Certainly she would've had bad dreams for some time if she had seen it. But knowing others cared enough about her to do all that warmed her heart.

Frank rounded the corner coming into town. Her eyes bugged, and she gasped. "Oh my god, Frank. Stop. Let me out." Amie rushed out of the car to stand at the new glass door for Wolf's Hair and Makeover Salon. Oh my god. This was so great. Of course, it was past eleven thirty, so the shop was closed. She had to find Sherri and congratulate her before she left.

Amie leaned against the door and cupped her hands around her eyes. The space was twice as wide as it was before, the vacant building sharing a wall with hers now gone. She had new chairs, washbasins, and booths. The place looked fresh and fabulous.

Frank put a hand on her shoulder. He held a sleeping Francis in his arms. "You want to see what happened to Dorothy's restaurant?"

She swallowed hard, hiding her eyes from where the restaurant was across the street. "I don't know." She looked into his eyes. "Do I?"

Frank shook his head. "I'm afraid it's not pretty."

Her heart squeezed. Dorothy loved her place and was going to redesign a part of it using ideas Amie and she had discussed. Amie turned, parted her fingers in front of her eyes, and saw it. She wanted to die. Fire-scorched cinder blocks marking the back and side walls were all that remained. Tears spilled from her eyes.

Frank held their son with one arm and pulled her close with the other, and kissed her head. "Walk with me around the corner." They turned onto the street where Bob's restaurant stood, safely out of the way of the RPGs used that horrible day.

The building had new glass doors and a new name: Bob's for Breakfast, Dorothy's for Dinner. Amie turned to Frank, almost jumping up and down. "Did they get back together? Are they sharing the space?"

"Mom said they were. And with the insurance money Dorothy received, they remodeled the place, and it's better than it ever was, she said."

Amie pulled on the door, but it was locked. Then she realized the place was empty. "Why are they closed? Nothing's wrong, is it?"

Frank kissed her again. "Let's get back in the car. Mom's waiting."

"But—"

Frank guided her along the sidewalk to the car. After belting Francis, making sure she was strapped in, and backing the car from the parking spot, they continued down the street.

"Now, this is another surprise, so close your eyes and don't open them until I say, okay?"

Amie giggled with anticipation. She loved surprises, but

giving them was more fun than receiving. She put her hands over her eyes to make sure she didn't give in to temptation and peek. What did Mom have outside that she couldn't see? Frank parked and helped her from the car, and they walked several feet in the grass, then stopped.

"You ready?" Frank asked. "Go ahead and look."

She dropped her hands, and the whole town shouted "Happy birthday!" Instead of Mom's place, they were in the park. A huge banner read *Annual Town Picnic Lunch*. Under that was a smaller banner: *and Amie's 26th Birthday*.

She couldn't hold back the tears that sprang to her eyes. This was too much.

Frank said, "This is all because of you, sweetheart. Not just your birthday, but the community coming together for the first time I've ever seen."

That didn't help the flood of drops rolling down her cheeks. Mom Dubois immediately went to the car and grabbed a waking Francis from the backseat, taking him in her arms to a group of playing children.

As Amie's eyes skimmed the women in the crowd, she saw the five suitcases' worth of clothing she'd brought when she'd first arrived. The clothes looked so much better on someone instead of hanging in her closet to perhaps never be worn.

A particularly tight group of women gathered around the main food table. Jeffry stood with them, laughing and talking like the group had been friends for years. He looked healthier than he had before. He wasn't as pale and his face was filled with joy. If anyone could get someone through a dark place in life, these women could.

She'd never been this happy, except when her son was born. She searched the area, looking for him. Then she saw Alice and her kit crew moving her way. Amie laughed.

"Alice, got your ducks—I mean, kits—all in a row?" Amie took the woman's hands.

"Gotta round up the young ones to eat." Alice gave Amie a hug then stepped back. "I'll talk to you all later." Amie watched the line of what looked like twenty kids with fluffy white hair marching in time. Sheesh. How did the woman do it? One was enough for her.

Mom and Butch, hand in hand, greeted them. Amie smiled and tittered and squeezed Frank's hand. He smiled at her, thinking her excited over his mother and Butch being a couple. His mom looked happy—not just her expression, but her whole body shined with happiness.

"Glad you're here," Mom said, giving her a hug. "Happy birthday, Amie. Hope your day is great."

She smiled up at Frank. "So far, it's been fabulous." She turned back to Mom. "And thank you so much for the surprise party. I was really worried people would be mad at me for hiding in the town and getting it blown up."

Mom and Butch laughed. He winked. "Being blown up was just about the best thing that could've happened. In more ways than one." He wrapped an arm around Frank's mom. She blushed. How adorable.

Mom added, "But don't thank me for the party. I wasn't the one who initiated it."

"Oh. Who did?" she asked. Behind Mom, Amie saw Mrs. Hagerty walking toward them. "Oh, no. Here comes the wolf bitch."

"Wait," Mom said to her. "Mrs. Hagerty." Mom gave the woman a hug, making Amie's mouth drop open. "Thank you so much for organizing this picnic for the town and Amie's birthday party." Amie's eyeballs joined her jaw on the ground. No way would this woman do something so nice after the words she'd said.

"You're welcome, Jean. It was my pleasure, really. I'd forgotten how much I enjoyed doing this sort of thing when I was younger. I guess since losing Howard I've become a little crusty around the edges."

"The edges?" Amie replied. Frank pinched her butt to shut her up. Amie squeaked, smiled, and hit his thigh. Just wait until they were alone—she'd show him what a pinch was. "I'm kidding, Mrs. Hagerty. Sometimes it takes getting out of your comfort zone to realize you're stuck."

The woman hung her head and covered her eyes. Amie glanced at Frank to see if he had the same reaction to what she was seeing. Mrs. Hagerty was crying? Mom hugged the older woman and patted her back.

"It's okay, Maurine. You don't have to say anything. We know you thought you were watching out for the town."

"I was, but that's beside the point. Someone could've died. Someone did die," the woman said. Amie looked at Frank's mom. Who died? She couldn't imagine losing anyone here. "Amie, Frank. I beg your forgiveness. After seeing the story in the newspaper, I knew Amerella had to be you. I put the idea into Colin's head about taking you to Vegas. He must have contacted them and told them you were here."

Amie didn't understand, but Frank stiffened and a growl came from his chest. Mrs. Hagerty shrank away from him.

"Frank, stop it. Now. You're scaring her."

He did, but his expression didn't soften. "Amie," he said softly, "Colin was the man who came to the house that morning."

She remembered. The wolf shifter wanting to get a bounty from Uncle Giuseppe. "Oh" was all she could say. But Mom Dubois had said the woman was trying to take care of the town. Amie understood the decisions that had to be made when you loved someone. Some were good, and some not so much.

Amie stepped up and gave the woman a hug also. "You may have put the seed in Colin's head, but it was only a seed. Colin had a choice, and he chose the one that got him killed. You did not force his hand. No forgiveness is needed since you did nothing wrong by trying to keep your town safe."

The elder cried even harder on Amie's shoulder. Not what she was going for there.

After a moment, the wolf shifter settled and stepped back. "I was wrong about you, young lady. You've been a godsend for this town. We'd all become too complacent, no longer living the life granted to us as we should every day. Thank you." The woman walked into the crowd and disappeared.

Again, Amie was speechless. She wasn't trying to change anyone in town while she was there, she was just making herself at home. Sorta.

"Okay," Frank said, "I gotta do this before I puke on my shoes."

Mom and Butch laughed. Seemed Amie missed the joke there. Frank released her hand and jumped on top of a vacant picnic table. "Can I have everyone's attention, please?" A round of "Shhh" and "This is it" floated through the crowd.

This was what?

"I'm going to do this the official way, so bear with me. I'm François Dubois, Jean's son, Amie's mate, and little Francis's daddy, as everyone probably knows by now. We'd like to thank everyone for coming out to the picnic today. It's the first I've seen the community come together— No. That's wrong. It's the second time the community has come together. Both times for my mate." Cheers rose. She could really kick Frank's ass right now for embarrassing her so much.

"So," he continued, "that's why I've chosen to do this publicly. Hopefully not humiliating myself in front of you all." He hopped down from the picnic table and kneeled on one knee before Amie. From his pocket, he pulled a gorgeous diamond ring.

Her heart stopped. Oh my god, he was going to propose to her again. The first time he did, she'd been overjoyed and in the same "situation" she was in now. How the past can repeat itself. She almost laughed. This time, though, no one was keeping them apart.

Amie realized Frank had stopped talking. She'd been so elated she hadn't heard a word of what he'd said. By the way he looked at her and how quiet everyone had become, she figured it was time for her to answer. "Yes, Frank. I'll marry you."

The town whooped and cheered. Frank slid the ring on her finger, then stood and lifted her in a hug, swinging her around. She laughed with sheer happiness she hadn't felt in a long, long time.

Francis ran over to them and demanded his daddy pick him up. "You're getting mawwied."

Frank nodded to his son and kissed the top of his head. "Yes. We are."

"We'll live together, right?" their son asked.

"Of course. We told you nothing is going to separate us. I love you both."

Amie cleared her throat, watching both of her loves turn to look at her. "Would you love one more person, too?"

"Who is it?" he asked.

Amie knew she had to make this quick or the surprise would be taken away from her. Thank goodness, her scent hadn't changed enough for him to know, at least that's what Mom told her. Frank wouldn't notice unless he really looked for it. "Take a deep breath, shifter."

Frank took a loud inhale of air, then his eyes widened in surprise.

Mom Dubois winked at Amie and yelled in the crowd. "This is awesome. I have two grandchildren now!"

Frank hugged Amie tight and kissed her neck. "How did you know when you're not shifter?"

She pulled back and met his curious gaze with a grin. "Francis noticed my scent change. I knew I had limited time to tell you before it wouldn't be a surprise any longer."

"This is the best gift you could have given me. Two kids."

She laughed and kissed his lips. "I aim to please, but don't get any ideas from the rabbits. I'm closing shop at three."

He gave her a wicked grin and rubbed his jaw by her ear. "I bet I can get you to change your mind."

Her body shivered and dirty mental images took over her brain. Yeah. She bet he could change her mind, too.

ACKNOWLEDGMENTS

My kids: Aiden "Pukibear"; Alan "Platano King"; and Angelina "Ballenita." You guys make my life brighter and happier. Thank you.

Tina Winograd—You're an amazing friend who is always there to help me with making my work superb. I can't thank you enough for being so freaking awesome!

My mom and sister: Thank you for always being so supportive.

My street team, reader group and readers: You all make writing so easy. Every time you ask me for more, it inspires me to keep going. Thank you.

Keep reading for an excerpt from

DANGEROUS MATING

Coming soon!

Kari Tomlin threw open the entrance door to the FBI building, stubbed her toe on the metal floor transition piece, then stumbled into a lady holding a cup of coffee, waiting in the security checkpoint line.

"I'm so sorry," Kari said to the woman's scowling face. The woman said nothing, just turned. Under her breath, Kari retorted, "Well, good morning to you, too." God, she hated being awake this early. Her brain didn't function until after seven a.m. And that's with two cups of coffee in her system.

She glanced at her watch. When her boss called forty minutes ago, he sounded as if aliens were attacking the planet. The director wanted to see her right away. Top secret information had arrived and they needed her.

She'd met the director once, if you called shaking his hand as he handed over her FBI certification a meeting. She'd never forget that day, not because she became an official FBI agent but because she tripped over a taped-down microphone wire on the stage and took out the podium. It was the fault of the stupid high-heel shoes she'd worn. She was more of a flip-flop kinda gal.

After getting through security, she hurried to the elevators. One started to close and she dashed between the doors, which left her facing the other occupants. There wasn't enough room for her to turn around. She barely fit, and her bag didn't. The briefcase crunched between metal before the security feature kicked in, and the elevator doors popped open.

"Oh, crap," Kari said. She pulled her briefcase toward her and turned around, which jostled everyone behind her. She cringed at the moans.

When she got off at the top floor, she rushed down the hall to the director's door. She took a deep breath and smoothed out her suit jacket, then knocked. She heard "enter" and opened the door.

Director Lancaster, the head of her division, grabbed his cup of coffee off the desk and leaned back in his chair. On the other side of the desk sat two older military men in highly decorated military uniforms. She didn't know the ranks of the armed forces, but both men had two stars on their collars. "And here she is now, gentlemen." Lancaster looked at her. "Come in, Miss Tomlin." She plastered on a fake smile and reminded herself to breathe.

"Good morning, sir," she managed to get out.

"Good morning, Miss Tomlin." He gestured to the two men. "These are Generals Smithton and White." She nodded and mumbled a good morning as they did the same. "Miss Tomlin, thank you for coming in early. We've received intel from the field we need decoded urgently. The CIA has had it for several hours and are making slow progress.

"I've been telling these guys," Lancaster gestured at the men sitting in front of his desk, "for a while now that you are a miracle worker when it comes to this kinda thing." The director winked at her. "And now we get to put our money where our mouth is, if you get what I mean."

She had no idea what he meant, but she'd play along. "I'll try, sir." He handed her a sheet with *classified* stamped on it. That was normal for her. Most of her work was fresh off the press with a get-it-done-yesterday deadline. "Do we know the originating country?" she asked as she scanned the lines of gibberish.

"Russian, we think," General White said.

"What about the intended recipient?"

The director answered, "Mexico, we're guessing."

Russia sending coded messages to Mexico—not what she'd expect.

"Do you need to go back to your desk?" the director asked.

"No," she said, "I have my laptop with me." She pulled her bag around, the one crunched by the elevator. Inwardly, she groaned. Please, don't be broken. "I just need a place to set up."

"Go on next door to the deputy director's office. He doesn't get here till noon most of the time."

"Thank you, sir." She hurried out. Standing in the hallway, she leaned back on the closed door and took a deep breath. Why was she so nervous? She'd met high-ranking people without flipping out. Too badly. But those people weren't depending on her to decipher something important enough to start a world war if she got it wrong.

Sitting behind the desk next door, she pulled out her laptop and set the paper in front of her. She stared at the strange symbols and their layout. Russia and Mexico. In her head, the patterns and similarities formed. She googled Russian language and took a minute to look it over. It'd been a while since she'd dealt with that part of the world. Ever since she started working for the FBI, where her primary focus had been the Middle East.

Skimming through the Russian alphabet, diphthongs, and sentence structure, facts and figures soaked into her head. She puzzled out the basic possibilities. Her mind filled in letter combinations and translated them into Spanish and Russian for decryption. She counted characters, looking for a hidden pattern. Then she saw the trick to solving. Every letter that corresponded with a prime number was a dummy character. Those fake characters being removed allowed for intelligible arrangements of other pieces.

She went through and crossed out the third, fifth, seventh, eleventh, letter up to the last. Her mind sorted and resorted. Then she noticed something about the structure. The words were not arranged in sentences. They seldom were. Those were too easy. After a quick mix in her brain, it was done.

Reading the message, she thought Russia was trying to get their asses in trouble. If they thought they could get Mexico to fight a war against the U.S., they had another thing coming. She closed down her laptop, stuffed it into her bag, and left the office.

She knocked on the director's door. Getting the go-ahead, she entered, trying to be more confident. She should be.

"I have the decoded message for you, sir."

The two generals gawked, then their eyes narrowed quickly. They didn't believe she'd done it. She'd gotten that reaction all the time. Nothing new. Ever since the childhood accident that nearly killed her, she'd been a wiz at math and puzzling solutions. She wished she had the same ability with her social and love lives, which were both in the toilet.

The director grabbed his cup of coffee and sat back in his chair. She came up to his desk and handed him the paper. When she scooted to the side, her elbow hit the picture frame on the corner of his desk. She quickly knelt to pick it up, apologizing profusely. She put her hand on the desk to help get her back to her feet and her hand knocked over a bronze flag statue, which in turn set a rubber band ball rolling across his desk.

She leaned over the desk to grab the ball and her fingers brushed over pens in a black mesh container, sending them sprawling. Still apologizing, she scooped the pens back into their holder. The rubber band ball was somewhere on the floor. Then she straightened from leaning over the desk and her elbow bumped the same picture frame to the floor.

She sighed. The two generals continued to stare at her again. This time for a different reason. So much for her coming across as a professional agent. That was the story of her life. Whenever she was on a roll, doing great at something, she'd ultimately end up with egg on her face.

The director leaned forward and put his coffee on the desk. "As I said, gentlemen, she's the best there is for decoding."

She looked at the military men. "Would you like me to explain the patterns or would you rather I just talk to your guys?"

"Just talk to our guys" was all they managed to say. Typical. Most people didn't understand the cryptography anyway. She took the proffered business card one of the generals presented and walked out of the room.

The card had the symbol of the CIA stamped on it. Looked important, unlike hers. Wait, scratch that, she didn't even have business cards. She figured someone had forgotten to order any or just deemed her unworthy of such distinction to have her name on something.

But despite all that, she was the first to know things no one else did or would ever know. The airplane crash over the Ukraine—it wasn't caused by local dissidents as the news reported. Nope. The world knew North Korea was working on nuclear capabilities, but had no idea about the biological chemicals the country was stocking by the ton.

And some things, she was sure the world was never meant to know. One was what really happened in the infamous Area 51 and the other about a non-human species blending in and living among us. What would the world be like, she wondered, if the public knew of this species? It'd probably go to hell in a handbasket quickly.

The funny thing was no one would believe her if she did tell them all she knew. That was one thing that kept her from having the meaningful relationships she craved with girlfriends and boyfriends. Her social IQ was about as low as it could go. Growing up as a freak to her peers started it. Now knowing little of the world beyond work, she had nothing to talk with others about.

She tried to get into the TV shows she overheard other women talking about. Oprah, Dr. Phil, Dr. Oz. But a lot of the things discussed were flat out wrong. Especially about foods. One would think organic meant coming from your grandmother's home garden. Not the case. So much so, she ate fruits and vegetables from cans. Preservatives were better than things used in the organic world.

Once, she dared to tell a few ladies she wanted to befriend in her apartment building about the hidden aspects of the food industry. They looked at her as if she were from a different planet. Who would they trust more? Dr. Oz with all his commercial backing or a person they hardly knew who wouldn't tell them where she worked or what her job was.

Well, piss on them. She didn't need friends who didn't get her. She could make it on her own. As long as batteries for her rabbit were in stock.

Ready to find
your next great read?

Let us help.

Visit prh.com/nextread

Penguin
Random
House